Lawyer-turned-herbalist China Bayles returns to the Deep South, where her family's legacy of silence is at last broken—and the past finally, unforgettably, speaks the truth. . . .

A frantic phone call from her mother brings China back to her family's Mississippi plantation—a place she'd forsaken long ago. But the late-spring air is thick with fear—and from the moment of her arrival, China knows that something has gone desperately wrong at Jordan's Crossing. An ancient property deed has surfaced—and the man who uncovered it has mysteriously vanished. And as the fates and fortunes of two very different families collide in frightening, unpredictable ways, China must face disturbing new questions about her family's past—and her own future. . . .

"Albert has created captivating new characters and settings dripping with atmosphere."
—*Publishers Weekly*

"Albert's characters are as real and as quirky as your next-door neighbor."
—*The Raleigh News & Observer*

"Albert artfully [brings] the down-home town of Pecan Springs alive."
—*The Dallas Morning News*

W9-BOI-337

continued . . .

Praise for the
China Bayles mystery series ...

"[China Bayles is] such a joy . . . an instant friend."
—Carolyn G. Hart

"A treat for gardeners who like to relax with an absorbing mystery." —*North American Gardener*

"One of the best-written and well-plotted mysteries I've read in a long time." —*Los Angeles Times*

"Albert's characters are as real and as quirky as your next-door neighbor." —*The Raleigh News & Observer*

"Mystery lovers who also garden will be captivated by this unique series." —*Seattle Post-Intelligencer*

"Gripping." —*Library Journal*

"Entertaining." —*Midwest Book Review*

"Cause for celebration." —*The Rocky Mount Telegram*

"The best." —*Booklist*

SUSAN WITTIG ALBERT

BLOODROOT

BERKLEY PRIME CRIME, NEW YORK

BERKLEY PRIME CRIME

An imprint of Penguin Random House LLC
375 Hudson Street, New York, New York 10014

BLOODROOT

A Berkley Prime Crime Book / published by arrangement with the author

BERKLEY® PRIME CRIME and the PRIME CRIME design are trademarks of Penguin
Random House LLC.
For more information, visit penguin.com.

ISBN: 978-0-425-18814-9

PUBLISHING HISTORY
Berkley Prime Crime hardcover edition / October 2001
Berkley mass-market edition / January 2003
Berkley Prime Crime mass-market edition / March 2008

PRINTED IN THE UNITED STATES OF AMERICA

20 19 18 17 16 15 14 13 12 11 10 9 8

Cover art by Joe Burleson.
Cover design by Judy Murello.
Interior text design by Tiffany Estreicher.

This is a work of fiction. Names, characters, places, and incidents either are the product of
the author's imagination or are used fictitiously, and any resemblance to actual persons,
living or dead, business establishments, events, or locales is entirely coincidental.

PUBLISHER'S NOTE: The recipes contained in this book are to be followed exactly
as written. The publisher is not responsible for your specific health or allergy needs
that may require medical supervision. The publisher is not responsible for any
adverse reactions to the recipes contained in this book.

Penguin
Random
House

Dedicated to the memory of my mother,
Lucille Franklin Webber
1909–2000

Acknowledgment

My grateful thanks, as always, to my husband and writing partner, Bill Albert. His invaluable advice and patient assistance may be invisible to readers, but I see it shining through every page.

Author's Note

Don't get out your map and start searching the state of Mississippi for the setting of this book, because you won't find it. Jordan's Crossing, the Bloodroot River, and the town of Chicory exist only in the virtual landscape of the imagination. However, if you're familiar with this beautiful state, you'll certainly recognize the Delta country of the Yazoo River, west of the old Natchez Trace and north and east of Vicksburg. This is the homeland of the Choctaws and Chickasaws, the location of Faulkner's fictional Yoknapatawpha County, the place where cotton was king until the abolition of slavery destroyed the plantation system and the boll weevil crossed the Rio Grande from Mexico and gleefully chomped its way north and east, destroying what was left. And yes, indeed, cotton *is* an herb, too, having been used medicinally in its native regions for many centuries. Medicinal uses are mentioned for it and other herbs in this book, but please do not use these pages as a treatment guide. If China Bayles were real, she would be horrified at the idea that you might use a murder mystery as a definitive handbook on the uses of medicinal herbs. (No, of course you wouldn't.)

Women who are out of touch with their motherlines are lost souls. They are hungry ghosts inhabiting bodies they do not own, because for them the feminine ground is a foreign place.

—Naomi Ruth Lowinsky

A woman writing thinks back through her mother.

—Virginia Woolf

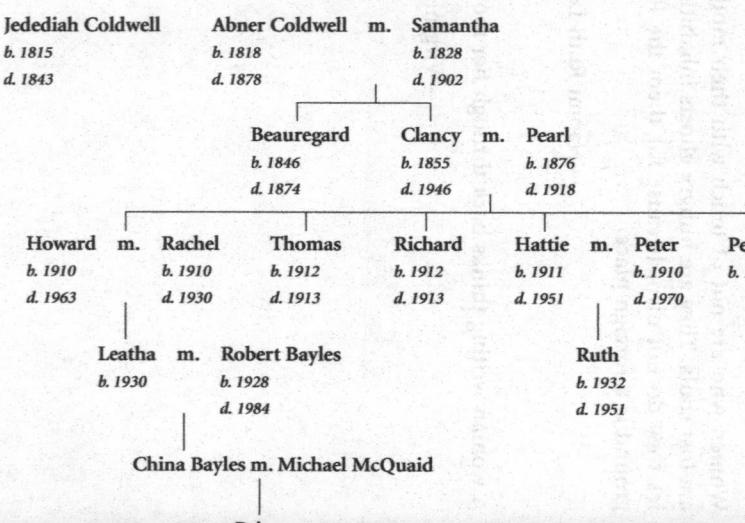

FROM THE COLDWELL FAMILY BIBLE
JORDAN'S CROSSING PLANTATION
CHICORY, MISSISSIPPI

Jedediah Coldwell
b. 1815
d. 1843

Abner Coldwell m. Samantha
b. 1818   *b. 1828*
d. 1878   *d. 1902*

Beauregard   Clancy m. Pearl
b. 1846   *b. 1855*   *b. 1876*
d. 1874   *d. 1946*   *d. 1918*

Howard m. Rachel   Thomas   Richard   Hattie m. Peter   Petulia
b. 1910   *b. 1910*   *b. 1912*   *b. 1912*   *b. 1911*   *b. 1910*   *b. 1915*
d. 1963   *d. 1930*   *d. 1913*   *d. 1913*   *d. 1951*   *d. 1970*

Leatha m. Robert Bayles   Ruth
b. 1930   *b. 1928*   *b. 1932*
                  d. 1984   *d. 1951*

China Bayles m. Michael McQuaid

Chapter One

Many wild flowers which we have transplanted to our gardens are full of magic and charm, while others are full of mystery. In childhood I absolutely abhorred Bloodroot; it seemed to me a fearsome thing. I remember well my dismay, it was so pure, so sleek, so innocent of face, yet bleeding at a touch, like a murdered man in the Blood Ordeal.

Alice Morse Earle
Old Time Gardens, 1901

For a long time, it has seemed to me that every chapter in my life's story has held a meaning I'm meant to understand, a lesson I'm meant to learn—and this one is no different. Before I went to Jordan's Crossing, I believed it was possible to cut myself off from a past I had rejected, to disinherit myself from my family and renounce its unhappy legacy. But the past, as someone has said, is always present, no matter how completely you reject its mysteries or pretend that they don't exist. I think now that everything that happened during those difficult days at Jordan's Crossing was meant to make me come to terms with what is in my blood, to force me (if you'll pardon the metaphor) to dig out my roots. But perhaps the lesson was even more specific than that: I was meant to rediscover the legacy I inherited from the women who bore me—as my friend Ruby Wilcox would say, from the motherline.

Whatever the reasons, I had a lot to learn during the days I spent with my mother at the place where she grew up, at Jordan's Crossing. Now, it seems to me that we were able to resolve only a very few of the mysteries. Yes, we found out who killed Wiley Beauchamp, and why. We discovered an unsuspected branch of the family tree. And we learned far more than it is comfortable to know of the ugly truths wrapped in the bloody history of the Mississippi plantation where as a child I spent the hot, still summers, rich in the resinous scent of pine trees and the moist green smells of the swamp. But the deeper shadows in that house, the darker enigmas, the most puzzling mysteries—these ghosts haunted my childhood, and haunt me still.

I think they always will.

In Texas, April is a spectacularly beautiful month. The meadows are an exuberant wildscape of bluebonnets, orange-red Indian paintbrush, and white prickly poppies— one of those hands-off plants that is defended by so many thorns that even a starving longhorn won't touch it. By the thousands, the tourists congregate in the Hill Country to warm their winter-chilled bones in the spring sunshine and marvel at the wildflower meadows, and when they've seen enough bluebonnets and Indian paintbrush to last for a while, they drive to Fredericksburg for Bill and Sylvia Varney's annual herb fair, or to Kerrville for the arts and crafts festival, or to Pecan Springs. And while they're hanging around Pecan Springs, they have lunch at Thyme for Tea and buy lots of pots of herbs and herbal products at Thyme and Seasons—enough to ensure that April is not just beautiful, it's profitable. You can't beat that.

My name is China Bayles. I'm the owner of Thyme and Seasons and the co-owner, with Ruby Wilcox, of a new tearoom called Thyme for Tea. In April, I'm lucky if I can find enough free time to scrub my teeth and flip a comb through my hair. In addition to the daily work in the shop and the tearoom, somebody's got to look after the herb gardens. April showers (definitely a good thing) are guaranteed to bring a fine flowering of May weeds (definitely bad) so the spring battle plan calls for me to show up at the shop around dawn and get started on the day's planting, mulching, and weeding chores. I try to leave by six in the evening so I can have dinner with my husband, McQuaid, and our thirteen-year-old son, Brian, but during the intervening hours, I go at a dead run all day.

In fact, April is so wild and woolly that Ruby and I often threaten that one of these years we're going to give ourselves a Spring Break of our very own. We'll throw our suitcases in the car and drive as far and as fast as we can, away from the tearoom and our shops and the gardens, far away from Pecan Springs. Who knows how far we'll go? The still-snowy plains of Manitoba, maybe, or the steamy jungles of Mexico, where there are no bluebonnets and no tourists.

Ruby Wilcox—six feet tall in her sandals, with an unruly mop of curly red hair, a face full of freckles, and an arresting sense of style—is the proprietor of the Crystal Cave (Pecan Springs's only New Age shop). Ruby is also my partner and very best friend, and while she frequently displays certain personal characteristics that can only be called, well, weird, I know I can always count on her to listen when I've got something on my mind.

On this bright, breezy morning on the last Tuesday in April, I had something on my mind. Her name is Leatha Richards, and she's my mother—although we haven't always been on the best of mother-daughter terms. While Ruby couldn't offer much help, she was willing, as always, to listen.

"Leatha's gone *where*?" Ruby sat down on the garden bench, folded her legs under her à la lotus, and closed her eyes. Ruby has taken yoga classes for years and is as foldable as a piece of rice paper.

"Mississippi," I said, slowly getting down on my knees. I'm not as supple as Ruby, who can bend straight over and touch her nose to her knees. (If you think this is easy, I invite you to try it.) I popped a dill seedling out of its plastic six-pack and snuggled it into an open space at the back of the kitchen garden. Dill is not only a tangy culinary herb (fine with fish, zippy in scrambled eggs, and especially famous for what it does to pickles) but is also useful in repelling witches—something to keep in mind if you have a problem along those lines. "She's at Jordan's Crossing," I added. "She's been there about two months."

Ruby opened her eyes. "You don't mean she's left Sam?" she asked, startled.

A few years ago, some fifteen years after my father's death, my mother married Sam Richards, who owns an exotic game ranch near Kerrville: exotic as in buffalo, antelope, wild sheep, and wild boar—animals whose bloodlines are almost extinct in the wild. The two of them live on Sam's ranch, which is a far cry from the palatial home in the affluent Houston suburb bequeathed to her by my father. And they seem to be happy together, which has come as some surprise to me. In the beginning, it was hard for me to imagine Leatha trading in her hairdresser and beauty spa for a home on the range, but so far it seems to have worked out.

I pulled cedar-chip mulch around one seedling and reached for another. "Aunt Tullie is sick," I said, pushing the trowel into the dirt. "Leatha's gone back to the plantation to help out."

My grandmother, Rachel Coldwell, died when my mother was born, and Leatha was raised by her father, Howard, and his sister Tullie at Jordan's Crossing, in a plantation house built during the bitter years following the Civil War. Aunt Tullie stayed on at Jordan's Crossing after her brother died in 1963, managing the plantation in the sternly autocratic style of her father and grandfather, keeping the place pretty much as it had been during her parents' lifetimes. (Or so Leatha told me—I hadn't been back since my early teens.) Tullie had to be in her mid-eighties now, and while I could not imagine her as anything less than absolute ruler over the kingdom of Jordan's Crossing, it sounded from Leatha's report as if she wasn't well. Not dying, exactly (at least not yet), but suffering from some sort of debilitating illness.

When the end finally came, Aunt Tullie's death would also be the death of an era—an era that had its roots in the bloodiest period of our nation's past and in the darkest depths of the Coldwell family history. *My* family history, although I had already and quite deliberately cut the Coldwell connection, leaf, branch, and root—which accounts for the fact that I've had little communication with Aunt Tullie. Except for the obligatory exchange of Christmas and birthday cards, I put my mother's family into a box, closed the lid firmly, and slid it onto a shelf in the back corner of my mind. It's not personal, mind you. After I entered high school and began thinking seriously about such matters, I began to hate the plantation and everything it stood for. I declared that I would no longer imagine myself in any way as a product of the Old South, with its brutal treatment of slaves, its contradictory veneration and exploitation of white women, its utter disregard for the dignity of human life. Like other women of my era, I decided to repudiate the patriarchal past and reinvent myself as a new kind of Southern woman, free to make her own choices, build her own life, write her own personal declaration of independence.

Ruby adjusted her orange tunic over her silky brown harem pants and closed her eyes again. The morning sun glinted off her bone-and-bead necklace, an African-style bib affair that made her look like a shaman.

"Mississippi in the spring." She sighed softly. "I did that once—Natchez. It was gorgeous. Azaleas, magnolias, live oaks draped with Spanish moss. Beautiful antebellum mansions, Greek Revival architecture, wide verandas, tall white columns." Her eyes popped open. "I've got it, China! Next year, let's go to your plantation for our Spring Break. We'll wear white dresses and Scarlett O'Hara hats and sit in the shade and sip frosty mint juleps and pretend we're Southern belles with a dozen adoring beaux."

"Whoa," I said, clambering to my feet. "You've got the azaleas and magnolias right, but the rest of it's all wrong. For one thing, it's not *my* plantation, it's Aunt Tullie's. For another, the Mississippi you have in mind is southern Mississippi, between Natchez and New Orleans. Jordan's Crossing is in the delta of the Yazoo River, too far north for live oaks and Spanish moss. And while the house is definitely antebellum, there's nothing even remotely Greek about it. There was a place like that once, but it burned. This house started out as a trading post, you see, on Choctaw Indian land. It's—" I stopped, thinking what I could say. "It's big," I said, imprecisely. "And old, and built out of native cypress, cut and milled on the plantation. But it doesn't have Greek columns and—" I stopped again, remembering my Sunday phone conversation with Leatha. "Anyway," I added, "there might not be a next year. Aunt Tullie's sick. And there are . . . well, complications."

Ruby cocked her head, curious. "What kind of complications?"

I smiled teasingly. Ruby tends to get excited about anything that sounds even vaguely supernatural, and I sometimes like to lead her on just a little. "Leatha hasn't been very specific," I replied, bending over to pull a weed out of the chive border. "But I think it's got something to do with Uncle Jed."

"And who is Uncle Jed?"

"Who *was* Uncle Jed," I amended, surveying the luxuriant rosemary that had flopped across the path like some loose-limbed Jezebel. The plant needed shearing, or people would break branches as they brushed past. Here in Pecan Springs, rosemary can grow five feet high and just as wide. I should have planted it farther away from the path in the first place. Now, all I could do was trim it back.

Ruby's orange eyebrows went up. "Uncle Jed isn't around any longer?"

Another teasing smile. "Yes and no," I said. "He's a ghost. At least," I amended, taking my clippers out of their pouch at my belt, "that's what people say he is. You can't prove it by me."

Which isn't exactly true, I thought, remembering a little uneasily the shadow like smoke twisting in a moonlit corner of my bedroom at Jordan's Crossing, when I was five or six. I might have been dreaming, of course, but I don't think so. I had seen Uncle Jed's smoky shape as clearly as—a few years later—I had seen Aunt Tullie and the witch woman and the skeletal hand reaching up out of the earth. The stuff of nightmares.

"A ghost?" Ruby's heavy bead bracelets jangled excitedly. "You have a ghost in the family and you've never even mentioned it?"

"It's just a story Aunt Tullie used to tell," I said drawing it out, leading her on. "Anyway, all old Southern houses have a resident ghost."

Ruby leaned forward. "Tell me, China," she commanded in an imperious tone.

"Well, if you insist." I clipped as I talked. "Jedediah Coldwell was my great-great-grandfather's older brother, you see. He acquired Jordan's Crossing back in the 1830s, when it was nothing but a log trading post on the Bloodroot River, plus a couple hundred acres of rich bottom land and wild swamp—Muddy Bottom, it was called."

The words began to come easily now, and the rhythms—Aunt Tullie's familiar words and rhythms, remembered from hot summer evenings on the veranda, when she was in a storytelling mood and I had been an eager audience.

"The land had been open to white settlement for only a few years, after the federal government—Andrew Jackson was president then—talked the Choctaws into trading their lands east of the Mississippi for territory in Arkansas and Oklahoma. The Yazoo Delta was the frontier in those days, and wild. The piney woods were full of game, and you could still find hold-out Choctaws and Chickasaws who had refused to leave, and bears and panthers, too, which the old-timers called 'painters' and whose screams sounded like a dying woman. The river bottoms were flat and fruitful and seductive, and the promise of rich soils and plentiful water enticed settlers from their worn-out fields in Virginia, Georgia, Carolina. It lured land speculators, too, and bad money and—"

"So?" Ruby demanded impatiently. "Cut to the chase, China. What happened to Uncle Jed? How did he get to be a ghost?"

"There was a fire at the trading post," I said, scooping the rosemary clippings into a basket. *"There's rosemary, that's for remembrance,"* Ophelia says; *"pray, love, remember."* This was one of the family stories I'd never been able to forget. "Uncle Jed and some of his drinking buddies had been carousing all night in front of the fireplace. After they stumbled off to bed, the soot in the chimney ignited the shingle roof. That's how some people tell it, anyway. Others say that Uncle Jed had cheated a Choctaw out of a section of land that was rightfully his under the terms of the treaty—that would be the Treaty of Dancing Rabbit Creek—and the man got even by putting a torch to the back wall. However it happened, Uncle Jed's cronies managed to escape, but he burned to death."

Aunt Tullie always concluded the story at this point with a grim smile and evident relish, as if she were saying to herself, *Good riddance to bad rubbish!* I was obviously too young to be entrusted with the unseemly details of Uncle Jed's riotous life, but I was old enough to realize that he did not occupy an honored place in Aunt Tullie's bloodline, her pantheon of paternal ancestors. Or perhaps she was smiling because his unfortunate ending had led to a fortunate outcome, at least as far as the Coldwells were concerned. For at Uncle Jed's death, Jordan's Crossing had come into the hands of his brother Abner, her grandfather, a Memphis lawyer who wanted to become a wealthy planter. Abner took possession of his new property and promptly married his rich neighbor's only daughter, Samantha, thereby adding nearly thirteen hundred acres and fifty slaves to his holdings. From Abner, the plantation (five sections at that time, or thirty-two hundred acres) had come to Aunt Tullie's father, Clancy, who was still a boy when the Civil War broke out, and on Clancy's death in the 1940s to her brother Howard, my grandfather. When Howard died, he passed it on to her, in gratitude for taking over the care of his motherless child. Perhaps Aunt Tullie's enigmatic smile was not a judgment on Uncle Jed but merely the expression of an understandable satisfaction with the way things had turned out.

"And now he's come back?" Ruby asked excitedly. "Uncle Jed, I mean?"

"He comes back periodically, when something happens to threaten Jordan's Crossing." I picked up the basket of rosemary clippings. "At least, that's what people say. But it's really just a story, Ruby. *I* certainly don't believe it."

Just a story. But there were those spiraling wisps in the shadows of my room and the faint but unmistakable odor of green cypress logs burning. And Leatha's odd comment, in our phone conversation on Sunday, about the past coming back to haunt the present. When I'd asked her what that meant, she only said, "There are ghosts here,

China. This is an unhappy place. And some of those ghosts are coming to life."

Ruby unfolded her long legs and stood up. "Why don't we get in the car and drive to Mississippi?" she said impetuously. "We could see for ourselves whether there's any truth to—"

"I don't think so, Ruby," I said. "Leatha's already been after me to come, but I told her that I've got too much to do here to go digging around my family tree."

Which is more or less what I'd said to my mother when she'd phoned from Jordan's Crossing the night before, to extend Aunt Tullie's invitation.

"Just for a few days, darlin'," she'd said, in that slow, sugar-sweet Mississippi drawl that she's never lost. (*Was it my imagination, or was her drawl flavored with gin and tonic?*) "You can relax and have plenty of time for yourself. It's lovely just now, with the azaleas in bloom." She'd paused and given an extra weight to the next few words. "Aunt Tullie is 'specially anxious for you to come, China. She's got something important she wants to talk to you about."

And then, uneasily, she'd added that enigmatic comment about the past haunting the present, and old ghosts coming back to life. Uncle Jed, no doubt, although he wasn't the only one. There was Great-grandmother Pearl, for instance, who committed suicide in 1918 by taking some sort of poison—digitalis, perhaps—a deeply mysterious event that has troubled the family down through the years. I've never seen Pearl's ghost, of course, although as a girl I often liked to think I caught a whiff of her lily of the valley scent on sultry evenings in the upstairs hall. Given the age of the Big House and the tumultuous times through which it has come, it would be something of a surprise if there weren't quite a few more ghosts lurking in the attic or the cellar or the family graveyard.

Aunt Tullie's invitation came as a surprise, too. I hadn't been back to the plantation since I was a bored, rebellious kid, and I couldn't think of a single reason why my mother's elderly spinster aunt should be anxious to entertain a grandniece whose obstreperous preteen behavior she had clearly considered unacceptable. I knew I'd enjoy the gardens, if they'd been kept up, and it was tempting to imagine myself in a rocking chair on the old veranda, iced tea at my elbow and a novel on my lap. But I subscribe wholeheartedly to Margaret Mead's observation that while there is such a thing as familial duty, it is not necessary to be intimate with one's blood relations. I remembered Aunt Tullie as stern and joyless, her step firm and unhesitating, her back straight as a poker, her dour spirit casting gloom over the whole place. I doubted that age and ill health had sweetened her temper, and I hoped that her legendary tantrums weren't driving my mother to drink.

"I couldn't go anyway," Ruby said, being realistic for a change. "Shannon's birthday is next week, and Amy and I are planning a big bash. And my checkup is scheduled for the day after the party."

Ruby had surgery for breast cancer at the end of December, a traumatic event that brought her and her two grown-up daughters, Shannon and Amy, closer together. It's brought us closer, too. The possibility of losing her—breast cancer is such a frightening thing—made me value our friendship in a new way. My eyes went briefly to her loose, gauzy top, which completely disguised the fact that she has only one breast. With a defiance that was typically Ruby, she'd refused reconstructive surgery, preferring, she said, to belong to the Tribe of One-Breasted Women. If I asked, she would be glad to lift her top and show me the permanent fern-and-flower tattoo she'd gotten recently to embellish the scar that arched across the flat half of her chest.

But I didn't. I said, instead, "Shannon is how old now—twenty-six?"

"Don't rush it," Ruby said, pushing her hair out of her face with both hands. "She'll be twenty-five." She took two deep breaths and added, "And don't let McQuaid forget about the party. It's Wednesday night, and he's definitely invited."

"I'm sorry, but he won't be there," I said, as we started down the path together. "He's scheduled to give a talk at a law enforcement conference in Baton Rouge." Brian and I would be batching it, and McQuaid's absence would give me a little extra catch-up time. I planned to finish my taxes, instead of waiting until the extension ran out. And when that was finished, I could write a couple of Home and Garden pieces for the next few issues of the *Enterprise*—in addition to all the daily stuff, of course. When you're self-employed, you work around the clock.

"Hey, China, it's your mother!" Laurel Wiley, my shop helper, had stuck her head out the back door and was holding up the cordless phone. Cupping her hand over the mouthpiece as she gave me the phone, she added, "She sounds sort of upset."

"If I know Leatha," Ruby said, "you're on your way to Mississippi after all." She waggled her fingers sympathetically, and she and Laurel went inside.

I put my basket on the step and sat down beside it,

feeling uneasy. When I was a girl, my mother's lack of personal authority, her apathy, her alcoholism, had filled me with confusion and pain. Like many daughters of my generation, just beginning to sense the possibilities of a new kind of power, I feared that my mother was a mirror of the self I would inevitably become. So I turned myself into my father instead—until I found the flaws in that pattern and was forced to begin inventing my own life, free of both of them (or so I thought).

But a few years ago, Leatha began going to AA and got control of her drinking, more or less. Since that time, the two of us have moved a long way toward repairing and refloating our derelict relationship. I've even begun calling her Mother when I speak to her, although she is still Leatha when I *think* about her. But her ongoing recovery hasn't been entirely without incident. A couple of times—when she and Sam had a crisis, or one of Sam's several children made life difficult—she's fallen off the wagon, and when that happens, the ghost of the woman she was comes back to haunt us both. I thought back to last night's telephone conversation (*had she been drinking when she called?*) and felt a swift apprehension. Was there a crisis now?

"Hello, Mother," I said into the phone, as lightly as I could. "What's up?"

"I need you, China." Her voice was taut and urgent, and low, as if she were afraid of being overheard. "I want you to come right away. Come *today*."

I cleared my throat. "How's Aunt Tullie? Is she—"

"Some days are better than others. But that's not why."

"Well, then, what *is* it? I told you last night: Unless it's really important, I can't just drop everything and—"

"I wouldn't ask if it wasn't important," she said, and I

thought that the longer she stayed at Jordan's Crossing, the more Southern she sounded: *I wudn't ask if it wa'n't impawt'nt.* "There's trouble here, China, and there's nobody to talk to. Nobody I can trust, anyway. And you're a lawyer. You can help."

Uh-oh. *That* kind of trouble. "Mother," I said carefully, "you know I don't practice now. And I've never done wills and estates, if that's what this is about." I used to be a criminal defense lawyer before I cashed in my retirement fund, moved from Houston to Pecan Springs, and bought Thyme and Seasons. I keep my bar membership current, just in case, but the old life has no appeal for me, and I hate it when people ask legal questions. "If you and Aunt Tullie need property advice or help with her will or whatever," I added, "you should find somebody local. Anyway, you must have a family lawyer. Can't he—"

"China," Leatha snapped, "this has nothin' whatsoever to do with your great-aunt's will, and the fam'ly lawyer is part of the problem. And if you keep on ditherin' back and forth and draggin' your feet, Aunt Tullie could be in *jail* by the time you get here. Is that important enough for you?"

I sucked in my breath. "In jail?"

"It's a distinct possibility," Leatha replied darkly. "The police haven't been here yet, but . . ." Her pause was pregnant with significance. "Well? Can you leave today?"

"I suppose, if Mother McQuaid is available to stay with Brian. McQuaid is going to a conference." I scowled. "What do the police have to do with anything? What the *hell* is going on there?"

"I can't go into it on the phone," she said evasively. "What time can I look for you?"

I glanced at my watch. It was just after nine. "If I leave

in a couple of hours, I suppose I could be there by ten or eleven—midnight at the latest."

"Good," Leatha said, and I could hear the relief in her voice. "I'll wait up. Do you remember how to get here? Take Route 61 north from Vicksburg. When you get to Middle Fork, go east to Chicory."

Middle Fork. Chicory. The names brought back images of dusty towns, unpaved streets arched with green trees shimmering in the summer sun, barefoot kids in straw hats, cane fishing poles over their shoulders, heading for the river.

"If I get lost, I'll call," I said.

"Drive safe, dear." The urgency came back. "But please hurry."

I turned off the phone and went into the tearoom. "You were right," I said with a sigh to Ruby, who was checking the menu. Thyme for Tea doesn't open until eleven-thirty, but Janet, our cook, was already in the kitchen, getting things ready for the day.

Ruby glanced at my face. "When are you leaving?"

"As soon as I can arrange it, if it's okay with you. McQuaid will be out of town, too, so I've got to call his mother and see if she can come and stay with Brian. I'm sure Laurel can manage the shop by herself, though, now that things have slowed down a little." I looked around at the tearoom, with its original limestone walls and hunter-green wainscoting, green-painted tables cheerful with floral chintz napkins and terra-cotta teapot centerpieces, pots of lush ivy and philodendron hanging from the ceiling. Janet was humming happily in the kitchen, the tables were laid for lunch, and I knew that Ruby could handle anything that came up.

"Of course it's okay," Ruby said. "You don't have to

worry about this place. Just be sure to leave a phone number where I can get in touch with you." She gave me an intent look. "Has Aunt Tullie taken a turn for the worse?"

"I don't think that's it," I said. "This is . . . different." *Jail?* I turned on the phone and punched in the McQuaids' number.

"Well," Ruby said, "if it turns out that Uncle Jed is causing trouble, you can always give me a call. I'm sure I can come up with something that will help, even long distance."

"Thanks," I told her, tapping my fingers impatiently. "But I'm sure I'll be able to manage."

Yeah, right. If I'd have known how the trip was going to turn out, I would have insisted that Ruby get in the car and go with me. She's the only one I know who's qualified to handle the weird things that happened in Mississippi.

"ARE you sure you don't want me to drive you?" McQuaid asked as I sat at the kitchen table, making a list for his mother, who'd said she'd be delighted to come and stay with Brian for as long as necessary. "I could drop you off at the plantation and then go back to Baton Rouge. It can't be more than a hundred and fifty miles extra."

"But then I wouldn't have a car," I objected. "I'd have to borrow Leatha's." At the disappointed look on his face, I added quickly, "It would be great if you'd come up after the conference, though. You've never seen the plantation, or met Aunt Tullie." A few years ago, on a visit to New Orleans, I'd introduced him to my father's mother, Grandmother Bayles, the China Bayles for whom I'd been named and from whom I inherited my love of gardening.

But Grandmother Bayles was dead now, and there was no one left on my father's side of the family. Besides Leatha, Aunt Tullie Coldwell was the only relative I had left, and this might be McQuaid's last chance to meet her.

McQuaid chuckled. "Your aunt sounds like one fearsome lady. Is that where you get your determination?" He put his hand over mine. "Listen, China. With Mom here to look after Brian, we wouldn't have to rush right home. We could check into a nice private B and B with a Jacuzzi, lock the bedroom door, and take off all our clothes." He waggled his eyebrows suggestively and put on an exaggerated leer. "Whad'ya say, babe? Just you and me and some good wholesome sex."

I love my husband's face. It's not handsome, but it has a certain rakish appeal that's emphasized by his crooked nose and the scar that zigzags across his forehead, under the loose thatch of dark hair. McQuaid is an ex-cop who is now an associate professor in the Criminal Justice Department at Central Texas State University, on sabbatical leave this year to recuperate from a shooting that happened when he was doing undercover work for the Texas Rangers. When he's feeling good, he walks slowly, with a limp; when he's tired or the pain gets bad, he leans on a pair of aluminum canes. But I'm thankful that he's walking at all. I still shiver when I think how much worse it could have been.

I picked up his fingers and kissed them. "All our clothes, huh? Now, that's something a girl can look forward to."

Holding my hand, he gave me a quizzical look. "Leatha didn't say what the problem was, or why the big rush?"

I shrugged my shoulders, being casual about it. "Just that if I didn't hurry, I might find Aunt Tullie in jail."

"Jail?" McQuaid exclaimed incredulously. "She wasn't serious, I hope."

"Probably not," I said. Thinking about it on the way home, I'd come to the conclusion that Leatha must have been overstating her concern, just to get me there. I couldn't believe that Aunt Tullie could be in any danger of arrest—unless she'd been driving the car and had hit somebody. That was possible, I supposed, and it would explain the business about legal advice. Criminal charges aside, Jordan's Crossing was a substantial financial asset, and under the right circumstances, Aunt Tullie would make a damned good target for a lawsuit.

I frowned. There was no point in worrying, since I had no idea what to worry about. I went back to the list, jotting down *Pick up Brian's band uniform at Jake's Dry Cleaners* and *BRIAN: NO OVERNIGHT GUESTS!*, then added the phone number at Jordan's Crossing and a big heart with an arrow through it, hoping that Brian wouldn't give his grandmother a hard time. But he's a good kid, usually. And Mom McQuaid raised his father with great success. She probably knows how to handle boys better than I do.

A half hour later, my suitcase was loaded in the trunk of my shiny white two-door Toyota (a replacement for my beloved old blue Datsun, which had rattled itself to death) and McQuaid was giving me a lingering good-bye kiss and wishing me a safe journey.

And then I was on my way, back to the blood relations I had repudiated and the past from which I had resolutely turned away. Back to the women who had gone before me. Back to the motherline.

Chapter Two

Bloodroot (*Sanguinaria canadensis*)

sanguinaria (san'gwi-nâ'i-a), *n.* [Mod. L. < L. (*herba*) *sanguinaria*, (herb) that stanches blood <*sanguis*, blood], a plant of the poppy family, with lobed leaves, white flowers, and large roots used in medicine; bloodroot.

sanguinary (san'gwin'ner'i), *adj.* [L. *sanguinarius* < *sanguis, sanguinis*, blood]. 1. accompanied by much bloodshed, murder, or carnage. 2 flowing with blood; bloodstained. 3. bloodthirsty.

consanguineous (kon'san-gwin'i-es), *adj.* [L. *consanguineus*, of the same blood; see CON- & SANGUINE], 1. having the same ancestor. 2. of blood relationship.

Webster's New World Dictionary

For years, I've had a recurring dream—a dream within a dream, I suppose you'd call it—about Jordan's Crossing. In the first part of my dream, the wheezy clock on the second-floor landing has just chimed midnight. My grandfather Howard is dying in a hospital in Memphis and my mother is with him, and I am with Aunt Tullie at the plantation. In the dream I am eight years old,

but my age hardly matters because I have always imagined myself as entirely grown up, never thinking that I
am a child or in any way vulnerable (a habit that has
persisted into my adult years). I am standing at the open
window of my second-floor bedroom, breathing in the
honeyed fragrance of the night and gazing out over the
wide apron of grass that curves down to the Bloodroot
River. The lawn is bordered with thick, mysterious shrub-
bery and overhung with tall pines, the breeze sighing like
a furtive lover among the branches, the moonlight sketch-
ing charcoal shadows across the pale grass. I have been
drawn to the window by the murmur of low voices and
the metallic clink of something—a shovel against stone?—
and now I see, at the foot of the lawn, a huddle of dark-
clothed people. One, a woman with a head the size of a
watermelon—is she wearing a turban?—holds a lantern
so that its shuttered light is cast in a small gold oval on
the ground beside the old wooden pergola, draped in
scented wisteria. Another, a man, wields a shovel. The
third—

The third is Aunt Tullie. I can see her lean, straight-
backed figure quite clearly now, for I am no longer standing at the window. I have slipped down the back stairs
and out the door and am creeping like a shadow along
my secret path behind the azaleas, the path no one knows
about but me and the whippoorwill calling from a swaying
branch. I am wearing my new pajamas—blue-and-white
striped cotton pajamas, with my name embroidered on the
pocket—and I'm barefoot. I can feel the twigs underfoot,
and the large, slippery leaves of the magnolias.

I keep to the shadows and move stealthily, so as not to
be heard or seen and sent back, under escort, to bed. This
slows my progress so that the man has already stopped

digging by the time I steal up to the group, close enough to see that he is wearing denim overalls and a straw hat. It is Old Homer, the ancient grizzled, toothless man who tends the vegetable garden and lets me pick peas off the vine and eat them, raw and sugar-sweet, while he sits against a sweet gum tree and packs his pipe with the tobacco I've filched from Grandfather Howard's humidor. I am close enough to see that the turbaned woman holding the lantern is the witch woman from Chicory, Marie Louise LaTour, who tells fortunes on the front porch of her cottage. And that Aunt Tullie, making a frantic noise, has fallen to her knees and with both hands is pulling something out of the hole Homer has dug. It looks like cloth, a sleeve, perhaps, and rotten, for it comes to pieces in her hands.

Then she is weeping: deep, despairing sobs, and for the first time in this dream, I am utterly terrified, for I have never seen my stern and implacable aunt moved by grief. Old Homer takes her by the shoulders, pulling her to her feet and forcing her away from the hole in the ground, back toward the house, muttering urgent words I can't hear. The witch woman in her red turban shutters the flickering lantern and follows them.

I am left alone in the pale moonlight, still chilled by Aunt Tullie's hysterical sobbing but irresistibly drawn to the hole in the moist earth beside the white-painted pergola, under the twisted trunks of the wisteria. What have they found? What is so sinister that it must be hidden under the dirt, so secret that they have to come looking for it at midnight, so terrible that it makes Aunt Tullie cry? I creep forward, my bare feet wet and cold, and peer into the hole, and what I see there is a hand, the flesh hanging from it in rotten ribbons, and on one skeletal finger a gold ring, carved with a design of twining ivy. The sweat breaks out over my body and the goose flesh rises on my arms as I stare at this awful, bony thing, so terrified that I can't pull my eyes away, can't move, can't even breathe.

After a few moments I shudder, swallow, and summon my strength to go back to the house. But as I turn, the witch woman steps in front of me, out of the shadows.

"You wasn't meant t'know 'bout this yet." Her voice is low and scratchy and her black face, looming over me, is inscrutable. "But don't fret, child. You'll have another chance to figger hit out. Now, g'wan back t'bed 'fore you catches yore death." She gives me a shove. "Git, I say!"

And then I am running across the flower beds, falling, and scrambling again to my feet, fleeing in terror from this fierce apparition. Later, when I am old enough to read William Faulkner's *Absalom, Absalom*, I will read these lines and feel that they describe my flight precisely: "a dream state in which you run without moving from a terror in which you cannot believe, toward a safety in which you have no faith."

In the second part of my dream it is morning, and I am waking to bright sunlight and remembering that I had dreamed about Aunt Tullie and the skeletal hand with the carved ring loose on its bony knuckle. I sit up and comfort myself with the reminder that it was just a dream—I have been dreaming this, and now I'm awake. But as I climb down from the bed, I see that the knees of my new pajamas are stained a bloody red, and that there is a trail of leaves and still-wet grass across the floor.

And so it is, every time I dream this dream. A terror in which I cannot believe. A safety in which I have no faith.

*   *   *

THE trip to Jordan's Crossing was uneventful—up I-35 to Waco, diagonally across northeast Texas to I-20, then east to Shreveport and across the river to Vicksburg, then east and north. It was dark when I crossed the Mississippi, but I knew it was down there beneath the bridge, wide and dark and mysterious, once the lifeblood of the entire continent, even now an important artery. I've crossed it hundreds of times in my life, I suppose, but the crossing always makes me shiver. The Mississippi, once the frontier, the edge of civilization, the farthest reach of our American imagination.

When I arrived at the Big House just after eleven, I found Leatha waiting up for me. But I didn't learn the reason for my trip that night, for she put her finger to her lips and hustled me and my suitcase up the stairs and down the hall to the back of the house, to the green bedroom, the same dark, high-ceilinged room where I'd slept as a child, with the same wedding-ring quilt on the same high, soft four-poster bed. And with only a hug and a few words of welcome, she left me to take off my clothes, pull my nightgown over my head, and climb into bed, shutting my eyes and turning my back resolutely on the pale window that looked out over the shadowed sweep of lawn. I was so tired from the trip that I fell asleep immediately. There were no dreams of bony-fingered skeletons, and if Uncle Jed came around, he didn't bother to wake me.

The next thing I knew, the sun was pouring cheerfully across the polished plank floor, and Leatha, wearing neatly pressed yellow walking shorts and a matching yellow blouse, was putting a tray on the bed. She wore her usual carefully applied makeup—peach lipstick, blue eye shadow, even mascara—but her graying hair was slightly straggly, she had a whole batch of new wrinkles, and I could see the skin sagging heavily under her eyes. She didn't look as if she'd slept as well as I had.

"Good mornin', dear," she said with forced cheeriness. "I've brought some tea and toast. I thought we might talk a bit before breakfast."

I sat up and rubbed the sleep out of my eyes. The clock on the landing was striking eight. Outside the open window, a wren sang lustily and I could smell the sweet, heavy scent of blooming wisteria. I glanced around at the green floral wallpaper, the gauzy white curtains and heavy green drapes, the delicate writing table between the two windows, the rocking chair, the mahogany pineapple-poster bed with the mosquito-net canopy that always made me feel like a visiting princess. I let out my breath.

"It's exactly the same," I said incredulously. "We've put astronauts on the moon, two women and a black on the Supreme Court, and watched the Berlin Wall come down—and not even the wallpaper has changed."

"Maybe not the wallpaper." Leatha handed me a cup of good, strong tea, not quite meeting my eyes. "But things are diff'rent, all right." She gave a heavy sigh. "You can't see it from where you're sittin' just now. But you will." She poured tea for herself, dropped in two lumps of sugar, and perched on the cedar chest at the foot of the bed, balancing her cup with practiced grace, as if she were at a sorority tea. "Thank you for comin', China. I'm glad you're here."

"You didn't give me much choice," I said, punching

the pillow behind my back and sitting up straight. "What's
up? And what's this about Aunt Tullie going to jail? You
weren't serious, were you?"

"It's complicated," Leatha said, nodding toward the
plate on the tray. "Have some toast. And there's jam, in
that pot with the strawberry on the lid." The corners of
her mouth turned up. "You used to love that little jam pot.
Do you remember it?"

"I remember breaking the strawberry off the lid," I said.
I picked it up and held it out. "See that crack? That's
where Queenie stuck it back together. I can't believe it's
stayed glued, all these years."

Queenie was the large, loving black woman who
cooked the meals, took care of the house, and was always
available to patch things up—things that got broken, feelings that needed mending, hearts that hurt. I'd been terrified that Aunt Tullie would find out what I'd done and
punish me, but Queenie fixed the jam pot without a word
and nobody was ever the wiser.

"Queenie died at Christmas," Leatha said, stirring her
tea. "I guess she took the secret to her grave." She shook
her head. "There's lots of that around here," she said, half
to herself. "Way too much of it."

I smeared jam on my toast and licked the spoon. Strawberry jam, made from the luscious berries that grew in a
thick border around the edge of the vegetable garden.
"Who takes care of the house now?"

"Queenie's daughter Darlene," Leatha said. "A couple
of part-time girls come in to help her. Old Homer's been
dead for fifteen years, and a woman does the garden now.
Aunt Tullie lets her live in that little cottage out by the
highway."

Darlene. When we first met, she had been a strong,

supple girl of ten to my eight, with dark-chocolate skin and glistening hair tight-braided all over her head, who could outrun and outclimb and outswear me any day of the week, who knew where to dig the best red wigglers and where to catch the biggest catfish in the Bloodroot River, and wasn't afraid of their barbed whiskers, either. She'd been the happiest and brightest part of my visits to Jordan's Crossing, the friend I needed, the sister I always wished I'd had. Like girls of that age, we swore to be true forever—and we were, for a long time. But Leatha and Aunt Tullie had some sort of disagreement when I was thirteen, and we didn't go to Jordan's Crossing after that. When Darlene stopped answering my letters the next year (she would have been sixteen then), I supposed I was too juvenile for her. Two years is a gap as wide as the Grand Canyon when one of you is in high school. It was a surprise (and a bit of a disappointment, too) to hear that Darlene was still at Jordan's Crossing. Her letters had always been full of fascinating stuff, and I was sure she'd run off to New York and become a famous writer.

"Darlene and I used to sneak into the kitchen and make mayonnaise-and-sugar sandwiches," I said. "Queenie never minded, but Aunt Tullie always threw a fit when she found out. She didn't like my hanging out with the hired help. And she didn't like it when I broke the rules."

The kitchen had been off-limits to me, like the road and the bayou and Darlene's house, although Darlene herself was supposed to keep an eye on me and keep me out of trouble. But Aunt Tullie had her hands full with the complex business of running the plantation her alcoholic brother was no longer capable of managing (and would have gambled and drunk away if he could). Darlene and I didn't pay much attention to her.

"I know about her rules," my mother said quietly, and I realized that she *did* know, because she'd been a child in this house, too, although her aunt was younger then and perhaps not so strict. Tullie had been only fifteen—the family photograph album showed her as a young, leggy teenager with molasses-colored hair and skin tanned dark by the summer sun—when my grandmother Rachel died giving birth to my mother, her only child. In desperation, I supposed, my mother's father, Howard, had begged his younger sister to take care of his motherless daughter (although perhaps this sort of arrangement was a service that an unmarried sister of any age was expected to render without objection). Leatha had told me once that Petulia (Tullie's real name, used only outside the family) had been ambitious for herself and eager to do other things—go to Newcomb College in New Orleans, where her older sister Hattie had gone; travel around the world, as her brother Howard had done; find work of her own; have a home of her own.

But her baby niece was sickly and required constant care, her brother was already given to bouts of heavy drinking, and her father had slipped into the series of depressions that sapped his vitality and darkened the last fifteen years of his life. Tullie was a purposeful young woman, and I imagined her striding through this thicket of difficulties, taking swift advantage of her father's and brother's inattention and learning to manage the business side of the plantation, as well as its domestic life. It couldn't have been long before she realized that Jordan's Crossing was to be her life's work—behind the scenes, of course, for her father and her brother took all the credit for her success.

As for Leatha, she had lived here until the last year of

World War II, when she was packed off to Greenville to stay with Aunt Hattie and go to high school. Leatha's daddy wanted her to be a debutante, and Aunt Hattie was an old hand at that, having just brought out her own daughter and seen her married to a promising young doctor, which was what being a debutante was all about in those days—and may be now, for all I know.

"How is Aunt Tullie?" I asked, toast in one hand and teacup in the other. Somewhere outside, a lawn mower had started, and the wren was singing louder, as if to drown it out. "She couldn't have been more than about fifty in the years I used to come here, but she seemed ancient, even then." I gave Leatha a crooked grin. "I was afraid of her, you know. The way she used to boss her plantation manager around—Ezra, his name was. And she wasn't very nice to Queenie, either, a lot of the time. She always seemed sour and angry, no matter how hard people tried to please her."

"She wasn't always that way," Leatha said. "When I was growing up here, she seemed lighthearted and happy. She had a smile and a hug for everybody."

"Are you sure we're talking about the same Aunt Tullie?" I asked wryly. "Somewhere along the line, something must have happened to change her."

"It did." The lines deepened around Leatha's mouth. "That's part of the reason I needed you to come." She looked away, out the window, and the hand holding the cup trembled slightly. "She's been sick for a long time— perhaps even when you used to come here. She has Huntington's disease."

The mower stopped and the wren broke off in mid-lyric. I swallowed the last of my toast, frowning, trying to remember something I'd read months before.

"Huntington's?" I said into the silence. "Isn't that some
sort of genetic—"

The door swung open and a white-haired woman in a
black dress stumped in, leaning heavily on a carved walnut cane with a large gold knob on top. She walked with
a peculiar gait and when she came to a stop, she stood
with her feet wide apart. She seemed to sway from side
to side, as if she were keeping time with a tune that no
one else could hear.

"Well, *here* you are, Leatha," she said sharply. "I've
been lookin' for you all over this house." She pulled her
thick white eyebrows together and gave me a penetrating
glance. "Still in bed, child? Isn't it time you came down
and had breakfast with your momma and me?" I knew
the next lines so well that I could have chanted them with
her, a morning mantra. "The sun's shinin' and there's
work to be done. Get up and get to it." All this was said
with an odd, jerky cadence, as if spoken in time to the
tune of her swaying.

"Good morning, Aunt Tullie," I said pleasantly. "How
lovely to see you, after all these years." I gave her my
best and brightest smile. "I was just telling Mother that it
seems as if nothing has changed. I feel as if I were twelve
years old again."

The dark eyes glinted and the thin mouth grimaced
oddly, and I could see that she was considering asking
me whether I was making fun of her—*makin' mock*, she
would have said. But she only thumped her cane on the
floor, nodded brusquely at me, and turned with a strange
twisting motion to my mother, as if she were giving a
little bow. "Come 'long, Leatha."

Obediently, Leatha put down her cup, mouthed, *Later*,
and followed her aunt out of the room. I climbed down

from the bed, pulled on the jeans and blue T-shirt I had worn the day before, and ran a brush through my hair. As I stared at myself in the wavy mirror over the dresser, the years seemed to dissolve and I thought that I didn't really look all that different from the last time I had seen my face in this glass—except for the gray streak in my hair, of course.

That wasn't true of Aunt Tullie, however. She seemed more rudely imperious than ever, if that was possible. But the woman I remembered had been wide-shouldered and tall, close to six feet tall in her prime, with dark hair twisted into a precise bun at the back of her neck and strong, angular features that bore a striking resemblance to those of her father. This woman's white hair was loose and unkempt and she was startlingly thin, her face shrunken to the bones, her shoulders bent. And there was that odd swaying, like a dance. I frowned. Huntington's? The name carried with it a vaguely disquieting recollection, but I couldn't pull up any details. If I were home, I'd log onto the Internet and have the answer to my question faster than I could take the encyclopedia off the shelf. Here, I'd have to wait and ask Leatha.

But we didn't have a chance to talk privately right away. The three of us ate breakfast—a Southern feast of scrambled eggs, bacon, grits, gravy, biscuits, orange juice, and coffee—at one end of a polished mahogany dining table that could seat sixteen easily; more, when the extra leaves were inserted. The dining room, an ornate affair with walnut wainscoting, was lined with the framed portraits of three generations of Coldwells—the rogues' gallery, I used to call it. During the interminable dinners with Leatha across the table from me and Aunt Tullie at one end (my father rarely came with us on these visits to my mother's family), I would study these enigmatic gilt-framed ancestors, to whom Leatha reintroduced me at each visit, as if to keep me from forgetting who they were.

There were Leatha's parents: Grandfather Howard as a debonaire young bachelor with a large diamond stickpin in his cravat, and Grandmother Rachel, newly married and posed with her pretty head turned over her shoulder, as if casting a regretful glance back at the girlhood she had just left. There was Great-grandmother Pearl, painted in late May of 1918, pale and wraithlike in a lemon-yellow dress with a lace collar, a bouquet of lilies of the valley held loosely in one hand, not a hint in her face of whatever despair or self-loathing would drive her to kill herself within the month. Beside her was her husband, my great-grandfather Clancy, dark and glowering, thin lips pressed together in an autocratic line, his gaze lancelike. He had died before I was born, but he was legendary as a disciplinarian and authoritarian, and I had always wondered what kind of happiness the fragile Pearl could have found in his stern embraces. To Clancy's right hung his fierce, one-legged father, Abner, who had inherited Jordan's Crossing from his brother, Jed, and then married thirteen hundred acres and fifty slaves in the person of delicate Samantha, painted as a prettily demure young mother with a baby on her lap and a young boy leaning against her spreading satin hoopskirt. Understandably, there was no painting of Jed, for he had died, sans portrait, before the Coldwell dream of a Southern empire had become a reality.

But there was still one more. At the far end of the room, above the walnut sideboard, hung a large framed picture of my own mother and father, painted from the photograph that had been taken on their wedding day, she seated, virginal in her white-satin wedding gown; he standing, his hand fixed firmly on her shoulder, as if to keep her from rising to her feet. When I grew up and began to understand the dynamics of their relationship, I thought that this was a perfect image of it. My father had always held my mother in her place, and she had always agreed to be constrained.

I was still studying the portraits, reminding myself of the cast of characters in the Coldwell saga, when a sweet-faced blond girl scarcely out of her teens came in with a pot of coffee and a plate of biscuits. Leatha introduced her as Alice Ann, one of the two part-time girls who helped Darlene with the house.

"How's your sister, Alice Ann?" Leatha asked as the girl put down the biscuits. "I understand that she's been sick the past few days."

Alice Ann put the pot on the table. She kept her eyes down, and her voice was almost a whisper. "She's . . . not too good, Miz Bayles."

"She'd feel better if she got herself back to work," Aunt Tullie snapped. "Laundry's pilin' up." She glared at Alice Ann. "And stop bangin', girl. Racket hurts my ears."

"But I didn't bang anything," Alice Ann protested. "I only—"

Angrily, Aunt Tullie reached for her cane as if to hit the girl with it. I watched, half-incredulous, as Leatha leaned over and put a cautioning hand on her aunt's arm. Alice Ann skipped nimbly out of reach. Then Leatha picked up a biscuit and put it on the old woman's plate.

"Have a biscuit, Aunt Tullie," she said, exactly as if nothing had happened. "Darlene made them especially for you."

As Alice Ann vanished from the room, I leaned for-

ward. Was this why Aunt Tullie was threatened with jail—
for striking the servants? Obviously, something was very
wrong here.

But Leatha gave me a warning head shake and remarked in a completely normal voice: "Alice Ann helps
Darlene in the mornings and goes to community college
in the afternoons. Her older sister Dawn comes around
two, after her morning classes, and does the bedrooms and
the downstairs. She gives Judith a hand in the garden, too.
But Dawn's had the flu for the past week." She handed
me the bowl of gravy and flashed an artificially bright
smile: We were making the best of things and that was
that. "We're doing our own rooms until Dawn gets back,"
she added. "And Darlene leaves in the afternoon, so we
have our main meal at noon and a light supper in the
evening. It's very quiet here, as you'll see, China. Nothing
much going on."

I spooned gravy onto my biscuit and peppered it lib-
erally. Whatever was going on with Aunt Tullie, it was
clearly off-limits as table talk. "And who manages the
plantation these days?" I asked, digging into my gravy-
soaked biscuit with a fork, which is how biscuits and bacon gravy are meant to be eaten. Darlene was an even
better cook than Queenie. If all her meals were like this,
McQuaid wouldn't know me when I got home.

"*I* manage the plantation," Aunt Tullie growled. Her
hand shaking, she reached for her orange juice and
knocked the glass over. Alice Ann appeared out of nowhere with a roll of paper towels and mopped up the
spilled juice, her lips pressed tightly together. Aunt Tullie,
scowling at me, didn't appear to notice that the sleeve of
her dress was wet where she had dragged it across the
spill. "I've been seein' to the plantin' and pickin' and

sellin' for sixty years, and I don't mean to stop anytime soon." At least, I think that's what she said. She was agitated and her speech came in such short, jerky phrases that I couldn't be quite sure.

I looked inquiringly at Leatha, who returned a hooded glance. "Wiley Beauchamp sees to the field work and the equipment," she said in a neutral tone, and smiled at Aunt Tullie, as if she were soothing a petulant child. "He does everything Aunt Tullie tells him to do."

"I remember Wiley," I said, with a little smile, although I couldn't picture him following anybody's orders, including Aunt Tullie's.

There's been a Beauchamp plantation manager at Jordan's Crossing for the last century: first Tobias, who worked for Abner before the Civil War and for Abner's son Clancy afterward; then Tobias's son Jacob, who worked for Clancy and then for his son Howard; and then Jacob's son Ezra, whom I remembered from my childhood. Wiley was Ezra's oldest: a lithe, dark-blond boy with a gap-toothed grin, skin tanned to a nutty color and wide, flat cheekbones. I had admired him not because he was handsome but because he was daring and unafraid and he let me go snake hunting with him in the dappled green twilight of Muddy Bottom. Once I watched him catch a five-foot diamond-backed rattler with a forked stick and a gunny sack. He sold the rattler to the red-turbaned witch woman in Chicory—the one I dreamed about—for a dollar.

"Wiley Beauchamp." Aunt Tullie snorted furiously. She dropped her coffee spoon on the floor and Leatha handed her another. "If that boy comes round here again, I'll blow his damfool head off. The nerve of a Beauchamp, tellin' a Coldwell that he's got a deed to—"

Leatha put her hand on the old woman's arm again. "It's all right, Aunt Tullie," she said soothingly. "There's no need to get upset. It's all been taken care of."

Whatever the disagreement had been, I wasn't going to hear about it this morning. Aunt Tullie bent over her breakfast, stuffing food into her mouth as if someone were threatening to take it away from her. (If she ate like that all the time, though, why was she so thin?) Alice Ann quietly poured the coffee, Leatha and I made small talk to fill the silence, and at last the uncomfortable meal was over. Aunt Tullie pushed back her chair and stumped clumsily out of the room, trailed by Leatha, who turned at the door and said, "Aunt Tullie takes a short nap around eleven. Let's talk then, shall we?"

On my own in the familiar old house, I went through the rooms, one by one, remembering the days I'd spent here as a child. As I'd told Ruby, this was no palatial Southern mansion with white-painted Greek columns. There had been a house like that once, according to Leatha, who was the official custodian of Coldwell history. It was designed by a French architect in the golden age of the 1850s and constructed by a small army of Abner Coldwell's slaves, with wide galleries, wrought-iron balustrades, and Italian black marble fireplace mantels. There were no photographs of it, but a drawing in the library showed its palatial exterior and sweeping lawns, surrounded by massive oaks.

But that house was destroyed by fire a decade after the Civil War. The blaze was fought by many of the same blacks who built it—freed men now—but their efforts to save the grand building failed. The Big House burned to the ground, reducing the marble mantels, the golden candelabra, the rosewood beds, and Abner Coldwell's antebellum dreams of grandeur to a heap of smoking rubble. Now, there was nothing left but weed-choked terraces and promenades and a marble step carved with the name *Coldwell*, where Samantha had mounted sidesaddle or stepped from her carriage.

Abner's son Clancy rebuilt the house—this house—on a smaller scale, on a different site a couple of miles away, closer to the Bloodroot River and not far from where Uncle Jed's burned-out trading post had stood. Designed for utility and comfort in the days when a palatial mansion was no longer practical or affordable, Clancy's Big House was constructed of native cypress cut from the nearby swamps, with bricks molded and fired in the plantation's own kiln. He built it against an east-facing slope so that it is two stories high in front and three in back, over the kitchen. The wide-railed veranda wraps around the front and the entire south side, and in the front is a wide oak door, framed in narrow stained-glass windows.

Inside, the house is divided down the middle by a long, high-ceilinged hall and a walnut staircase. In Clancy's day, the right half belonged to the women: a parlor with an Oriental carpet, a red velvet settee, and a crystal chandelier (saved from the original mansion), where Coldwell ladies did their needlework and received their callers; and beyond that the dining room with its gallery of silent ancestors and a small music room containing Great-grandmother Pearl's player piano. The other half belonged to the men: a large library opposite the parlor, where Coldwell men smoked their cigars, drank their whiskey, and played poker; and the large plantation office, with its own entrance and the only telephone in the house, installed sometime in the early 1960s. The four bedrooms were upstairs, and the kitchen (instead of being detached and reached by a covered walkway as it was in older plantation homes) was at the back, below the dining room, reached by the narrow back stairs that also led to the upper floor.

After my quick tour—which assured me that the house was exactly as I had left it, no changes in the placement of the furniture, the same drapes and wallcoverings, the same carpets—I headed for the kitchen, where I could smell the unforgettable aroma of chicken stewing. A wiry woman turned from the cupboard at the sound of my entrance. She had skin the color of honeyed molasses and tightly curled black hair cropped close to her head, and her gold-rimmed glasses were pushed down on her nose. She was dressed in sexy, skin-tight black jeans and a yellow T-shirt with *UCSB Writers in Residence* printed on it.

"China!" she exclaimed, throwing her arms open wide. "China Bayles! Your momma said you'd be comin'. I am *glad* to see you, girl!"

"Hey, Darlene," I said happily, walking into her embrace. "Climbed any big trees lately?"

Darlene threw her head back with a hearty laugh. "I've still got scars from the time we shinnied up that old beech down at the fishin' camp. Remember when we locked Old Homer into the tool shed and made Uncle Jed noises? He hollered so loud, they could hear him over at the cemetery."

I nodded and stepped back. "And the time we stole the plate of fried chicken out of the dumbwaiter? And ate a whole bucket of tomatoes out of the garden?" I sobered. "I was sorry to hear that your mother's gone, Darlene. She was always good to me."

"Momma was good to ever'body," Darlene said, turning to put a stack of plates on the shelf. "She lived a long, sweet life and there wasn't much pain at the end. You can't ask for much more than that, I reckon."

Alice Ann came in just then and unloaded a tray of dirty dishes from the dumbwaiter. She pushed up her sleeves and began to wash them in the sink, not saying a word. Darlene put a lid on the stew pot, poured two cups of coffee, and motioned with her head. We carried our coffee out the back door, to a pair of rusty red metal chairs—the old-fashioned springy kind—that were set under a tall pine at the edge of the lawn, beside a clump of purple verbena.

Darlene sat down, her head tilted, her amber eyes studying me critically. "Well, girl, I gotta say you look good. Filled out some from your scrawny days." She settled back. "Momma kept me up on your doin's. Told me you're some kind of big-time fancy lawyer down in Houston." A grin twitched at her mouth. "Said you keep folks outta jail, even when they deserve to be there."

"Used to," I corrected. "I quit doing that seven or eight years ago. I've got my own business now. An herb shop and a tearoom. And a husband and a thirteen-year-old son," I added. "They came in one package. The husband and son, I mean."

"That right?" Darlene flicked a mosquito off her arm. "Me, I've never had children. Never had a marriage strong enough to make me want to risk adding a kid to it." She paused. "If you're into herbs, I'll have to take you out to Martha Edmond's place. She's got a lot of plants that the Choctaws and Chickasaws used in the old days. She studies 'em."

"I'd like that," I said, thinking that it would be nice to get out and see whether the places I remembered had changed as little as Jordan's Crossing.

There was a brief silence. Down at the foot of the garden, close to the spot where the old wooden pergola used to stand, I could see a straw-hatted figure in a loose white tunic and pants, shoveling mulch out of a wheelbarrow around the azaleas. I couldn't tell whether it was a man or a woman.

"Who's that?" I asked curiously. "Can't be Old Homer. Mother said he was dead."

"Could be Old Homer," Darlene said with a little laugh. "You know what they say about this country. Folks die here, they never leave." She pointed. "In fact, Homer died right about where Judith is workin'. Just keeled over in the grass beside that old pergola, Momma said. Heart attack. Miz Tullie had it tore down after that. The pergola, I mean."

"Judith?" I asked.

"Judith Lightfoot. Come here from Oklahoma five, six years ago. She takes care of the garden. Said she wanted to live near where her people come from."

"Her people?"

Darlene grinned. "Judith's full-blood Choctaw. Remember that big ol' mound over in Winston County? Nanih Waya? She says the Creator made the first people there. They came up out of a hole and got together in tribes. The Muskogees moved off to the east, into Georgia, and the Cherokees, too, only the Cherokees got lost because of a big fire and ended up farther north. The Chickasaws tagged along after the Cherokees, but the Choctaws liked it right here, so they settled down. When the Creator figured he'd made enough people, he stopped up the hole and told everybody to stay put, right where they was. That was their blessed place, and they wasn't supposed to leave it." Darlene's voice trailed off, as if she were reflecting on the legend's significance for her own people, who had come all the way from Africa, from their own blessed place, but not by divine design. After a moment she added, as if in a postscript, "Anyway, after Old Homer died, the garden kinda got swallowed up. You know how it is around here—a couple of years and the weeds and wilderness take back their own. But Judith came along and asked if she could work on the place."

"I'm a little surprised that Aunt Tullie agreed," I said. "The garden was never one of her priorities."

"I was, too," Darlene replied. "But the two of them seem to have reached some sort of understanding. Judith wants to make it into a display garden, she says, where people can come and look at flowers." She jerked a thumb over her shoulder. "Miz Tullie lets her live in that old cottage up at the fork of the road. She's also doing some kind of internship with Martha Edmond on native plants."

"Well, she's done a good job here," I said, glancing around the yard. "The garden looks even better than it did when Old Homer took care of it." The azaleas and hydrangeas were blooming, as were white bridal wreath bushes and iris, and the lovely floppy peonies, red, white, and pink.

Judith Lightfoot took her wheelbarrow and disappeared in the direction of the old potting shed. There was another silence, broken only by the chattering of a querulous squirrel and, at last, by Darlene's wry chuckle. "You prob'ly wonder what I'm doin' here, too, but you're too mannerly to ask." She grinned at me, exaggerating the dialect. "For all yore sass, you could be a po-lite little white kid when you felt like it. Butter wouldn't melt on yore tongue."

"I figure you'll tell me when you get around to it." I grinned back. "You always were a blabbermouth. Remember the time you told on me for hunting snakes in Muddy Bottom with Wiley Beauchamp? Aunt Tullie near skinned me alive, while you and Wiley watched through the window, holding onto one another and laughing your heads off."

"Them was the glory days." Darlene's mouth tightened and there was something bleak in her eyes. "After high school, I went to college up in Knoxville. I even got a year of journalism school before the money ran out. After that, I signed on as a reporter with a newspaper in Greenville."

"I *knew* it!" I exclaimed. "You always were a good writer—no, not just good, marvelous! Only I didn't think of journalism. Your stories were more fancy than fact. I had you figured for a novelist."

She raised her eyebrows. "Yeah, well, I guess I got some of that in me, too. After a couple of years I headed east like the Muskogee and got myself married to another reporter. That lasted about as long as it takes to tell it, and I turned around and went west, all the way to California. But Momma got sick last year and there was nobody to take care of her but me, so I came back. I figured after she died I'd head on back to California, but somehow I haven't got around to it yet." She sighed. "You know what they say about how the Delta country stays in your blood. Anyway, I've got Momma's house to live in, and your aunt needed somebody to cook and look after this place. I come over early in the mornin' and leave as early as I can in the afternoon so I can have time for my own work."

"Writing?"

She nodded. "Short stories. My life, the folks I grew up with, the dried-up towns, the tired old houses, the cotton fields, the swamp." She pushed out her lower lip, considering. "If they work out the way I'm hoping, maybe they'll be a book. If not—" She shrugged, philosophical. "If not, I'll go back to California, I guess. Or maybe I'll just stay here. It feels good that I'm livin' in my momma's old house and workin' at my momma's old job. And havin' the time to do my own writin', too." She lifted her hand. "There's a symmetry to it that pleases me. Blood echoing blood, life renewing life. It feels as if a part of me has been starved where I've been, and I've come back here to the Delta to nurture and heal it."

I heard the shift in Darlene's speech and knew it reflected the different layers of her experience, emotional and intellectual, in the world beyond Jordan's Crossing. I had no reason to disbelieve her schematic version of her life, but something about the way she told her story made me sure that she had left out several chapters—painful ones, probably. A black woman in journalism in the 1970s would've had a hard time of it, and she'd have to be twice as good as the rest just to keep her job. Perhaps she had been running from something ugly when she came back to Jordan's Crossing. But that was none of my business.

"I understand," I said, and changed the subject. "I'm worried about Aunt Tullie. She seems to have some serious coordination problems." I paused, thinking about what I had seen and heard at the table. "Her temper's awfully short, too, and she doesn't seem all that . . . well, rational."

"Tell me about it." Darlene's wry glance suggested that she might have been on the short end of that temper a time or two. "I'm glad your mother came back here to take over, China. I know it's hard on her, this constant watchin' every day, all day. But I just flat had to refuse to look after Miz Coldwell anymore. Cooking and managing the girl is one thing, and I'm glad to do it. But nursing is something else. I couldn't take that mouth of hers. Or the cane." She shook her head darkly. "This may be the old plantation, but the old plantation days are long gone."

I frowned. Yes, I could see Aunt Tullie flaring into a rage and striking out violently at Darlene, or whoever happened to make her angry. "She never was a happy woman, but I didn't think she'd actually hit people," I remarked.

"Well, at least she's not hittin' the bottle," Darlene said with a grin. "Momma used to say that the Coldwells ran to drink and the Beauchamps ran wild, and that both of 'em was crazier than bedbugs. Something in the blood, I guess. Prob'ly a good thing most of them died young." She brushed away an inquisitive yellow jacket. "If you want, I'll stop by and pick you up after supper this evening, and we'll drive out to see Martha Edmond and her gardens. She's the local historian—used to teach history at Ole Miss and knows all there is to know about Chicory and the plantations around here."

I nodded, still thinking about Darlene's earlier remark. It hadn't occurred to me before, but it was true that the Coldwells had died young. At seventy-one, Leatha was already fifty years older than her mother had been when she died, and thirty-something years older than her grandmother. And Leatha's father had died at fifty-three, after a successful career of drinking himself to death. Her grandfather Clancy, if I remembered right, took the prize for Coldwell longevity, having made it to ninety-one. He was old enough to remember being left as the man of the house when his daddy, accompanied by his plantation manager and an African slave named Moses, rode off to defend Vicksburg and the Confederacy against Grant's Union army. And he had lived to see the United States defeat Germany twice and drop a couple of atom bombs on Japan.

"Hey, Darlene," a husky voice said, and the straw-hatted, loose-shirted figure of Judith Lightfoot emerged from behind the azaleas. Even up close, she had what Ruby calls "that unisex look." She was tall and strong-featured, with dark, almond-shaped eyes and short, dark hair. Her hands were large and callused from working with tools. "Do you know when Dawn's coming back to work?"

Darlene shook her head. "Haven't heard," she said. "But I sure wish she'd hurry up. I'm gonna have to put Alice Ann on some of her chores, and she's not half the worker her sister is. Judith, this is China Bayles, Miz Tullie's grandniece. She's here from Texas for a visit."

"Leatha's daughter?" Judith asked, as we shook hands.

"That's right," I said. "I was just admiring the way you've shaped up this garden. It's looking better than I've ever seen it." I grinned. "Old Homer would turn over in his grave if he heard me say that. He couldn't imagine anybody growing prettier peonies than he did. His secret was burying chicken guts around the roots."

"I'll stick with manure tea," Judith said, pushing her hat back on her head. "I'd be glad to show you around," she added, "but not this morning. I'm headed over to Martha Edmond's place. She's teaching me about native plants." She frowned at Darlene. "I called Dawn at home last night, but her mother said she was too sick to come to the phone. I'm worried about her. It's not like her to miss so many days. What's it been now? A week?"

"Just about," Darlene said. She pushed herself out of her chair. "I went to school with the girls' momma. Reckon I'll give May Rose a call and find out what's goin' on." She squinted at Judith. "Dawn doesn't seem like the type to head for New Orleans, but you never know. Girls these days, they're pretty wild. To tell the truth, I'm glad I didn't have one of my own. I don't think I could cope."

"Alice Ann might go off without telling us, maybe, but not Dawn," Judith said emphatically. "Not without telling *me*, anyway."

I stood up too. "May Rose?" I asked. "Would that be May Rose Maxwell?"

"That's her," Darlene said, "only it's Hayworth now. Prettiest cheerleader Chicory ever had. Sexy, too. Drove the boys hog wild. You remember her?"

"May Rose is indelibly etched in my memory." I grinned, thinking of the slender, willowy blond with the tip-tilted nose and the pretty feet. "Remember when you two blackmailed me into being your beauty slave? I had to paint your toenails and roll up your hair on big foam rollers and give you a cucumber facial. If I didn't do it, you threatened to tell Aunt Tullie that I stole two dollars out of the sugar bowl to buy Lucky Strikes for Wiley, so he'd let me ride on the back of the tractor."

Darlene laughed. "Red toenail polish and Lucky Strikes and ridin' on the tractor. Wish life was that simple now." She sighed. "Well, I got to quit bein' lazy and get somethin' on the stove for dinner, or Miz Tullie will bust my tail."

"You'll call Dawn's mother when you get a chance?" Judith persisted.

"I've got a better idea," Darlene said. "China and I are goin' over to see Martha Edmond tonight. We can pick you up and stop off at Dawn's house. If we show up at the door, May Rose will have to let us in."

"I wouldn't count on it," Judith said. "But I guess it's worth a try."

Chapter Three

LILY OF THE VALLEY

The root is small, and creeps far in the ground, as grass roots do. The leaves are many, against which rises up a stalk half a foot high, with many white flowers, like little bells with turned edges, of a strong, though pleasing smell. . . . It is under the dominion of Mercury, and therefore it strengthens the brain, recruits a weak memory, and makes it strong again: The distilled water dropped into the eyes, helps inflammations there. . . . The spirit of the flowers distilled in wine, restores lost speech, helps the palsy, and comforts the heart and vital spirits.

Nicholas Culpeper
Complete Herbal, 1649

The Big House, like most old houses, contains its share of family relics, some on display, such as the collection of blue-and-white porcelain tableware on the dining room sideboard under my parents' portrait, others hidden away in drawers and cupboards. When I was ten, I spent the long hot summer with Aunt Tullie at the plantation. When I wasn't getting into trouble with Darlene, I occupied myself by studying my Coldwell ancestors and the people who were involved with them at Jordan's

Crossing. Seeing my interest, Aunt Tullie had pointed out the Family Record page in the front of the family Bible, pulled out the old photograph albums, and opened the secret drawer under the bookcase, which was filled with papers and memorabilia: old dinner menus and guest lists, a few newspaper clippings and envelopes full of family documents. I copied the family tree and took it home with me, where Leatha occasionally told me a few family stories—not eagerly, but more like a reluctant librarian allowing a pestering child into the adult section. I always had the feeling that there were more and better stories behind the people on that piece of paper, but my mother didn't want me to know what they were.

Now, while I was waiting for Leatha to put Aunt Tullie down for a nap so we could talk, I browsed idly through the photograph albums that lay on the rosewood table in the library. Many of the familiar pictures were faded and some of the pages—those that dated back almost a century—were coming apart. I was there, of course, skinny and spindle-legged and missing two front teeth, hugging the ragged lop-eared rabbit I called Fancy because she'd once worn a lace collar. There was my grandfather Howard, a few months away from a painful death from lung cancer, sitting on the veranda with Leatha, a bottle of Jack Daniel's and two empty glasses on the table between them. There was Aunt Tullie at fifteen, the infant Leatha in her arms and my much younger grandfather Howard behind her, peering over his sister's shoulder at the baby with a bewildered look, as if he were trying to remember how this improbable child had come about and why its mother wasn't there to take care of it. He held a whiskey in his hand in that picture, too.

I paused over the photograph, remembering that Howard's father, Clancy, had also been a heavy drinker. Perhaps my mother's alcoholism had a genetic cause rather than being the result, as I had always thought, of an empty, meaningless life. If that was true, I hadn't inherited it, thank goodness—unless you count my workaholic compulsions.

I turned the page again. There were more photographs of Aunt Tullie at various stages in her life: in her twenties, with ten-year-old Leatha at the top of Lookout Mountain, the wind blowing her loose hair, her face lively and excited; in her thirties, dressed in men's work clothes and sitting on a tractor, her capable hands strong on the wheel; in her forties, already dour and gaunt-faced, standing in front of her grandfather's monument in the Coldwell family cemetery.

But my favorite—the one I had always lingered over when I was a child—wasn't pasted on a page, but tucked in at the back of the album, almost as if it were an afterthought. It was a photograph of Aunt Tullie and her older sister, Hattie. Both girls were dressed alike—frilly white dresses, white stockings, bows in their hair, patent leather slippers on their feet—but they didn't look alike. Hattie was blond and fragile, like her mother, Pearl, while Tullie was dark haired and dark eyed, her father's angular features already stamped on her child's face, making her look older than her years. They were standing in front of their nurse, a strikingly beautiful brown-skinned woman with exotic eyes and the romantic name of Sapphire. Sapphire had been married at fourteen to the plantation manager, Tobias Beauchamp, who had celebrated his fiftieth birthday on their wedding day. Tobias seems to have been plenty virile, though, for Sapphire bore him a number of sons, the eldest of whom had taken his father's place as plantation manager. Wiley Beauchamp, who had allowed me to go with him on his snake-hunting expeditions, was Sapphire and Tobias's great-grandson.

I closed the photograph album and went to the secret drawer under the bookcase, dropping to my knees on the floor. It wasn't really a secret drawer, of course—everybody in the house knew it was there. But that's how I thought of it as a child, and that's how I thought of it now, with a child's shiver of pleasure. The paneling looked just like the wooden paneling under all the other bookcases, except that it had a little keyhole at the top, with a small brass key in it. You turned the key and the hinged panel dropped down to reveal a drawer you could pull out.

When I was a child, I hadn't had much interest in the old papers in the drawer, mostly letters and incomprehensible lists and notes. But now, with time on my hands and nothing special to do, it seemed to me that sorting and organizing this clutter might be a good project, with Leatha, perhaps, if she were interested. As I pushed the papers around, my eyes fell on something I had never seen before, a leather-bound journal with the owner's name embossed in small gold letters on the cover: Pearl Campbell Coldwell, my great-grandmother—the one who had committed suicide in 1918.

I opened the little book carefully. As I did, I smelled the unmistakable scent of lilies of the valley, as fresh as if I had just picked a handful from the shady bed along the north side of the house, where Great-grandmother Pearl had planted them. I raised my head, thinking surely that the wind had wafted the fragrance through an open window, but the room was closed against the midday heat. I lifted the journal and sniffed, and as I did, something fell out—a yellowed clipping from the Chicory *Gazette* announcing Pearl's death; and a fragile spray of pressed white flower bells, paper-dry and translucent with age. I tucked the clipping into the book and sniffed again at the flowers, but the petals that crumbled in my fingers were far too old and brittle to be the source of the fragrance. It was a puzzle.

I slid the drawer back, closed the panel, and turned the key, my thoughts intent on the journal I still held in my hand. If it had been in the drawer when I was a child, I would surely have discovered and read it, curious as I was about my Coldwell ancestors. But it was just as well I hadn't found it then, because I was too young to have understood all that it meant. I would read it now, and see what I could learn about my great-grandmother: my mother's father's mother, the pale, wraithlike Pearl. I may have declared my independence from the Southern patriarchy, but that didn't mean that I couldn't learn some important lessons from a woman who had lived her life in the South and whose Southern blood flowed in my veins.

A trio of white wicker rocking chairs with fern-printed cushions were arranged on the front veranda, relics of a slower-paced past when people had time to sit for a leisurely moment and read the Chicory weekly newspaper or write a letter. As I sat down, I pictured Pearl here, too, and for an instant, the remembered fragrance of lilies of the valley came back to me. I imagined her leaning over my shoulder to see what I was reading, then seating herself quietly in the chair alongside me, a little frown between her eyes, as if she might be worrying about my response to what she had written in her journal.

But it was the other way around, wasn't it? How

would *she* feel about an inquisitive, impertinent great-grandaughter who had already rejected her Southern family and what it stood for, reading these private thoughts, intruding into this long-ago inner world? Wouldn't she be offended?

The moment this question came into my mind, however, I heard the answer, as if it were a light, breathy whisper in my ear: I was *meant* to read Pearl's journal. There was something important in these pages that I was intended to know, that I *must* know, if I were to understand . . .

Understand what? I frowned. *Excuse me—what am I supposed to understand?* But the whisper had fallen silent and there was no clear answer to this question, which hung in my mind like a leaf slowly turning at the end of a spider's thread. If Ruby were here, of course, she would've insisted that I had just been visited by Pearl's ghost, who had given me special permission—a mandate, even—to read what she had written. But since I didn't really believe in ghosts, I didn't share Ruby's confidence in the ability (or the willingness, perhaps) of those in the spirit world to interact with the rest of us. Anyway, I had plenty of other things to keep me occupied while I was here. I didn't need to be killing time by—

This internal debate was interrupted by the sound of a car coming down the drive, and a moment later, the county sheriff's car pulled up and parked behind my Toyota in front of the house. Two uniforms got out, taking their time about it. They wore regulation mirror sunglasses and were chewing gum, and if I'd been the casting director for *Smokey and the Bandit*, I'd have picked both of them out of the lineup first thing.

While the shorter one jotted down my license plate

number and went back to the car to call it in, the taller one came to the foot of the veranda steps and took off his cap. Chivalry and civility are alive and well in Mississippi.

"Mornin', ma'am," he said with a slow smile. "How're you this mornin'?"

"Just fine." I put the journal on the table beside me and got out of my wicker rocker, matching his casual tone. "What brings you folks out here?" I nodded toward the car. "Your partner doesn't need to trouble the dispatcher to run a check. If he wants to see my driver's license and proof of insurance, I'd be glad to get it for him."

The deputy cleared his throat. "Oh, it's no trouble, ma'am. No trouble at all. We're just needin' to talk to Miz Petulia. She at home this mornin'?"

Before I could answer, the double doors opened behind me and Leatha came out. She smiled pleasantly—I had the impression that she had seen the car and prepared herself—but her eyes were dark and I could see the strain in her face. She set the small tray she was carrying—two glasses of iced tea and a dish of grapes—on a small table beside the wicker rocker and straightened.

"Miz Tullie is sleeping, Officer." Her voice was languid, soft and innocent as a Mississippi morning. "She's quite elderly, as I 'spect you know, and not at all well. I'm her niece, Leatha Richards. Is there anything I can do for y'all?"

The cap went back on, the bill low over the sunglasses. "When do you reckon Miz Petulia's goin' to wake up, ma'am?" The deputy was polite but firm. "Hate to bother her, but we got some questions we need to ask."

"What kind of questions?" I stepped forward, putting on my take-charge face. "What's this about, Deputy?"

The sunglasses swiveled in my direction, the chin came up. "I don't think I caught your name," the deputy said.

"China Bayles," I said firmly. "I am Miss Tullie's great-niece. I am also an attorney. If you'll let me have your questions—" I paused and looked at the nameplate on his pocket. "If you'll let me have your questions, Deputy Green, I'll be glad to see that you get answers. If my aunt has any to offer. She may not be able to help you, of course."

"Ah," Deputy Green said. His mouth had tightened at the word *attorney*. "Well, Miz Bayles, I sure hate to intrude on a sick lady, but what we gotta find out is whether Miz Petulia knows anything 'bout what might've become of Wiley Beauchamp."

Beside me, Leatha tensed. If the deputy had noticed it, he didn't give any sign.

"Wiley Beauchamp?" I frowned. "Is he missing?" The other deputy had finished calling in my license tag and had come up the walk to stand behind Deputy Green. He was taking notes.

"Now, how'd you come to know that, Miz Bayles?" Green's smile was slow and friendly, his tone pleasant. "Your aunt mention somethin' about it?"

"Deputy Green," I said crisply, "when Miss Tullie is awake and able to answer your questions, you will have answers. In the meantime, I suggest—"

"How about you, Miz Richards?" Green turned back to Leatha, still pleasant. "Do you have any idea of what might've become of Wiley after he left here on Sattidy evenin'?"

Leatha's eyes opened wide and she took a deep breath. "Why no, Deputy. I have no idea at all. He was here, of course, just after supper. I suppose you know that Wiley was—*is* my aunt's plantation manager." She swallowed and went on hurriedly. "He often comes over to talk business. It was something about equipment repairs that night, if I remember correctly. One of the tractors needed work. But he didn't stay more than a few minutes."

"That so?" Green asked, as if he were surprised. "That ain't what we heard he come over here for. Accordin' to his neighbor, who is a close friend of his, he'd turned up an old property deed amongst Ezra Beauchamp's papers." He glanced in my direction, making sure I was listening. "Course, we could be wrong. But the way we understand it, Wiley showed this old deed to Colonel Blakeslee, who said it looked legal to him. He advised Wiley to git together with Miz Petulia as soon as he could and see what she might be willin' to do 'bout it. That's what the neighbor says, anyhow."

"A . . . deed?" Leatha laughed unconvincingly. "Really, I don't think—I mean, this is news to me. I was there all durin' the conversation, and I can promise you that Wiley didn't mention a thing about it."

"Now, that's just real odd," the deputy said in a musing tone. "Y'see, Wiley told his neighbor 'round six o'clock that evenin' that he was comin' over here to talk to Miz Petulia, the way Colonel Blakeslee told him. And nobody's seen hide nor hair of him since. He didn't show up at his Saturday night poker game, and his neighbor, he called the sheriff yestiddy. Says it's not like Wiley to go off 'thout tellin' him, 'specially since they was figgerin' to go fishin' together on Sunday mornin'. So we thought we'd check here, 'cause this is where he was headed."

"If we hear anything from him," I said, "we'll be sure to give you a call."

"You do that," Deputy Green said. He turned as if to go, then turned back. "By the way, Miz Richards, didn't I hear you say that Wiley *was* your aunt's plantation manager? Far as his neighbor knows, he still is."

"Is that what I said?" Leatha made a nervous gesture. "Just a slip of the tongue, I guess. My aunt has been talking about making some changes in the plantation management, and I suppose that's what I was thinking of."

"Oh?" He raised one eyebrow. "She fixin' to fire Wiley Beauchamp?"

"I don't think that's quite what she has in mind," Leatha said in a tentative tone, "but everything's still in the talking stage, so I'd appreciate it if you wouldn't say anything to Wiley about it."

There was a silence. Out in the squad car, the radio crackled and the other deputy pocketed his notebook and went to answer it. The registration check had come through, and he was hearing that I had no outstanding warrants and was not considered a threat to society.

"Secret's safe with me, ma'am," Deputy Green said reassuringly. He lifted his cap. "You ladies have a nice day, now. And be sure and let us know if y'all hear anything from Wiley."

"Oh, we will," Leatha promised earnestly. There was a long silence as we watched them get in the car and drive away.

I sat down in the rocking chair, the journal forgotten. "All right, Mother," I said grimly, "I want the whole story. Top to bottom, with all the details. What's this about a deed?"

"A deed?" A pucker appeared between Leatha's eyes as she handed me a glass of iced tea. "I'm afraid I don't know anything about—"

"Mother," I said, "do you think I'm a dimwit? On Sunday you call me and tell me there's trouble at Jordan's Crossing—ghosts from the past coming back to haunt the present, if I remember correctly, and something about needing legal advice. On Tuesday morning, you call me and beg me to come and help. If I don't hurry, I might find Aunt Tullie in jail." I was gathering steam. "On Wednesday morning the cops show up and—"

"Not so loud, please, China," Leatha begged. "The windows are open. The servants might hear."

Darlene and Alice Ann weren't servants, and I doubted that they had any interest in our family argument, but I lowered my voice, making up for it by putting on my lawyer's face. "On Wednesday morning," I continued, "the county Mounties turn up looking for Aunt Tullie's missing plantation manager who, coincidentally, was last seen on his way here to discuss an old property deed." I pulled my eyebrows together fiercely. "Now you tell me about that deed, Mother, or I will throw my suitcase in my car and drive straight back to Pecan Springs. I swear it." It wasn't an altogether empty threat.

"Oh, you couldn't do that!" Leatha cried. Tears had sprung to her eyes. "I need you here, China. You've *got* to stay. You're the only one I can count on!"

I put the glass on the table, sat back in the rocking chair, and folded my arms across my chest. "Let's have the truth, then, Mother. And nothing but the truth, so help you God."

Leatha pressed her lips together, swallowed, then said, "Wiley was here, after supper, the way I told it. And he did say something about a tractor that wasn't working."

"What *else* did you talk about?"

She put down her glass and fished a handkerchief out of her pocket to wipe her eyes, smearing her mascara. "He said he'd finally gotten around to cleaning out his father's family papers—Ezra died about three years ago, you see. In the bottom drawer of the desk, in an old envelope with a notebook and some other papers, he found a property deed." She blew her nose.

I waited. When she didn't go on, I said, "A deed to what?"

"To six hundred and forty acres of Jordan's Crossing." Her voice was muffled. "The land includes the spot where we're sittin' right now. It includes this house."

"This house?" I stared at her. "Why, that's the most ridiculous thing I've ever heard of, Mother. You're Aunt Tullie's closest kin. When she's gone, this house will come to you. Nobody would *ever* have deeded this property to Ezra—"

"Not to Ezra." She fanned herself with her hand. "To Ezra's grandfather, Tobias. The paper was signed by your great-great-grandfather. By Abner Coldwell."

It took me a moment to digest this. I remembered Aunt Tullie telling me about the Beauchamps, whose story seemed to be woven almost inextricably into Coldwell history. The first Beauchamp, Tobias, was closely related through his Choctaw mother to Greenwood Leflore, the Choctaw chief who had been rewarded with a thousand acres of land for signing the Treaty of Dancing Rabbit Creek, through which the Indians gave up their land. Having eventually parlayed this thousand-acre tribute (a bribe, some called it) into fifteen thousand acres of fertile Delta land, the formidable Leflore went on to become a member of the Mississippi House of Representatives and then the state Senate—and might have gone further, if he had not opposed secession. He was *persona non grata* after that, of course.

Abner Coldwell apparently recognized something of Leflore's resolute enterprise and canny business sense in the young Tobias Beauchamp, for he made him his book-keeper, giving him the authority to do the plantation's business during its owner's frequent absences. And in May of 1862, when Abner rode off to join the Confederates defending Vicksburg against Ulysses S. Grant's federal troops, Tobias Beauchamp rode beside him. Lucky thing, too. Abner Coldwell found himself fighting along-side the Missourians of Cockrell's Brigade, desperately trying to hold Graveyard Road. He lost his right leg and would have lost his life if Tobias had not crawled into the deadly Yankee artillery fire to pull Abner to safety and stanch the spurting blood.

This was all family legend, of course—and legends are often exaggerated. But when Abner came back to Jordan's Crossing to recover from his wound, he promoted Tobias Beauchamp from bookkeeper to plantation manager: not an overseer on horseback, driving the slaves in the cotton fields with a blacksnake whip, but the owner's legally designated agent, who could decide what seeds and equip-ment to buy and from whom; where, and how much to plant; where to ship the cotton to market; when to sell and at what price. After Abner's death, Tobias continued to serve Abner's son Clancy in the same capacity, holding the position until the year the *Titanic* went down, when he turned it over to his son Jacob. Jacob relinquished the job to his son Ezra during the Depression, and now it belonged to Wiley. This long association with the Cold-wells and the succession of one son after another to his father's position had certainly benefitted the Beauchamps, who lived down the road in a comfortable white frame house built on land that Jacob had bought from a planter who went broke during the Depression. But it had also been undeniably fortunate for three generations of Coldwells, bringing stability to the plantation's management and probably ensuring its financial survival.

I broke the silence. "Did you see the actual deed?"

"I guess so," Leatha said. "It looked awfully old." She gave me a hopeful glance. "But maybe it's a fake, China. Something he dreamed up to try to trick Aunt Tullie into giving him money or land or something. I can't *imagine* that Great-grandfather Abner would have been so foolish as to have given Tobias the land that this house was built on."

Personally, I didn't think Wiley Beauchamp would make up something like this. Rattlesnake-hunting is a sport where you have to be decisive and quick-witted, but you don't move an inch until you know the odds are in your favor—and then you strike like greased lightning. I hadn't seen Wiley since we were kids, but the boy I knew would never have been stupid enough to wave a bogus deed under Aunt Tullie's nose. If she called his bluff and they went to court—which was the inevitable outcome of a property disagreement of this magnitude—he'd have to submit the document for expert scrutiny. If it turned out to be fraudulent, he'd be in big trouble. Anyway, the man had a job for life, as had his father and grandfather and great-grandfather before him. I doubted that Wiley Beauchamp would bet a sure thing against a forged property deed.

"What was the date on the document you saw?" I asked.

"Is that important?" Leatha frowned. "Wait a minute. I think he pointed it out. January, maybe—1864, I think."

January 1864. And Tobias Beauchamp had dragged Abner Coldwell from the jaws of a Yankee hell in May of 1863. Perhaps Abner had been so grateful for his deliverance that he made the young man a generous gift of land. In the context of Abner's gratitude and perhaps his desire to secure the Beauchamp loyalty, I could understand the deed of land—but the house? Knowing the Coldwells' pride in this place, it didn't make sense.

And then I thought of something. "This house. When was it built, exactly?"

"In 1879," Leatha said promptly. "Or maybe 1880. The original house burned the year after Great-grandfather Abner died. Why?" And then her face cleared. "Of course! Abner couldn't have given Tobias *this* house. Clancy built it after his father was dead! That changes everything, I'm sure."

I shook my head. "I don't think so, Mother. I don't know about Mississippi property law, but in Texas, if somebody builds a house on your property, whether by mistake or by design, it's your house." But if Tobias held title to this land, why had he allowed Clancy to build the house here? And why had a gift of over six hundred acres been kept secret through three generations of Beauchamps? None of it made sense.

"Did Wiley leave a copy of this deed with you?" I asked.

"He said he'd give us a copy later," Leatha replied. "I wanted him out of here, to tell the truth. Aunt Tullie was pretty upset."

"I can imagine," I said, thinking about the way she had snapped at Alice Ann this morning. I wouldn't have been surprised if she'd taken her cane to Wiley in a fit of Coldwell temper. "The deputy mentioned somebody named Blakeslee. Colonel Blakeslee. Who is he?"

Leatha made a wry face. "He's the family lawyer. That was one of the things that made Aunt Tullie so furious, you see. She can't imagine why the Colonel is taking sides with Wiley on something as important to the Coldwells as this."

"Maybe because Wiley's on the right side of the law," I said grimly. I stood up. "I want to see Blakeslee. We need to get to the bottom of this as soon as we can." I gave her a sharp look. "Why did you lie to the deputy, Mother? Wiley will turn up in the next day or two and tell the police that he showed the deed to you and Aunt Tullie. It's going to look as if you're hiding something."

Leatha chewed on her lip. "I didn't tell him because—" She stopped. "We have to talk about this, China. About Aunt Tullie's illness."

"What does Aunt Tullie's illness have to do with what you told the police?"

"It's complicated." She gave me a sideways look. "I guess you don't know about Huntington's."

"Not really," I said. I sat back down. "I can see that Aunt Tullie's got the shakes, though, and some pretty serious motor problems. She has speech difficulties too." I frowned. "Is it something like Parkinson's?"

"Well, sort of," Leatha replied slowly. "Both are movement related, but they don't have the same cause, and there's a treatment for Parkinson's." She didn't look at me. "There's no cure for Huntington's, although the medications have helped to control the worst of it, at least until the past few weeks. The disease is progressive, and things have been getting worse."

"In what way? Those jerky movements, you mean? I seem to remember that she was always fidgety and nervous, but nothing like this."

Leatha's face was set and her eyes were dark. "It's not just the movements, China. The disease causes personality changes, too. She's always been a little hard to get along with, but recently she's begun having terrible tantrums. She simply loses control." She looked at me. "You saw what happened this morning at the table."

I certainly had. "I thought she was going to hit Alice Ann."

"Her outbursts are getting more violent," Leatha said soberly. "The paranoia is worsening, too. And the hallucinations."

"Hallucinations?" I asked, startled.

Leatha's fingers picked at the yellow fabric of her shorts. "She sees ghosts. People from the past. Her mother and father and her nurse, Sapphire. Oh, and somebody named Brent, whom I've never heard of." Her hands twisted in her lap. "They're as real to her as we are."

I frowned. "Are these hallucinations part of the disease?"

Leatha nodded wearily. "She doesn't sleep well, either. She gets up at night and wanders around." Her smile was rueful. "You'll probably hear her. She bumps into things and makes a racket. I'm afraid she'll fall down the stairs or something. I've gotten to the point where I'm afraid to leave her alone, even at night. I'm learning to sleep with my eyes open."

I studied my mother, noticing again how exhausted she looked, and defeated, too, as if she didn't know where to turn. This kind of situation would be difficult enough for a young woman, and Leatha certainly wasn't young anymore. This could do her in, as well as Aunt Tullie.

"When did you find out about her condition?" I asked.

"After I came here, at the beginning of March. I knew she'd been in poor health, but I didn't know what the problem was. She was diagnosed five years ago by a neurologist, but she didn't tell me, or anyone else." Leatha made a face. "She *still* hasn't told me, in fact—but I found the doctor's reports and called him." She shook her head. "It's a scary disease, China, and so *secret*. That's what bothers me as much as anything else. I've been going back through the generations, trying to piece things together, trying to figure out where it came from and who had it. But it's hard. All these years, and everything hidden, like my daddy's drinking and his daddy's before him. There's nothing to hold on to. Just lies and secrets."

Some of this wasn't making much sense, but we could straighten it out later. There were more practical matters to attend to. "Who was taking care of Aunt Tullie before you came?"

She sighed. "Darlene, for a few months. Before that, Queenie. She was able to manage Aunt Tullie pretty well, but after she got sick last year, things sort of fell apart. Anyway, Darlene certainly isn't the answer. Aunt Tullie doesn't get along with her." Leatha's lips were quivering at the corners and I could see that she was close to tears. "I need to figure out some way to manage her care, at least by the end of summer. And you and I need to decide what we're going to do about—"

"Absolutely," I said firmly. "You can't stay here indefinitely. Sam is a patient man, but two months is a long time. And summer is *forever*." I paused. "Is it too soon to start thinking about a nursing home?"

Leatha looked away. "I'm sure that Aunt Tullie is less

anxious and confused in her familiar surroundings than she would be anywhere else," she said slowly. "It would be good to keep her here as long as possible. And the local nursing homes aren't set up to handle difficult or violent patients. It's not going to be easy to find a facility that will take her."

"I can see the problem." Unfortunately, I couldn't see an immediate solution to it. "You haven't answered my question," I added after a moment. "What does Aunt Tullie's illness have to do with what you told the police?"

"Can't you guess?" She wasn't looking at me.

"I hope to hell she didn't *shoot* him," I said fervently.

"Oh, no, nothing like that!" Leatha exclaimed. "She only hit him."

"Hit him! With *what*?" But the minute I asked, I knew the answer. "She smacked him with her cane, didn't she?"

"She's strong, China. She hit the side of his head." Leatha shuddered. "It made an awful sound. Like a baseball bat whacking a watermelon."

"It didn't knock him out, did it?" I asked, alarmed.

She looked rueful. "I'm afraid so. Just for a few minutes, though. He came around really fast, and he said he was all right. He didn't seem badly injured, just a little dizzy is all. I tried to get him to lie down but he jumped in his truck and drove off. I cleaned up the blood myself and—"

"Blood?" I was horrified. "Aunt Tullie hit Wiley Beauchamp hard enough to knock him out and draw blood and you didn't call—"

"Oh, he wasn't hurt." Leatha flapped her hand nervously. "You can't hurt a Beauchamp. My father always said they had the hardest heads in the world."

"But nobody's seen him since he left here," I pointed

out. "Maybe she gave him a concussion. Maybe he stopped his car beside the road someplace and got out and wandered off into the swamp. Maybe he lost consciousness and—"

I stopped, feeling panicky. The potential consequences of severe cranial injury weren't pleasant to contemplate. If Wiley had crawled off into the snake-infested bayou and died, the local constabulary would be on Aunt Tullie like white on rice. What's more, my mother had cleaned up the blood and failed to report the assault, making her an accessory after the fact, not to mention her obstruction of justice with that lie to the police. Aunt Tullie probably couldn't be convicted in criminal court, because her defense attorney would marshal a parade of expert witnesses to testify that organic impairment inhibited her ability to form the requisite intent to commit a crime. But that wouldn't buy us much in the civil proceeding that was bound to follow. A successful lawsuit would wipe out Jordan's Crossing. I made a hollow noise deep in my throat.

"Don't worry, China," Leatha said reassuringly. "If Wiley had parked beside the road, the police would have found his car by now." She leaned over to pat my arm. "Really, dear, I'm sure there's nothing to worry about."

Inside the house, there was a crash, an angry cry, and a scream of pain. Leatha heaved a long, despairing sigh and stood up. "Oh, God, now what?"

Whatever it was, I didn't want to know.

Chapter Four

Chicory (*Cichorium intybus*, succory). Grows wild along roadsides and in neglected fields through North America.

Uses: The plant has been grown in large quantities in Europe for many years to supply the demands of the beverage industry for roasted chicory root as a coffee additive or substitute.... In folk medicine, chicory root is valued primarily as a mild nonirritating tonic with associated diuretic and, particularly, laxative effects. It is said to protect the liver from, and act as a counter-stimulant to, the effects of excessive coffee drinking. Chicory root is valued in Egypt as a folk remedy for tachycardia (rapid heartbeat). The bruised leaves are considered a good poultice and are applied locally for the relief of inflammations.

Steven Foster and Varro E. Tyler, Ph.D.
Tyler's Honest Herbal

After considering the various directions a telephone conversation might take, I decided to drive into Chicory and talk to Colonel Blakeslee in person. I wanted to watch his face as we talked and try to get some measure of the man. His calendar must not have been terribly crowded, because Leatha's phone call got me the two-thirty slot.

Lunch was a big meal, with stewed chicken and dumplings, mashed potatoes, string beans, and lemon meringue pie. Darlene was showing off. Afterward, I replaced Pearl's journal in the drawer under the bookshelf in the library, then went upstairs and put on a plaid blouse and the only skirt I had brought, a denim wraparound. It wasn't power dressing but it would have to do, since I hadn't packed for a conference with a lawyer. While I was at it, I unpacked the clothes I had brought, hanging some in the closet and putting others into the empty drawers in the bureau in my room. Then I added a little lipstick and put on a pair of gold earrings. I was ready to meet Colonel Blakeslee.

Chicory, Mississippi, a town of thirty-five hundred souls, used to be named after a Choctaw chief. But in 1935, the Garden Club got up a petition to change it, for reasons that everybody knew but nobody would acknowledge. After a few months of wrangling about whether the town ought to be called Chicory or Sycamore, the Garden Club held a plebiscite and Chicory won, by a narrow margin. But no matter what it's called, the town is still the same: a grid of dusty streets laid out between a sprawling farm-implement depot on the north and a cotton gin on the south, the whole affair tied loosely together by Highway 49, which runs north to Greenwood and Memphis and south to Jackson and Hattiesburg and Gulfport.

The hard, fierce sun glared down as if it still resented the name change, the thermometer was stuck somewhere around 90 degrees, and the humidity was high enough to sweat juice out of a watermelon. But the four large magnolia trees, one at each corner of the courthouse lawn, were beautifully layered with waxy white blooms. Their scent hung heavy in the air as I parked in front of the feed store and walked past the Confederate veterans' monument to Robert E. Lee Street.

Colonel Blakeslee's office was over the drugstore, up a flight of narrow stairs that led to a surprisingly wide, high-ceilinged hallway. The first door on the right bore the modest announcement that this was the office of Colonel Cyrus P. Blakeslee, Attorney at Law. The reception room inside might have been a stage set for a turn-of-the-century movie: green leather sofa and chair, dark oak desk, wooden filing cabinets, period-style lighting, framed antique prints of black folks working in the cotton fields.

But the young blonde at the secretary's desk was contemporary enough—short-short red skirt, beads and bangles, and talonlike nails—and the computer in front of her, on which she was doing the billing, made it clear that the wooden filing cabinets were only stage props. The really serious business—the boilerplate files that long ago took the place of seat-of-the-pants lawyering—lived in the computer, where they could be called upon to serve in any conceivable legal situation. Jennifer (her name, according to the engraved nameplate on her desk) informed me that he'd just gotten back from his lunch with the mayor and tripped gaily into the colonel's office to see if he was ready for me. He was, apparently, for she ushered me in with a bright smile.

The inner office was a walnut-paneled replica of the outer, with the addition of heavy green draperies and a wall hung with framed diplomas, gilt-edged certificates, Chamber of Commerce citations, and the usual collection of testimonials to exemplary citizenship, personal integrity, and all-around good character—the sort of thing lawyers like to hang on their walls to assure their clients that they have nothing to fear. As I contemplated this encouraging display, Colonel Cyrus P. Blakeslee turned from the coat tree where he had just hung up a rumpled gray suit jacket. He was a tall man and hefty, with an amiable smile, a ruddy complexion, and graying hair, a little sparse on top. He might have been in his mid-seventies, a decade or so younger than Aunt Tullie, but he was still robust and hearty.

"Join me in a cup of coffee?" he asked in a down-home Andy Griffith drawl. "Chicory-au-lait. N'Awlins finest."

I was primed to say no to coffee, but chicory is something else again. I like its mellow bitterness—a contradiction in tastes, but there it is. "Sounds real good to me," I said, matching his folksy tone, and watched him pick up the phone to ask Jennifer-honey to please bring us thirsty folk some good ol' chic'ry coffee with plenty of cream.

Without waiting for directions, I sat in the burgundy leather chair in front of his desk. "Thank you for seeing me," I said. "Did your secretary tell you who I am?"

"Miz Petulia Coldwell's grandniece," he said. He loosened his blue silk tie—a prominent spot of barbecue sauce testified to what he had eaten for lunch—and sat down across from me. He pulled his pale, thin eyebrows together, a little frown appearing between them. "I don't s'pose you thought to bring any—"

I took a folded sheet of paper out of my shoulder bag and handed it across the desk. It was a short letter of introduction that I had typed on the ancient portable in the plantation office and to which Leatha had forged Aunt Tullie's loopy and indecipherable scrawl. We had agreed that Aunt Tullie would be agitated by any mention of Colonal Blakeslee, Wiley Beauchamp, or the property deed, and that we would not bring up the subject until it was absolutely necessary.

Colonel Blakeslee gave the letter a quick glance and handed it back. "How is your aunt?" he asked. "Ain't seen her much lately."

"She hasn't been well," I said cautiously, not sure how much he knew.

"Age catchin' up with her, I reckon, like it does all of us." There was a gusty sigh. "Last time I was out to the plantation, she seemed awful nervous." The Colonel gave me a measuring glance. "China, eh? So you're Leatha's girl. You look like your mother. Got that Coldwell mouth." His smile was congratulatory, as if he were bestowing some sort of honor upon me. "Strong fam'ly resemblance 'mongst you Coldwells. Something about the eyes, an' the look around the mouth." Another glance under the pale eyebrows, sharper now and more inquisitive. "Didn't Miz Tullie tell me you went through law school? University of Texas, I b'lieve she said."

I nodded. "I don't practice, though." I hoped my tone was disarming. I had no idea how far this man could be trusted, and he might be less wary if he thought of me simply as Leatha's girl. "I own a small business in the Texas Hill Country."

Jennifer came in just then with a tray and two cups of hot chicory coffee, creamy and sweetly bitter. After a few sips and an appreciative sigh, the Colonel sat back in his chair, tented his thick fingers under his chin, and frowned.

"Well, I s'pose we might as well get down to cases," he said. "If you ask me, this deed's a bad business. I wouldn't've expected Wiley Beauchamp to come up with somethin' like that." He made a wry face. "And if he did, wouldn't't've expected him to come to me about it—'cept that Miz Tullie's obviously failin', and I reckon he figured he'd have to talk to me, one way or t'other. I handle your aunt's legal affairs, as I s'pose you know."

I nodded. "It might be a good idea if you and I had a talk about Aunt Tullie's estate," I said. "I'd like to be able to discuss the details with her and my mother." I knew that Jordan's Crossing was supposed to be left to Leatha, although I hadn't actually seen the will. "But for right now, maybe you could just tell me what you and Wiley talked about. He's an old friend," I added with a disarming smile. "We used to go rattlesnake hunting together. And of course, the Beauchamps and the Coldwells have been almost like family." That was a stretch, but strict truth wasn't the goal here. I needed to get as much information as the Colonel was willing and able to give me, and at this point, I didn't know which side he was on.

"You got that right." His chair creaked as he leaned back. "Both fam'lies, they go back a long ways together. Back before the war." The war, of course, was the War, fought to protect the slave economy from the damyankees who wanted to stomp the South into the dirt and keep it from ever risin' again. "Wiley came in here . . . let's see, last Friday, I b'lieve." He consulted some inner calendar. "Yep, Friday morning it was. He was waitin' for me when I got back from the Baptist Pancake Breakfast, sittin' in that there chair where you're sittin' now, his legs crossed and a smile on his face, purty as you please. 'Thout even waitin' for me to get my coat off, he pulls out this old envelope and flaps it down on the desk."

The Colonel sat forward, reached for a carved wooden box, took out a cigar, and lit it with a wooden match that he struck against the sole of his shoe. I sat stoically as he exhaled a cloud of choking blue smoke. Leaning back in his chair again, he went on with his story.

"So he tells this long tale 'bout how his daddy Ezra kept all the fam'ly papers in a big ol' desk. Says he hadn't got around to sortin' 'em until last week 'cause it was such a terrible job. Great big mess of letters, invoices, even some slave bills of sale goin' back to Tobias's time. And this envelope, with a deed in it."

"Did you see it?"

"He showed it to me. It was so old and brittle, it was splittin' along the folds. I wanted to make a copy, but the machine wasn't working and Wiley didn't want Jennifer to take it over to the bank for copies. But I made some notes." He opened a drawer and took out a sheet of paper. "The deed conveyed one full section of land—Section 12—to Tobias Beauchamp, his heirs and assigns forever etcetera, in return for one dollar and services rendered. It was signed by Abner Coldwell and dated January 16, 1864."

"During the War," I said slowly.

"The winter after Abner got back from Vicksburg, minus the leg he left there." The Colonel sucked on the cigar and puffed out another cloud. "I looked the deed over good, and saw that it was signed and witnessed all right and proper. Not havin' a section map in the office, I couldn't confirm the legal description, but Wiley said he'd checked it against the map on the wall in the plantation office. Accordin' to him, the six hundred and forty acres of Section 12 starts at the main road and goes all the way back to the river. It includes the old river landing and the house that your great-grandfather Clancy built on the property after this transaction supposedly took place." He reached for his coffee cup and squinted at me through the smoke. "As opposed to Abner Coldwell's big ol' mansion, which burned down around the time he died. You know about that, I s'pose?"

I nodded as the blue cloud enveloped me like a noxious shroud. I was practicing shallow breathing. "I know that for some reason that's never been clear, Clancy decided not to rebuild where his father's house burned. Instead, he built the present house closer to the site of Uncle Jed's old trading post."

"Which just happened to be on the river section that his father had deeded to Tobias Beauchamp more than a decade before," the Colonel said. He drained his cup and set it down. "If you believe that deed, o' course."

"That's what I don't understand," I said. "Why in the world would Abner give land to Tobias? And why *that* particular section? It had the river landing, which would have made it the best of the five or so sections he owned." I was exaggerating my puzzlement. I did have a few ideas on the subject, but I wanted to hear what the Colonel might come up with.

He shrugged. "Could be all sorts of reasons." There was a long pause. Outside, a horn blared. The Colonel eyed me. "You ever hear 'bout Davis Bend?"

I shook my head. This had the makings of a story.

The Colonel pulled out a lower drawer of his desk and put his feet on it. "Davis Bend was a big plantation over on the river, up 'bove Vicksburg. It was owned by Joseph Davis, who was Jefferson Davis's blood brother, although as I understand it, Joseph didn't share in the convictions that made ol' Jeff the president of our ephemeral Confederacy." His tone had grown dry. "Anyway, Joseph had a smart young slave he was right fond of, name of Benjamin, who he taught to read and do numbers. After a while, Joseph made Benjamin his manager, and the two of them worked that plantation side by side for quite a few years, before and durin' the war, although o' course by the time it was over, Benjamin was a freedman. After the war, Joseph took it into his head to set Benjamin up as a planter, so he sold him Davis Bend—or gave it to him, was what it amounted to, 'cause he didn't charge anything like market value. Under the Black Code of Mississippi, Benjamin couldn't own it outright, so they had to come up with some kind of lease. When Benjamin did get to own it openly, that ex-slave became the third largest producer of cotton in the entire nation." He puffed reflectively on his cigar. "Somethin' to ponder on, I reckon."

It certainly was, and I could see the possible analogy. "So you're suggesting that Abner Coldwell wanted to set Tobias up as a planter?" I frowned. "Tobias was a Choctaw, wasn't he? There was no legal barrier to his ownership of the land, as there was for blacks."

"Right. Under the Treaty of Dancing Rabbit Creek, an Indian could hold land in Mississippi as long as he became a citizen of the state, which meant forswearing his tribal allegiance. A number of them did, y'know, including Chief Leflore, who was Tobias's blood kin. Under the treaty, y'see, a Choctaw could lay claim to a section of land for himself and a quarter-section for each natural child, and after he'd lived on it and improved it for five years, he'd get a deed to it. So some of the Indians didn't go west, the way the government intended them to. Some stayed and tried to make a living on the land, or had it stolen by lawyers and speculators." He looked at me. "Some say that's how Jed Coldwell got that section in the first place. Stole it from some Choctaw."

We were getting off the subject. "But if Tobias Beauchamp held clear title to the land," I said, bringing us back, "why did he allow Clancy Coldwell to build the Big House on it? Have you checked the courthouse? Is there any record of this so-called deed being filed?"

The Colonel made a whistling noise through his teeth. "The original Davis County courthouse burned about the time Grant got hisself elected for a second term. Wasn't much of a courthouse, anyway, just a log lean-to stuck up next to the jail, where the county clerk kept a trunk full of old land records. If there was a filing, it got burned up."

He paused and narrowed his eyes, using his cigar to signal a new paragraph. "I asked Wiley the very same question you're askin'. About the house, that is. I could imagine Abner givin' Tobias that land—after all, Tobias did save his hide when the Yankees blew off that leg at Vicksburg, and Tobias helped make Jordan's Crossing into a mighty fine plantation. But why the hell did he let Clancy put that house on land that rightfully belonged to him? Was there some kind of a deal between Tobias and Clancy? A quitclaim, maybe? If so, why ain't there a record of that too?"

"Maybe there is. Or *was*." I leaned forward. "What did Wiley say when you asked him these questions?"

The Colonel rubbed his jaw. "He said he didn't have any idea why it happened, but it didn't matter, 'cause any fool could see that the land and the house both belonged to the Beauchamps, meanin' him, since he's the last of 'em."

I sat back. "What's your advice, Colonel? What do you think Aunt Tullie should do?"

"Your aunt won't like it," the Colonel said soberly, "but

I think she oughta try to reach a settlement. Otherwise, this thing will go to litigation, which she is likely to lose. Wiley's got time on his side. The least harm he can do is to tie up her estate so it can't be probated. That's if the deed is gen-u-ine, o' course."

"I can't believe that Wiley would try to accomplish something like this with a forged document," I said. "He's too smart for that."

"I'm with you there." The Colonel gave a wry, assenting chuckle. "Ol' Wiley's a hell-raiser, y'know. Had more'n his share of lady friends, but allus managed to duck out before they got to the church. Offhand, I'd say it don't look like there's gonna be another generation of Beauchamps—unless Wiley takes it into his head to find him a wife." Another chuckle. "Which he might, if he thinks he's got a section of land and a house to pass on."

Wiley wouldn't be anxious to find a wife if he was lying facedown in the swamp, his skull caved in by a whack from Aunt Tullie's gold-headed cane. I suppressed a shudder.

"He took the original away with him, o' course," the Colonel went on. "Said he was going to put it where nobody could get at it but him. I suggested a safe-deposit box at the bank, but he said he knew a better place." He shook his head. "You never could tell those Beauchamps a dad-blamed thing. Ol' Ezra was that way, too. They allus got a better idea."

"I'll search the family papers for a record of a later transaction," I said. "Maybe Clancy bought the land back from Tobias. Maybe there's some sort of quitclaim." I didn't think it was as simple as that, but anything was possible.

The Colonel sucked on his cigar. "You've got quite a

hunt on your hands. That office is full o' papers, and so is the attic. No Coldwell could ever bring hisself to throw anything away."

"I'm sure you're right," I said, wondering just how high the temperature might be in the Big House attic. "Did Wiley say what he planned to do about this situation?"

"He asked my opinion," the Colonel replied, "and I told him he'd best hightail it out to Jordan's Crossing and have a serious sit-down talk with Miz Tullie." He tapped his cigar into the ashtray. "I figured a few words from her oughta take some of the starch outa him. If there was a second deed or a quitclaim or something, she'd know right where to lay her hands on it. She's a sharp old lady, 'specially where property is concerned."

"I'm not so sure her memory can be trusted these days," I said. "Have you talked with her lately?"

"Not for a while." The Colonel sighed. "Sure hate to see Miz Tullie get old. She's kept that plantation goin' since her daddy died, which was right after I came home from the Pacific. That brother of hers, Howard, he never was good for much." He frowned. "What's the problem? Not Alzheimer's, I hope."

"Something like that," I said vaguely. I was beginning to like this lawyer, but some instinct told me not to share the symptoms of a disease I didn't yet fully understand. Leatha and I would be talking to the Colonel in the next few days, though, after I understood more about what was going on. If Aunt Tullie hadn't done it already, she would need to execute a durable power of attorney, giving Leatha the power to make decisions on her behalf.

I stood up. "Oh, by the way, a couple of deputies came out to the house this morning," I added, as if it were an afterthought. "They were looking for Wiley. He seems to have gone off without letting anybody know where he was headed."

"Is that right?" The Colonel pushed himself out of his chair. "Well, as I said, Wiley's a hell-raiser. All of those Beauchamps have always been a little squirrelly. My mother, God bless her, used to say that Tobias's wife, Sapphire, was the most beautiful woman she ever saw. Mixed blood, you know, French and Choctaw, maybe African, too. But there came a time when Tobias wouldn't let her out of the house. Some folks said it was 'cause he was crazy jealous, her bein' so much younger than him, thirty-some years I think it was. But my mother said it wasn't that at all. Said she had some sort of bad sickness." He shook his head sadly. "Wiley's father, Ezra, he had a mental problem in his last days, too. They had to put him in the state hospital down at Jackson. And Ezra's sister Belle, she killed herself. Come to think of it, Wiley's brother did, too. Bad luck seems to run in the fam'ly. But o' course folks don't talk much about things like that."

I nodded. "If Wiley turns up here, could you let me know? Mother says there's a tractor that needs repair." I didn't think it was a good idea to tell the Colonel that Aunt Tullie had walloped Wiley with her cane.

"Sure thing," the Colonel said. "And if you find a document that supersedes the Beauchamp deed, you'll let me know?"

"Oh, you bet," I said.

OUTSIDE, the afternoon sun seemed to burn even brighter and hotter than before, and the pavement shimmered in the dizzying heat. As I turned the courthouse corner on my way to the car, I saw a very old woman wearing a purple muumuu and a wine-red turban shot through with gold and brown threads, sitting on the scarred wooden bench in the green shade of a magnolia tree, a brown-paper shopping bag at her feet.

I stared at the mummified old face, the skin shrunk tight against the bone, and felt the goose bumps rise on both arms. A voice in my head asked, incredulously: *Is it possible? Can this woman actually be the same Marie Louise LaTour who used to tell fortunes on her cottage porch?* Another voice, from the general region of what Ruby calls my left brain, replied more skeptically: *Oh, come off it, China. Of course it's not possible. That was thirty-five years ago, and she was an old woman then. She's been dead and gone for almost a quarter of a century.*

The old woman was watching me, too, silent and inscrutable as a buddha, and now she slowly lifted a hand, beckoning. I hesitated for a moment, and the skeptical voice scolded: *This is absolutely absurd, China. Get in the car and go back to the plantation. You've got enough on your plate without asking for some silly hocus-pocus.*

But I couldn't go to the car. The woman's ancient eyes—so dark that they were like deep black pools—were fixed on mine, drawing me slowly toward her, and I was powerless to do anything about it, the way a dream makes you powerless. There was a tinny buzzing in my ears and the air around us vibrated, charged with some sort of vital energy. As I came closer, we were surrounded by an immense and reverberating silence, and it seemed as if the whole town had come to a dead stop. If I had been able to glance over my shoulder, I'm sure I would have seen cars and trucks and passersby frozen in their places.

" 'Lo dere, child," the woman said softly. "I bin waitin' fer you." She reached for my hand and clasped it, her brown hand cool and leathery, like a familiar old glove, her low voice cracked and raspy like the voice in my dream, but mild and somehow comforting. "Don't fret. You'll figger out all dose old myst'ries soon 'nuf. An' you'll have help, when de need comes." She grinned, showing missing teeth. "You come see me, I'll help."

I stared at the woman, the present moment receding like a dissolving thought in the green shade, her eyes—the pupil and iris so black that they seemed like huge empty holes—drawing me inside her, into the vastness of all that her eyes had seen, all that her memory held. It was as if I were kneeling beside a dark pool in the swamp, peering through the pale green algae on the surface, down and down through layer after layer of teeming swamp life, down to the deep, drowned roots of long-dead cypress trees. Beneath the surface of what was happening in this present moment—an ancient black woman, sitting regal as a queen on the courthouse bench in the cool shade of a magnolia, beckoning to a younger white woman casually passing by on the sunstruck street—lay the vast and unplumbed mystery of the past, and I was falling into it as if I had plunged headfirst into that black pool in the swamp, diving deeper and deeper, the water silently closing over my head, leaving no trace of me. I was suddenly terrified. My life, other lives, too, depended on my finding something long hidden among these drowned roots, but I had no idea what I was seeking or how I would know when I had found it.

I held onto my last breath and made a determined effort to open my eyes under the black water. But there was no water, no pool, no swamp, just Chicory's courthouse square and the old woman on the bench. I coughed, tried to speak, cleared my throat and tried again.

"What am I supposed to figure out?"

She sighed and shook her head, as if in rebuke, as if she were disappointed. "You gots to let dem ol' skeletons rest, fer now, leastways. Yo're jes like Miz Tullie, wantin' to know too much too soon." Her voice became stern. "I tol' her den an' I'll tell you now: de answer'll come when yo're ready to know what hit means, an' all de diggin' an' de askin' and de pushin' won't hurry hit along one li'l bit." She gave my hand a squeeze and let it go.

I stood there staring at her, speechless. "How do you know—"

"G'wan back home, girl," she said. "Yore momma needs you." She tilted her head, regarding me compassionately. "Yore momma needs you *bad*. She gots somethin' to tell you, somethin' 'pawtant. An' you gots to pay 'tention. So g'wan, you hear?"

And suddenly I woke up from the dream, if that's what it was. My ears stopped buzzing, the electric air stopped vibrating, and the courthouse clock struck the half-hour. Behind me, a car horn honked, a couple of black kids on in-line skates flung themselves noisily down the concrete sidewalk, dodging an angry white woman, who yelled, "What you think you're doin', you little hoodlums?"

I blinked. *What was I supposed to say?* "Thank you," I managed.

The old woman nodded. A breeze lifted the leaves, shifting the sunlight onto her face, and I saw that she wasn't as old as I had thought, no older than Aunt Tullie probably. "Yo're welcome," she said in that rusty voice, putting both hands on her knees and pushing herself painfully erect. "Reckon it's time fer me to git on home."

"My car is just down the street. Can I give you a lift?"

She picked up her shopping bag. "D'ruther walk, thank

'ee. Need to stretch my ol' legs. You tell Miz Tullie I'm sayin' a li'l prayer fer her. An' tell her to let all dem ol' ghosts lie. Ain't much she kin do 'bout 'em now, anyways."

Then she turned and walked away, humming tunelessly, the purple cloth clinging to her swaying hips, the shopping bag banging against her leg.

Chapter Five

Bloodroot (*Sanguinaria canadensis*)

Common Names: Red Puccoon, Indian Plant, Tetterwort

Features: Indigenous to eastern North America. A monotypic genus of the Papaveraceae family. The small herb is often difficult to find in its woodland home, where the sheltered places and leaf mould is ideal for its survival. The thick, palmately lobed leaf is lapped around the bud, which swiftly outgrows its protector, loses its two fugacious sepals and opens into a star-shaped flower, one to each stem, with several fleshy white petals and a mass of golden stamens in the center. The flower closes at night or on shady days and is among the early spring flowers, often cultivated in gardens. The whole plant is very brittle and succulent and when broken, especially at its thick, fleshy root, an acrid red juice bleeds from the divided sections: the root is about the size of a man's little finger. The taste is bitter and harsh. The whole plant is medicinal, the root being the part chiefly used.

Alma R. Hutchens
Indian Herbalogy of North America

The old woman's words were still ringing in my ears, and I half-expected Leatha to be waiting for me on the veranda. But apparently she didn't need me, at least not at the moment. The house was quiet and I guessed that both she and Aunt Tullie were upstairs taking naps, for which I was grateful. If I had any hope of finding documentation of a subsequent land transaction, I had a big chore ahead of me. While I certainly couldn't accomplish much in the hour or two before our early supper, I could at least figure out the size of the job and decide on a plan of attack.

I hadn't spent much time in the plantation office when I was a kid. The room had its own separate entrance at the back of the house so employees could come and go without traipsing down the hall. It was the place where Aunt Tullie and Grandfather Howard (when he was sober) carried out serious business, and it was off-limits to a noisy young girl who had a talent for sticking her nose into places she didn't belong.

Like the rest of the house, though, the office hadn't changed much over the years, unless you counted the fax machine on the table in the corner or this year's farm-equipment calendar on the wall above it, with a photograph of the latest tractor model. There was the old walnut desk that I remembered, and an oak swivel chair that would probably go for a couple of hundred dollars at an antique store. On top of the desk was a still-life arrangement out of an earlier time: my grandfather's portable Underwood typewriter; his wind-up clock, its hands stopped at half-past five; and a metal ring of old skeleton keys. There was also a green-painted gooseneck desk lamp and the telephone—a black phone with a bell that gave a ghostly tinkle every time you turned the round dial.

Beside the desk was a gray metal filing cabinet, circa World War II, and along the opposite wall two more file cabinets. A musty, old-house odor hung on the air, a smell compounded of dry rot, moldy wallpaper, and damp plaster, and I wondered, not for the first time, what would happen to this place once Aunt Tullie was gone. Leatha would sell the plantation—or at least I hoped so. What my mother didn't know about raising cotton would fill a book. Surely she wouldn't try to hold onto the place just because it had been in the Coldwell family for four generations.

But then I remembered the reason I was here. If the deed Wiley had dug up was genuine, the house and the land on which it was built could go to the Beauchamps, not to Leatha—which aside from the unhappiness it would cause Aunt Tullie, might not be such a bad thing after all. The house was over a century old, and it had never been very well maintained. It undoubtedly needed tens of thousands of dollars of repairs. And as far as the land was concerned—

A stained, fly-specked map of Township 18 of the North Range of Davis County had been tacked to the wall above the desk ever since I could remember, and I went over to study it. At one time, Jordan's Crossing had been a 3,200-acre rectangle comprising five sections of land, each of them one square mile in area, laid side by side and numbered 12 through 16. But Sections 16 and 15, at the eastern end of the plantation, were now marked through with a big red X; presumably they had been sold by Aunt Tullie or her father or grandfather and no longer were part of the plantation. The westernmost piece, Section 12, was bordered by the Bloodroot River. It was the piece against which Wiley was staking his claim.

I turned on the desk lamp and swiveled it upward so that it illuminated the map. There was no doubt about it. In Abner's day, Section 12 had been the finest of his five sections. It would've boasted the richest and deepest soil, bordering as it did the Bloodroot River, and it included the river landing, which a century ago had been vital to the plantation's economy. Barges brought supplies up the Bloodroot to the landing, where they were reloaded with bales of cotton and floated back downstream to the Mississippi and then to New Orleans, where the crop was sold for the best price.

Now, of course, the old landing wasn't worth much. The Bloodroot River was no longer navigable, except by canoe or flatboat, and there was nothing left of the busy landing except the old fishing camp where Darlene and I hung out as kids, slowly slipping back into the swamp out of which it had been carved. I had no idea whether Section 12 had been continuously cropped, or whether the weeds and the wilderness had reclaimed it, too. But I was still left with that unanswered, unanswerable question: Why had Abner given this valuable piece of property—the heart of his holdings—to Tobias?

I turned, glancing around the room. But perhaps the deed was not genuine, or perhaps there was a subsequent repurchase or quitclaim, and I would find it in one of those three metal file cabinets. There were labels on the drawers and a neat, organized look about them that suggested that their contents might be neatly organized as well. Maybe it wouldn't be as difficult to find what I was looking for as I had feared.

No such luck. When I opened the top drawer of the nearest cabinet, I saw a jumble of bank statements from several years back, canceled checks, invoices for seed and fertilizer, and employment records, all tumbled loosely together as if by some careless or malicious hand. When I looked in the other drawers and the other file cabinets, I found the same thing, for earlier years. What we had here was one hell of a mess. I doubted that the attic would yield anything more promising.

The door opened and I turned as Leatha came in, her yellow blouse wrinkled, her hair disarranged from sleeping. "I didn't know you were back," she said. "I was going to phone Sam." She crossed the room and sat down in the desk chair, wearily, as if her nap had brought her no real rest. "But maybe we'd better finish our talk while Aunt Tullie is still sleeping. Did Colonel Blakeslee tell you what he thought about that deed?"

I perched on a corner of the desk. "If it's genuine—and that can be determined only by examining the original document—he's going to advise Aunt Tullie to reach some sort of settlement with Wiley. Otherwise the case is likely to go into litigation. If she dies before the question is resolved, it could tie up the entire estate for years."

Leatha rubbed her eyes with the back of her hands. "Oh, dear," she said sadly. "Haven't we got enough to worry about?"

"You said that Wiley had the original deed with him that night. Is that correct?"

"That's what he said," she replied. "Why?"

"I'm just wondering where it is," I said. If something had indeed happened to Wiley, that deed might never be found. On the other hand, if he was out of the picture, we could stop worrying about his claim—although we might have other things to deal with that were potentially even more worrisome, such as a criminal charge of assault with a deadly weapon, or a civil suit for wrongful death.

"What are we going to do?" Leatha asked. She seemed slightly dazed, as if she was not yet quite awake. I thought how lost and vulnerable she looked, and I hoped once again that she wouldn't start looking for answers in the bottle. We had enough problems without Leatha falling off the wagon.

"The Colonel and I agreed that I should go through the family papers and see if I could find a record of any subsequent land transfer," I said. "If Tobias Beauchamp held clear title to this property, it's hard to imagine that he would've allowed Great-grandfather Clancy to build this house on it."

Leatha looked around with a shudder. "You've got a job, I'm afraid. The Coldwells were never very good at organizing, but it's been worse lately. Last week, I found Aunt Tullie in here, dumping out one of those file drawers. She goes through the house that way, too, turning everything upside down." She sighed. "When I was a child, Wiley's father, Ezra, kept this office in apple-pie order. If you asked him for a document related to the land, he'd know exactly where it was to be found."

"If that's true," I said grimly, "there isn't any point in looking. There won't be any document to find."

Leatha looked up at me, her eyes widening. "Because Ezra destroyed it?"

"Or Jacob, his father. All the Beauchamps, from Tobias on down, have had access to this office, haven't they? But I'll give it a try anyway." I looked at my watch, wondering if I should climb up to the attic. "What time is supper?"

"In another hour." Leatha leaned forward and put one hand on my knee. "But we need to talk, China. About Aunt Tullie's condition and what it means to us. To you and me, I mean. There are some things about this that I don't think you understand."

Hearing the tension in her voice, I brought my attention back to her. "I understand that we have to start making plans to find her the right kind of custodial care," I said. "And that we need to get her to execute a durable power of attorney in your name."

"A durable—" Leatha frowned. "What's that?"

"It's a legal document that will give you the authority to act on Aunt Tullie's behalf. You can write her checks, pay her bills, file her tax returns, manage her health care— whatever needs to be done. If we don't do this now, while she's still halfway capable of understanding what she's signing, we might end up asking a Mississippi court to appoint you as her guardian."

"Wouldn't that be easier?" Leatha's question was plaintive. "Aunt Tullie's not going to like this power of attorney thing. She'll think she's signing away her rights."

I shook my head firmly. "Going through the court system is infinitely more difficult, Mother. We'd have to file a petition, allege her incapacity and the reason for it, and get medical experts to testify that she is no longer competent." I put my hand over Leatha's. "It's a costly adversarial proceeding that includes legal representation and a jury trial, designed primarily to safeguard Aunt Tullie's rights. It would be terribly humiliating for her, and for us."

"Then I suppose we have to persuade her to do it," Leatha said wearily. She pulled her hand away and turned her head, not looking at me. "But that isn't what I was talking about, China. I don't think you understand about Huntington's. About the disease itself, I mean."

I regarded her. "It's something like Alzheimer's, isn't

it? Except that people develop odd movements." Now that I thought about it, I vaguely remembered that it used to be called Huntington's chorea, after the Greek word for dance.

"It's like Alzheimer's in the sense of being both degenerative and progressive and eventually fatal," Leatha replied slowly, as if she had memorized the words. "But it's hereditary, too, you see."

I watched her as she spoke—not so much listening to her words as seeing the lines around her eyes and mouth, the streaky gray in her disheveled hair, the trembling of her thin fingers—and I felt a new kind of tenderness toward her, almost a protectiveness. I had not been the dutiful daughter she wanted, and she had not been the mother a girl needs, able to declare herself as an independent woman and stand her ground against a neglectful and sometimes abusive husband. But that was in the past. This was the present, and we were confronting a very difficult situation. I had to do whatever I could to help her deal with Aunt Tullie.

Leatha took a deep breath. Her voice was urgent. "China, dear, I don't think you're *hearing* me. According to the doctor, this disease of Aunt Tullie's is caused by a faulty gene. A dominant gene. Some people think it can skip generations, but that's not true. Every member of the family has a fifty-fifty chance of developing it." She said the words slowly, definitively, emphatically. "*I* might have the gene for Huntington's. And if I do, *you* might have it, too."

I must be missing something. This horrible disease was obviously a living nightmare for Aunt Tullie. But I couldn't see how it affected mother and me, except as family members who loved her and wanted to arrange for her care.

"This doesn't make sense, Mother. Aunt Tullie and your father were brother and sister, and I can understand that he had a chance to inherit this faulty gene you're talking about. But Grandfather *didn't* have Huntington's. He died of stomach cancer. And if he didn't have it, he couldn't pass it on to you, and you couldn't give it to me. So we're in the clear. There's nothing for us to worry about—except how it affects Aunt Tullie, and what we can do to make this easier for her." And if that wasn't quite enough, we could worry about the deed Wiley had come up with, and his disappearance.

Leatha was shaking her head, slowly and rhythmically. "But Huntington's often doesn't appear until later in life, China. Some people think that if symptoms haven't shown up by the time you're fifty-five, you're in the clear, but that's just not true. It's hard to say for sure because I only saw her five or six times a year, but I don't think that Aunt Tullie began to exhibit symptoms until she was in her sixties. Your grandfather was only fifty-three when he died. He could have had the gene and didn't live long enough to develop the disease." She paused and looked anxiously at me. "Now do you see why I'm worried?"

I saw, and I was stunned. A late-onset hereditary disease was like a genetic time bomb. People could pass it on to their children without any idea that one of their genes carried a death sentence. And it could be part of our genetic inheritance, my mother's and mine. It could be in our blood.

Leatha tilted her head. "In fact, it's hard to trace the disease in our family because all the Coldwells died young. Except for Dad's father, Clancy, of course, who was never sick a day in his life until he died of a heart attack on his ninety-first birthday. But Dad's sister Hattie and her daughter were both killed in a car wreck when Hattie was only forty. Dad's twin brothers died when they were babies, before the First World War. There's no way to tell who had the gene and who didn't."

There was a heavy silence. A frantic fly buzzed in the window, and the old clock tick-tocked magisterially, as if it were measuring out the remaining moments of healthy life the two of us might have. This wasn't just Aunt Tullie's nightmare. It was my mother's nightmare. It was mine.

Leatha seemed very still and far away, as if she were searching back through her memory for moments long forgotten. "When I first learned about this, I refused to believe that you and I were in any danger. I denied it. Maybe I had to, because the possibility that I might have given this to you was too painful to accept. The denial was a kind of temporary shelter, you see. A refuge. A place to hide."

She caught the corner of her lip in her teeth, was silent for a moment, then went on. "But I've moved past that now, China. I'm ready to face the truth. And now that I've started thinking about it, I realize that my father could have been exhibiting symptoms before his death. I remember hating to go anywhere in the car with him, because he was such a crazy driver, so jerky and unpredictable. And he was always terribly fidgety, just like Aunt Tullie. He couldn't sit still for a minute. We blamed all this on his drinking, of course, and the family doctor in Chicory agreed. But according to the book I'm reading, doctors frequently misdiagnose Huntington's, even today, after the gene has been identified. Thirty or forty years ago, only a handful could actually recognize the disease. And lots of families hide it, even when they know the truth, because the disease is just so *awful*. Personality changes, loss of mental ability, uncontrollable physical movements—" She wrapped her arms around herself, shuddering. "And then there's the insurance problem, and the difficulty in finding a nursing home that's equipped to handle people who have it, and—"

I made a strangled noise. Oh, God, the insurance problem. If my health insurance company found out that there was a fatal genetic disease in our family, they might refuse to renew my policy. And what was I going to tell Mc-Quaid? That he'd married a woman with a ticking time bomb attached to one of her chromosomes?

Leatha managed a small smile. "I guess you can't blame people for pretending it doesn't exist, or hoping that it's something less scary—Parkinson's, maybe, or alcoholism." She pulled at a loose lock of her hair. "I struggled so hard against my own drinking habit when you were a child, but being an alcoholic just seemed inevitable. I always thought I'd inherited it from him, from my father. Now I just hope that's *all* I inherited."

I looked at my mother as if I were seeing her for the first time. Perhaps I was. As a kid, I had never seen her struggle against alcohol; I'd only witnessed her surrender and I'd judged her harshly for it. If I'd known—if I'd bothered to learn about her fear that she had inherited a predisposition to alcohol—would that have made a difference in the way I felt about her? And if I had been her ally instead of her judge, would she have been stronger?

This was treacherous ground, though, and I needed to back away from it, move to a safer place. I took a deep breath. "Have you told Sam?"

She nodded. "He was here for a couple of days last month, and he noticed immediately that something was seriously wrong. He's so supportive. He located the book for me, and as I come up with new questions, I telephone him, and he gets on the Internet to look for answers. He calls himself my research assistant." Her smile was wry. "You can see I've gotten really involved with this—you might call it an obsession. But there are certain things that you and I have to know in order to plan our lives."

For an instant, I felt slightly disoriented. I'd never thought of my mother as "planning" her life. It had always seemed to me that she went with the flow, passively letting things happen to her. This was a different Leatha than the one I knew, and I was having trouble adjusting.

Leatha shook her head. "You know, this is so ironic, China. All my life, I've been proud of the Coldwells, and especially of the women—Aunt Tullie; her mother, Pearl; her grandmother, Samantha. I brought you here when you were a little girl because I wanted you to understand them and love them as I have. Whether you like it or not, Jordan's Crossing is home. You'll inherit it eventually, and I wanted you to know something about your inheritance." She swallowed hard. "I couldn't have dreamed of *this* kind of inheritance. It seems terribly . . . cruel."

The musty room was very still and warm, and the old walls seemed to close around me like a coffin. I took a breath, then another, but the air itself was fouled. I got down from the desk and walked to the door that led out into the yard, flinging it open. I stood on the step, breathing in the clean, fresh scent of honeysuckle and wisteria and lilies of the valley, following with my glance the long green curve of the lawn as it fell toward the river. After a moment, feeling more in command of myself, I turned and forced a smile.

"It's a good thing I haven't had any children of my own," I said. I clasped my hands against my breast like the heroine of an old-fashioned melodrama. "You and I are the last of our line, Mother. If we've inherited the curse of the Coldwells, it will die with us."

I chuckled and Leatha laughed, a thin, high laugh. But both of us knew it wasn't funny.

Chapter Six

MARTHA EDMOND'S COMFORT COOKIES

> 1 cup sugar
> ½ cup butter or margarine
> 1 egg, beaten
> 1 cup grated zucchini
> 2 cups flour
> ½ teaspoon cinnamon
> ½ teaspoon cloves
> ½ teaspoon salt
> 1 teaspoon baking soda
> 2 tablespoons finely chopped basil, fresh
> 1 cup chopped nuts

Preheat oven to 375 degrees. Cream sugar and butter; add egg and beat. Add grated zucchini alternately with dry ingredients, mixed together. Stir in basil and nuts. Drop by small spoonfuls onto greased cookie sheets and bake 12–15 minutes. Makes three dozen.

Supper—ham sandwiches, canned vegetable soup, and strawberry shortcake—was a subdued affair. I was glad to notice that there was no wine on the table, a small thing, perhaps. But when my mother is drinking, she loves wine, and its absence was an indication that she was in control of herself. Leatha and I made casual small talk on comfortable, homey topics: McQuaid's conference, Brian's school stuff, Ruby's health, things going on at the shop. Aunt Tullie, who was caught up in some sort of mumbled debate with an unseen guest at her elbow, seemed scarcely to know that we were there, even when she dropped the strawberries, breaking the dish and making a mess that we jumped to clean up. I would have liked to broach the subject of the durable power of attorney, but it was painfully obvious that we were going to have to find a moment when Aunt Tullie was more lucid and attentive than she was now.

After we'd eaten, Leatha and Aunt Tullie went for a walk in the garden while I made a quick phone call to Ruby and another to McQuaid. I was glad to hear that everything seemed fine back in Pecan Springs (Ruby reported that a busload of tourists had spent several hundred dollars in the shops and the tearoom) but when McQuaid asked me how things were going at the plantation, I hedged. I certainly couldn't tell him about Aunt Tullie's disease—not until I had learned more about it and understood its frightening implications for my mother and me. The deed and Wiley's disappearance were still open questions, and I couldn't tell him about my encounter with the witch woman without sounding totally weird and off-the-wall. Anyway, there was too much stuff for me to process for myself, let alone share with him. So I made evasive noises, told him I loved him very much, and let it go at that.

After we said goodbye, I carried our few supper dishes down to the kitchen and washed them, leaving them to drain beside the sink. I was just wiping the counter when

I heard a step in the hall and the door opened.

"What you doin' here, girl?" Darlene inquired severely. "That's the hired help's job. You wash them dishes, won't be nothing for Alice Ann to complain about in the mornin'."

"Force of habit," I said with a grin, drying my hands on a terry towel. "At home, the only help I have are two males. It's usually easier to do it myself."

"Yeah, I've been there." Darlene was still wearing her *UCSB* T-shirt, but she had changed her jeans for a pair of black biker's shorts and added a bright yellow cap, the bill turned backward. "You ready?"

"Ready for what?" I asked stupidly.

"Girls' night out. We're pickin' up Judith and stoppin' at May Rose's house to say howdy to Dawn. Then we're drivin' out to see Martha Edmond. She's expectin' us." She gave me a look. "You forget we planned all this?"

"Sort of," I said. "It's been a busy day." I was tempted to tell Darlene part of what had gone on since I saw her this morning, but something—a certain instinctive wariness in me, or perhaps something in Darlene—held me back. After all, how much did I really know about this woman? How far could I trust her?

So I went out to the garden and told Leatha I was going out with Darlene for the evening, then followed her to her old car, a dusty green Ford two-door with the right rear fender caved in, the seats and floor littered with candy wrappers and empty soft-drink cans. Darlene drove down the road a short distance, then turned into a short graveled drive and stopped in front of a weathered gray cottage with blue trim around the windows and the porch and a rusted metal roof. The entire front was covered with pink roses.

"Judith's place," she said, and tapped the horn.

"It's pretty," I said admiringly. There were gauzy white curtains at the windows and an unruly mass of delphiniums, snapdragons, and daisies along the path. A weeping willow hung over the tiny green yard, which was bordered by hydrangeas, iris, and roses. It was like a little jewel box.

"She's got it fixed up real nice inside, too," Darlene said. "Dawn's been helpin' her paint it." She sighed. "It's been a good arrangement for Judith and Miz Tullie both. Sure wish it could go on."

I gave her a curious look. "Any reason why it can't?"

"Wiley's got some sort of weird bee in his bonnet," Darlene replied soberly. She pushed her gold-rimmed glasses up on her nose. "Judith told me this morning that Wiley came to see her last Friday. Ordered her out by the first of next month. Wasn't very nice about it, either." She tapped the horn again, briefly.

"But Aunt Tullie won't let him kick her out," I protested. "She told Judith she could live here. Anyway, there must be a lease."

Darlene gave a short, hard laugh. "You really think Miz Tullie remembers what she told Judith? And no, it was just an oral agreement, no lease or anything like that, so Judith can't prove what Miz Tullie said. Wiley, he's been actin' like he owns the place, and it don't look like there's anything anybody can do 'bout it."

I frowned. "We'll just see about that. Aunt Tullie's still in charge, and if she can't deal with this little problem, Leatha and I sure as hell can." It would be a pleasure, actually. Wiley only thought the Beauchamps held title to this section of land. As far as I was concerned, that claim was still to be proved, and that might take a hell of a long time.

Darlene gave me a sideways look. "You heard that Wiley's skipped town?"

"I heard that he hasn't shown up for a couple of days." I shrugged. "Maybe he's in the sack with one of his girlfriends."

Darlene, unsmiling, ran her hands around the wheel. "The police came around to see me this afternoon. They said he's been officially reported missing. They wanted to know if I'd heard from him."

"Why did they think he'd get in touch with you?" Darlene knew Wiley, of course—they'd grown up together at Jordan's Crossing. But that was a long time ago, and she'd been gone for most of her adult life, hadn't she? Was there something here I was missing?

Darlene didn't answer. Judith came out of the door just then, closing and locking it behind her. She was wearing white jeans, a white cotton shirt with the tail out, and rope sandals, and her dark hair was brushed into a thick, shiny helmet. I pulled the seat forward and she climbed into the back, holding a large bouquet of sweet peas and lilies of the valley. After we'd exchanged greetings, she said to Darlene, "I brought these flowers for Dawn. Did you call May Rose?"

"Nope," Darlene said, shifting into reverse. "Figgered we'd just barge right on in. That way, she can't tell us to hold off visitin' until she's got the place shined up. You know May Rose—never wants anybody to see her or her house unless both of 'em are picture perfect."

*   *   *

BUT May Rose Hayworth was no longer picture perfect, by any stretch of the imagination. She lived in a nice section of town, in a fifties ranch-style brick house set back from the street under a couple of large pecan trees. But the square of green grass out front hadn't been cut in recent memory, the ferns in the hanging baskets had turned crisp and brown for lack of water, and the open garage was a chaos of loose papers and women's magazines, broken furniture, and discarded clothing.

And while May Rose herself might have been the prettiest cheerleader Chicory High ever saw, the passing years hadn't been kind. The kelly-green tights and floral-print top she was wearing when she opened the door did nothing to conceal the fact that she had gained about fifty pounds, most of it settling in her belly and breasts. Her pale, moonlike face was puffed and blotchy under clumsily applied makeup, and her even paler hair, thin and dark at the roots, could have done with a shampoo. Her eyes widened when she saw the three of us clustered on her front porch, but she didn't invite us in.

"You remember China Bayles," Darlene said, with a wave in my direction. "The mouthy little kid we used to bully into paintin' our toenails? She's here visiting her aunt."

May Rose gave me a cursory glance and a nod. "You should've phoned," she said to Darlene. "I could've saved you a trip. Dawn's sick. She can't have company."

"Oh, that's all right," Judith said, in that low, husky voice of hers. "We won't stay but a minute. Dawn's been out for over a week now, and I . . . we just want to let her know we're thinking about her."

"She's all right," May Rose said briefly. There was no

emotion in her voice. "Just a case of flu, is all. You know how these girls are. Get a little sore throat and they use it as an excuse to skip classes for a week."

"Not Dawn," Darlene said firmly. "She's not like that. She's a good worker."

"You're not her mother," May Rose said. "You don't know her like I do." She reached for the flowers. "I'll see she gets these."

Judith held onto the bouquet. "I'll give them to her myself."

"Well, you can't," May Rose said flatly. "She's contagious."

Darlene tossed her head. "Oh, for cryin' out loud, May Rose. It's only flu, not smallpox. Anyway, we won't all go in. China and I will stay here and Judith can take her the flowers and cheer her up a little. Then you'll be rid of us."

May Rose folded her arms across her breasts, bra-less and heavy as melons under the green-print top. Her pouty mouth was set in a stubborn line and something—apprehension? fear?—had come into her eyes, despite her obvious efforts not to display any emotion. "Doc Waters said no visitors, and that's it, far as I'm concerned," she said. "You wanna leave the flowers, fine. If not—" Her shrug was meant to be casual.

With an angry noise, Judith thrust the flowers into her hand. A few of the little white lilies of the valley fell to the floor. "Tell Dawn I'm thinking of her," she said tautly. "She needs to hurry and get well so we can . . . so we can start setting out the transplants."

"And Alice Ann and I have a mountain of laundry to do," Darlene added with a grin. "Tell that girl to get back on the job so her sister and me don't have to work our fingers to the bone. You give her that message, May Rose, do y'hear?"

May Rose's mouth was suddenly trembling and she bit her lower lip to hold it still. "I will," she said in a muffled voice. "I'll tell her." And then, as an afterthought: "Thanks for coming. I really appreciate it." She shut the door.

" 'Preciate, my fanny," Darlene said disgustedly, as we went back to the car. "What's wrong with her? She's actin' like we're tryin' to kidnap her precious baby."

"There's something funny going on here," Judith muttered, getting into the back seat and slamming the door. "I'll bet May Rose found out that Dawn is moving into my place. She's locked her up."

Darlene raised her eyebrows. "Dawn is movin' in with you?"

Judith turned her face away, and I had the feeling that she'd said more than she meant to. She answered slowly. "Dawn turned twenty-one in January, and you'd think her mother would let her be her own woman. But no, she still insists on a curfew for both those girls. She's got rules about who they can hang out with and who they can't."

"May Rose was always pretty religious," Darlene said. "Catholic. I 'spose that's it."

Judith didn't seem to hear her. "Anyway, Dawn says she's had enough. A couple of weeks ago, she asked if she could fix up that old porch on the back of my cottage for a bedroom. I said sure, go ahead." She made an angry noise. "Of course, that was before that jerk Wiley decided to kick me out."

Darlene fastened her seat belt and put the key in the

ignition. "China says maybe Wiley doesn't have the last word on that subject." She threw a meaningful glance at me.

I turned to look at Judith over my shoulder. "I'd be glad to see what I can do," I offered. "At the least, I can let Aunt Tullie know what's going on."

Judith shook her head darkly. "That won't do any good. She's too sick to do more than yell at him. The minute she turns her back, he does exactly what he wants." A sly look came into her eyes. "Anyway, I've already dealt with the problem. Wiley's not going to shove me around any longer."

I let that pass. "Maybe if you talked to Alice Ann, she'd tell you what's going on with her sister."

"Now, *that's* a good idea," Darlene agreed. "Judith, first thing tomorrow you get Alice Ann off by herself and see what you can find out 'bout why her mother won't let us near her sister." Cheerful again, she turned the key and put the car into gear. "Y'all ready to go see Miz Martha? When I called, she said she's got a visitor she wants us to meet. Some professor lady from Louisiana."

Judith wrinkled her nose. "A stuck-up professor lady, if you ask me," she said darkly. "She's over here from Baton Rouge doing a research project. A book about women and plantation life in the Old South."

Darlene grinned and tapped my knee. "She wants to study a plantation, maybe she ought to come to Jordan's Crossing. Huh, China?"

"Oh, sure," I said with an uneasy laugh. "She can dig up all our old family secrets." *All those nasty secrets, including inexplicable gifts of land, alcoholism, hereditary disease* . . .

Judith leaned forward. "I've changed my mind about

going to Martha's, Darlene. I spent the afternoon there, working in the garden. I want you to drop me off at Marie Louise's."

Darlene frowned. "How you gonna git home from there, girl? You're not thinkin' of hitchhikin', are you?"

"What if I am?" Judith asked. "I can take care of myself."

"Marie Louise LaTour?" I turned again. "I saw her this afternoon, sitting on a bench in front of the courthouse. I had no idea she was still alive."

"She's not." Darlene laughed scratchily. "That was her ghost you saw. Likes to hang out on that bench and scare folks."

I sucked in my breath, startled.

"Darlene's only fooling you, China," Judith said. "Marie Louise is in her eighties, but she's still very much alive."

Darlene looked at Judith in the rearview mirror. "What you goin' to see Marie Louise about? You wouldn't be plannin' to ask her for some kind of charm to use 'gainst Wiley, would you?"

Judith grinned mirthlessly, her lips stretched across her teeth. "I thought you didn't believe in that witchy stuff, Darlene. Anyway, who needs a charm to deal with that jerk when you've got a brain and your own two hands?"

"Don't you do it, Jude," Darlene cautioned. "That'll get you in a pot of trouble."

To me, Judith said, "I drop in on Marie Louise every now and then to talk about the old days. She's a little bit Choctaw, you know. She even remembers my great-grandmother. I enjoy hearing her stories."

"Oh, right," Darlene said. "Listen, while you're getting that charm, get one for me, too. Tell Marie Louise I need money. Five or six grand would be fine. Ten, if she's got it to throw around."

We all laughed.

THE sun was setting into a bank of clouds to the west and a pink-tinged thunderhead loomed behind us as we followed a winding road out of Chicory, heading toward the wooded bluffs that rise up at the eastern edge of the rich and level plain of the Yazoo Delta. While we drove, Darlene replied to my questions about Judith.

"Way I understand it," Darlene said, "she moved to this part of Mississippi 'cause her family came from around here, back in the 1840s."

"That's when the government took this land from the Choctaws?" I asked, remembering the story Colonel Blakeslee had told me that afternoon. "They gave it to the white settlers and the Indians had to leave?"

Darlene nodded. "Yeah, but Judith's family didn't leave right away. There was something in the treaty that allowed the Choctaws to stay and claim property if they gave up being members of the tribe. Her great-great-grandfather filed to settle on the land he was living on, and after a while the government recognized his claim and gave him a deed. Then somebody came along and cheated him out of it, and they left. That's the short version. If you want the whole story, you'll have to ask Judith." Darlene paused. "She didn't tell me, but I think she even knows where it used to be—her family's property, I mean."

I was silent for a moment, looking out toward the west at the vast expanse of fertile alluvial plain and newly plowed fields, a smudgy line of willows and darker sweet gums and cypress growing along a meandering stream. I was thinking about the connection between the land and the people who lived on it and made their living from it. What kind of livelihood had Judith's people earned from this land, so many years ago? Did they grow crops? Did they hunt and fish?

Darlene broke into my thoughts. "That's where we're going," she said, pointing toward the bluff. We turned off the main road and she began to fill me in on Martha Edmond, who—in addition to having a remarkable garden full of native herbs—was said to know more than anyone else about Chicory and the surrounding country. She had grown up here and then gone off to get her undergraduate and graduate degrees and teach in the History Department at Ole Miss, returning six or seven years ago to live on the farm that had belonged to her mother and father.

The Edmond place was an old white farmhouse perched so high on the bluff that on a clear day (if there was such a thing anymore), you might've been able to see across the Mississippi into Arkansas. When we drove up, Martha was outdoors pulling weeds in the daylily bed behind the white picket fence. She had to have been my mother's age, but she looked younger, lithe and tanned in a sleeveless red blouse and denim cutoffs, her salt-and-pepper hair cut in a pixie under a wide-brimmed white straw hat. She was diminutive—not much over five two—and barefoot, and the hand she offered me was dirty. I had to smile at that. I had found a woman after my own heart.

"I'm glad to meet you, China," she said with an elfin smile that made her look even more girlish. "Your mother may not remember me, but we knew one another years ago, when we were children. She went somewhere else to high school, though, and we lost track of one another after that."

"Greenville," I said. "She lived with her aunt Hattie and went to high school there." *Aunt Hattie. The aunt who died before she could know whether she had the same disease that now afflicted her sister.* "I'm sure Mother would be pleased to see you," I added, a little clumsily. "Why don't you come over and—" I was about to ask her to lunch when I thought of Aunt Tullie and decided that might not be a good idea. "And have a chat some-time," I concluded, feeling foolish.

"I'd like to do that," Martha said, appearing not to no-tice my fumble. "And perhaps I'll bring my house guest, too, if you wouldn't mind. She's working on an oral his-tory project about Southern women. I've suggested that she might talk to your great-aunt."

"China's into herbs," Darlene said, before I could think of a tactful way to suggest that this wasn't a good idea either. "I told her that she just has to see your garden."

Martha glanced around at the large expanse of herbs and flowers, and up at the darkening sky. Twilight was falling over the valley, and the air was growing dusky. To the north, I could see occasional lightning streaking through the cotton-candy thunderhead, now tinged with purple. It looked as if it might rain in the next hour or two.

"I'm afraid we can't do it justice this evening, Darlene." She turned to smile at me, her eyes clear and bright. "Why don't you come over and spend tomorrow morning with me, China? That's when the plants will be at their best, especially if we get a shower tonight. We can take all the time we want, then have some lunch."

"I'd like that," I said, meaning it. I wasn't sure what was on tomorrow's agenda, but I could certainly take a couple of hours off to enjoy a garden.

She nodded. "Good. You two sit on the porch, and I'll get us something to drink. Perhaps Amanda will join us."

Amanda turned out to be Amanda Gleason, the research historian who was staying with Martha. She came down from upstairs where she'd been working and introduced herself to Darlene and me, while we were sitting side by side on the porch swing.

My first impresssion of Amanda was that of a taut, tense woman who had something serious on her mind. She was quite thin and tall, in her late thirties, with wide-set brown eyes, a strong nose over a firm mouth, and shiny brown hair cut in a precise pageboy that swung forward at the angle of her jaw. She had the look of a woman who was expecting something to happen, who was waiting for someone—not just anyone but some person in particular—to appear. She wore no wedding ring, which somehow didn't surprise me, and there was a passionate intensity about her that I found both fascinating and a little bit frightening. I guessed that, as a researcher, Amanda Gleason had entered the right profession. She was clearly committed to finding things out.

She focused on me, scrutinizing my face. "So you're staying at Jordan's Crossing," she said, after introductions. "You're one of the Coldwell descendants?"

"I suppose I am," I said. "But I've been away so long that I don't really think of myself as a Coldwell." I might have added, *Actually, I'm not a Coldwell at all. I renounced that connection decades ago*. But I didn't feel comfortable sharing confidences with this woman.

Amanda sat on the edge of her seat, regarding me with

what seemed an unusual curiosity. Her eyes were very bright, her glance avid. "Did Martha tell you that I'm anxious to interview your aunt for my research project?"

"She did," I said, "but I really don't think you'll be able to get any information from Aunt Tullie. She isn't—"

"Whatever is convenient for your aunt will work for me," Amanda went on, as if I hadn't spoken. She took a small calendar book out of a pocket of the loose beige shirt she wore over beige slacks. "Is she free most mornings?"

I frowned. "My great-aunt is ill," I said. "She may not be able to see you at all."

Amanda let out a small, explosive breath. "Oh, I'm so sorry," she said. She looked at me, intent and questioning, as if she were searching for something in my face. "Has she been sick long? What's wrong?" It was not a casual question, although she added, as a polite afterthought, "Nothing serious, I hope."

I was about to offer a snappish reply to these impertinent questions when Darlene got me off the hook. "Anything can be serious when you're eighty-five," she said gravely. "China and her mother are just trying to make things as easy for Miss Tullie as they can. I'm sure you understand."

Amanda blinked, as if she had just this instant realized that I wasn't alone on the porch swing. "Oh, yes, of course," she replied quickly. "I didn't mean—" She lifted her hand and brushed back her hair, making a visible effort to ease up, to soften her intensity. "I'm afraid this research project is almost too important to me," she said ruefully. "I've lived with it for a couple of years now, and—"

She broke off as Martha came in carrying a tray with

a pitcher of iced tea, four glasses, and a plate of cookies. "Has Amanda told you about her project?" she asked.

"Not the details," Darlene said dryly. "Just that it's very important." She took a cookie from the plate Martha offered her, and bit into it. "Ummm," she said. "These are good, Martha. What are they?"

Amanda didn't give Martha a chance to reply. "I'm exploring the real-life experiences of women who lived most of their lives on plantations," she said, as if this were a practiced speech. "I've been working with the diaries and letters of nineteenth-century women, but I want to include the stories of women of our own day, as well. I'm interested in demythologizing the women of the South, because I'm convinced that we don't know the true story of their lives. I want to correct the idea that they were fragile or saintly or sexless, or that they all lived the aristocratic life we saw in the prewar scenes in *Gone With the Wind*. I want—"

"Well, then," Darlene remarked, in a deceptively mild tone, "I suppose you're studying white women. Not us blacks."

Amanda seemed flustered for a second, but quickly recovered. "Well, yes, I'm afraid that's true. Unfortunately, I have to focus, or the study will be too broad."

"Right." Darlene began to push the swing with her foot. "I only raise the question because black women were never considered fragile or saintly or sexless. We've been mythologized, sure, but not in those terms." Her voice was dry. She paused and added, "There's at least one very good book on your subject already: *Within the Plantation Household*, by Elizabeth Fox-Genovese. The subtitle, if I remember it correctly, is *Black and White Women of the Old South*—a broad focus, strongly factual. I'm sure you must have read it, though, since it's been out for nearly fifteen years."

Darlene paused, as if she were waiting for Amanda to say that she knew all about the book. But Amanda was leaning back in her chair as if she weren't quite sure what to say. That was odd. You'd think that she'd have read what sounded like a major work in her field. For a moment I considered the possibility that this project wasn't the real reason for Amanda's being here, that behind it lay some other agenda that she wasn't talking about but which was terribly compelling. Then I checked myself. There was no reason not to take this woman at face value. I was being overly suspicious and critical just because I didn't like her.

Martha handed me a glass of iced tea. "The cookies are made with zucchini and basil," she remarked to no one in particular. "My mother used to call them 'comfort cookies.' She always baked them for my sister and me when we were feeling bad about something." She smiled at Darlene. "Have you finished that project you were working on, Darlene? The last time we talked, you were getting ready to send off a first draft."

"It went to my editor last week," Darlene said. She made a wry face. "I expect she'll want lots of revisions. Editors always do. Gotta get their way, regardless. Meanwhile, I'm workin' on somethin' new."

Amanda was readjusting to this new view of Darlene. "You're a writer, too, then," she said, getting back into the conversation. She glanced at Darlene's yellow *UCSB Writers in Residence* T-shirt. "I should have guessed. You've been in the program at Santa Barbara? Nonfiction?"

"Darlene is about to publish her second book of short

stories," Martha said quietly. "Her first won a major literary prize."

Amanda looked startled. I glanced at Darlene in some surprise, for she hadn't mentioned the book, let alone the award.

Darlene picked up another cookie, making an appreciative noise. "Martha, these comfort cookies are *fine*. Give me the recipe and I'll try it out on Miz Tullie. She's a reg'lar cookie monster."

Martha laughed, a light, easy laugh that dispelled whatever tension might have remained. I turned to Amanda.

"Look, I really don't think you'll be able to learn anything very helpful from Aunt Tullie. But my mother grew up at Jordan's Crossing and I'm sure she'd be glad to share what she knows of her grandmother and great-grandmother. There may also be some documents—"

I checked myself. There *were* documents, such as the journal I had found this morning and probably others, in the secret drawer and up in the attic. I thought they could be shared, but that decision wasn't up to me. Leatha or Aunt Tullie were the ones who should determine whether any of the family papers should be put into the hands of a researcher—especially into Amanda's hands.

Amanda leaned forward, her expression almost greedy. "I'd be glad to meet your mother," she said. "She's ... let's see if I've got this right. Her mother was Tullie Coldwell's sister?"

"Her father and Aunt Tullie were brother and sister," I replied, a little puzzled at this interest in the Coldwell genealogy. And where had she gotten her facts? From Martha?

"I see," Amanda said. She didn't relax. "I'm sure your mother has a great deal of information that would be very helpful to me. I'd love to see her."

"I'll check with her," I offered. "I'll be here in the morning for a tour of Martha's garden. I'll let you know then what she says."

"Well, then, that's settled," Martha said. She leaned back in her chair. "Now, China, let's hear about you. Darlene tells me that you own an herb shop. I'm dying to know all about it. What kind of shop is it? Do you have gardens? And did Darlene tell me that you and your friend have some sort of café or tearoom, too?"

For the next half hour or so, while the dark thickened, the storm grew nearer, and the nighthawks began to swoop low over the fields hunting for insects, Martha and I chatted about herbs, with Darlene chiming in every now and then and Amanda listening, not saying much, although I couldn't shake the feeling that she was still studying me, with that same searching look.

After a while, Darlene stopped rocking the swing and sniffed. "Hey, I can smell rain," she said.

"*Smell* rain?" Amanda asked doubtfully.

"Sure. Can't you?" Darlene asked. "It's like the good wet earth is saying thanks." She touched my arm. "Maybe we better be on our way before the storm hits. You ready to call it a day, China?"

"It's been a long one," I replied, agreeing, and we said our thanks and good nights. I was about to shake hands with Martha, when she reached up to give me a hug.

"Tomorrow," she reminded me with a smile. "The garden and I will be waiting." To Darlene, she added, "Here's a care package for the trip home," and handed her several cookies wrapped in a paper napkin.

But the long day hadn't come to an end just yet. There was an even longer night ahead.

Chapter Seven

Black-haw (*Viburnum sp.*) Folk names: Cramp bark,
May Rose, Red elder, wayfaring tree

"Black-haw is a little tree with black or blue berries
on it, which are good to eat. The bark of the root
or of the tree is used as a tea. It's wonderful ladies'
medicine. It's good for men, but there is something
in it that ladies need. It's one of the finest remedies
for a lady's monthly troubles and hot flashes."

Tommie Bass, Appalachian herbalist
in *A Reference Guide to Medicinal Plants:
Herbal Medicine Past and Present*
John K. Crellin and Jane Philpott

Darlene tuned the car radio to a country music station, and as she drove, we listened, not talking
much. Neither of us felt compelled to remark that Amanda
was borderline pushy and insensitive, although both of us
were probably thinking it. I broke the silence just long
enough to chide Darlene for not telling me about her literary prize, and she retorted that it hadn't been a major
milestone in her life and she'd be just as glad if I skipped
it.

"What I'm writing right now," she added, "matters a
lot more to me than what some folks said about things I

wrote a few years back." Darlene obviously wasn't impressed by her own achievements. We munched on Martha's cookies and listened to the radio in a companionable silence.

We were still on the main highway when the car was rattled by a booming thunderclap that seemed to come from directly overhead. A flash of lightning lit the blackness and rain began to splash down in fat splatters on the windshield, then came down so heavily that we might have been driving under a waterfall. Darlene slowed to a crawl, but in a few moments, just before we reached the turnoff to Jordan's Crossing, we heard a siren and saw flashing lights behind us.

"Hell's bells," Darlene muttered, pulling over onto the narrow shoulder. With a scowl, she turned on the overhead light and reached for her purse to get out her wallet. "It's a cop. What the devil does he want?"

"Whatever it is," I said, "he must think it's pretty important. When he gets out of the car, he's going to get seriously wet."

But it wasn't us he was after. Siren wailing, the sheriff's car raced past, followed in less than a minute by an EMS ambulance, its lights also flashing. Then, as we watched in surprise, the two sets of taillights turned off onto the gravel road to Jordan's Crossing.

My heart jumped into my throat and I made an anxious sound. Had Aunt Tullie suffered some sort of attack? Had Leatha fallen ill? But they wouldn't call the police for something like that. Maybe there'd been a break-in, and someone had been injured or killed. I narrowed my eyes. Maybe Wiley Beauchamp had shown up to confront Aunt Tullie about the deed and she had whacked him again— fatally, this time.

"Follow that ambulance, Darlene," I said urgently.

But Darlene was already shifting into first gear, spinning her tires on the gravel. "Hang on to your hat, girl," she said between clenched teeth. "We gonna *fly*."

My fears about what Aunt Tullie might have done to Wiley were relieved almost at once, for the squad car and the ambulance didn't stay on the plantation's main road. A half-mile from the highway, just past Judith's cottage, they turned off onto a narrow grassy lane between overhanging trees. We followed, Darlene's old Ford bouncing along through the dark, thirty yards or so behind the red taillights of the ambulance. It was a noisy ride, with thunder booming above us, grass and weeds whisking against the underside of the car, and twiggy bushes scratching the sides like fingernails on a chalkboard—a difficult ride, too, because the road twisted and turned like a corkscrew. After a while, it became a track, and we seemed to be driving through an impenetrable jungle of briar and cane, under a heavy canopy of oak and gum and hickory. Where the hell *were* we? Where were we going?

And then we turned a corner and all of a sudden I knew. It had been over thirty years since I'd been this way, but I recognized an old shed off to the left, at the corner of a small open field—the first field ever cleared and cultivated on the plantation, way back in Uncle Jed's day, my grandfather had told me. We were driving across Muddy Bottom, heading toward the Bloodroot River, the shallow, slow-moving stream that had once been the lifeblood of Jordan's Crossing.

"This is the way to the landing and the old fishing camp, isn't it?" I asked, bracing myself with one arm against the dash and thinking that the ambulance was probably part of some sort of rescue operation. A fisherman struck by lightning, maybe, or somebody who'd come out here from town and managed to lose himself in the swampy bottoms that fringe each side of the river. This is wicked country, when you don't know your way around in it—and even when you do, it's pretty hard to avoid the snakes and deep, flooded holes. If you get bitten by a poisonous snake, you can die, slowly and painfully. If you fall into a hole, you can drown. Take your pick.

"Yeah, this is the Muddy Bottom road, all right," Darlene replied grimly, as we skidded around another sharp corner, sliding on wet grass. "But it's a hell of a night to go fishin'."

"Somebody probably figured the catfish would be biting," I said, and chuckled. "Don't you remember telling me once that the fishing was good just before a rain?"

"Did I say that?" Darlene asked. She flashed me a grin, her teeth white in her dark face. "Yeah, reckon I did. Hey, maybe you 'n me can get in some fishin' before you head back to Texas." She hit the brake hard to avoid a small furry mammal ambling unhurriedly across the road in the glare of our headlights, under the black-haw trees, their blossoms gleaming white in the headlights.

"Possum mama," she muttered. "Lookit. She's got babies tucked in her fur, goin' for a ride in the rain. Maybe she's found 'em a new place to live." She looked around, shivering. "Wonder what else is out there in those bottoms. A night like this, lightning and thunder and rain, a person can still believe in panthers and bears."

"Not any longer, surely," I said. "My grandfather said they killed the last bear in these woods the year his father built the Big House." *The year Clancy built the house on the land Abner gave to Tobias*, I thought, and wondered if there was some sort of symbolic connection between Clancy's house and the last bear.

Darlene grunted. "Yeah, that's what they say. But these woods are deep. No tellin' what's still hidin' in there. Judith's great-great-granny maybe." She released the clutch. "Makes a good story, anyway. For all the city folks know, we could have man-eatin' 'gators swimmin' in our rivers."

The possum family had disappeared and we drove on through the dark, more slowly and cautiously now. The rain had subsided to a drizzle, and the track was getting muddy as it slanted down into the river bottom. A giant owl swooped low through the beams of our headlights, looking startlingly like a pterodactyl, and just off the road, in the brush, I saw a shadowy deer, watching silently as we drove past.

Then, through the trees, we could see emergency flood-lights illuminating the rotting dock and the grassy ramp where Darlene and I used to launch Aunt Tullie's old red rowboat, and men in muddy boots and yellow slickers standing around, talking. The ambulance was there, its flashers still turning, and a couple of police cars, and a wrecker, backed halfway down the steeply sloping ramp.

A wrecker? Some inner caution made me put a hand on Darlene's arm. "Let's pull off," I said, and reached over and cut our headlights. "I'd like to see what's happening before we announce our arrival."

"Sure thing." Darlene turned off the lane into the weedy yard of the ramshackle fishing cabin, which didn't look much different from the way I remembered it. It was constructed of cypress logs, with a shake roof and a screened-in porch. It had been built back in the early part of the century so that Clancy Coldwell and his friends could fish and hunt and get drunk—built, it was said, from some of the unburned logs left from Jed Coldwell's old trading post. As the crow flies, it was probably less than a half-mile from the house to this point on the river, although it certainly seemed farther. In the old days, there had been a trail that Darlene and I, and Wiley, too, put to good use whenever we wanted to come down here and hang out. It was probably long since overgrown and impassable.

Darlene parked and we got out of the car, shivering in the cool of the storm-washed air. We crept around the cabin and peered out from behind an old log shed with a rusty metal roof that used to be full of empty barrels and wooden boxes where the rats and the red wasps nested. From here, we had a good view of the flood-lit ramp. I could hear vehicle engines running and the crackling of the police and ambulance radios and the low sound of men's voices. The bluish glare of the emergency lights shone out over the slow-moving water of the Bloodroot River, giving the wet weeds and dripping cypress an oddly festive gleam. The river's surface was blank and smooth. The rain had stopped falling.

"What do you think is goin' on?" Darlene asked in a low voice into my ear.

At the edge of the water, a man in a blue poncho made a windmilling motion with his arm. "It's a-comin'," he called. "Bring'er up easy, Jack."

The gathered men were silent now, watching intently. A man standing beside the wrecker—Jack, I guessed—pushed harder on a lever and the wrecker's powerful winch began to whine. The light glinted along a heavy cable running out into the black water, just as a pale-faced man in a wet suit emerged from the darkness, wading up the ramp. Off to one side stood a pair of preteen boys, T-shirts and cutoffs plastered to their skin, watching open-mouthed. They were wet and cold and obviously scared. One of them was holding a cane fishing pole, a black-and-white dog pressed against his leg.

"They're winching something out of the water," I said, low. "Probably the boys' car."

The kids looked too young to be driving, but that doesn't mean anything in this rural area, where boys—and girls, too, sometimes—drive farm equipment almost as soon as they can walk. Maybe they hadn't put on the brake, and Dad's car had coasted gaily down the steep ramp to go for a swim in the river. They were probably scared of the licking they were going to get when they got home. And if I knew modern kids, even rural kids, they'd called the wrecker on a cell phone. Brian thinks he's terribly deprived because he's the only one in his crowd who doesn't have one, but since there's no contest between convenience and possible brain cancer, McQuaid and I have held the line.

Darlene nudged me with her elbow. "It's a pickup truck," she whispered. "Look, you can see the rear end comin' out of the water."

A pair of deputies in yellow slickers came to the river's edge in front of us, as the man in the wet suit climbed out and sat on the edge of the dock to take off his flippers. There was a sudden flare of lightning and an almost simultaneous roll of thunder, loud enough to wake the dead. I jumped. Darlene clutched my arm.

"Anybody in there?" one of the deputies asked, aiming his question at the diver.

"Yeah," the man in the wet suit said. "The driver. From the looks of him, he's been in the water three-four days.

Turtles have been chewin' on him pretty bad."

"Anybody else?"

The diver got to his feet, shaking his head. "Nope. Passenger door was open, though, and there's a pretty good current running out there. Could've been somebody else with him. Maybe it'd be good to put out a boat when it gets daylight, check the shore."

A murmur ran among the clustered watchers, and they shifted and stirred uneasily. "Who is it?" somebody asked in a hushed voice, as the pickup came heavily out of the river, ribbons of duckweed draped over the cab, water streaming off it like water off a drowned dinosaur hulk, silver in the glare of the emergency lights.

"Looks new," somebody else said. "Anybody recognize that truck?"

"Sweet Jesus Lord." Beside me, Darlene made a choking sound and turned her head away. "That's Wiley's truck."

I felt a sudden cold at the pit of my stomach. *Wiley's truck? Wiley was dead in the river. Had been dead in the river long enough for turtles to chew on him.*

The two deputies were still standing in front of us at the river's edge. "Hey, Banjo," the shorter one said. "Ain't that the new Dodge Wiley Beauchamp bought off Tom Ratliff's lot last week? He had it to the fish fry Friday night."

"By God, Charlie, I b'lieve you're right," Banjo replied, and I realized that he was the taller of the two deputies who had visited Jordan's Crossing that morning. Deputy Green. "Well, reckon we can cancel that APB. If Beauchamp was tryin' to get outta town, he didn't make it very far, poor bastard." He raised his voice. "Hey, Joe, get on the phone and tell the coroner to get his ass out of bed and get out here. We got a dead man for him."

Her hand across her mouth, Darlene was already headed back to the car. I wanted desperately to know the cause of death and a few other things, such as whether the truck's ignition was on and if it was in gear. But I wanted almost as badly to keep our presence a secret from the deputies. It was time Darlene and I got out of there, while everybody was intent on the gruesome thing they had fished out of the Bloodroot River.

It started to rain again as we drove off, finding our way by the glow of the floodlights and the intermittent flashes of lightning. We weren't followed, but as a precaution, Darlene didn't turn on the headlights until we were out of sight of the camp.

When the dash light went on and illuminated our faces, I saw to my surprise that Darlene was weeping, shoulders shaking, tears streaming freely down her cheeks, her lower lip caught between her teeth to keep from making a sound.

I was chilled through and bone weary when Darlene dropped me off at the house. I wanted to say something comforting, but since I had no idea what her relationship to Wiley had been and why she felt his death so deeply, I wasn't sure what to say. I contented myself with a quick wordless hug as I got out of the car, and whispered that I would see her in the morning.

There was a green-shaded light burning in the downstair hall, but the rest of the house was silent and dark, with that oppressive darkness that seems to belong to old houses, heavy with the burden of decades of bad dreams. I didn't want to wake Leatha and Aunt Tullie, so I crept up the stairs and down the hall as quietly as I could. It was this second-floor hall where I had sometimes smelled Great-grandmother Pearl's perfume, but all I could smell tonight were musty carpets and old dust. At least, I thought, with a wry gratitude, I didn't have to contend with old ghosts.

Once in my room, I shut the door before I turned on the bedside lamp. If I'd wanted to do some serious reading, I'd have to find a bigger bulb, for this one was so dim that the corners of the room were dusky and there was barely enough light to read the clock on the bureau. Eleven-fifteen. Time to call it a night. I kicked off my muddy shoes and glanced at the bed. The wedding-ring quilt was turned down and the big feather pillows plumped up invitingly—my mother, taking care of her daughter. She had put something on the bedside table, too: a small, silver-framed snapshot of a woman sitting at a writing table with a pen in her hand. *Rachel*, I thought, *the mother my mother never knew*. Next to the photo was Pearl's leather-bound journal.

I frowned. I distinctly remembered putting the journal back where I had found it, in the drawer under the bookshelf in the library. But perhaps Leatha had seen it on the table on the veranda and—family historian that she was—wanted to encourage me to read it by placing it here. Under other circumstances, I might have been annoyed by her motherly manipulation, but I was too exhausted for that tonight.

Still, in spite of the inviting bed, I was too wired to go to sleep right away. I couldn't shake the image of Wiley's truck coming up out of the water, his corpse in it. So I turned off the lamp, opened the screened window, and sat down in the oak rocking chair beside it—the chair, my mother once told me, where she had nursed me as a baby. The rain-washed air that stirred the gauzy curtains was cool and fresh; the storm's fireworks and sound effects had moved off to the south, and a full moon was shining fitfully through a trailing veil of luminous clouds, casting a frostlike sheen over the lawn that sloped down to the river.

The same river where Wiley drowned, I thought, *presumably on the night he disappeared. On Saturday night, after Aunt Tullie hit him hard enough to draw blood.*

I felt the cold again in the pit of my stomach. Had Aunt Tullie hit Wiley hard enough to split his scalp *and* give him a concussion? Had he driven down to the old fishing camp to look around and think what he was going to do with the property, once Aunt Tullie handed it over to him? I pictured him sitting alone on that steeply sloping ramp, passing out from his injury, his new truck coasting slowly and inexorably into the river, carrying the unconscious man to his death. *The passenger door was open*, I reminded myself. *Maybe someone else had been with him. But who? And why hadn't the person come forward?*

I couldn't answer those questions. I only knew that the coroner was going to spot that head wound and draw his own inevitable conclusions. When that happened, the deputies would be knocking on our door. Aunt Tullie probably wasn't competent to make a decision about this, so Leatha would have to take the initiative, and fast. First thing in the morning, I would advise her to phone the sheriff's office and ask Deputy Banjo Green to come out and take her statement about the events of Saturday night, and Aunt Tullie's as well. There was no need to let on that we knew anything about the discovery of Wiley's body, but it was imperative that the truth be told as quickly as possible, so we couldn't be accused of hiding something even more incriminating than the assault.

I sat in the rocking chair for a long time, thinking about this situation and its various possible outcomes and trying to come up with a contingency plan. But the discovery of Wiley's body, horrible as it had been, hadn't driven the other horrible question out of my mind—the question of my inheritance. My *genetic* inheritance. Did Leatha carry the Huntington gene, and if she did, had she passed it on to me?

Surely there was an answer to these questions. Hadn't there been some recent developments in genetic testing that made it possible to know for sure whether you were going to get these inheritable diseases? If so, should I encourage Leatha to be tested? If her test was positive, should *I* be tested? How would Leatha's life change, how would *my* life change if we carried the gene?

But these questions had no immediate answers, and the effort it took to stay focused was making me dizzy. I sat for a few moments thinking nothing at all, except that I was really very tired, tired enough to go to sleep right here in this . . .

My head lolled uncomfortably to one side, waking me, and I sat up with a jerk. The clock on the landing was chiming midnight. There was no point in sleeping in an uncomfortable chair when I could be in bed. I was getting up when my eye was caught by a huddle of shadows at the foot of the garden, down by the old wooden pergola. I caught the murmur of low voices and something that sounded like the clink of a shovel. Then the shadows moved apart and I saw that they were people, two people, and they seemed to be looking for something on the ground, or in the ground perhaps. Had the deputies somehow followed the old trail up from the landing? Had they—

Then one of the figures holds up a dim light, a lantern, and I see that it is a woman, that she is wearing a long caftan-like garment and that her head is wrapped in a turban. The light falls on the man wielding the shovel. It is Old Homer, dressed in denim overalls and his ragged straw hat.

But Old Homer is dead. He's been dead for fifteen years. It must be Judith down there, and for some unknowable reason, she has brought Marie Louise LaTour here with her and the two of them are burying something beside the old pergola. But Aunt Tullie had the pergola torn down fifteen years ago, when Homer died. I must be dreaming.

That's it. I put my palms flat on the windowsill, and said it out loud. "I'm dreaming. This is a dream. You can wake up now, China, any time."

Somewhere in the moon-glazed dark, an owl hoots low and breathy, *whoo-who-who*, as if he is secretly amused by these goings on. A June bug whirs like a mechanical wind-up toy against my cheek. I brush it off and it lumbers off into the night, flying clumsily, like a tiny, shiny brown airbus. The owl and the June bug are undeniably real, but the lantern still burns at the foot of the garden, and the huddled shadows continue their work.

I try again. "This can't be happening," I say. From the sycamore tree, pale and ghostly at the edge of the grass, comes the mocking confirmation of a whippoorwill. The shadows merge and separate and now I see that there are three: the turbaned witch woman with the lantern, old Homer or Judith or whoever that is with the shovel, and—

And Aunt Tullie. She is crying. I can hear her clearly,

for I am no longer at the open window. I have crept noise-lessly down the back stairs and past the metal lawn chairs where Darlene and I sat this morning with our coffee, and I am slipping along my old secret path behind the azaleas and black-haws. I am barefoot, and the grass is wet—why am I barefoot? Oh, yes, now I remember: My shoes were muddy from the old fishing camp, and I took them off to keep from tracking mud and grass across the bedroom floor. The grass is wet under my feet and I can smell the fresh scent of leaf mold as I step across the damp ground. *I can smell the rain coming, can't you?* Darlene says in my mind. Far off to the south, the dying lightning flickers. *Sweet Jesus Lord, that's Wiley's truck truck truck. . . .*

Judith, or is it Old Homer, has leaned the shovel against the white-painted pergola, and Aunt Tullie, weeping, has fallen to her knees, digging feverishly with her hands. I try my best to be silent. But as I move closer, Marie Lou-ise hears my step among the leaves. She turns and raises her lantern.

"That you, China Bayles?" she asks, raspy, disapprov-ing. "You jes cain't leave it alone, can you, child? G'wan back to bed. You wa'n't meant t'see this yet."

"She wants to see, let her see," Old Homer says. It really is Old Homer, grizzled and toothless, grinning. *You know what they say about the Delta.* It's Darlene's voice again. *Folks die here, they never leave.* Old Homer died right here, keeled over with a heart attack, but he's stand-ing there beside the shovel, grinning, beside the white-painted pergola, torn down after his death. *Folks die here, they never leave.*

Aunt Tullie is still on her knees, still weeping, still dig-ging with her hands, pulling something out of the hole. It's cloth, it's that sleeve, that rotten old sleeve and it comes to pieces in her hands. *It must be Old Homer's sleeve*, I tell myself. They've buried him right where he died, right where he keeled over with a heart attack. This is *his* grave.

But Old Homer is standing here, lifting his hat and wiping his sleeve across his wet forehead, making little wheezing sounds. I move closer and fall to my knees beside Aunt Tullie; I peer into the hole and see that she has unearthed that damned hand with its ribbons of rotting flesh that I used to dream about, on one skeletal finger a wide gold ring, carved in an ivy design. And then I notice that she has also scraped away the earth from the face, and I can see it and learn at last who has been lying in this makeshift, unmarked grave for so many years. Homer, perhaps. But no.

It is Wiley Beauchamp, his face half-eaten away by the swamp creatures. I suck in my breath, thinking that I have to run to the telephone, to call the police and tell them that somebody has made a stupid mistake and stuck Wiley's body into a hole in our garden and they need to come and get him so he can be autopsied. But before I can jump to my feet, the flesh on his face begins to melt, flowing like scummy swamp water off his skull until it is no longer possible to recognize him—or her. This might be the skeleton of Aunt Tullie's mother or father, that ancestor in whose blood swam the gene that sentenced half of the offspring to a terrible death. Had my mother inherited that death sentence? Had she passed it on to me? The sweat breaks out over my body and the goose flesh rises on my arms as I stare at the bony skull grinning mirthlessly up at me, the answerless questions circling like vultures in my head, hoping that there will be something left of the corpse for them to feast on.

Beside me, Aunt Tullie gets clumsily to her feet, still weeping, and begins to dance and cavort in an obscene parody of what I know now is Huntington's chorea. I turn my head, not wanting to watch her bizarre movements. As I do, I notice that the ring has fallen off the skeletal hand and is lying on the grass. It bears an inscription inside. It says—

Marie Louise takes the ring from me, sighing as if she is disappointed. "You gots to let dem ol' skeletons rest, girl. I tells Miz Tullie an' I tells you: De answer'll come when yo're ready to know what hit means, an' not before." She bends closer, her voice compassionate. "Now g'wan back where you b'long. Hit ain't yore time. Y'hear?"

I hear, and I don't argue. I scramble to my feet and run, leaving Aunt Tullie in her mad dance, and Old Homer beginning to dig again, and Marie Louise holding her lantern. I am suddenly terrified by the idea that if I don't get back to my room I might find myself lost somewhere between the time it is in the garden (whatever that is) and real time, the time where McQuaid and Brian and Ruby live, *my* time. I sprint across the grass and duck under the black-haw tree by the door and bound up the stairs and fling myself into my bedroom, breathless and dizzy.

After a moment, hearing nothing but the blood beating in my ears and my heart pounding in my chest, I make my way to the window. The moon shines into an empty garden. I sink down in the rocking chair and watch to be sure no figures reappear, then find my eyelids closing, my head falling to one side.

I jerk upright and push myself out of the chair. *It must have been a dream*, I tell myself, *a variation on the old, awful nightmare*. But as I stand and begin to strip off my clothes for bed, I see that my feet are dirty, and that there is a trail of leaves and still-wet grass across the floor.

And when I go to the bureau and pull open the drawer to get the nightshirt I put there when I unpacked, I find a pair of pajamas lying on top, neatly folded. A pair of child's blue-and-white-striped cotton pajamas, my name embroidered on the pocket. They have been washed and pressed, but a brownish-red stain, like old blood, is still faintly visible on both knees.

Chapter Eight

QUEENIE'S ROSEMARY BISCUITS

2 cups flour
1 teaspoon baking powder
1/2 teaspoon salt
1/2 teaspoon baking soda
2 teaspoons sugar
2 tablespoons butter
1 tablespoon fresh or 1 teaspoon dried rosemary leaves,
   chopped very fine
3/4 cup milk

Preheat oven to 400 degrees. Sift the flour, baking powder, salt, baking soda, and sugar together in a large bowl. Cut the butter into pea-sized lumps in the flour mixture. Add rosemary and milk and mix with a fork to form a soft dough. (Do not overmix.) Roll out dough 1/2-inch thick on lightly floured board. Cut into circles with a biscuit cutter and place close together on a greased and floured baking sheet. Bake 20 minutes. Serve hot. Makes 12.

I woke with a start in bright sunshine. The clock said seven-thirty and the mockingbird on the magnolia branch outside the window was insisting that it was time to be up and about the day's work. I jerked upright and threw off the quilt, already anxious. I'd meant to get up at dawn and wake Leatha for a talk before Aunt Tullie was up. We had to phone the sheriff's office this morning, and I needed to explain to her why it was so important to call them before they called us.

Laugh if you will, but the first thing I did was check the bottoms of my bare feet. They were clean and so were the sheets, so I hadn't climbed into bed with dirty feet. I couldn't see any traces of grass or leaves on the floor, either. What had happened last night in the garden must have been just another version of that recurring dream, the old plot interlaced with the more disturbing of the recent realities—Wiley's death and my new knowledge of Aunt Tullie's illness, of its terrible possibilities for my mother and me.

But when I got up and went to the bureau to check, those child's pajamas were still folded neatly in the drawer, their knees stained brownish-red. When I turned around, I saw that Pearl's journal, on the table beside the bed, was open to the first page, as if I had fallen asleep reading it, even though I knew positively that the little book had been closed when I turned out the light, and that I had not read a line in it. And when I glanced at the silver-framed snapshot beside the journal, I realized that it wasn't my grandmother Rachel seated at a writing table, as I had thought, but my great-grandmother Pearl, and that the table was positioned between two tall windows, exactly like the table that stood in the very same place, between the windows in this very room. And as this realization came to me, I smelled it again: the sweet, unmistakable scent of lilies of the valley, filling the room.

I stood still for a moment, the skin prickling along my

arms. This seemed like spooky stuff, but I was sure that there were rational explanations behind everything that was happening. My mother had to have put the pajamas in the drawer and the journal and photograph beside the bed. And somewhere in this room, perhaps in the bureau or the writing table, there was a source of the scent I was smelling.

And why not? Judging from the photo, this was probably Pearl's bedroom, and the photo and the journal belonged here. On a hunch, I picked up the framed photograph and pried off the cardboard backing. On the back of the picture was written, in my grandfather's distinctive hand, *May 15, 1918. The last photo of Mother, taken in her room.* I glanced back at the writing table and for an instant I could almost see her there, pen poised over her journal, so completely absorbed in it that she had no idea that someone was about to take her picture. And when I looked back at the snapshot, I could see that, yes, she *was* writing in her journal, or at least in a little book that looked very much like it. The photograph—as pictures often do—gave both Pearl and her journal a kind of reality that had seemed lacking before.

But what about those pajamas in the drawer, the ones with my name embroidered on the pocket? There was no doubt that they were real—I could touch them and feel the weight of the fabric and see the brown-red stain on the knees. I caught my breath, thinking of something. The stain was obviously real, which meant that at least some of what I had thought was a dream might have been real, too. Or perhaps I had invented the dream as a way of explaining the stains I had somehow gotten on my pajamas.

Frowning, I put the frame back together and set it down. I began to dress, pulling on a green T-shirt and denim shorts, wishing that Ruby were here. She would love all these ghostly happenings, the dream that was all mixed up with reality, the eerie scent of lilies of the valley. Ruby might be able to tell me what was going on. She was an expert on the supernatural.

The supernatural. I stood in front of the mirror, tugging a comb through my hair, frowning at my reflection. I glimpsed an irony here, and not a very subtle one, either. I was the one who insisted that things that went bump in the night always had a logical, real-world explanation. Now my left-brain world had filled up with bewildering gardens and bedrooms populated by bewitched characters in a dream that didn't feel like a dream, and I wanted Ruby to explain it to me in words I could understand.

Ruby. For a moment, I felt a deep, insistent longing for her. Back in Pecan Springs, she would be getting up about now and making coffee. I could go downstairs and phone. I could talk this business over with her, could arrange it in some kind of logical narrative. She might help me find some answers.

But as I put down the comb and turned to look for my shoes, Marie Louise's half-rebuking voice came unbidden into my mind—*De answer'll come when yo're ready to know what hit means, an' not before.* Anyway, I didn't have time to call Ruby. I had to talk to Leatha before breakfast and tell her what had happened. We had to call the sheriff's office and tell Deputy Green that—

As if my thought had triggered it, the telephone rang— that unforgettable, old-fashioned ring of an old-fashioned rotary-dial phone—downstairs in the plantation office. I didn't stop to put on my shoes. I flew down the stairs, two at a time, bursting through the office door, getting to the phone as it rang for the third time.

I caught my breath as I reached for it and answered with as much control as I could summon. I had to be cool. I didn't want Banjo to think this phone call flustered me.

But it wasn't the deputy. It was Darlene.

"That you, China? Would you please tell Miz Tullie and your momma that I won't be in this mornin'?" She forced a pathetic cough. "It's that flu of Dawn's. I think I'm comin' down with it. I feel awful."

I didn't believe her. She sounded awful, all right, but I knew it wasn't the flu. It was what had happened last night at the fishing camp. There was some mysterious connection between Darlene and Wiley, some *important* connection. Darlene wasn't the kind of woman to go into a tailspin over the death of a childhood playmate.

Darlene coughed again, even less convincingly this time. "There's plenty of eggs in the icebox, and bacon and juice, and Momma's rosemary biscuit recipe is on the wall beside the stove. That's the one Miz Tullie 'specially likes."

"But Darlene—"

"Tell Miz Leatha I'll be back as soon as I can," Darlene said. "Tomorrow, I hope." She hung up.

I had just put down the phone when it rang again. It was Alice Ann. She had decided to quit—she and Dawn both. "I'm sorry," she said contritely. "It's bad to leave you in the lurch this way, but . . ." Her voice trailed off.

"I'm sure you have your reasons," I said. "If you'll come by, we'll write a check for what we owe you both. And thanks a lot for all your good work."

I was still holding the phone when the door opened behind me. "Was that Sam?" Leatha asked hopefully. "He's visiting his daughter, and I was hoping he'd call." She must have overslept, too. She'd thrown a floral wrapper over her pink nightgown and her face, without makeup, was soft and lined and very vulnerable.

"It was Darlene," I said, replacing the receiver. "She has the flu and won't be in this morning. And the second call was from Alice Ann. She and Dawn have both quit."

The minute the words were out of my mouth, I wished I could take them back. I didn't know how strong Leatha was, or how much she could handle. I could've saved the news about Dawn and Alice Ann for another time. Our business with the sheriff's office was far more urgent.

"Oh, no!" Leatha exclaimed, running her hand distractedly through her hair. "*Both* of the girls? What in the world is going on?" She sighed. "Well, we'll manage somehow. We have to. I'll get dressed and go down to the kitchen—"

"Coffee first," I said firmly. "Darlene's put me in charge of breakfast. And we're not saying another word until the coffee is brewing." And I steered her toward the stairs to the kitchen.

Ten minutes later, Leatha and I were sitting at the kitchen table with mugs of hot coffee, and I had just finished telling her about the discovery of Wiley's body. She had gone pale and there was a panicky distress in her eyes.

"Do you *really* think we have to call that deputy, China? Maybe he won't make the connection." Her hand fluttered, as if she were trying to wave this all away. "Maybe Wiley died from something else entirely. Drugs or something."

"Drugs are a possibility," I agreed. "But like it or not, Mother, I am still a member of the bar. As an officer of the court, I have an obligation to—"

"I know all about that," Leatha said wearily. "Your father was a lawyer, too, remember? He was always talking about his obligations. But couldn't we *wait*? At least until we know how Wiley died."

I put my hand over hers, making my voice sympathetic. "The sooner we do this, the better, I'm afraid. If you'd rather, I can make the call."

That suggestion seemed to relieve only some of her anxiety. "Would you?" she asked nervously. "You're more comfortable talking to the police than I am."

As she said this, it suddenly occurred to me that there might be more to the story than I had heard so far. "We need to tell the *whole* truth, Mother," I said firmly. I frowned, and modified that directive slightly. There was one truth I didn't want the police to hear. "Except that I don't want them to guess that we already know about Wiley's death," I added. "Darlene and I didn't declare ourselves last night, down at the fishing camp, and they might think it's a little strange that—"

"I know, darling, I know," she said. "I'll pretend I haven't heard anything about it." She stood up. "But please do what you can to keep them from talking to Aunt Tullie. It will only upset her, and she might say something that—" She stopped, her eyes sliding away, then coming back to me, pleading. "It's not that I'm hiding anything, China. There's nothing to hide, really. It's just that this is *so* difficult."

I believed her—almost. I rose, too, and put my arms around her. For a moment we just stood together, holding one another. Then I said softly, "I'll make the call,

Mother. And then I'll make us some breakfast. You get dressed and take care of Aunt Tullie. We'll get through this somehow."

She stepped back. "Thank you," she said. She pressed the back of her hand against her mouth, and I saw she was crying. Her fingers were trembling, too. Her whole hand was shaking, even though it was pressed against her mouth. Uncontrollable movements. A sign of . . .

I cleared my throat. I'd drive myself crazy if I started watching my mother for symptoms. "Better not thank me until Aunt Tullie approves those biscuits," I said. Then I remembered about the journal. "Oh, by the way, Mother, thank you for putting Pearl's journal and her photograph on my bedside table. And where did you find my old pajamas?"

Leatha gave me a puzzled look. "Pearl's journal? Pajamas? I don't know what you're talking about, China. I didn't put anything in your room." She smiled. "I did turn your bed down, though."

I stared at her. If she hadn't put them there, who had?

If Aunt Tullie could tell the difference between Darlene's biscuits and mine, she didn't let on. And if Deputy Green was surprised at my request that he come out and take my mother's statement, he didn't show it, either. We met him on the veranda at nine-thirty and led him into the front parlor, where he actually took off both his cap and his sunglasses. I wasn't sure what Leatha had done to keep Aunt Tullie occupied, but she didn't put in an appearance while we entertained the police.

Leatha told her story straightforwardly, without flutterings or embellishments. Too straightforwardly, maybe. To my ear, she sounded rehearsed. Not by me, though. Even if I'd had the inclination, there hadn't been time.

The deputy looked up from his notebook, pursing his lips. Without his sunglasses, I could see that he had clear, dark eyes and a direct look to go with his strong jaw, and I wondered where he had gotten the nickname Banjo. I put it out of my mind quickly. I had heard that name last night, at the old fishing camp. I wasn't supposed to have been there.

"Let me see if I've got this straight," he said. "On Saturday, Wiley shows up here about six-thirty and stays for twenty minutes."

"About that long," Leatha amended. "I wasn't watching the clock."

"Yes, ma'am," the deputy said dryly, and made a note. "When he tells Miz Petulia that he's turned up this old property deed, she gets mad and whacks him 'longside the head, inflictin' a wound—" He narrowed his eyes. "About how long a cut would you say it was, Miz Richards? And on which side of his head?"

"On the left side. Aunt Tullie is right-handed." Leatha screwed up her face. "I guess it was a couple of inches, three, maybe. Above his ear. But I wish you wouldn't put down that she got mad. She has a neurological disorder, you see, that makes her—well, lose control. She doesn't understand what she's doing."

I flinched. A three-inch scalp wound. It's a wonder it didn't kill him on the spot.

"Yes, ma'am," the deputy said, not looking up. "And he was out for, how long do you guess?"

"It couldn't have been more than a minute or two," Leatha replied somberly. "He picked himself up right away and walked out."

"How'd he look?"

"Angry, I suppose you'd say. If it'd been a man who hit him, he probably would've hit him back." Leatha brushed her hair out of her eyes. "I couldn't blame him, could you?"

The deputy glanced up, the corner of his mouth twitching. "'Scuse me. I mean, did he act woozy or anything?"

"Of course not," Leatha said quickly. "Apart from the bleeding, he was just fine. He wasn't staggering, if that's what you're asking."

"And you mopped up the blood? You've got somebody who cleans for you, don't you? How come you didn't just leave it?"

My mother gave him a superior smile. "Being a man, I guess you don't know how fast a bloodstain sets. If you don't get after it right away, you'll be living with it forever. As it was, I couldn't get it all." She stood up. "I'll show you."

We trekked down the hall to the plantation office. The deputy frowned at the faint, scrubbed-out stain on the carpet and made a few more notes. "I'll have to see the weapon," he remarked.

"Here it is," I said, taking Aunt Tullie's gold-headed cane from beside the file cabinet. At breakfast, thinking ahead to this moment, I had snitched it and substituted her second-best one. It was quite different, but she hadn't noticed a thing. In the process, I had spotted the tiny flecks of blood in the crevices of the carved gold knob. Wiley Beauchamp's blood. And it was entirely possible that this was the weapon that had killed him.

The deputy examined the cane carefully, no doubt thinking the same thought. "I'm gonna have to take this with me."

Leatha was alarmed. "But what will Aunt Tullie say when she—"

I put my hand on her arm. "It's okay, Mother. We'll think of something to tell her."

"And what about that deed?" the deputy asked. "Did he leave it with you?"

Leatha shook her head. "He took it with him," she said. "Of course, for all we know, it could have been a fake."

"What do you think, Ms. Bayles?" The deputy looked at me. "Real or phony?"

"I didn't see it." I shrugged. "Anyway, we can't make a judgment about its validity without an expert appraisal. And it can't be appraised unless we have access to the original. We don't know where it is until Mr. Beauchamp tells us."

Maybe, I thought, it's in the truck—and if it is, it's been soaking in river water for several days. But I couldn't raise that possibility without giving away what I knew, so I kept my mouth shut.

The deputy's eyes narrowed. "Sounds like a pretty good motive to me," he said.

I wasn't going to be tricked, if that's what he was up to. "A motive for swinging at him?" I asked. "Sure, it was a motive. How would you like it if somebody walked up to you and claimed to have a deed to the land under your house?"

The deputy pursed his lips. "I don't reckon it's absolutely necessary this mornin', but sooner or later, I'm gonna have to talk to Miz Petulia." He eyed Leatha. "You say she's got some kind of neurological problem. Alzheimer's, is it? I 'spose you got a paper or somethin' from the doc that says she's sick."

"It's not Alzheimer's," Leatha said quickly. "I have the

doctor's report that explains what it is. I'll run upstairs and get it for you."

"Better yet, Mother," I said, "why don't you also get the doctor's name and telephone number, and Deputy Green can call him directly? That way, he can ask all the questions he wants about Aunt Tullie's condition."

"That'll work," the deputy said, closing his notebook.

"Has Wiley turned up yet?" I asked, when Leatha was out of the room. "What have you heard from him?"

"As a matter of fact, he has," the deputy said. He looked at me without expression. "He's turned up dead."

"Dead!" I echoed, in what I hoped was a tone of mingled surprise and shock. "That's terrible! Was it an auto accident?"

"Not 'xactly." He was being very cool, very professional. "'S matter of fact, he was found right down the road a piece. At the old fishin' camp. That's on this property, I understand."

I noticed that he hadn't let it slip that Wiley had been found in the river, and I was glad that Leatha was out of the room. I frowned. "The old camp? Yes, that's the old river landing, where the barges used to dock. It belongs to Jordan's Crossing." I shook my head. "That's really too bad. What happened? He was fishing, I suppose. Did he fall into the river or something?"

"Something," the deputy said, still cool.

"What was the cause of death?" I persisted—perhaps unwisely, because he gave me a canny look.

"Why're you askin', Counselor? Thinkin' he might've died from that blow to the head?"

That was exactly what I was thinking, but I didn't want to admit it. "People die for all sorts of reasons," I said. "I'd sure hate it if what happened here had anything to do with his death. Of course, Miss Coldwell can't be held legally responsible for her actions."

"I don't know about that," the deputy said sourly. "But you gotta admit that she stood to gain from his death. Wiley's the last of the Beauchamps. With him gone, there's nobody to make a fuss about that deed, assuming it was genuine."

I didn't have to answer, because Leatha came in with a slip of paper. She handed it to the deputy. Before she could speak, I said, "Mother, I'm sorry to have to tell you this, but Wiley's dead. They found him down at the old fishing camp."

Her gasp was a credible substitute for surprise. I turned to the deputy. "When did you say he was found?"

"I didn't." He paused. "But it was last night, late."

"Oh, no!" Leatha's expression was exactly the right mixture of wide-eyed consternation and regret. "Oh, I am *so* sorry." She looked at the deputy. "How did he die?"

"That information isn't available yet," the deputy said. He put the slip of paper with the doctor's name and address into his notebook. "Thanks for your help, ladies. I can see myself to the door. I'll call if there's any more questions."

I didn't exactly breathe a sigh of relief when he was gone, but it might have sounded like that. I looked at the clock and saw that it was now after ten.

"I promised Martha Edmond I'd come over this morning and take a tour of her garden." At the look on Leatha's face, I was immediately guilt stricken. I added, quickly, "If we can get Judith to stay with Aunt Tullie, would you like to come with me? You need a break."

"I'd love to," Leatha said happily. "I haven't seen Martha in years." She glanced out the window. "Judith was working outside a moment ago. Let me see if she can come in for a little while. How long will we be gone?"

"Martha mentioned lunch, but if you don't think that's possible—"

"There are sandwiches in the refrigerator," Leatha said firmly. "I'm sure Judith can cope for a few hours. You're right. I need a break."

Chapter Nine

As far as native people were concerned, every plant was the Creator's gift to the people and had its own particular uses. These include plants we would never think of as herbs—the magnolia tree (*Magnolia grandiflora*), for instance. In Mississippi, the Choctaw women washed the skin with a decoction of the bark to relieve the itching of prickly heat and mashed the bark to be used in a steam treatment for dropsy (what we now call congestive heart failure). They also chewed the bark of the buttonbush (*Cephalanthus occidentalis*) as a remedy for toothache, and brewed a decoction of the root to treat colds and fevers. This knowledge wasn't written down, of course, but passed from mother to daughter in a centuries-old oral tradition.

Martha Edmond
"A Mississippi Indian Herbal"

Martha and Leatha renewed their acquaintance with warm hugs and a few tears, and after a moment or two, Martha put on her wide-brimmed straw hat and led us into her extensive garden, which was full of an amazing variety of flowers and shrubs. She had all of the familiar herbs, of course—rosemary, thyme, sage, fennel and dill for the butterflies, lemon balm and lemon verbena for tea, many different artemisias, St.-John's-wort, tansy, and more.

But the most interesting part of Martha's garden was in a separate corner, screened by a row of buttonbushes and elder trees, the elders heavy with their white umble-like spring flowers, the clusters as large as saucers. The plants in this section were native herbs collected from the wild as seeds or cuttings by her and her mother and grand-mother, both dead now. Martha cultivated these herbs, she said, so that she could study and photograph them for a book she was working on. When it was done, it would be a comprehensive survey of the great variety of plants used by the Indians in this part of Mississippi.

Martha shoved her hands into the pockets of her brown shorts. "After all," she remarked with a smile, "a Choctaw woman couldn't very well get into the car and drive to the local Wal-Mart when she needed a new basket or a broom, or wanted some tea, or caught a bad cold—or something more serious."

She pointed to a plant with square stems and lance-shaped leaves. "That's bedstraw, or cleavers. This variety is *Galium boreale*. Northern tribes, like the Cree, for in-stance, used the root to make a red dye. The Choctaws, on the other hand, used the whole plant as a contraceptive and as an abortifacient." At Leatha's puzzled look, she added, "That's the word people use to describe an herb that can cause an abortion."

"I didn't realize that herbs could be used for anything like *that*," Leatha murmured thoughtfully. She picked a leaf and twirled it in her fingers.

"That's what the women of every culture used before surgical abortions became available," I put in. "Plants were safe and effective, and the wise women in the villages passed along the information about how to use them from one generation to the next."

"There were lots of herbal abortifacients," Martha remarked. She took off her straw hat and fanned herself with it. "Rue, parsley, and pennyroyal are probably the best known in the European tradition. In America, the Indians used what was locally available to them. Queen Anne's lace, or wild carrot, was one possibility. White crownbeard was another." She pointed to a tall, raggedy-looking plant with winglike ribs running up the length of the central stalk.

"I didn't know that this plant was an abortifacient," I said in surprise. "In Texas, we call it frost-weed. And not just because it has white flowers, either. In the first hard freeze, the stems split at the bottom and the frozen sap is extruded in little curls and ribbons of ice. It's also called tick weed, because it seems to attract seed ticks."

Martha pulled off a leaf. "Did you know that it's also called squaw-weed?" She wrinkled her nose at the word. "One book claims that the name came about because the women made the dried leaves into a tobacco substitute." She rubbed the leaf between her fingers. "But when you know that crownbeard was used as an abortifacient, you can guess the *real* reason behind the name. I have the feeling that the mixed-blood traders who called it squaw-weed might have been afraid of the power this plant gave women to control their bodies, so they wanted to disparage it."

I nodded, agreeing, and my admiration for Martha Edmond rose another notch. This beautiful woman not only knew her plants, but respected the healing traditions of wise women and the special bond that seems to have existed for eons between women and plants.

"That looks like a yucca," Leatha observed, pointing to a plant with stiff, swordlike leaves. "We have plenty of yuccas in Texas."

"You also have this plant," Martha replied, "although it isn't really a yucca. It's *Eryngium aquaticum.* Around here, the Choctaws and Chickasaws called it rattlesnake master, or button snakeroot. Back in the 1700s, a trader named James Adair saw Indians chewing the root, then blowing the pulp onto their hands before they handled the snakes they used in their rattlesnake medicine songs and dances." She touched a spiky leaf. "My grandmother, who collected this particular plant, used to say that maybe they were using it to put the snakes to sleep. The root of a different variety of *Eryngium* was used by some of the Plains Indians as a sedative."

"Your grandmother had a good idea," I said, thinking how wonderful it was to look at a plant and remember that it had belonged to your mother, or to her mother, or perhaps even to *her* mother. I pointed to a small patch of plants growing in cool, moist shade. "And that's bloodroot, isn't it?" I paused. "I suppose it's finished blooming already."

"Right," Martha replied. "It blooms very early, before the leaves are completely unfurled—beautiful white blooms, like stars. In the summer, it's a wonderful ground cover." She smiled affectionately. "This little guy is one of my favorites. I wish more people would use it in their gardens. It's highly toxic, of course, but most poisonings occur when the plant is being used medicinally—which doesn't happen much anymore."

"We can't grow it in Texas," I said. "It's much too hot and dry."

Martha nodded. "This little patch of three or four plants has multiplied from a single root that my mother dug years ago in the northeastern part of Mississippi, in the foothills of the Appalachians."

"There's some of it in the garden at Jordan's Crossing," Leatha said, "under the azaleas."

"There is?" I asked in surprise. "I didn't know that." But then I remembered my dream, and running across the garden, falling to my knees beside the azaleas. And those brownish-red stains on the knees of my pajamas. Not blood stains, as I had thought, but bloodroot.

Martha was nodding. "My mother gave a start of it to Tullie, years and years ago, and I'm sure it's still there. Where it's native, it was powerful medicine—I suppose because the juice looks just like blood."

"It was used as a dye, wasn't it?" I asked.

"Right. The Iroquois dyed cloth and stained basket fiber with it—it was one of their favorites. Medicinally, it was used to treat coughs and stomach and urinary troubles. They also brewed a tea that they believed made the heart stronger and cleansed the blood of impurities. And they used it as a love charm."

"A love charm," I repeated thoughtfully. "I suppose that was because of its association with the heart."

"Perhaps." Martha put her hat back on. "The red juice and its connection with the blood and the heart seems to have given it an important role in the sacred tradition. The Iroquois burned the leaves as a cleansing smoke to purify someone who had seen a dead person. And tribes in other parts of the country—the Ojibwa, the Ponca, the Potawatomi—used it to paint special identification marks on their faces, so that everyone would know at a glance what clan they belonged to. That was important, you know," she added. "Clan membership was at the heart of the tribe's social organization. Bloodroot must have been powerful medicine, if they used it for clan markers."

"Interesting," I murmured, thinking that nowadays, clans and families would be traced through their DNA. And that the Coldwell connection might not be hard to spot. We—some of us, anyway—had a special marker: the gene that was responsible for Aunt Tullie's condition. I shivered and pushed the thought away. The day was too bright and pretty to darken it with such reflections.

"Oh, *here* you are, China," Amanda said eagerly, coming along the path. "Did you ask your mother about my talking with her?"

I had totally forgotten about Amanda and her academic pursuits. "You can ask her yourself," I said shortly, and made the introductions, hoping that Leatha wouldn't be too rude to this irritatingly pushy person.

But to my surprise, the two of them seemed to hit it off immediately. "I'd love to tell you what I know about the Coldwells and Jordan's Crossing," Leatha said with enthusiasm. "What especially are you interested in?"

"Oh, just *everything*," Amanda replied. I could see that she was pleased, even relieved perhaps, with my mother's response, and I couldn't help wondering why this was so important to her. "Let's go sit on the porch, and we'll have a glass of iced tea while we talk." The two walked off with their heads together.

Martha raised her eyebrows. "As if they'd known each other all their lives."

"Right," I said dryly. "How did you happen to invite Amanda here?" I didn't add, *She doesn't seem like your type*, but I think Martha understood.

"I didn't invite her, actually," she replied. "Let's go snip some fresh parsley and dill. While the two of them are talking, you and I will see to our lunch and I'll tell you all about it."

The old farmhouse kitchen had been remodeled to include new appliances, but no amount of renovating could destroy its Deep South past. Tall white cabinets reached to the ceiling on either side of the window over the sink, which was open to the honeysuckle-scented breeze. The walls were covered with ivy-print paper above a white-painted wainscot, and the floor was polished pine planks. One long shelf held a row of lidded jars filled with dried herbs, and in the middle of the room stood a table covered with a green-checked cloth and surrounded by four green-painted chairs. An old black cookstove occupied one corner, stacked with antique tins and baskets, but the main dish for our lunch—a fragrant, basil-rich tomato pie—was baking in the oven of a modern gas range.

With a pair of quilted mitts, Martha slid the pie from the oven and set it on top of the range to cool, remarking that the recipe was an old family favorite, handed down from her great-great-grandmother. Then she went to the refrigerator and took out a large bowl of chilled cucumber soup. While I sliced a loaf of homemade herb bread, she began ladling the soup into bowls, talking as she worked.

It turned out that Martha had been introduced to Amanda Gleason through a mutual friend from the University of Louisiana, who had called to say that a colleague was looking for a place to stay while she did some research in the area. Since the friend knew that Martha had an extra room that she occasionally rented out and a special interest in local history, she thought it would be a good match.

"And it is, more or less," Martha said, lining up the four bowls. "I admire what Amanda's doing, although I must admit that she's a little intense for me." She glanced at me, and I wondered if I had been terribly transparent. "I could also wish that she had read more widely in Southern women's history before she began this project. Her teaching field is economics, not history." She frowned. "I have a hunch that she's really after something else, although I have no idea what that might be. She hasn't told me a great deal about herself."

I thought back to my fleeting impression of the night before: that Amanda had a different agenda from the one she had shared with us. "Well, perhaps she'll get what she wants from Mother," I remarked. "Anyway, working with her will give Mother something else to think about besides Aunt Tullie. This is the first time she's left Jordan's Crossing in weeks and weeks."

"Caregiving is a full-time job," Martha agreed. "I know. I was here with my mother for the last two years before she died." She picked up a handful of dill sprigs. "I'll ask some of the women in the community to help me organize some relief for Leatha until you've made a different arrangement for Tullie. It's too much for Leatha to do alone, and I suppose you can't be away from your business very long. Who's pinch-hitting for Leatha today?"

"Judith Lightfoot." I put the bread on the small board Martha had taken from the cupboard and added a crock of herbal butter and a couple of sprigs of rosemary. "It's her day to do garden work, so she was there anyway."

"Judith's very competent," Martha said, and then added, candidly: "But I'm not sure she'd make a good caregiver. She's inclined to be impatient with people who don't meet her expectations." She tilted her head. "You know that she works with me?"

"I heard that she's doing an internship in native plants," I said, thinking that Judith's irritation with May Rose certainly confirmed Martha's thumbnail description. "It's good of you to share what you know."

"Good of *me*?" Martha's light laugh was amused. "Judith is a big help in the garden—I've got the best of the deal. It's really too bad that Wiley's decided to move her out of that cottage. I hope your aunt will intervene. That section of land belonged to Judith's family before the Coldwells took it, you know. Living there, she feels as if she's come home." She began arranging cucumber rings and dill sprigs on top of the soup. "Would you get the lemonade out of the fridge, please? The glasses are over the sink."

I didn't fully understand Martha's comment about Judith and the land, but that could wait. "I don't suppose you've heard about Wiley," I said, getting out the pitcher of lemonade. "He's dead. His body was found last night, at the old fishing camp." I went to the cupboard. "We heard it from the sheriff's deputy. He stopped by this morning to see if we knew anything about it."

Martha was staring at me. "Oh, dear," she said softly. She shook her head. "Oh, that's really too bad. Was it— did he kill himself?"

I put the glasses on the table. "What makes you ask that?" Under the circumstances—knowing what I knew about Aunt Tullie's attack on Wiley—I hadn't considered suicide as a possibility. I had no idea what the investigation would reveal, but it was certainly something to think about.

"I don't think I should—" Martha moved uneasily. "Oh, I suppose there's no harm in talking about what's past and gone," she said. "There's a long history of suicide in the Beauchamp family, you see. Wiley's older brother Ray drowned himself ten years ago, and his aunt Belle jumped off the bridge at Vicksburg."

"Oh, yes," I said. "Colonel Blakeslee told me about them." *Bad luck seems to run in the family*, he'd said.

She frowned, reflecting. "It's not just those two, as I recall. One of Wiley's grandfather's sisters hung herself when I was a girl, and there was talk at the time that her brother had shot himself. But he lived in New Orleans, and I don't think anybody around here knew for sure what happened."

"It sounds like a pattern," I said, as I filled the glasses from the pitcher. If it came to constructing a defense strategy for Aunt Tullie, it would certainly be a possibility. Maybe Wiley had been drinking, parked on the ramp, and decided to end it all by coasting into the river. I shivered. I wouldn't elect to die by drowning, but there's nothing rational about suicide. In my former life as a lawyer, I had seen people choose all kinds of unimaginably painful methods of self-destruction in order to escape an unendurable life.

"The Beauchamps have made some important contributions to the community," Martha said, putting the soup bowls on a tray. "The Coldwells always seemed to hold themselves aloof, out there on the plantation, and the Coldwell women didn't mix much. But Wiley's mother, Sissy, and his grandmother Eliza were both active in the Chicory schools, and they helped to get the Family Clinic and the Visiting Nurse program started."

I put the bread on the tray beside the soup bowls, thinking of something Martha had said a few moments earlier. "You mentioned that the section of land where Judith is living once belonged to her family. What did you mean by that?"

"Why, didn't you know?" Martha asked, in some surprise. She took a knife from the drawer and began to slice the tomato pie, first into quarters, then into eighths. "That's a very old story. I would have thought you'd already heard it, being a Coldwell."

"I'm only part Coldwell," I reminded her with a wry grin. "And that part isn't always enthusiastic about the relationship."

Martha's pixielike eyebrows went up. "Perhaps some time you'll tell me why," she said. "The story I'm thinking of goes back to one of your ancestors. Jed Coldwell. The first Coldwell of record."

"Oh, yes," I said, with a little laugh. "The occasionally ghostly Uncle Jed."

"Really? I'm not surprised to hear that he comes back, given his abrupt and painful departure." I was about to make some skeptical comment about ghosts, but she was going on. "He had the idea of building a trading post on that particular section of land because it was close to the Natchez Trace and on the Bloodroot River, which in those days was used like a highway. But that section belonged to a Choctaw named Sam Weaver and his wife, Rachel, who had been granted it under the terms of the treaty. Sam Weaver owned a half-section, and Rachel Weaver owned the other half. That didn't mean much to Coldwell, though. He just moved onto the land and built that trading post."

"I think I've heard some of this story," I said, remembering Aunt Tullie's old tale about Uncle Jed cheating an Indian out of the land. "But I had no idea that a Choctaw *woman* owned that land."

Martha took four floral-print napkins from a drawer, rolled them around silverware, and put them on the tray. "There were three women named in the Dancing Rabbit treaty, and Rachel Weaver was one of them. The Choctaws were a matrilineal people, you see. Descent was traced through the motherline, and control of property— cooking pots, blankets, animals—was traditionally in the hands of women."

Now I was making the connection. "And Rachel Weaver was one of Judith's ancestors?"

"Her great-great-grandmother, I think." Martha got out four plates. "Anyway, after Jed Coldwell had been squatting on the land for a couple of years, he discovered what he claimed was a 'defect' in the Weavers' title to the property. Rachel Weaver had apparently failed to co-sign the deed to her husband's property, and Sam Weaver hadn't co-signed her deed. They argued that the land agent hadn't told them this was necessary, but it didn't help. Coldwell pointed out this so-called 'defect' to the federal government's land commissioners, the grants were voided, and Coldwell bought the property for a dollar an acre. The Weavers didn't get a penny, of course."

"What a rip-off!" I exclaimed angrily. "They were robbed!"

"There was lots of that going on back then." Martha was matter-of-fact. "The land seemed unbelievably rich, and settlers and speculators were after it. The Indians were peaceable and most couldn't read English or understand property law, so they weren't any match for the thieves. Anyway, Coldwell built his trading post beside the river, on the Weavers' land. But it burned, and he died in the fire."

"That's the part of the story I remember," I said. "In fact, Aunt Tullie used to say that the place was burned down by an angry Indian who thought he'd been cheated."

"It could have happened," Martha said. "The Weavers were forced to follow the tribe to Oklahoma Territory. I don't suppose it'd be any great surprise if they put a torch to the trading post before they left." She looked around. "Now, what am I forgetting? Oh, yes, dessert." She went to the fridge and took out a bowl of fresh sliced peaches.

"So Judith came to Jordan's Crossing with a purpose, then," I mused. "To live on the land that once belonged to her ancestors."

"It's important to her," Martha said. "She feels a deep connection to it. That's why she was so upset about the prospect of having to leave the cottage." She picked up the tray. "Of course, I'm terribly sorry to hear about Wiley Beauchamp, but fate has a way of shaping our lives, and even the darkest clouds have silver linings. Perhaps now Judith will get to stay at Jordan's Crossing—at least as long as your aunt is alive." She nodded toward the tomato pie. "If you'll bring that and the pitcher of lemonade, we'll have our lunch out on the porch."

As we went down the hall toward the porch, where Leatha and Amanda were sitting close together, laughing and chattering, the thought crossed my mind that Aunt Tullie wasn't the only one who stood to gain by Wiley Beauchamp's death. Now that Wiley was gone, Judith Lightfoot's possession of the cottage was secure, at least for the foreseeable future.

Which led to yet another possibility. Perhaps Judith hadn't left the matter entirely in the hands of fate. Maybe she had painted the silver lining on that dark cloud, all by herself.

Chapter Ten

As lily of the valley blooms in May it was customary
to decorate churches with them at Whitsuntide. . . .
In the West of England, to plant a bed of lily of the
valley was a bad omen, an invitation to an early
death.

Josephine Addison
The Illustrated Plant Lore

Leatha and Amanda were so deeply engrossed in
each other that Martha and I spent the entire lunch
hour talking between ourselves, mostly about the traditional uses of native plants. In fact, Amanda and my
mother got along so well that before we left Martha's
house that afternoon, Leatha had told her that there was
a large cache of family documents at Jordan's Crossing
and that she could take her pick. As we drove home, I
couldn't help feeling annoyed about this.

"Are you sure it's a good idea to let a total stranger
paw through our family papers?" I asked. "We haven't
even seen Amanda's credentials, for Pete's sake. We have
no idea whether she is who she claims to be. How do we
know we can trust her?"

"Of course we can trust her," Leatha replied calmly.

"It's funny, but I have the feeling that Amanda's not a stranger. From the moment I met her, I felt as if I'd known her all my life."

"I could certainly see that," I retorted. "But any lawyer will tell you to be careful who you give the family papers to. I'm sure Colonel Blakeslee would agree with me."

Leatha turned. "Do you distrust Amanda because you're worried about those papers, China, or because you simply don't *like* her?"

I had to laugh. "It shows, does it?"

"I'm afraid it does. *Why* don't you like her?"

"I wish I knew," I said, trying to be honest. "But somehow I have the feeling that Professor Gleason has more on her mind than this research project. She has another agenda, and we don't know what it is."

But the minute the words were out of my mouth, I could hear how petty and mean they sounded and I wished I could take them back. My dislike of Amanda was entirely intuitive and had no more validity than my mother's instinctive liking for her. And now that Wiley was dead and it wasn't likely that anyone would pursue that old property deed, there couldn't be anything of vital or current importance in all those old family documents. What harm could there be in Amanda's going through them? I might not like the woman, but what kind of trouble could she cause? And if I were being completely and brutally honest with myself, I'd have to concede that there might be some jealousy involved here. I had seen the way Amanda cozied up to my mother, and I didn't like it.

I opened my mouth to apologize, but the damage had already been done. Leatha turned away, hurt.

"I'm sorry you feel the way you do," she said stiffly. "I've already invited Amanda over this evening to talk and perhaps meet Aunt Tullie. If you'd rather not see her—"

"You go right ahead," I said in a careless tone. "I have other plans for tonight." That wasn't true, but I didn't want to hang around and spoil my mother's evening. If she liked Amanda, who was I to be churlish about it? I changed the subject.

"Speaking of family papers, I'm curious about your grandmother's journal." I glanced at her. "You're *sure* you didn't put it by my bed last night?"

"I've already told you I didn't," Leatha said. "I didn't even know that Grandmother Pearl had kept a journal." She smiled slightly. "I was thinking about those pajamas you mentioned, though. Were those the ones with the bloodstained knees? The last time I saw them, they were in a trunk in the attic."

"Those are the ones," I said, wondering how they had gotten from the trunk to the drawer. "But that stain isn't blood. It's probably bloodroot juice. I fell in the garden once when I was wearing them. When Martha said that her mother had given Aunt Tullie some bloodroot, I realized I must have broken off one of the plants and gotten the juice on my pajamas." I laughed self-consciously. "In fact, until I saw those old stains this morning, I thought I'd dreamed the whole thing."

"Dreams are like that," Leatha replied. "They get mixed up with reality. Do you remember that old family tale about Uncle Jed being burned alive? I have no idea whether the story is true, but I often dream about him when I'm staying at Jordan's Crossing. Every time he appears in a little eddy of gray smoke that smells like burning cypress. I always wake up thinking the place is on fire." She paused. "I dream about Grandmother Pearl, too. I can even smell that lily of the valley perfume she loved so much."

I frowned. Leatha had dreamed those dreams, too? I came back to my earlier question. "If you didn't put Pearl's journal in my bedroom, who did? Could it have been Aunt Tullie?"

Leatha gave a little shrug. "There are only the three of us, so I suppose it must have been." She smiled. "I'll bet Amanda would love to see that journal. It's just the kind of thing she's looking for."

"I'll bet she would, too," I said in the most noncommittal tone I could manage. But if it was up to me, Amanda wasn't going to get the chance—at least, not until I'd read it first.

WHEN we drove up to the house, Judith was pruning branches from the shrubs in front of the veranda. "Miz Tullie's having a nap," she said, "so I thought I'd just do a little clipping. Don't like to waste time."

"I hope everything went okay," Leatha said anxiously. "Did you have any . . . trouble?"

"She was awf'ly restless," Judith said. She was wearing a red headband. She pulled it off and wiped the sweat from her forehead with the back of her hand. "And all that jerking and flailing around—" She paused and added bluntly, "What's wrong with her?"

"She has a kind of neurological disorder," Leatha said quickly, before I could speak. "She can't always control her movements."

"Can't control her temper, either." Judith pulled her headband on again and dropped her pruning shears into a loop in her leather belt. "But after she had a sandwich, things went better. So maybe she was just hungry."

"I'll go upstairs and see how she's doing," Leatha said, and disappeared. When she was gone, I looked at Judith, thinking about dark clouds and silver linings.

"Did you hear about Wiley Beauchamp?" I asked.

She was bending over to pick up a bundle of clipped branches. She looked up, her eyes slitted, her face guarded.

"What's there to hear?"

"He's dead," I said.

Eyes on my face, hands empty, she straightened slowly. "Dead!" It was an exclamation, not a question, and it was jubilant and triumphant, rather than surprised. It sounded like a response to information she'd been hoping to hear.

"Yes," I said, and waited.

She stood as if paralyzed, rooted to the ground. Then, obviously making an effort to be casual, she said, "So how'd he die? Wiley was a crazy driver, no sense at all. Did he run that new truck of his into a tree?"

"They found him in the Bloodroot," I said. "Didn't you see the emergency equipment last night? It went right past your place. Sirens, lights, the whole thing."

"I didn't get home until late last night," she said. "You and Darlene dropped me off at Marie's. Remember?" She shifted from one foot to the other. The expression in her dark eyes was unreadable, but thin, hard lines had appeared like parentheses around her mouth. She let out her breath. "When did it happen? How?"

There was nothing at all remarkable about her questions, of course. They were exactly the kind of questions you might ask when something like this happened to an acquaintance. Except that Wiley Beauchamp wasn't just an acquaintance. He was the man who had threatened to evict her from her home, from the very land from which her ancestors had once been evicted. And his death released her from that threat.

"It happened at the old fishing camp," I said. "He apparently drowned sometime after Saturday evening."

"Saturday evening?" An odd, involuntary look crossed her face, an inward-turning expression of fierce concentration, as she recalled something. What was she thinking of?

"That's what the police say," I said, watching her face. I was remembering another expression I had seen earlier—the sly look that had come into Judith's eyes when Darlene questioned her about Wiley, and her answer: *I've already dealt with the problem. Wiley's not going to shove me around any longer.* How had she dealt with him? What had made her so sure that Wiley was going to leave her alone?

She bent over to pick up the pruned branches. "Well, if anybody's thinking that I'm going to grieve over that bastard, they can think again. As far as I'm concerned, it's a damned good thing he's dead." And then she walked off, carrying her bundle of clippings.

After a few moments, I went into the house and down the hall to the plantation office, where I dialed Colonel Blakeslee's number. It took a few minutes for the secretary to round him up—I could hear her go to the door and call him, as if he were somewhere down the hall. When he finally came on the line, a little breathless, I told him that my mother and I wanted him to draw up a durable power of attorney giving Leatha the ability to manage Aunt Tullie's finances and her health care.

"Gettin' to that point, is it?" he asked sympathetically.

"We're not quite there yet, but it's a good idea to be

prepared." I paused. "By the way, have you heard—"

" 'Bout Wiley?" the Colonel asked. "Ran into Banjo Green in the post office a little bit ago, and he told me." I could hear the sound of his chair creaking as he leaned back. He was probably putting his feet on the desk. "Kinda strange, wouldn't you say? Him dyin' that way, I mean." His voice was thoughtful. "I always figgered some young girl's daddy would get him. I never expected anything like this."

"Have they learned the cause of death yet?"

"The body's gone to Jackson for autopsy, but Banjo said it looked to him like a drownin'." There was a pause. "However, it 'pears he'd been hit on the head, too. Could be a contributin' cause, maybe." Another pause, a longer one this time. "Banjo said there was some kind of fracas out your way on Sattidy night, when Wiley showed that deed to Miz Tullie."

"You might say that," I replied dryly. "She took after him with her cane. Swatted him pretty hard. Leatha was there and witnessed the whole thing. She gave Green a full statement this morning."

The Colonel cleared his throat. "Well, I 'spect there's plenty of extenuatin' circumstances. If you need help, you holler, hear? The county attorney's an old friend of mine. We can prob'ly come up with something. Be a pity for Miz Tullie to end up in court, her age and all."

Bless the good old boys, I thought fervently. "We'll let you know the minute we need you," I said aloud. "But for starters, let's get that power of attorney drawn up and signed." I wanted Mother to be able to manage Aunt Tullie's defense, if it came to that. We'd probably avoid a criminal charge, but the idea of a wrongful death civil case still bothered me. Everybody said that Wiley was the last of the Beauchamps but he might have left somebody behind who claimed to have standing to sue, especially if they figured there was a chance of getting their hands on Aunt Tullie's money.

"There's something else you may be able to do for us, Colonel," I went on. "With Wiley gone, we've got to arrange to get the plantation's work done. Maybe you can come up with an idea. And pretty quick, too." Once the cotton is up, there's cultivating and spraying, all according to a schedule. If the work isn't done, there's no crop. And if there's no crop, there's no income.

"Yore momma didn't raise no dummy," the Colonel said in a tone of paternal approval. "But I'm afraid it ain't gonna be easy to find a plantation manager who can get along with Miz Tullie."

"After she's signed that power of attorney, we'll be able to take her out of the loop." I wasn't quite sure how we were going to accomplish this, but it was clear that we'd have to do it, sooner or later. Aunt Tullie obviously couldn't manage the plantation's business, and neither Leatha nor I had the necessary knowledge and experience. We'd have to find somebody to help us keep things from falling apart.

We agreed that the Colonel would bring the papers over for signature at nine-thirty in the morning, and I hung up and went upstairs. I heard voices in Aunt Tullie's bedroom and opened the door.

The square, high-ceilinged room was exactly as I remembered it, with cabbage-rose wallpaper, a marble-faced fireplace against one wall, a large armoire against another, and a full-length cheval mirror in the corner, ornately framed. Aunt Tullie was dressed and lying on the chenille spread with a green crocheted throw over her legs, as if she had just awakened from a nap. Leatha was sitting in the upholstered wing chair next to the bed.

"I was just telling Aunt Tullie what a grand time we had at Martha's today," she said brightly, in the tone that people use in the company of invalids and old people.

"Martha Edmond is a busybody," Aunt Tullie grunted sourly. "Knows way too much about everybody in this county." She turned to me and I saw how tense and drawn she was. Her eyes had a dark, hollow look and her hands fluttered spasmodically, like injured birds. "Sort of person *you'd* like, though," she added in a scornful tone. "All those weeds she goes to so much trouble to grow."

As I perched on the side of the high bed, I could smell musty perspiration and thought that Aunt Tullie could do with a bath. The three of us chatted for a few minutes, while I tried to assess her mental condition. Although her glance wandered and she was frequently inattentive, she seemed to respond to the flow of the conversation more or less logically. But her speech was slurred and abruptly cadenced and her arms and legs and head jerked involuntarily. The longer we talked, the more difficult it was for her to frame a coherent answer.

Finally, she turned to me with an abrupt movement and said, "You're 'sposed to talk to Pearl, China. She told me she's got something she needs you to know."

My skin prickled. Talk to Pearl?

Leatha leaned forward and put her hand on the old woman's arm. "But your mother is dead, Aunt Tullie," she reminded her quietly. "She died when you were only three years old. Don't you remember how you used to take me to the family cemetery when I was a little girl? If you don't remember it, I certainly do. Somebody planted lilies of the valley on her grave and over the years they spread all through the grass. We always picked a few to decorate the church on Sunday morning."

Aunt Tullie's old face creased in a frown, as if she were trying to make some sort of sense out of what Leatha had said. "If she's dead, how come I see her every time I look in that old mirror over there?" she asked querulously, nodding toward the cheval mirror. "Smell that perfume of hers, too." She plucked at the chenille tufts. "Anyway, she's not my mother."

"What a thing to say!" Leatha trilled a light laugh, humoring her. "Of course she's your mother, dear! You're only imagining that you see her. All of us Coldwells have vivid imaginations. In fact, I've seen her myself, in dreams."

"How'd you know you were dreaming?" Aunt Tullie countered. She glanced back at me. "You need to talk to her," she repeated, saying each word clearly and emphatically, as if to be sure that I heard and obeyed.

"Tell you what," I said. "I have Pearl's journal—the one you put beside my bed last night. I'll read that first. Then if she still wants to talk, I'd be glad to—"

"Journal?" A look of irritation crossed Aunt Tullie's face and her voice became shrill and petulant. "I don't know anything about any journal."

"You didn't put her journal in my room, or her picture on the table?" I would have added the pajamas, but I could see that she was already upset.

"If Pearl left a journal, she hid it from me," Aunt Tullie said angrily. "*Everybody* hides things from me. First my daddy and my brother, then Wiley Beauchamp, and now you!" She slammed her hand on the bed and her mouth twisted bitterly. "Get your fannies out of here, both of you. Go on back where you came from and leave me alone! I don't need you, and I don't want you. Go home!"

Leatha leaned over her, stroking her hand. "There, there, dear," she murmured soothingly. "It'll be all right. How about a nice glass of milk? Shall I get it for you? Or maybe a little dish of ice cream?"

I somehow doubted that a glass of milk or a dish of ice cream would improve Aunt Tullie's temper. I stood up. "See you later," I said to the room in general, and left, hoping that she'd be in a better mood in the morning. In this state of mind, she'd probably throw Colonel Blakeslee out of the house. And all that business about talking to Pearl—she was already hallucinating. It was obvious that we needed to get her to sign that power of attorney as soon as possible.

In the meantime, though, there were a couple of things I needed to do. I headed for my room, took my old pajamas out of the drawer, and examined the brownish-red stains closely. The fabric wasn't ripped, as it certainly would have been if my knees had been scratched enough to bleed. I wasn't an expert on a thirty-year-old bloodroot stain, but that's what it looked like to me.

I folded the pajamas again and put them back in the drawer. If the stains were real, the bony hand I saw must have been real, too. Somebody had been buried beside the old wooden pergola at the foot of the garden. Who was it? And why had the discovery of the body made Aunt Tullie weep with such fierce anguish? It was high time I learned the truth about the frightening scene that had haunted my dreams for so many years. And I knew exactly who to ask for answers.

But first there was Pearl's journal.

Chapter Eleven

In the language of flowers, honeysuckle meant sweetness of disposition because of the sweet scent of the flowers. It also implied a bond or meant "captive of love," suggested by the plant's twining growth habit that embraces trees and other plants. The common name woodbine comes from Middle English and refers to the ability of the plant to tie or bind as it grows and climbs.

Bobby J. Ward
A Contemplation Upon Flowers:
Garden Plants in Myth and Literature

Honeysuckle (*Lonicera canadensis*) was used by the Iroquois as a blood purifier, a sedative, and as an antidote to homesickness.

Daniel E. Moerman
Native American Ethnobotany

I wouldn't have been surprised if Pearl's journal had been returned to the drawer in the library by some ghostly housemaid, but the leather-bound book was still lying on the bedside table where I had left it. I tucked it under my arm, went down to the kitchen and poured myself a glass of iced tea from the pitcher in the refrigerator, then went out to sit in the rocking chair on the veranda. It was a warm, sleepy afternoon, the sunlight spilling in golden puddles across the soft green grass, the languid breeze stirring the leaves, the cicadas buzzing with that metallic monotony that always signals the coming of summer. A good afternoon to read. I opened the book, half-expecting to catch a whiff of those lilies of the valley again. But all I could smell was the honeysuckle that climbed one end of the veranda.

The first page was dated in the top right-hand corner: May 15, 1918. There was no other heading and no introduction, and except for the gold-embossed name—Pearl Campbell Coldwell—on the leather cover, no way to tell until I began to read who had actually written this. But reading wasn't easy, not at first, anyway. The ink had faded to a pale sepia and the steeply slanted, heavily ornamented handwriting was hard to decipher. The sentences, too, were a challenge: long and complex, with an oddly poetic rhythm and an old-fashioned and almost Biblical syntax.

After a moment, I found myself reading aloud in a low voice, murmuring the words. But when I had read a few lines, I stopped and leafed through the rest of the pages, then looked back at the date with a dawning chill of understanding. This was not a journal made up of a series of consecutive entries, as I had originally thought. It was one long, unbroken narrative, written only a week or so before my great-grandmother had committed suicide.

I felt an almost electric surge of anticipation. Perhaps these pages would answer the question that had haunted the family for over three-quarters of a century: *Why? Why had Great-grandmother Pearl killed herself?*

May 15, 1918

> *I have considered deeply what I mean to do & feel*
> *compelled to set down an explanation for it: cer-*
> *tainly not for the benefit of my husband Clancy (I*
> *intend to conceal this book so that he does not find*
> *& destroy it when I am dead) but for my dear chil-*
> *dren Howard and Hattie and perhaps others who*
> *may at some future time be able to read & under-*
> *stand. And for myself as well, to clarify matters and*
> *set my heart at ease by telling the story, as much*
> *of it as I presently know and understand. There are*
> *too many ghosts at Jordan's Crossing already. I*
> *know, for I have often seen them, Jed and Samantha*
> *and even Abner, all restless & resentful. I do not*
> *wish to become one of their number, & hence hope*
> *to rest my heart in this writing, which is as much a*
> *justification of what I intend to do as explanation*
> *of my reasons for doing it.*

Puzzled, I glanced back up at the long first sentence.
For my dear children Howard and Hattie. Hattie, of
course, was the aunt with whom Leatha had lived while
she went to high school in Greenville, and Howard was
Leatha's father, my grandfather. But why didn't Pearl
name her other daughter? Aunt Tullie was three years old
when these pages were written. Why had her mother left
her out? A snatch of conversation echoed, ghostly, in my
mind. *She's not my mother,* Aunt Tullie had said. *Of
course she's your mother, dear,* Leatha had responded.
My eyes widened. What if Leatha was wrong? What if—?

But all this was profoundly mysterious, and I had no
clues from which to begin to decipher it. Perhaps there
was something here that would explain. I went back to
my reading.

*Since the story is a long one I must begin at the
beginning, with the land & this house, & say emphatically that I believe it was wrong of Clancy to
build this house on this ground, on the very section
of land—Section 12—that his father Abner Coldwell
gave to Tobias Beauchamp in 1864. Of course I was
not yet born when the gift was given (Clancy himself
was not above ten years of age at the time) & had
no idea until recently that the place where this
house now stands once belonged to Tobias, nor did
I know the reason Clancy's father Abner made this
inexplicable gift. As I have been told (at least, this
is how Tobias related the story to me), when Abner
gave Section Twelve to Tobias, he also executed a
will bequeathing two full sections to Clancy & two
to Beauregard, Clancy & Beauregard being his two
living sons by his wife, Samantha. (Beauregard, I
should say here, was blown to bits when a steamboat exploded on the river above Vicksburg, before
his father's will was proved, so Clancy inherited his
dead brother's two sections as well as his own.) But
after his father Abner was dead, Clancy, now come
to manhood, canceled the gift of land to Tobias,
making it null & void & revoking it by means of a
quitclaim deed that he forced Tobias to sign. Having no choice in the matter, Tobias complied, re-
nouncing his title to the land. (Upon hearing
Tobias's tale, I found the original deed he described
among the family papers and have returned it to
him. I have said nothing to Clancy about this, of
course.)*

So *that* was how it was done, I thought, and wondered
briefly what leverage Clancy had used to force Tobias to
sign the quitclaim, and where the quitclaim was now. It
didn't matter, since Wiley was the last of the Beauchamps,

and he was dead. But I didn't pause long, for what I was reading was deeply compelling. I went back to it.

> *I have pieced the story together in this way from disconnected fragments Clancy has dropped from time to time like clues to a mystery, deliberate & taunting, wanting me to be party to this affair so that I am by virtue of my knowledge complicit in his guilt. And of course from Tobias also, who gave it to me not in fragments but in full detail & undoubtedly with malice, to destroy whatever love might remain in my heart toward my husband. But I who have been so long bound by ties of love to a man who misused my trust and betrayed my faith now refuse absolutely to be any longer bound to him. And so this explanation or justification is also (& perhaps most importantly) a declaration of my refusal to be held captive. It is a declaration of my independence.*
>
> *But still the story must be set down & the reasons . . .*

Inside the house, the telephone rang, startling me out of my reading. I picked up a honeysuckle blossom that had blown onto the table and used it to mark my place. Taking the book with me, I hurried to answer the phone, thinking it might be McQuaid. It was Deputy Green.

"Thought you'd like to know some more details about Wiley Beauchamp's death," he said without preamble. "His truck ended up in the river down at the fishing camp, with him in it. The autopsy report says he drowned."

"I see," I said gravely.

"However," he went on, "the report says that he was likely suffering from a mild concussion." He paused to give his words greater significance. "Caused by a blow to the left side of his head."

I ignored that, for the moment. "Did the autopsy yield any evidence of alcohol? What about drugs?"

"He'd apparently had a couple of beers. There was a plastic-ring six-pack of Bud in the truck cab, with four unopened cans, two missing. But he probably wasn't drunk, and there was no sign of drugs, either. From the looks of the stomach contents—what was left of a barbecue sandwich and some coleslaw—the coroner says he died within six or eight hours of the meal he ate at Elmer's Bar-B-Q, which was around five on Saturday afternoon." The deputy paused and added, in a meaningful tone, "I 'spose you can guess where we're headed with all this."

It didn't take a rocket scientist to establish the trajectory of official thought on this matter. But Green wanted to make sure that I understood. "We figure he parked on the ramp to take a look at the river and passed out from that concussion. It was an easy coast into the water. He prob'ly never knew what was happening."

"I guess you'll want to talk to Aunt Tullie," I said. I looked at the clock and was surprised to see that it was nearly five. "It's much too late this afternoon, though, and she isn't at all well today. How about tomorrow morning? Around ten, say?" Colonel Blakeslee would be here, and if I guessed right, Aunt Tullie would already be angry about being asked to sign a power of attorney. She'd put on a performance for Deputy Green that would likely convince him that he was dealing with a raving lunatic.

"I reckon ten o'clock will work," the deputy said, in a tone that implied that he was doing us a big favor to hold off the posse. "You can guarantee she won't leave town?"

"And just where the hell do you think she'd go?" I

asked irritably, and then added: "Sorry. Yes, of course I can guarantee that she'll be here." I paused. "By the way, did you happen to find any fishing tackle in the truck?"

"No," the deputy said. "You thinking he planned to go fishing?"

"I was just curious about why he went to the river in the first place," I replied. "Especially on a Saturday night. Knowing Wiley, I would have thought he'd be down at the Wagon Wheel dancing the Cotton-Eyed Joe."

"Your guess is as good as mine," the deputy said.

I'd just hung up when Leatha came into the room. I told her about the conversation with the police, and when she looked distressed, reported what the Colonel had said about being friends with the local county attorney.

"I seriously doubt that a prosecutor would waste time bringing criminal charges against anyone in Aunt Tullie's condition," I added, "but if he's inclined to, the Colonel can probably make him see reason." I didn't want to mention the possibility of a wrongful-death suit in civil court. Leatha had enough on her mind without worrying about *that*.

"I certainly hope the Colonel can handle it," Leatha said. "I'm very sorry about Wiley, but the police have got to understand that Aunt Tullie really doesn't know what she's doing. Why, she doesn't even know her own mother! Justice couldn't possibly be served by charging her with a crime."

I frowned, thinking about Pearl's failure to name Tullie as one of her children. "What do you suppose made her say that? About Great-grandmother Pearl, I mean."

"Who knows?" Leatha said. "Aunt Hattie sometimes used to tease her about being adopted. But that was because Tullie takes after her father, tall and dark-complected, where Hattie was small and blond, like her mother. There's nothing rational behind it, though. You could see for yourself that the poor thing was hallucinating—all that stuff about Pearl wanting to talk to you."

"That was pretty weird," I agreed.

Leatha looked up at the clock. "I'm going to try to get her to take a bath and wash her hair, which she's not particularly keen on. While we're doing that, would you see what you can put together for supper? Just soup and sandwiches would be fine."

I would much rather fix supper than try to get Aunt Tullie into the tub. I opened a can of mushroom soup, made grilled cheese sandwiches, and dressed sliced tomatoes with fresh chopped basil and Italian dressing.

An hour later, we were sitting at the table. Aunt Tullie, smelling fresh and with her hair still wet, ate sullenly but with a good appetite. Leatha and I talked about Sam and McQuaid and our families, and I felt a sharp pang of homesickness for Pecan Springs—for my family, my house, even my shop. I'd only been gone for a couple of days, but it felt like forever.

And at the rate things kept happening here, it might take that long for me to get back home.

A few minutes before Amanda was due to put in her appearance, I got in my car and drove off. I'd lied when I told Leatha earlier that I had plans for the evening, but I really did now. Most of the ghosts at Jordan's Crossing weren't under my control, but there was one ghostly incident I thought I could exorcise if I asked the right questions of the right people. I intended to learn what had *really* happened on that long-ago summer night, the night I watched Aunt Tullie weep over that skeletal hand.

Marie Louise LaTour lived in a shotgun cottage at the end of a dusty street on the eastern edge of Chicory. The yard was busy with chickens chasing grasshoppers through the sparse grass. The path to the front porch was bordered with multicolored pansies and lined with white-washed bricks stood on edge in a saw-toothed pattern. The cottage's board-and-batten siding had probably never been painted, but the front porch was festive with pots of red geraniums and white petunias, and almost smothered by a wisteria vine heavy with purple blossoms.

Nervously, I knocked at the screen door. I could hear the melodious warble of a canary from somewhere in the dark interior, and the spicy fragrance of red beans and sausage mingled with the sweetness of the wisteria. I knocked again, and the canary stopped singing. After a moment, Marie Louise shuffled to the door.

"You come jes' in time fer supper," she said, as if she had been expecting me. She pushed the screen open. "I've already eat, but yo're welcome. There's 'nuff for a plateful, an' I ain't washed the dishes yet."

"I've eaten, too," I said, feeling suddenly relieved that there appeared to be no replay of the spooky circumstances of yesterday's conversation. We were two ordinary women having an ordinary conversation. The subject might be painful, but there was nothing uncanny or supernatural about it. "Why don't we sit outside? It's cooling off a little, and there's a breeze."

"I reckon," she said, "long as you don' mind a few skeeters. Dey's fierce round here." She opened the door and stepped onto the porch. She was wearing the same voluminous purple muumuu she'd had on when I saw her in town, and a heavy necklace of seeds and beads and small animal bones hung around her thin neck. Her head was bare and her wiry curls fit close to her head like a gray wool cap.

With a wheezy *whumph*, she lowered herself into the wooden rocking chair. I sat on the edge of the porch close to her feet and leaned against a post. The chickens had scattered, the breeze had dropped, and the air was still and heavy, as it is before a storm. The sky was clear when I'd started out but it had turned hazy and the sun was dropping into a bank of bloodred clouds. Another evening thunderstorm seemed to be brewing.

I opened the bag I had brought and took out the pajama bottoms. "I was wearing these the night I saw you and Old Homer and Aunt Tullie in the garden," I said. "The night the three of you dug up the dead body."

There was a long silence. Somewhere behind the bushes, a rooster crowed. The sound seemed to split the air like a lightning bolt.

The old woman's eyes had darkened. "Happened a long time ago," she said, smoothing the pajama fabric with her gnarled hand. "You wuzn't more'n a mite." She looked at the stained knees. "Scratch yoreself, did you?" she asked, half-amused. Then she held them up for a closer look. "Looks like you fell down in dem bloodroots used to grow in de garden." She shook her head. "When dat juice sets in, hit ain't never gwine wash out."

Her words seemed to hang in the air between us, vibrating, heavy with meaning. I licked my lips. "I had nightmares for years," I said. My voice was a husky whisper, and I had to clear my throat. "In fact, I thought the whole thing was a nightmare. I didn't know it was real until I found those pajamas this morning and realized that it had actually happened."

She refolded the pajamas and handed them back to me. "Could've been a nightmare," she said quietly. "*Wuz* a nightmare fer pore Miz Tullie. You wuzn't meant to see hit. Nobody wuz but us, Old Homer and me, and we already knew."

"Knew what? What did you know?"

Her lips were pressed tight together. Sphinxlike, she shook her head.

I swallowed. "I may have been just a kid, but I saw what happened that night and I never forgot it. And now that I know I didn't dream it, I want to know what it was all about. Who were you digging up? And why was he buried in the garden?" I paused, hearing what I had said. "Was it a man or a woman?"

She shrugged carelessly, lifting one shoulder, letting it fall. "He's dead and gone. Ashes to ashes and dust to dust, as de good book says. And din't I tell you yestiddy dat you gots to let dem ol' skeletons rest?" She bent forward and thrust her wizened face close to mine. "Anyway, what's hit to you who he wuz, Miz China?" she demanded sharply. "Why does you want to know?"

Her question pinned me, her glance held me frozen, sent me inside myself for an answer. I'd declared my independence from the Coldwells. Why was I poking around in a past that had nothing to do with me? Shouldn't I be searching for a way to help my mother cope with Aunt Tullie's illness, rather than fooling around with this old stuff? The questions buzzed in my head but the answers, stubbornly, refused to come.

Finally I said, "I don't know why I need to know. Maybe it's only because I've dreamed about that corpse so often that it seems like part of my life." For an instant, I saw those bony fingers reaching up out of the forgotten grave, glimpsed the carved gold ring, wide, like a wedding band, and heard Aunt Tullie's keening wail. "But somehow I think it's more than that. I think I'm *supposed* to know, for reasons I don't understand yet. I'm supposed to find out so I can—"

I stopped. So I can *what*? What am I supposed to do with what I learn? Is it all an academic exercise, like Amanda Gleason's research into the lives of plantation women?

The old woman put her hand on my shoulder. Her fingers felt cold and twiggy. "Hit ain't yore story, girl. Hit's Miz Tullie's. You want to know who de dead man wuz, you ask *her*. If she don't want to tell you, let hit go."

I considered that. Yes, it was Aunt Tullie's story, but it was the dead man's story, too. And if his death was a part of our family's story, that made it mine, whether I liked it or not. Anyway, nobody had a right to keep such things secret.

I shook my head stubbornly. "There are questions that have to be answered and stories that have to be told, no matter who wants to keep them quiet." I paused, and a new thought came into my mind. "Was it . . . Aunt Tullie didn't *kill* him, did she?"

"O' course not." Marie Louise made a dismissive gesture. "Don't be ridic'lous."

I looked at her, startled. "But *somebody* in our family killed him," I said, suddenly understanding. "Maybe it was an argument, maybe it was an accident. But however it happened, it was something that had to be kept secret. You don't bury a man in a garden unless you're trying to hide his death." I thought back to Pearl's suicide, to the pages I had read that afternoon, to the pages I had yet to read. "Did Great-grandmother Pearl have anything to do with it? She killed herself—was it because of that man? Was he her lover? Maybe her *husband* killed him. Clancy, I mean." Although none of that would explain Aunt Tullie's grief. Why would she weep over someone who died when she was still a young child?

The old woman heaved a heavy sigh. "Yo're jes like yore aunt, child. Allus askin' questions, allus wantin' to know what's what. I kin see yo're not goin' to rest till you's found hit out." She tilted her head, looking at me as if she were taking my measure. "And maybe yo're right, maybe now is de right time, after all dese years. There's somebody else wants to know, anyway. Wants hit even more dan you do. *Needs* hit even more dan you do."

"Somebody else?" I asked, surprised. "Who?"

She grinned and a teasing light came into her eyes. "You don't know dat yet, Miz Smarty-pants? Well, git busy an' find hit out." She stood up, gathering her skirt in one hand, and straightened her shoulders. Lifting her chin, she gave me an oracular look. "If'n you want to know who wuz buried beside dat ol' pergola, you go hunt in de graveyard. Miz Tullie had him put dere."

"The graveyard?" I asked in surprise, and then felt silly. If you wanted to bury somebody, the cemetery was the usual place. "Which graveyard?"

She looked down at me as if pitying my ignorance. "Why, *yore* graveyard, o' course. The Coldwell graveyard. Where else would she put him?"

And with that, she went inside and latched the screen door. The canary began to sing again.

Chapter Twelve

The Ancients were well acquainted with rosemary, which had a reputation for strengthening the memory. On this account it became the emblem of fidelity for lovers. It holds a special position among herbs from the symbolism attached to it. Not only was it used at weddings, but also at funerals.

Maud Grieve
A Modern Herbal, 1931

As for Rosemarine, I lett it runne all over my garden walls, not onlie because my bees love it, but because it is the herb sacred to remembrance . . . that maketh it the chosen emblem of our funeral wakes and in our buriall grounds.

Sir Thomas More, 1478–1535

Put rosemary leaves under thy bedde and thou shalt be delivered of all evill dreames.

Banckes' Herbal, 1525

 Twilight was hastened by the ominous clouds rising up from the northwest, and it was almost dark by the time I reached the family cemetery, off the main road not far from the site of Abner Coldwell's grand mansion—the one that had burned after the Civil War. Abner probably chose the place as a burial ground because it was the highest spot on the plantation, safely above the Bloodroot's frequent winter and spring floods and shaded by the spreading branches of hickory and sycamore trees. From the cemetery, I could glimpse the green-shingled roof of the old church, where the people from the plantations all around had once come to worship. But the building had fallen into disuse at some point in the last quarter-century, when the dwindling congregation moved its worship services to Chicory, and now I could see that the steeple had been blown down and the roof was half gone.

At first glance, the graveyard didn't seem to be in any better shape. Like most Southern rural families, the Coldwells felt a deep affection and respect for their family cemetery. The survivors—the women, mostly—had always made regular visits to keep this small plot carefully tended. They painted the wrought-iron fence and benches to keep the metal from rusting; they mowed the grass and raked the leaves; they filled the urns with flowers. They gave to the dead the same care and compassion as they had given the living.

But when I got out of the car in the fading light, I saw that the graveyard, like the church, had an abandoned look, sad and derelict, as if the Coldwells no longer cared for their own. As I stood there looking, it occurred to me that this was a sign of our times, and that there must be many small family cemeteries just like this one throughout the South. The older folks had moved to assisted living facilities or nursing homes; the younger ones had gone to the cities in search of new livelihoods and new identities; and there was no one left behind to tend the graves of the ancestors, no one to remember.

But that sociological explanation let me off the hook too easily. I was one of those who had gone away, who no longer remembered. Did I have a right to cut myself off from my past and from those who had gone before? What *was* my obligation to the people who had given me life, to those who were buried here? A dark melancholy washed through me, and the low, sad sighing of a pair of mourning doves echoed my thoughts. A cold breeze from the coming storm swept up the hill, swirling the fallen leaves, and I shivered.

The Coldwell cemetery had obviously gone untended since Aunt Tullie became seriously ill, and the invading wilderness had taken advantage of the human inattention. The gate hung at a crazy angle, one hinge rusted through, and the headstones and grave markers were half-hidden behind thick veils of weeds and grasses. The flowers planted on the graves had run riot through the grass— lilies of the valley in fading ribbons of white; waves of blue forget-me-nots; white and gold and yellow iris grown into thick clumps. Several urns had fallen over, and the iron benches showed patches of red rust. Leatha and I should load the lawn mower and garden tools into the car and spend a day here, cleaning it up. But a one-shot effort wouldn't mean much; to keep the wilderness at bay, somebody would have to pay regular attention to this place. After Aunt Tullie was gone, there'd be no one left but Mother and me, and we lived hundreds of miles away, in a very different world.

Over my shoulder, somewhere among the shadowy trees, a great horned owl hooted eerily, reminding me that it would soon be too dark to see. I'd better get on with my errand. I pushed the gate open and stepped inside the fence, feeling the past settle heavily upon my shoulders. When I was a little girl, Aunt Tullie used to bring me with her when she came to put fresh flowers on the graves. She'd point out the headstones to me, one by one, and we'd say the carved names until I knew them, and the relationships, by heart. She would encourage me to connect the characters in our family stories, to see them, not as individuals, but as part of our clan. It was like reading the Family Record page in the Bible. It was a family history lesson.

But our family history had a much more ominous significance now that I had learned about Aunt Tullie's illness, and as I thought of this, a sinister shadow seemed to wheel across the evening sky. I shoved my hands into my pockets and stood still, realizing that the secret of her frightful genetic inheritance—and Leatha's and mine, as well—was buried somewhere in this cemetery. Somewhere among these graves was the Coldwell who had sentenced those who came after to a dreadful end. Who was it? Where did Aunt Tullie's dying begin?

In the far northwest corner, under a rough stone with a bronze plaque on it, was Jed Coldwell, the man who (if Martha was right) had stolen the section of land from Judith's ancestors to build the trading post that became his funeral pyre. But since Jed had died childless, he couldn't have bequeathed his genes to the rest of us. That particular honor went to my great-great-grandparents, Abner and Samantha, who lay in the center of the cemetery, their graves marked by a symmetrical polished granite monument taller and more substantial than any of the others.

According to the dates carved in the stone, Abner Coldwell had died in 1878. His wife, Samantha, had survived him by more than two decades, dying two years into the new century. Samantha had borne Abner six children, four of whom died, unnamed, as infants, their small graves marked only by identical flat stones engraved with identical angels. Beauregard was buried next to his mother (not all of him, however, for he had been blown to pieces in that steamboat accident and some of his body parts had not made it back home).

The second son, Clancy, was the only one left to carry on the name, and he and his wife, Pearl, and their descendants had their own section of the cemetery. Clancy's resting place was marked with an imposing granite marker engraved with a carved cotton boll and a Confederate flag, as befitted a son of the South, and a long list of his accomplishments, probably not terribly remarkable in view of the many years he'd had to achieve them. I noticed a few straggly bloodroot plants growing in the shade of the monument, and thought that Tullie must have planted them there. I looked back up at the carved stone. His death on July 10, 1946, at the grand old age of ninety-one, made him the longest-lived Coldwell on record—and probably took him out of the running as the carrier of the Huntington's gene.

Which more or less pinned the blame for this inherited disease on Clancy's wife, Pearl, I realized, as I moved a few steps to stand beside her weed-covered grave. Was she the parent whose genetic legacy had sentenced Aunt Tullie to death? As I stared at Pearl's simple flat marker, decorated only with her name, the dates of her birth and her death, and the words *Wife and Mother*, I wondered whether I might find the answer to this question in the still-unread pages of the leather-bound book in which she had recorded her reasons for killing herself. Perhaps Pearl—who had come from Memphis, if I remembered correctly—had seen the disease in her mother or her father or her brothers and sisters. Little was apparently known about it in 1918, but perhaps she had begun to trace its advance in herself and could not bear to inflict it upon her family.

Pearl's grave was on the far side of Clancy, her twin boys Thomas and Richard (who had died of a fever before they were two) buried together at her feet. Her daughter Hattie and Hattie's daughter Ruth, killed together in an auto accident, had been buried in Greenville. But her son Howard lay nearby, under a respectable marker, beside his wife, Rachel, who died giving birth to my mother. Leatha's parents, my grandparents. I looked around, thinking that all of us gathered here in this unkempt plot, inside this rusting fence, were related by blood or by marriage. All of us had a common heritage, most of us shared a common genetic package. And for those of us who were descendants of Pearl, that package might contain a lethal gene.

For whom? For Aunt Tullie, certainly. For my mother's father, who might have died before his genetic time bomb went off? For my mother? For me?

The sun was gone now, the light was failing, and a breeze rattled the nervous leaves of a cottonwood tree. I shivered. It was impossible to ignore these urgent questions and their brutal and deadly implications, but they had nothing to do with my reason for coming here tonight. I was searching for the answer to an entirely different question, and I had to get on with it before it grew too dark to see. I was looking for the man who had haunted my dreams for decades, who had been buried in our garden and reburied with the Coldwells.

But where is he? I wondered, looking around. There were only fifteen or so graves here, and their markers were all recognizable, all familiar. There was nothing new, nothing—

No, there it was. In the far corner, I saw a rosemary bush, its mounded green shape almost hidden behind a screen of thick weeds. I made my way toward it, burrs catching in my socks and on the legs of my jeans. Beneath the rosemary was a polished marker, flat in the ground, the carved name obscured by a tangle of grass. I bent over and brushed it aside.

> ### *Brent Holland, USMC*
> ### *1913–1946*
> ### *Beloved*

And beneath I read Ophelia's lovely words, from Shakespeare's *Hamlet*:

> ### *There's rosemary, that's for remembrance;*
> ### *Pray, love, remember.*

I frowned. Our family tree was no more complicated than anybody else's, and I'd memorized every branch. As far as I knew, there was no one named Brent Holland located anywhere on it. And if he wasn't a Coldwell, why had Aunt Tullie buried him in the family cemetery?

I looked again at the scanty evidence on the gray granite marker. Brent Holland had been born before World War One and died after World War Two, at the age of thirty-three. He was roughly contemporary with Pearl and

Clancy's children, Howard, Hattie, and Tullie, and his death in 1946 could have had nothing to do with Pearl's suicide in 1918. He had been a Marine. He had also been someone's beloved. Whose? Aunt Tullie's?

An uneasy silence hung like a pall over the graveyard and the grass and weeds stirred restlessly, as if the unhearing, unknowing dead were themselves eager to learn the answer to my question. I bent over once again and pushed the lush lower branches of rosemary aside. The marker was a double one designed to span two graves. But the other half was still smooth: no name, no dates, no clue to the identity of the person who expected to be buried here.

And then, in the dusky, murmuring twilight, I saw it all again, as clearly as if it were happening in front of me. The huddled group at the foot of the moonlit garden, beside the old pergola. Old Homer with his shovel, Marie Louise with her shuttered lantern, Aunt Tullie on her knees, weeping hysterically, clutching that grotesque hand with its rotting ribbons of flesh, a hand that wore a gold ring carved with a design of twining ivy, emblematic of fidelity and love. A wedding ring. Brent Holland was Aunt Tullie's husband. She had buried him here, and when she died, she expected to be buried here beside him.

I sucked in my breath, startled. So far as I knew—so far as Leatha knew, too, I was sure—Aunt Tullie had never been married, had never even had a lover. *Being Miss Coldwell is enough of a job for one woman*, she'd always say when I asked, and laugh that abrupt, half-angry laugh of hers that, even as a child, had struck me as a kind of bleak self-mockery. *What would I want with a husband?* she'd scoff. *Haven't I got enough to do to take care of this place, without taking care of a man, too?*

I bent again to break off a fragrant sprig of rosemary, holding it up to my face, filling my nose with its resinous scent. Aunt Tullie had spoken those sardonic words in the 1960s, when I was a young child. But what if she hadn't always felt that way? What if she had once dreamed a different dream? What if—on some distant, romantic day, full of hope for a future filled with love and the promise of children—she had gone off to marry a young Marine named Brent Holland? Perhaps they had taken a train together to New Orleans or Atlanta or even New York for a hasty wedding and a sweet, stolen honeymoon. Thousands of young people did that in those years, all over the country. And after the weddings the young wives hurried back to the home front to work and watch and endlessly wait, while their husbands went half a world away to fight, many to die.

So maybe Tullie had come home to weather the war at Jordan's Crossing, and Brent had gone to Guadalcanal and Saipan and Iwo Jima, each of them thinking that their wedding and their honeymoon might be all the time they would ever have together. And maybe she didn't tell them at home that she was married, or wear the ring that matched her husband's. From what I knew of him, her father had been an authoritarian who insisted on making all the important decisions for his family. Maybe she had kept her marriage a secret from him and from her brother Howard—and of course from her niece Leatha. Maybe Tullie hadn't said a word to anyone about it, had just gone on with her life as before—and then the war was over and her Marine came back to Mississippi to claim his bride.

And then what? Did he take one look at her and decide that she wasn't the woman of his romantic dreams? Or did she spend a few days with him and realize that the marriage was a dreadful mistake that would never work? Or had her father or her brother—

I broke off. This kind of speculation was downright silly. My narrative was woven of nothing more substantial than romantic formulas. I was constructing the entire plot out of the least, the slightest of clues: a dead man's name, a barely glimpsed ring (perhaps not even a wedding ring), an anguished cry on a dark night. It hadn't happened the way I thought. And even if it had happened exactly that way, even if I were right in every particular, my story ended too soon. This was a mystery, not a romance.

Why had this man been buried in our garden? If Tullie had put him here, under this enigmatic headstone, who had put him *there*, with no headstone at all? Who killed Brent Holland?

The anxious breeze fingered the grasses and rippled the leaves, and in the dying light I could almost hear the dead, too, asking their own nervously proprietary questions. *Who is this stranger, Tullie, and what was he to you? And what is this Brent Holland to* us, *that he should be buried here with the Coldwells and their kin?*

I went back toward the gate, retracing my steps through the tangled grass. Where should I turn next in search of the truth? I had traced the story this far only with the help of Marie Louise. If I went back and told her what I surmised, she might be willing to tell me more. But she had reminded me that this was Aunt Tullie's story—should I ask *her* to tell me what had happened?

I turned as I closed the gate. Now that I knew where to look, the rosemary in the far corner stood out clearly, its disciplined shapeliness a striking contrast to the unrestrained, wildly exuberant weeds surrounding it.

There's rosemary, that's for remembrance; pray, love, remember.

A forked-tongue flicker of lightning split the western sky and thunder rumbled, low and threatening. Somehow it didn't seem right for me to disturb Aunt Tullie with my questions. Perhaps this was a truth that was too terrible to remember, too ugly to tell. And since the Coldwell line would die with me, there was no one else who needed, or even wanted, to know what had happened to Brent Holland back in 1946. Maybe I should take Marie Louise's advice, and let the old ghosts lie where they were buried, in the weed-choked Coldwell graveyard, in the heart of an old woman who would soon lie here, too.

But even Marie Louise had agreed that perhaps it was time that the story was told. And as I stood there, her final, cryptic remark echoed in my mind like a haunting voice: *There's somebody else wants to know. Wants hit even more dan you do.* Needs *hit even more dan you do.*

I frowned. Who? Why?

And how did Marie Louise know this?

Chapter Thirteen

Bloodroot (*Sanguinaria canadensis*). According to *Native American Ethnobotany*, by Daniel E. Moerman, the Ponca Indians of South Dakota and Nebraska used bloodroot as a love charm, rubbing the juice on the palm of a young bachelor. The Micmac Indians (Nova Scotia, Prince Edward Island, and New Brunswick) used the same plant both as an aphrodisiac and as an abortifacient.

Cotton Root *Gossypium herbaceum*. Herbal authority Maud Grieve (*A Modern Herbal*, 1931) reports that cotton root bark was used as an abortifacient by slaves in the South. Appalachian herbalist Tommie Bass tells how to prepare it. "You peel the bark of the root before the frost; take half a teacupful [of a decoction made by boiling the root in water for 10 minutes] four times a day. Sometimes it's had very dangerous reactions." One Shaker community offered cotton root bark "to promote uterine contractions," and an Appalachian root and herb dealer, C. J. Cowle, actively marketed it in 1857, offering it for sale for fifty cents a pound.

It was only nine o'clock. If I went back to Jordan's Crossing now, I'd probably run into Amanda, and I didn't need that. Anyway, I had another idea. Darlene's house was on the way. I'd stop and talk to her for a few minutes. Her mother Queenie had been with the Coldwells since before I was born, and if I remembered correctly, she was Old Homer's cousin. There was a good chance that Queenie had known about Brent Holland—either about his death or his subsequent disinterment and reburial—and that she'd told her daughter about it. At this point, I'd settle for second- or even third-hand information.

Darlene was living in her mother's old house, newly painted white and with a new green metal roof, behind a white picket fence fringed with orange daylilies. I parked and went through the rose-arbor gate. The air had grown very still and the lightning was flickering crazily in the west, but the rain was holding off. Through the open living-room window I could see a glowing computer monitor where Darlene had been working. Inside the house, a dog was barking fiercely, and as I came up the path, the porch light went on and the door opened. I could see Darlene's form silhouetted against the light. She was wearing leggings and a close-fitting halter top. She was barefoot.

"It's only me, Darlene," I said. "No need to panic."

"Who's panicking?" she retorted, and unlatched the screen. "I got my enforcer right here." The dog was large and black, of indefinable heritage but fully equipped with a great many sharp teeth and a built-in suspicion of strangers who came up to the door after dark. "Be quiet, Jake," she said firmly. "China's your buddy. Go lie down in your corner."

Jake wasn't quite ready to take her word for it, so we spent the next moment or two getting acquainted. I rubbed his ears, he sniffed my tennis shoes and socks. Not quite satisfied, he sniffed both knees, then returned to my socks.

"Jake seems to think you've been somewhere interesting," Darlene remarked.

"The Coldwell cemetery," I said. "Maybe he smells old ghosts."

"Maybe so," Darlene said equably. "He was Momma's dog. No tellin' what tricks that lady taught him. You want a glass of wine?" she added, as Jake went to his corner, having apparently decided that I was harmless. "I'm going to have another. You might as well join me."

"Good idea," I said approvingly. I gave her a close look. "I hope your flu is better."

"Some," Darlene said without expression. "You sit down. I'll be right back."

But I didn't sit down. While she was getting our wine, I wandered to the book shelves that filled one wall—a recent addition, I suspected—and glanced at the titles. Darlene collected Southern women writers. Alice Walker, Flannery O'Connor, Katherine Porter, Eudora Welty. Her own book of stories was there, too, a handsome hardcover published by the University of Louisiana Press. It was called *Working Girl*. I took it down and studied the picture that appeared on the back, a casual photo of Darlene in jeans and a loose shirt, sitting in a rocking chair on a porch—the porch of this house, I realized after a moment—with Jake at her feet. The endorsements and snippets of reviews glowingly praised a "new literary talent," a "fresh voice in fiction," a writer with a "clear eye for compelling detail, a fine ear for the rhythm of speech, a compassionate heart." Across the top of the jacket was a banner: *Winner of the Webbley Prize for Southern Literature*. I was impressed. I opened the book at random and read the first few paragraphs in a story called "Courting Daisy." I was even more impressed.

I was still reading when Darlene came back into the living room carrying a half-empty bottle of white wine and one glass. There was an empty glass beside the computer. She filled both of them and handed one to me.

"You're hiding your light under a bushel out here in the country," I said, replacing the book on the shelf. As I did, a framed photograph caught my eye. A high-school graduation photo, probably. A young man with high, flat cheekbones and a shy, gap-toothed grin. He was wearing a jacket and tie, his brown hair slicked back Elvis-style. On the bottom of the photo was written, in a boy's awkward script, "From Romeo."

"Nah," she said. She sat down in a lumpy, slip-covered chair. An orange tabby appeared out of nowhere and jumped into her lap. "For me, this is where it all starts and ends, right here. The prizes and the critics—they don't mean anything. The only thing that counts is the story that takes shape in my head." Stroking the cat, she nodded toward the computer. "And the story that comes out of that machine, of course. If I never get another prize, it won't hurt my feelings one bit." She took a swallow of wine. "Although I do have to say that the money spends nice. Buys lots of kitty food and treats for Jake. Right, Jake?"

Over in the corner, Jake thumped his tail appreciatively.

I sat down on the sofa, thinking that maybe Darlene was a little drunk. Not much, just a little. "It was a cash prize?"

"Yeah. Royalties, they don't amount to a hill of beans. My name ain't exactly a household word." She grinned.

"If I was writin' to make money, I'd be writing romances, I guess. I read the other day that romance outsells all the rest of the fiction that gets written in this country."

"But the prize means you don't have to work?"

She stretched out her legs and the cat, dislodged, jumped down. "Not exactly. It's enough for me to live here for a couple of years, especially since Momma finished paying for the house before she died. What I get from Miz Tullie pays for my insurance, stuff like that." She took another swallow of wine and tilted her head curiously. "Not to change the subject, but what were you doing in the graveyard tonight?"

"I was looking for somebody," I said. The cat had joined me on the sofa. I sipped my wine, stroking its silky orange fur. "Somebody named Holland. Brent Holland. Did you ever hear of him?"

"Oh, sure." She repeated his name thoughtfully, wiggling her bare toes. "He was Miz Tullie's significant other, back before the Second World War. They were even engaged for a while, Momma said. But he died in the war, the way I remember. He wouldn't be in your fam'ly cemetery."

"But he *is* in our family cemetery," I replied. "And according to the marker, he died in 1946, *after* the war." I hesitated, wondering how much to tell her. "I have reason to believe that he wasn't buried there until sometime in the 1960s," I said. "Around '63, maybe."

"That's weird," Darlene said decidedly. She drained her glass and got up to pour another. "The way Momma told it to me, Miz Tullie's father didn't want her to have anything to do with Brent Holland. Ordered him off the place, or something like that. He joined the Marines and went to the war, and Miz Tullie's heart was broken. Momma said he was the love of her life." She held up the bottle inquiringly, and I shook my head. She sat back down. "Momma was a romantic. When I was in high school, we put on *Romeo and Juliet*. Momma, she flat loved it. Cried buckets when May Rose died. She was Juliet."

We were wandering away from the subject, and I brought her back. "Why didn't Aunt Tullie's father like this guy?"

Darlene lifted the glass in a mock salute. Her tone was sarcastic. "Because he was a Beauchamp, that's why. The Beauchamps were good enough to work for the Coldwells, but they weren't near good enough to marry." She became philosophical, but there was an undertone of bitterness in her voice. "Fam'lies are like that, y'know. 'Specially in a rural area like this, where they live close and go way back together. There's a pecking order. There's also racism. The Beauchamps have some black blood in 'em, along with their Choctaw. Tobias Beauchamp married a Creole woman, y'see. Sapphire. She was black enough to put them off limits, far as the Coldwells were concerned."

"But Brent Holland wasn't a Beauchamp," I objected.

"That's all you know about it," Darlene said with a short laugh. "Brent was raised by the Beauchamps, which made him one of 'em as far as Miz Tullie's daddy was concerned. And he worked on the plantation, along with Wiley's daddy, Ezra, who was about his age. I guess that's how they came to fall in love, Brent and Miz Tullie. She managed the plantation work, 'cause her brother didn't take much of an interest and her father, he was gettin' on in years." She shook her head reflectively, swirling the wine in her glass. "Momma always said Tullie should have married him and left home first chance she got, the way her sister Hattie did. That was the only way she was ever gonna be free of that father of hers. He was a bastard. A first-class, hell-raisin' tyrant. Some of the stories Momma told about him would make your hair curl."

I was silent for a moment, thinking. If I was right, Aunt Tullie *had* married Brent Holland. But instead of going away, she'd remained at home, taking care of her father and her brother and the plantation.

"I wonder why she stayed here during the war," I said after a minute. "There were lots of opportunities for women. She didn't have much education, but she could have gotten a job almost anywhere."

"Sure, there were opportunties," Darlene said in a practical tone, "but this is the South. Southern women didn't do stuff like that back then. Maybe her daddy told her she had to stay. Or maybe it was her choice. Remember what I said about the Delta getting into your blood? Lots of folks never want to leave. Or maybe it was the security. If Miz Tullie didn't have much of a life except for the plantation, she at least had that. It might've been hard for her to walk away from something that could support her for the rest of her life."

"I suppose," I said. I glanced at the graduation photo and changed the subject abruptly. "I'm curious—why do you keep Wiley's picture on your shelf?"

Darlene's smile became thin and dark. "I don't know. For old time's sake, I guess." She drained her wineglass. "We were . . . I had a crush on him when I was in high school."

"So that's why he signed himself Romeo?"

She shook her head, still not looking at me. "He was Romeo in the play." The small smile became grim, then vanished altogether. "There wasn't a part for a black, of course. Even when they did *Othello* the next year, they gave the lead to a white boy. Us blacks, we got to manage the props, pull the curtains, hand out the programs."

"Is that why you cried when you saw them pulling Wiley's truck out of the water?" I asked gently. "Because you had a crush on him when you were in high school? Or was there something more between you?"

I could see her struggling. She wanted to talk about it, but she wanted to keep it private, too. The silence lengthened.

Finally, she said, "Well, I s'pose I might as well tell you. It's long over with, anyway. It was more than a crush. I was in love with him. It was ridiculous, of course—me, a big, gawky black girl, in love with the cutest white boy in the class."

"White? But you said the Beauchamps were—"

"That was as far as the Coldwells were concerned, and the other old-time white families." She lifted her chin defiantly. "Compared to me, Wiley was white. *I* was at the bottom of the pecking order, way down below the Beauchamps." Her voice became angry. "And don't tell me it's any different now, China, because it isn't. Here in Mississippi, a white boy who dares to date a black girl is risking his reputation. And a black boy who gets mixed up with a white girl—he's risking a lynching."

The anger had turned to a bitter sadness. I retreated to safer ground. "Did Wiley know how you felt?"

She made a despairing noise. "Know? Of course he knew. And I was dumb enough to think he cared. Especially after . . . after I gave myself to him. We used to meet at the fishing camp a couple of nights a week. It was a lot better than making love in his old pickup, 'cause there was a bed." She smiled a little. "A bunk, actually. The mice had made a nest in it, but that didn't matter to a couple of hot-blooded kids."

"Oh," I said lamely. I could see now, or thought I could.

"You're probably thinking I was a fool," she said.

"I'm thinking that you were young. When we're young, we think with our hearts, not our heads. Or with our bodies."

"I came to terms with this a long time ago," she said. "I don't know why I'm letting it get to me now." After a moment she added, almost as if it were of no importance, "He didn't love me, of course. It was all an act. But that wasn't entirely his fault. I *wanted* him to act like he loved me, whether he did or not. And why shouldn't he take what I was so anxious to give? It wouldn't have mattered at all, to anybody, if I hadn't gotten pregnant. Of course, my mother found out and made me tell her who the father was. Then she marched straight off to Wiley's mother."

I whistled under my breath. "Wiley's *mother*?"

"Yeah." Darlene grinned. "My mother had no fear. She said it wasn't just me that made this baby, and the Beauchamps oughta take their share of the responsibility. Wiley's mother—Sissy, her name was—was a fine woman, very active in the community, and of course Momma knew her. Mrs. Beauchamp and her mother-in-law helped set up the clinic and the Visiting Nurse program and did all kinds of good things for Chicory."

I nodded. I had heard about the Beauchamp women from Martha Edmond.

Darlene went on. "Momma wanted me to go to college, and she was convinced that having a baby would drag me down. So she tried every way she could to get me a safe abortion. There were plenty of old folk-remedies around and Momma knew all about them, but she didn't want me to do anything like that. She hunted for a doctor who'd do it, but of course it was illegal back then." She sighed. "Finally, Momma went to Wiley's mother and told her, straight out. I guess Miz Beauchamp confronted Wiley about it, and he was man enough to say it was true. So Miz Beauchamp, she got me the abortion, and she made Wiley give me money out of his bank account that he was supposed to be saving for his own college expenses." She turned her face toward me, impassive. "And you know what? All that wild, crazy love in me turned into hate the minute he handed me that money. And I didn't just hate him for buying me off. For years afterward, I hated *myself* for being bought."

"Oh, Darlene," I said, putting out my hand. "I'm so sorry."

"Well, don't be," she said bleakly. "I wasn't the first black girl to give herself to a white boy 'cause she loved him. I've always been sorry about the baby, but Momma was dead-on right about that. He wouldn't have had a daddy and I wasn't the mother he deserved—not at eighteen, anyway. And Wiley's money put me through college, and *that* changed my life." She gestured toward the bookshelf. "You never can tell, you know? If it hadn't been for Wiley getting me pregnant, maybe I'd never have read any of those books. And if I hadn't read them, I couldn't have written mine."

I nodded. I could understand that. I've made some big mistakes in my life, but afterward, I could see that they took me places where I wouldn't have been willing to go all by myself.

Her mouth twisted. "All that stuff was going through my mind last night, when I realized it was Wiley's truck they were pulling out of the Bloodroot. I stopped loving that boy when I was still a girl, and I've got no cause to hate the man. But I sure hate to think of him dead." She paused. "Have they found out how the truck came to be in the river? Do they know how he died?"

"Deputy Green called this afternoon," I said. "Wiley

apparently drowned sometime on Saturday night. Unfortunately, he and Aunt Tullie had a squabble early that evening, and she whacked him with her cane—hard enough to give him a concussion. The police think it might have contributed to his death."

"Uh-oh," Darlene said. "So maybe he was parked on the ramp, passed out, and just kinda coasted into the river? Bad news for Miz Tullie, I reckon. But in her condition, no jury in its right mind would—"

The telephone's ring jarred the silence. Jake lifted his head, and Darlene got up to answer it. Her end of the conversation, which was punctuated by silences, gave plenty of clues to what was being said on the other end.

"Yeah, hi, Judith. What's happening? . . . No, I've got company." She grinned at me. "Well, who d'you think? Denzel Washington? China, that's who. . . . Yeah, well, why don't you come on over? It's still early, and we're just sittin' here, keepin' comp'ny with a bottle of wine. I've got another if you're thirsty, or you can bring your own poison."

The next silence was longer, and as she listened, she began to frown. Finally she said, "Hey, hold on. Are you sure you can believe that stuff Alice Ann is telling you? After all, her mother—" Another silence. "Yeah, right. Sure, I know, but—" Then, after a minute: "Listen, Judith, before you do anything you might be sorry for, I think you ought to look into it a little more. Talk to Dawn's girlfriends at school. They'll likely know where she's gone, even if her sister doesn't. You're not going to get anywhere threatening May Rose with—"

The next silence was very long. Jake got up and went to stand at the door. At a nod from Darlene, I opened the screen and let him out. The cat jumped down from the sofa and padded into the kitchen, and a moment later, I heard him lapping water. Darlene was saying, "Look, I know how you feel about Dawn. . . . yeah, I *do* know, believe it or not. But if you want to find her, don't mess with May Rose. Do your oooown detective work, and leave Dawn's mother out of it. . . . Yeah, you're welcome. G'night." She banged down the phone.

I looked questioningly at her. "What's going on with Judith?"

Darlene sat down again. Then, realizing her glass was empty, she got up and refilled it. "Alice Ann just left Judith's place. She came over to tell Judith that Dawn isn't sick at all. She's run away from home."

"I guess that explains Alice Ann's call this morning," I said. "Right after I finished talking to you, she phoned to say that she and Dawn both were quitting."

"And it also explains why May Rose wouldn't let us in last night." Darlene turned her glass in her fingers. "Dawn wasn't even there."

"Well," I said, "kids *do* take off—although that doesn't explain why May Rose had to lie about it. Why didn't she just tell us that her daughter left home?"

"Judith says she doesn't believe that's what happened," Darlene replied. "She says that Dawn would have told her if she was leaving town." She frowned, then added, more carefully, "Or rather, that she wouldn't have left town at all. She would have come to live with Judith, the way they planned."

"So Judith and Dawn—" I paused, leaving the rest unsaid.

But Darlene knew what I meant. "Yeah. At least, that's Judith's story. I've seen the two of them together, and they seemed like very good friends. As far as being lovers . . ." She shrugged. "You can't tell about people just from looking at them. Anyway, Judith thinks May Rose found out what was going on and shipped Dawn off to stay with a relative or something. She intends to confront her, and she wants me there, as a witness, I guess. But I think Judith would learn more if she did some asking around first. Even if May Rose sent her off, Dawn is bound to have said something to *somebody*."

"There's another possibility," I said. "Maybe Dawn doesn't care for Judith as much as Judith cares for Dawn, and she's chosen this way of letting her know."

"I suppose," Darlene replied doubtfully, "although, knowing Dawn, I'd say she's more straightforward than that, and more responsible. I think she'd tell Judith how she felt, not just run away from the situation."

"It's a mystery," I said, standing up and stretching. The clock on the wall over Darlene's desk said it was ten o'clock. Amanda had no doubt come and gone by now, and it was safe to go home. "I'm outta here," I said. "Are you feeling well enough to show up for work in the morning, or am I doing the biscuits again?"

"I'm feelin' better by the minute," Darlene said. "Thanks for coming over tonight, China. Talking helps."

"Yeah, it does," I said. I took her wineglass and set it on the table, then reached for her hands to pull her out of her chair. "A hug would help some, too."

We held each other for a few moments, then pulled apart. She ruffled my hair. "For a mouthy little white kid, you turned out okay."

"It was your momma's biscuits," I replied.

Chapter Fourteen

St. Vitus dance. This disease affects mostly the muscles and the limbs, and consists of an involuntary motion of both. A jerking of the limbs prevents their obeying the will, and the patient in vain essays to do what he wishes at the first attempt.

Treatment: Extract of skullcap, two drams; extract of chamomile, two drams; extract of boneset, one dram; quinine, one dram; cayenne, one scruple; oil of valerian, half a dram. Beat well together and make ninety pills. For an adult, one pill every two or three hours.

A. E. Youman, M.D., 1878
Twenty Thousand Receipts
in Nearly Every Department of Human Effort

Bloodroot as a treatment for St. Vitus dance. According to Alma R. Hutchens (*An Indian Herbalogy of North America*, 1991), a tincture of bloodroot was used in equal amounts with tinctures of black cohosh, lobelia, and squill to treat St. Vitus dance.

The rain was still holding off when I got home. I had expected the house to be silent and dark, as it had been when I got home late the night before. But the porch and hall and parlor lights were burning and a small red sports car with Louisiana license plates was parked out in front. I gritted my teeth. Darn it. Late as it was, Amanda Gleason was still here, insinuating herself into my mother's confidence.

I suppressed a sigh, climbed the steps, and opened the front door. Aunt Tullie had no doubt already gone to bed, leaving Leatha and Amanda to sort through the family papers or chat or whatever was keeping them so late. But recalling my churlish behavior of the afternoon and its effect on Leatha, I was determined to be civil to Amanda, no matter how big a nuisance she was or how much she irritated me. After all, she cheered my mother up—and there was precious little for Leatha to be cheerful about these days.

Blinking in the bright light, I went into the parlor. Amanda and Leatha were both there: Amanda in T-shirt and jeans, sitting cross-legged on the floor with a photograph album on her lap; Leatha on the sofa, holding a wadded-up handkerchief, her eyes and nose slightly red. She'd obviously been crying, but when she saw me, she smiled through her tears.

"China, I'm so glad you're back!" she cried out excitedly, as I stood in the door. "Something absolutely wonderful has happened! You'll be so surprised."

"No doubt," I said dryly, glancing at Amanda's upturned, jubilant face. She looked as if she'd just stumbled into a streambed littered with gold nuggets. All my good resolutions vanished and I added, in a sardonic tone, "I suppose you've been busy digging up old family connections, huh? So what is it? Are you some long-lost cousin?"

Amanda dropped the album, scattering loose photographs, and scrambled to her feet. "How did you *know*?"

she cried, running across the room to fling her arms around me. She began to laugh and then to sob, half-hysterical, as if the tension holding her together had snapped, like a rubber band. "How could you possibly guess?"

I took a step backward, away from her clutching hands. "Guess what?" I looked at Leatha, narrowing my eyes. "What's going on here?"

"You'll never believe it, China," Leatha said. She blew her nose. "Tell her, Amanda, dear. Tell her what we've found!"

"It's amazing, totally amazing," Amanda babbled. Tears brimmed in her eyes and her cheeks were wet. "We've discovered that you and your mother are my cousins!"

She went back to where the album had fallen and picked up a photograph of Aunt Tullie—the one I'd always liked so much, with Sapphire and Hattie. "And your aunt Tullie is my *grandmother*!" She thrust the photo at me as if it were her possession, as if she thought I'd never seen it before. "I've found her at last, after all the years of searching!"

I stared at her. "Your grandmother?" I managed finally. "Is that what you've come looking for?" I'd been right. There *was* another agenda. I gave her a stern look. "All that stuff about a research project, about women's history—it was all a lie?"

"Well, not quite," she said uncomfortably, putting the photograph on the coffee table. "This thing has been a research project for me, and it does involve women's history. But I thought I needed a cover story, in case I was wrong. I didn't want to embarrass any of us." She wiped her eyes with the back of her hand. "I've been down so many blind alleys, you see. I'd almost given up hope of finding my grandmother, and I had no idea I'd find her alive. And now I've found a whole new family, as well! It's almost too good to be true."

Aunt Tullie's *granddaughter*? Too good to be true, indeed. But then I thought of the enigmatic marker in the cemetery, of the stranger Aunt Tullie had buried among the close-knit kindred of Coldwells. That romantic story I'd conjured up might be much closer to the truth than I could have guessed, even after Darlene had confirmed Aunt Tullie's romantic relationship. And I'd obviously left out a very important chapter in Aunt Tullie's romantic tragedy: a pregnancy, a birth, a child. Brent Holland's child, Amanda Gleason's father or mother.

But all this speculative stuff was a long way ahead of the facts. If Aunt Tullie had never revealed that she'd been married, she'd certainly never let on that she'd been a mother. Nobody in the family seemed to be aware of it, including her father, her brother, and her niece. When was this pregnancy supposed to have occurred, and why didn't anybody know anything about it? What had Aunt Tullie done with the baby?

But there were other issues. Jordan's Crossing—its land, its buildings, its assets as a farming business—was worth several millions of dollars. In my previous incarnation as a criminal lawyer, I'd seen frauds and phonies who were motivated by far less. Currently, my mother was the beneficiary of her aunt's will. If Amanda was Tullie's granddaughter—a hypothetical that would have to be carefully documented before I was willing to accept it—did she think she could simply elbow Leatha aside and step into her place as Aunt Tullie's major beneficiary?

And there was something else, perhaps the most consequential of all, at least as far as Amanda herself was concerned. Looking at her, I couldn't see any family resemblance. But if Coldwell blood really did flow through her veins, she was as much at risk for Huntington's disease as Leatha and I. I doubted that Amanda would be so delighted with her new-found family when she learned that the Coldwell birthright included a kicker: a nifty little time bomb, ticking away in her genetic closet. When you come right down to it, Huntington's disease isn't something you'd be thrilled to inherit along with the family silver.

I turned to Leatha. "Have you told Amanda about Aunt Tullie's illness?"

Amanda took a deep breath. "China, I know all about Huntington's. It killed my mother, a few years ago."

I turned back to her, staring. "Killed . . . your mother?"

"Yes," she said in a matter-of-fact tone, as if she were announcing that it was raining, or that it was time for a sandwich. "And I've tested positive for the disease myself. Someday, I'll end up just like my mother and my grandmother, unless they find a cure for it first. And surely they will," she added. Her voice became fervent now. "They've *got* to. There are too many of us waiting to die."

Leatha's eyes were shining through her tears. "Huntington's is what led Amanda to us, China. She felt she had to trace the genetic line that was responsible for her disease."

I wish I could tell you that my skepticism evaporated like a raindrop on a hot brick, but it didn't—not entirely anyway. The Huntington's gene was certainly part of the factual documentation that would prove Amanda's claim, along with the other necessary proofs. Somewhere, there had to be a record of her mother's birth and an explanation for the fact that nobody within the Coldwell family knew anything about her. And if it was a question of inheriting the estate, I'd insist that she provide a DNA profile that proved her Coldwell connection. But we could get to that.

"You've met Aunt Tullie?" I asked, with less of an edge. "You've seen her condition?"

"We talked for a few minutes this evening," Amanda replied. "But she seemed agitated, and I didn't think it was a good idea to tell her who I am." She held out her hands. "Anyway, I needed to tell you and your mother first. I wanted you to understand, and I hoped you'd help me break the news. It may not be easy for her. I'm sure she has lots of feelings about . . . what happened. About giving up her baby, I mean."

Leatha looked up at me, patting the sofa beside her. "Why don't we all sit down and get comfortable? Amanda had just begun to tell me how this happened when you arrived. Go back to the beginning, Amanda. China must be absolutely *dying* to know the whole story."

That was putting it mildly, I thought, settling myself next to my mother. The whole idea was absolute, utter weirdness, as Ruby would say. But life is stranger than fiction. And there was that double grave marker in the cemetery—

"It began when my mother was finally diagnosed with Huntington's disease." Amanda had taken the chair across from us. Her shoes were off, her knees pulled up under her chin. She was obviously settling in for a long story.

" 'Finally?' " Leatha asked. "It took a while?"

"It took a *long* while." Amanda ran her fingers through her brown hair, loosening it. "Enid—that's my mother, Enid Freeman Gleason—was always nervous and fidgety, even when I was a girl. She began to get worse when my father died, about fifteen years ago. She wasn't fifty yet, but she'd get confused easily, and she'd sometimes get lost when she went downtown. Her speech began to slur, her movements were jerky, and she stumbled and fell a lot. Her sisters thought she had something called St. Vitus dance, but since she was a heavy drinker, I blamed her behavior on alcohol. Our family doctor seemed to agree, but when Mom started having terrible headaches, he sent her to a neurologist. He noticed her erratic movements and said she had something called Tourette's syndrome. Then another doctor got into the act and decided she had multiple sclerosis. Nobody seemed very sure, one way or another. But at least Mom had quit drinking. And either way—MS or Tourette's—we figured it was something we could learn to live with."

"It must have been very difficult for both of you," Leatha said sympathetically. "Are you an only child? Were you living with your mother?"

"I had a brother, Ralph Jr., but he drowned in a neighborhood swimming pool when he was four and I was six. At the time when all this was happening with Mom, I was studying economics at the University of Tennessee at Knoxville. When she got worse, I moved her to an apartment nearby. But eventually I had to move in so she wouldn't be alone at night." Amanda smiled crookedly. "Working with her physical disabilities was hard enough, but the psychological stuff was much harder. She had long, black depressions and she flew off the handle at the least little thing. I had to manage a lot of stuff behind her back—legal affairs, her disability claim, things like that— because anything involving paperwork or the bureaucracy frustrated her to the point of rage." Amanda hugged her knees. "When I tried to talk to the doctors about this, they said it was a normal result of her difficulty in coping with her growing disabilities."

"But it wasn't," Leatha said. "I know that from being around Aunt Tullie. The anger and the depression—that's classic Huntington's. That, along with the movement problems."

Amanda nodded. "I found that out when I stumbled across a short piece about Huntington's disease in the newspaper. I called the doctor who was named in the article, and he agreed to see Mom right away. The minute he laid eyes on her, he knew. He said that her movements were called chorea, and that it was a genetic disease that she had inherited from one of her parents. He told me I was at risk, too."

"That's tough," I said. This woman had been through a great deal and I was beginning to feel like a jerk for questioning her credibility. But having the gene for Huntington's didn't automatically make her Aunt Tullie's granddaughter. Apparently lots of other people had the disease, and *they* weren't Coldwells.

"You know how tough it is," Amanda said quietly. "You're both at risk yourselves. But you also know that it's something you have to deal with and move on. You can't let the disease control your life. Anyway, once we got the right diagnosis, it was easier to cope. We found some medications that worked. She was calmer for a while and the movements were better controlled, and I began to feel optimistic. But then the chorea started to get worse and she was having trouble sleeping at night. Then her depressions intensified. It was rough on both of us. I was in the Ph.D. program by that time, but I took a leave and got a job teaching at a community college so there'd be some money coming in."

"It's too bad you had to give up your education," Leatha exclaimed.

Amanda made a rueful face. "Don't think I did it out of the kindess of my heart. I hated having to quit, and there were times when I almost hated Mom for making my life so hard. Then when I got tested and came up positive—well, that made everything so much harder. I knew that marriage was no longer an option, even if I found the right guy, because I'd never want to be a burden to him. And of course, kids are simply out of the question."

She took a deep breath, signaling a new chapter. "One day while I was at class, Mom put on her parka and walked out of the house. When I got home and found her missing, I began looking. The weather was bitterly cold— December 16, it was—and I was terribly afraid for her. I searched everywhere—the mall where we liked to shop, the hospitals, the morgue, homeless shelters. It was a nightmare." Her eyes filled with tears. "Finally, I called the police. They brought in some dogs that followed her scent to a nearby reservoir. They spent several days dredging, looking for her body, but they never found even a trace of her. The police think she killed herself. I didn't want to accept it, but after a while I had to. I'd rather think she committed suicide than imagine the alternatives. Somebody kidnapping and raping and killing her, I mean. Or wandering lost for days, before she finally died of exposure."

I shivered and groped for Leatha's hand. She turned her head and we exchanged glances. I could see the deep, cold fear in her eyes and knew that both of us were thinking the same thought: Was this how it would be for us at the end? A long, slow slide into a dreadful death?

Leatha's fingers tightened around mine. "I don't know which would be worse," she said somberly. "Losing your mother suddenly that way, never knowing exactly what happened—or watching her die, inch by inch."

Amanda looked down, sighed, and looked up again. "I've wondered about that, too. Maybe she thought ahead to the end, and hoped it would be easier for me this way. Or maybe she just got to the point where she couldn't bear it anymore, and wanted to make it easier for herself. It's something I'll never know."

I let go of Leatha's hand. This was a terrible story and I felt a deep sympathy for Amanda, who had handled the situation far better than I would have. But the lawyer in me knew that it didn't take us any closer to identifying Amanda as a Coldwell.

"When did you start looking for your grandmother?" I asked, trying to make my tone neutral.

Amanda took a deep breath. "When Mom was gone and I had time to think about what happened, I could see that it didn't make any sense. The genetic thing, I mean. You see, both of Mom's parents had lived into their eighties, and neither of them showed any signs of the disease. What's more, Mom had three sisters, and not one of them had symptoms."

"Then it couldn't have been in the family!" Leatha said excitedly.

"Exactly," Amanda replied. "So where did it come from? That was when I began doing some serious genealogical research. I ran up against all kinds of brick walls until I finally located Grandma Freeman's youngest sister,

Mom's aunt, who lived in Canada. She was in her nineties and healthy as a horse. She's the one who told me the truth. My mother and her sisters were all adopted."

"Adopted!" Leatha exclaimed.

Of course, I thought. That's the only way this could have happened. Different children from different parentages brought together as a family, one of them with a genetic disease. But adopted children have no way of knowing their genetic background. That's one of the most powerful arguments for forcing adoption agencies to open their birth records.

Amanda nodded. "They adopted four girls, all very young, within the space of three years, so the children had virtually no memory of an earlier life. Grandma and Grandpa Freeman wanted a big family. They were both very religious—Catholic—and they thought it was better if the girls were raised to believe that *they* were their natural parents. The Freemans gave their daughters a wonderful home and none of the girls ever imagined that they were adopted. In fact, the truth would probably never have come out if it hadn't been for my mother's illness. But when I finally made Grandma's sister understand why I was asking, she told me that Mom had been adopted as a newborn infant in late December 1942—she remembered the date, she said, because it was after the first anniversary of Pearl Harbor. She wasn't sure, but she thought Mom came from an orphanage somewhere in Louisiana."

"It must have been strange," Leatha said, "finding out that your family wasn't related by blood. Of course, that doesn't make them less of a family," she added hurriedly.

"No, of course not," Amanda agreed. "I've always been close to my Freeman aunts and their children, and they're still my family. But when I realized that I had no other blood relatives in the whole world, I felt terribly lonely—disconnected, somehow. I wanted to find my *real* family. And for some reason, it was important for me to know how the disease had been transmitted—who in the family had had it and how it came to me. So I left Knoxville and moved to Baton Rouge. I got a job teaching at a community college and started to search."

"I imagine that must have been a real challenge," Leatha said. "Your mother's adoption was a long time ago. Most of those orphanages probably aren't in existence any longer."

"It took a long time," Amanda replied. "I couldn't spend as much time on the search as I would have liked, because I was teaching. My heart wasn't in it, but I had to make some money. Anyway, I finally found out that Mom had come from St. Anne's Catholic Orphanage in New Orleans, which was closed in the 1970s. It took a long while to track down the records, which had been moved to the diocese offices, and even longer to persuade the sister in charge to give me access. She kept insisting that all their records were sealed to protect the birth mothers and that I'd have to get a court order, which I knew would take forever. But when I provided a letter from Mom's doctor explaining about Huntington's and the genetic situation, she relented and allowed me to make a copy of my mother's birth record, and from there I checked the parish records and got her birth certificate. Mom was born on December 20, 1942, to Petulia Coldwell." To me, she added, "I'll bring you a copy of the parish certificate, China. I'm sure you'll want to see it."

The birth certificate, with Aunt Tullie's name. Well, that took care of the documentation. I looked at Amanda. My cousin, no doubt about it.

Amanda laced her fingers together. "The search didn't end there, unfortunately. The address on the birth certificate turned out to be false. It took me another two years to find the real one. The name Coldwell is more common than you would think."

"I don't suppose Aunt Tullie wanted anybody to know about the baby," Leatha remarked quietly. "Especially her father. Clancy ruled the family with an iron hand. I've sometimes wondered whether Pearl—she was his wife—killed herself just to escape from him. She took something. Digitalis, my father always said, although nobody ever knew where she got it."

"Pearl was Tullie's mother?" Amanda asked, and when Leatha nodded, she said, "Maybe she killed herself because of Huntington's. As *my* mother did. So perhaps she was the one who brought the disease into the family."

I nodded. Amanda and I had reached the same conclusion by different routes, mine in the family cemetery earlier that evening. I thought again of Pearl's journal. It was beginning to seem likely that something there would confirm our suspicions.

"I don't know much about the circumstances of Pearl's suicide," Leatha said. "That happened before I was born, back in 1918, and was very mysterious. She left a note, but it didn't really explain anything."

She also left a journal that would probably explain a great deal, I thought. I'd finish it tonight, and see what I could learn.

Leatha was going on. "Everybody in the family was afraid of Clancy Coldwell, you see. One of his daughters, Hattie, got married and moved away as soon as she could, but Tullie and Howard, his son, both stayed here. Howard was my father," she added to Amanda. She smiled a little.

"Daddy always took the course of least resistance, especially where *his* father was concerned."

I gave Leatha a curious look. "What do you remember about 1942?" I asked. "You would have been twelve that year, right?"

Leatha nodded, frowning thoughtfully. "The early forties were very difficult years. It was wartime, of course. A lot of the men were gone and it was hard to find laborers to work in the cotton fields. Aunt Tullie was gone, too, for a while—she had to have some sort of operation, or at least that's the way I remember it. When school started in 1942, she took me to Greenville to stay with Aunt Hattie. I did sixth grade there and I didn't come back until after school was out the next year."

"So Aunt Tullie might have been away from Jordan's Crossing during the last four months of her pregnancy," I said. "She could have given the baby up for adoption, come back home, and pretended that nothing had ever happened." I thought again of the marker in the cemetery and turned to Amanda. "Was the father's name on the birth certificate?"

Amanda shook her head. "The line was blank." She turned to Leatha. "Do you have any idea who my grandfather might have been?"

Leatha frowned. "She was seeing somebody about that time. In fact, I think they might even have been engaged, although her father made sure it never came to anything. He was bitterly opposed to it, for some reason." She smiled slightly. "I remember thinking at the time that it was very sad that Grandpa didn't approve, because the young man looked so handsome in his uniform. He was a Marine."

"Who was he?" Amanda asked eagerly.

"One of the Holland boys," Leatha said. "I've forgotten his name, I'm afraid."

"Brent," I said. *Beloved.*

Leatha turned to look at me, surprised. "How do you know, China?"

I wasn't ready to tell them yet about the grave in the Coldwell cemetery. "I suppose I heard it somewhere," I said evasively. "Wasn't he one of the Beauchamps?"

Outside, the wind had begun to rattle the leaves, and a branch tapped against the window. Leatha paused for a moment to listen to the coming storm, then said: "I don't think he was a Beauchamp. He and his brother were raised by the Beauchamp family, though. I recall that they were Sapphire's nephews—her sister's children." She leaned over and pointed at the photograph that Amanda had put on the table. "That's Sapphire, Amanda. She was your grandmother's nurse. My father's, as well. Wasn't she beautiful?"

But Amanda had her mind on other things. "This Brent Holland," she said excitedly. "Do you suppose he was my grandfather?"

"The only way to know for sure is to ask Aunt Tullie," Leatha replied.

"And she might not remember," Amanda replied regretfully. "I used to ask my mother about my father and the early days of their marriage, and she'd always tell me she couldn't remember him at all. It made me sad. When someone is forgotten, it's as if he never existed."

We all fell silent for a moment, listening to the rising wind. *There's rosemary, that's for remembrance,* I thought sadly. *Pray, love, remember.*

"Brent Holland," I said at last. "Whatever happened to him, Mother?"

"I don't think I ever heard," Leatha replied. "Maybe he was killed in action. Or maybe he came back and my grandfather chased him off. As I said, Clancy was terribly opposed to the match." She shook her head, bemused. "You know, all of this just seems impossible. It never occurred to me that Aunt Tullie might have had a child. I've always thought of her as being so... oh, I don't know. Virginal, I guess. Like Elizabeth the First, the Virgin Queen. Married to Jordan's Crossing, in the same way Elizabeth was married to England."

"As I remember the movie," I said dryly, "Elizabeth had one or two major flings before she married England."

Leatha looked doubtful. "But Aunt Tullie has never been the kind to have flings. Of course, I'm thinking of the way she was later. She was different before the war. She was a very happy woman, always laughing, even a little flirty."

"Laughing?" I asked in surprise. "Aunt Tullie *laughed*? I remember her from the sixties, and all I can recall is that sour look on her face."

"You're right," Leatha agreed. "You know, now that I think of it, something must have happened to change her during the early forties. By the time I was in high school, she was an entirely different person. Bitter, I'd say. And sad. Of course, now that I know about Huntington's, I'd have to say that she might have been in the very early stages of the disease."

Lightning flashed and an instant later, thunder rattled the windows. "Maybe she was sad because she had to give up her baby," Amanda said quietly. "And bitter because the man she loved didn't come back from the war."

But he did come back from the war, I thought, and ended up dead, in our garden. I frowned. He died in 1946, according to the marker in the cemetery. Was that also the year Brent Holland had come back to claim her? Did Tullie know that he had returned? Or did she know nothing at all until the summer when she and Old Homer and Marie Louise unearthed his body? The summer I was eight years old. The summer of 1963, seventeen long years after Brent Holland's death.

I opened my mouth to tell Leatha and Amanda what I knew, but the lawyer in me made me close it again. We were talking about a man who might be Amanda's grandfather, and I didn't want to make any mistakes. I needed to confirm some of these facts before I shared my suspicions. Perhaps Marie Louise could help. The thought of her brought something else to mind, and I turned to Amanda.

"Do you know someone named Marie Louise?"

She gave me a blank look. "I don't think so. Is she a member of the family?"

"No," I said slowly. If Amanda didn't know Marie Louise, how did the old woman know about Amanda? But I'd have to process that question later. There was something else I wanted to know.

"Did you ever see Aunt Tullie wear a ring?" I asked Leatha. "A wide gold band, like a wedding ring, carved with an ivy design, maybe?"

"I never saw her wear it," Leatha replied, "but there's a ring like that in the top drawer of her bureau. I saw it just this morning, when I was putting her clean underthings away. I noticed that it was engraved, but I didn't get a chance to look because she came in just then, and I didn't want her to think I was snooping. You know how paranoid she is." She gave me a puzzled look. "Where did you see that ring?"

"It's a long story," I said, "and it's getting late."

Amanda looked at her watch. "Omigosh, it *is*. I've got to go." She pushed her feet into her shoes. "Martha will be worried."

"It's storming," Leatha said. "Would you like to stay all night? There's an extra bedroom."

Amanda shook her head. "I told Martha I'd be back. Knowing her, she's probably waiting up for me. But thank you." She stood up. "Maybe I'll take a rain check."

"It's been a wonderful night," Leatha said tearfully. We were all three standing, and she put her arms around both of us. "Now I have *two* fine girls."

I waited for the jealousy to flicker, but it didn't. Maybe I was beginning to come to terms with Amanda and our relationship—although certainly not with the genetic disease we might share. I couldn't ever adopt Amanda's philosophical attitude toward Huntington's. I hated what it had done to Aunt Tullie, and the thought of what it might do to Leatha and me was like an icy lump in my stomach.

"I'd like to come over in the morning and talk with my grandmother," Amanda said. "Would that be okay?"

"Tomorrow is going to be rough," I replied. "The family lawyer is bringing a power of attorney for Aunt Tullie to sign, and the police are coming to ask some questions. She got into an argument with a man and slugged him with her cane."

"That doesn't sound good," Amanda said soberly.

"It isn't," I agreed. "He died." And because he's dead and the deed has disappeared, I caught myself thinking, Amanda will be able to claim Jordan's Crossing.

There was a silence. "And after all that," Leatha said, "I'm taking her to the doctor in Jackson. I'll call you when we get back, and we can make our plans."

"That'll be fine." Amanda hugged Leatha, and then me. "Thank you for being so understanding, China," she whispered. "I'll never have children, but at least now I know I have someone to share the rest of my life with. I have a *real* family."

Some family, I thought ironically, its surviving members united by the fear of inheriting one ill-behaved gene. But I squeezed her hand and said good night as warmly as I could. Amanda had to go to sleep with the certain knowledge that she had inherited the Huntington's gene. I could go to sleep with the possibility that I hadn't. There was a significant difference between the two.

But before I slept, I intended to read the rest of Pearl's journal.

Chapter Fifteen

> God forgive us, but ours is a monstrous system, a
> wrong and iniquity. Like the patriarchs of old, our
> men live all in one house with their wives and their
> concubines; and the mulattoes one sees in every
> family partly resemble the white children. Any lady
> is ready to tell you who is the father of all the mu-
> latto children in everybody's household but her
> own. Those, she seems to think, drop from the
> clouds. . . .
>
> Mary Boykin Chesnut, 1832–1886

Outside, the storm had grown savage—pounding rain, thunder rattling the windows, lightning like a fireworks display. When I went to my room and shut the door, I didn't light the lamp immediately. Instead, I stood by the window for a long time, watching the wind-whipped trees, eerily illuminated by flashes of blue-white lightning. The evening had been like that, too: full of fierce flashes of insight and recognition, sudden *ah-ha*s brilliantly illuminating the dark of what I didn't know. From Marie Louise's front porch to the cemetery to Darlene's house and back to Jordan's Crossing—each stopping point had been like a stage on a journey into the past and toward the truth, teaching me something new, showing me something I hadn't known. And suddenly I heard that echo again: *There's somebody else wants to know. Wants hit even more dan you do.* Needs *hit even more dan you do.* I leaned my forehead against the cool window pane, half-smiling to myself. I'd have to tell Marie Louise that Miz Smarty-pants had figured out that much, at least.

After a few moments, I turned on the light, took off my clothes, and pulled my sleep shirt over my head. Curled up in bed, the house quiet and dark against the violent rattling of the storm, I opened Pearl's journal. I understood her relationship to her husband Clancy rather differently now that I knew about his tyrannical behavior, and I could see it reflected in the lines I had read earlier:

> But I who have been so long bound by ties of love to a man who misused my trust and betrayed my faith now refuse to be any longer bound to him. And so this explanation or justification is also (& perhaps most importantly) a declaration of my refusal to be held captive. It is a declaration of my independence.
>
> But still the story must be set down & the reasons . . .

The light beside the bed dimmed for a moment, then grew bright again. Ghosts, maybe? Uncle Jed playing tricks with the electrical system? No, more likely a strike on a utility pole. The power grid probably covered thousands of acres, and if one transformer took a hit, a lot of houses went dark.

The light stayed bright and I went back to my reading, but not for long. The next sentence stopped me again, this time with astonishment.

*Clancy's father Abner gave the land to Tobias as
his birthright, for Tobias was the bastard son of
Abner by the freewoman Rosa Beauchamp, who was
part Negro and part Choctaw, being a niece of the
great chief Greenwood Leflore.*

Tobias Beauchamp was Abner Coldwell's *son*? But I
shouldn't be surprised. All of the clues had pointed in that
direction, and now that I knew the situation, I could see
their significance. And this wasn't an isolated event. I'd
read recently of DNA evidence proving beyond doubt that
Thomas Jefferson, a father of our country, also fathered
at least one illegitimate child (and probably more) by his
slave Sally Hemings, who herself was the illegitimate
mixed-blood daughter of Jefferson's father-in-law by *his*
slave. This sort of thing—the master sleeping with the
female servants—was part of the ugly sexual dynamics of
slavery and a common practice among plantation owners,
to whom these people were only property, to be used at
the owner's whim and will. I wondered whether Abner's
wife, Samantha, had known about what her husband did,
and if she had known, how she felt about it. Did she
simply accept it without question, or did she hate it, seeing
in it the seeds of a great tragedy whose poisonous roots
would creep through all the generations to come?

I went back to my reading with a mix of emotions:
anger, apprehension, sorrow. This was the truth about the
Coldwells. How much more of it did I want to know?

*Tobias lived with his mother on the plantation (this
is what Tobias has told me) & was educated &
trained by his father Abner, who secretly preferred
him in his heart to his legitimate sons borne him by
his wife Samantha. And as a token of this affection*

& preference & in gratitude for Tobias's devoted service at Vicksburg (where he no doubt saved his father's life) & his able administration of the plantation's accounts, Abner deeded Tobias one full section of land (the river section, which is the best land, for it included the landing on the Bloodroot River), so that Rosa Beauchamp's son might receive his rightful & irrevocable share in his father's estate without being named in his father's will, which Samantha's sons were certain to challenge in a court of law on grounds of illegitimacy & thereby rob their half-brother of his birthright, which his father intended him to have.

And so the deed was drawn & for the next fourteen or fifteen years, Tobias (named by his father as plantation manager) quietly & without calling attention to his actions recorded in a separate ledger the costs & incomes pertaining to the property his father had given him. And because Tobias was a careful and skillful manager & knew the best markets & how to receive the highest prices for his father's cotton & his own, & because he held title to the river landing & hence was able to charge landing fees against his father's accounts (as Abner, he says, instructed him emphatically and repeatedly to do), he began to accrue substantial earnings to himself. I should also add that these accounting transactions were a private matter between Tobias & his father. The other sons, or son rather (Beauregard having been killed in the steamboat explosion), knew nothing of this business. For (& here was the mistake, Tobias says, & I do agree) Abner did not take Samantha's sons into his confidence. Beauregard & Clancy were wayward & wild, with little concern for their father's business, & Abner relied on Tobias to fill the place these two sons

might have filled. And then Beauregard was dead
& Clancy alone was left & soon thereafter Abner
died as well, and there was only Clancy & Tobias.

I paused for a moment, thinking that my earlier question—why Abner gave away the best land—was now answered. And who could blame him? He had two legitimate sons who showed little interest in his business affairs and one illegitimate son who did: He would naturally prefer the son, bastard or not, who cared about the plantation. But with Abner's death, Tobias would have lost his mentor and his protector, and would have become vulnerable to his half-brother's jealousy and anger. The next paragraph confirmed this:

And when Clancy was left to deal with the business
of his father's plantation (this is Clancy's story now,
as he has told it to me), he began to see that Tobias
as plantation manager had not done as he should,
but had been blatantly stealing from the accounts,
appropriating both goods & monies to himself, a
fraud quite easily perpetrated (these are Clancy's
words) upon a sick old gentleman who felt a pe-
culiar affection for the reprobate who was defraud-
ing him. Clancy says he discovered the evidence for
his suspicions when he found and confiscated cer-
tain ledgers Tobias had compiled. Tobias, con-
fronted, claimed that Abner had given him the land.
He produced the deed, which Clancy (and now this
is Tobias's account) forcibly took from him, threat-
ening to offer the ledgers in court as proof of To-
bias's dastardly and most ungrateful chicanery
(Clancy's words). If Tobias did not sign a quitclaim
that rendered null & void the gift of the land, he
would be summoned before the magistrate (who at

the time was Judge Tobias Coldwell, Clancy's first
cousin) on charges of embezzlement. Tobias (his
story now), fearing that if the matter came before
Judge Coldwell, he would be found guilty of theft
& would lose not only the land but his livelihood &
perhaps his liberty, agreed to sign the quitclaim in
return for Clancy's assurances that he would not be
prosecuted.

So that was how it had happened. Clancy had used the
account books as the basis for a blackmail threat, forcing
Tobias to give back the land. So what happened next?

I was turning the page when the light flickered,
dimmed, and went out. *Damn*, I thought, tasting a sour
frustration. I sat there in the dark for several minutes,
hoping the power would come on again, but it didn't. I
thought of getting up and trying to locate a candle, but I
had no idea where to look, and anyway, the house was
pitch-black.

After a few minutes more, I put the journal on the table,
turned the lamp off so it wouldn't wake me when it came
on, and slid down under the blanket. The story of
Clancy's ill-treatment of his half-brother Tobias was a
compelling page-turner, but it would have to wait until
tomorrow. It had been a long, eventful day. I was so tired
that I fell asleep almost immediately and didn't wake until
Leatha knocked on my door the next morning and an-
nounced that Darlene was about to serve breakfast.

"WELL, that wasn't so difficult now, was it?" Colonel
Blakeslee remarked, when Aunt Tullie had listened to his
explanation of the reasons for giving Leatha her power of
attorney and had agreeably signed the documents he'd

brought. "I reckon you'll sleep a lot easier at night," he added, "knowin' that your closest kin is watchin' out for your best interests."

Leatha gave me a questioning glance, and I knew what she was thinking. Amanda Gleason, not Leatha, was Tullie's closest kin. What kind of a role would she expect to play in her grandmother's health care? And if her story held up (and I was ready to concede that it would), Jordan's Crossing would belong to her. What part would Aunt Tullie's granddaughter want to play in its management?

But we could answer those questions later. Right now, there were more pressing problems—such as the impending visit by the sheriff's deputy. I was grateful that this was one of Aunt Tullie's lucid mornings. Slowly and carefully, trying to downplay all of the story's horrible aspects, I told her that Wiley had driven his truck to the river on Saturday night, and that by some accident he had drowned there.

"Deputy Green wants to talk to you about what happened while Wiley was here that evening," I said.

Aunt Tullie scowled. "You mean, he wants to know how hard I hit him."

"Something like that," I said. "All you have to do is answer his questions truthfully."

"And don't tell him any more'n he asks," the Colonel added. "Jes' answer his questions."

"I'll tell him I feel sorry 'bout hitting Wiley, and worse about him drowning," Aunt Tullie said, "which is the gospel truth." She sighed heavily and twisted her hands. "I feel even sorrier when I think of all the work that's got to be done around here. Now I've got to hire somebody to fill his shoes. And unless I've lost count, there's no more Beauchamps."

"I think we've got the work covered, Miz Tullie," the Colonel said, his voice smooth. "China asked me yestiddy to start thinkin' about it, and I'm puttin' together a list of possibles to fill in the rest of this season. For next year, you might oughtta consider leasin' out the land. It won't be hard to line up somebody who'd be glad to take it over."

"Lease it out?" Aunt Tullie gave him a scandalized look. "My father would turn over in his grave, and his father, too." She fell silent for a moment. "But with the last Beauchamp gone, it just don't seem right to carry on," she said jerkily. "They've been as much a part of this land as the Coldwells, over the years. I never imagined we'd outlast 'em."

I thought about what I had read the night before. The ironic truth was that the Beauchamps *were* Coldwells, if you traced the line back through the generations. Tobias Beauchamp was Abner Coldwell's son, and had just as much Coldwell blood in him as Aunt Tullie's father, Clancy. He'd been born on the wrong side of wedlock, that was all. It seemed very sad, somehow, that Wiley had died before I understood that the two of us shared a common ancestor: Abner Coldwell, our mutual great-great-grandfather.

And then I thought of something else. Was it possible that Clancy had objected to Tullie's engagement to Brent Holland because they were *related*? But the minute the question popped into my mind, I knew that the answer was no. The Holland boys may have been raised by the Beauchamps, but they had been related to Sapphire, Tobias's wife. Brent and Aunt Tullie weren't blood kin.

There wasn't any more time to speculate. The county sheriff's car had pulled up out front, Deputy Green was knocking at the door, and it was time for Aunt Tullie's interrogation, Colonel Blakeslee and I standing by to be sure that her rights were protected.

I'd been nervous about the interview, but on balance, I had to say that it went pretty well. Aunt Tullie answered Banjo's questions forthrightly enough, although her speech was becoming slurred and he had to ask her to repeat herself several times. His difficulty in understanding irritated her, of course, and her frustration and anxiety made her move more erratically and speak less comprehensibly. But finally the deputy had what he came for: her account of the altercation between her and Wiley. And he had more. He'd have to report to the county attorney how hard it would be to convince a jury that Aunt Tullie was competent to form the requisite intent to commit a crime.

There was one other thing. The deputy mentioned the deed, and I asked the question that had been on my mind since the day before. "Did you happen to find the deed in the truck?"

The deputy looked at the Colonel, then back at me. "We found a document in the glove compartment," he said slowly, "in an envelope. We're pretty sure it's the deed, but it's kinda hard to tell. There's not much left of it. I'm 'fraid it's been soakin' for a few days."

I regarded Banjo thoughtfully. He was a competent lawman, and it had certainly occurred to him that if someone had murdered Wiley in order to retrieve that deed, the murderer would have taken it out of the truck before the truck went into the river. With a little nod, he looked back at me. There was probably no need to put this understanding into words.

When the deputy had gone and Leatha had taken Aunt Tullie upstairs to get ready to go to Jackson to see the doctor, I walked with Colonel Blakeslee out to his car. We exchanged observations about the interrogation, both of us having arrived at pretty much the same conclusion. The Colonel reiterated his offer to talk to the county attorney and remarked that he thought we'd probably heard the last of the deed. But at the end of the path, he turned to look at me.

"What's wrong with her?" he asked bluntly. "I've seen Alzheimer's, and that ain't it."

We went through the gate. "You're right," I said. "It's Huntington's disease."

The Colonel whistled under his breath. "I've read about that. Pretty awful stuff." He looked at me sharply. "Genetic, ain't it? Which means that you and your momma—"

"Leatha and I are aware of what it could mean for us," I said quietly. "All this is pretty new to us, though. For right now, we're just trying to meet Aunt Tullie's needs and make plans for her future."

He gave me a sympathetic look. "If there's anything I can do to help, you be sure and let me know." He paused. "Where do you think this thing came from? Not from Clancy, I'd say. He was healthy right up to the end. His daddy, too."

"We're guessing that Pearl carried the gene," I said, "and that she died before the symptoms developed. It's also possible that my grandfather had it as well."

"What your grandfather had," the Colonel said dryly, "was the D.T.'s. But maybe Huntington's is why Pearl killed herself. It ain't the kind of thing you want your kids to watch." He shook his head. "Old Tobias's wife had something like that. My mother used to say that poor woman jes' couldn't sit still, no matter how hard she tried."

"You've been a friend of the family for a long time," I said, thinking of Amanda, and Tullie and Brent. "I've been doing some research into the family history, and I wonder if you might be able to answer some questions for me."

"Will if I can," the Colonel said, leaning against the car. He produced a cigar and lit it. "What's on your mind?"

"Does the name Brent Holland mean anything to you?"

"Well, well," the Colonel said softly. He exhaled a cloud of blue smoke. "Where'd you dig up that old story?"

"I've heard that he and Aunt Tullie were once engaged," I said, "but that Clancy was against it. I haven't talked to Aunt Tullie about it yet, but I'm beginning to think that they might have gotten married without telling her father."

The Colonel eyed the tip of his cigar. "You *have* been doin' some research. I figured that old tale was dead and buried."

"You knew Brent?"

"He was older'n me, but yeah, I knew him. My mother, you see, knew the Beauchamp women pretty well, so I grew up with the Beauchamp fam'ly gossip. Brent and his brother—their mother died and they were raised with the Beauchamps. Brent and Tullie musta started gettin' together on the sly, because first thing anybody knew of it, they was engaged. But Clancy, he pitched a fit and Tullie pretended to break it off, like a good girl."

"Why?" I asked. "Why was Clancy opposed?"

"Who knows?" The Colonel shrugged. "Maybe 'cause he didn't think of it first. Or maybe 'cause he thought of Brent as a Beauchamp, and the Beauchamps weren't good enough to marry into the Coldwells. Tobias's wife was Creole, y'see, so there was some black blood in the fam'ly—not 'nough to show, but ever'body knew 'bout it. Anyway, after Brent joined the Marines, him and Tullie went down to New Orleans and got themselves married."

"Did she tell her father?"

"Don't know that she did. I wouldn't't've known anything about it myself, if my mother hadn't told me. Wiley's mother told her, was how she knew. Real Romeo and Juliet story, she said it was."

"What happened to Brent after the war?"

"Nobody seems to know." The Colonel puffed on his cigar. "He came home and hung around Chic'ry for a while, then he was gone. Mother said she kept expectin' Miz Tullie to follow him wherever he'd went off to, but she never did. She just kept on takin' care of this place, same way she's done almost to this day. And the Beauchamps, they never heard from him again."

"He was gone? Just like that?" I thought of the lonely grave at the foot of the garden where Brent Holland had lain for seventeen years. "Didn't anybody wonder where he went?"

The Colonel pulled his pale eyebrows together. "You gotta remember how tough the times were back then, China. The boys were home from the war, but we weren't out of the Depression by much. There wasn't a job to be had in Chic'ry, o' course. The only jobs were in the cities, and Miz Tullie, she'd never be able to live in the city. She's got Delta in her blood. I figgered the two of them realized it was hopeless, and jes' decided to go their separate ways. There was stories, o' course, but they was prob'ly jes' tales. You know, guys gettin' drunk and talkin'."

"Did you ever hear about a divorce?"

"No, cain't say I did." He eyed me narrowly. "What's behind all these questions? What're you gettin' at, China?"

"What I'm getting at," I said, "is that Aunt Tullie had a child, a daughter, in 1942. The baby was placed in a New Orleans orphanage, and adopted. She died a few years ago, but her daughter—a woman named Amanda Gleason—has been searching for her mother's family for years. And now she's found us. She's Aunt Tullie's granddaughter."

The Colonel pulled in his breath and whistled it out. "Well, I'll be danged," he said softly. "I'll be *gol*danged." He thought for a minute, sucking on his cigar. "You sure about this? There's quite a bit of money involved, y'know. Miz Tullie's estate is gonna be worth a fair amount."

"We'll know more when Amanda produces the documentation," I said. "She obtained her mother's birth certificate from the parish registry in Louisiana. And she's tested postive for Huntington's. If there's any doubt, a DNA test would resolve it."

The Colonel shook his head slowly. "Cain't argue with that, I reckon. My lord, who'd've guessed it?" He was silent for a moment, and then asked: "What does Miz Tullie say about all this?"

"I wanted to piece together more of the story before we broke the news to her." I paused. "There's one thing more, Colonel. If I told you that Brent Holland died and was buried at Jordan's Crossing in 1946, would you care to hazard a guess as to how he died?"

He gaped at me. "Died . . . and was *buried*?"

I jerked my thumb over my shoulder. "At the foot of the garden," I said grimly. "Beside the old wooden pergola. He was dug up in 1963. I know, because I saw it, one night that summer. Marie Louise LaTour told me that Aunt Tullie had him reburied in the Coldwell family cemetery, and I found his grave there last night."

"Sweet Jesus," he breathed. "So Tullie's brother really did it, after all."

Now it was my turn to stare. "My *grandfather* killed him?"

The Colonel's mouth turned down at the corners. "Well, I cain't say that for a fact, o' course. Howard told me once that Clancy had ordered him to shoot Brent. Said he'd done it, too, jes' the way his daddy told him. But I figgered it was the bottle talkin'. When your grandfather got drunk, his stories were pretty wild. I never knew whether to believe him or not."

I stared at him, half-sick, not knowing what to say.

He looked at the tip of his cigar. "So Brent was murdered after all," he muttered to himself. "I'll be a son of a gun." He shook his head and repeated it, amazed.

"I'll be a son of a gun."

Chapter Sixteen

For a poultice, a mixture was made of 2 parts ground slippery elm bark, 2 parts corn meal, and 1 part each of bloodroot, blue flag, ragweed, chickweed, and burdock, with warm water added to the required consistency. This was used on fresh wounds, abscesses, inflammation, congestion, eruptions, and swollen glands.

Alma R. Hutchens
Indian Herbalogy of North America

Bloodroot contains alkaloids similar to those of the opium poppy, including sanguinarine, which can depress the central nervous system. Overdoses cause vomiting, irritation of mucous membranes, diarrhea, fainting, shock, and coma. Most poisonings reported were from medicinal preparations.

Steven Green and Roger Caras
Venomous Animals & Poisonous Plants

When the Colonel had driven off, I turned and stood looking at the Big House, thinking of the terrible secrets hidden under its silent roof, concealed within its walls, buried in the vast, green land itself: land that had been stolen from its Indian owners by a Coldwell; tended by Coldwell slaves under a monstrous system that deprived human beings of their liberty; stolen again by another Coldwell from his half-brother; and used as a secret burial ground for the body of a murdered man—and these were only the crimes I had uncovered. The land itself was innocent; like the Indians and the slaves brought here from their homeland, it was a victim of Coldwell outrages and iniquities that brooded over us all like a savage, unrepentant ghost. What would it take to purge these stains, wash away the spilled blood? In the shadow of those awful questions, it didn't take much to imagine that Aunt Tullie's disease was the retribution imposed upon all Coldwells by those whose land and liberty and lives we had taken.

Somberly, I stuck my hands in my pockets and walked around the house. I opened the back door and went into the kitchen, where Darlene was just finishing up the breakfast dishes—by herself, since Alice Ann had quit. She looked quizzically at me when I came into the room.

"Well?" she demanded. "You gonna tell me what that deputy was doin' here this morning?"

I picked up the coffeepot and poured a cup. "Remember what I told you last night? About Aunt Tullie smacking Wiley on Saturday, a few hours before he died? The deputy was here to take a statement from her." I held up the pot. "Want a cup?"

"Sure," Darlene said. She dried her hands on her apron. "I hope it went okay."

"As well as could be expected." I added sugar and cream—real cream, which I never have at home—and sat down at the table. "Even if the blow she struck is ruled a contributing cause of his death, I don't think the county attorney will attempt to prosecute her."

"That's good," Darlene said. She brought the coffeepot to the table and poured a mug for herself. "That poor old lady's got enough problems without havin' to go to court."

I looked at her. "The best way I know to untangle a knotty mess of facts is to talk them over with somebody else," I said. "I'm trying to make sense out of a story I've picked up in bits and pieces. Mind if I tell it to you? It might help me get it straight."

"Well, sure." She sat down. "Stories are my life's blood, you know. This a good one?"

I sighed. "It's certainly complicated enough. You'll have to judge whether it's good." I began with the tale Amanda had told us last night, adding the story of Tullie and Brent and including the chapter the Colonel had told me just a little while before. In an effort to get it all clear in my mind, I told her everything I knew, including the name of Brent's killer. The only thing I left out was the part about Huntington's disease, which just might be the family's well-earned curse. I was a character in that part of the story, and I wasn't ready to share it just yet. I didn't think I could bear seeing the undisguised pity on Darlene's face, and hearing the echo of her unspoken question, the question that had no answer: *Is China going to end up like poor Miz Tullie?*

Darlene evidently thought it was a good story, or at least suspenseful, because she was hanging on every word long before I came to the end. "Wow," she whispered reverently, when I was finished. "Whoever said that life is stranger than fiction got it right, huh? Never in a million years could I have thought up a plot like this one. A forbidden love affair, a clandestine marriage, a baby given up for adoption, even a *murder!*" She shook her head. "So

Clancy ordered his son-in-law's execution, huh? Momma always said the older that man got, the more pure devil there was in him. Good thing he didn't live any longer than he did. Lord knows what other wickedness he might've dreamed up."

I thought of what I had learned from Pearl's journal the night before. The devil that was in Clancy had raged there a long time before he directed his son to murder his daughter's husband. It was in him when he forced his half-brother Tobias to surrender the land their father had given him, and when he brought all that misery and anguish to Pearl. But that early family history had no bearing on the story I was telling, so I'd left it out.

Darlene was still shaking her head. "Poor Miz Tullie. Do you think she had any notion what a terrible thing her father had done?"

"I don't know," I said. "I'm sure she had no inkling that Brent was buried in the garden until she and Marie Louise and Old Homer dug him up in 1963. But whether she knew or even suspected that her father had ordered her brother to kill him—"

I stopped. Leatha had said that Tullie had been a happy young woman before the war. Was it the twin losses of her husband and child that had turned her so dour and morose? Or was it the knowledge that her father and brother had murdered the man she loved? And if she knew how Brent Holland died, when did she find this out?

A shadow darkened the light. Darlene and I looked up to see Judith framed in the doorway. Seeing her, I was reminded of the last time we'd talked, the day before, and I knew what I wanted to ask her. But not right away. She clearly had something else on her mind.

"Well, hi, Jude," Darlene said cheerfully. "Thought

maybe you wasn't comin' to work this mornin'." She nodded at the coffeepot. "Pour yourself a cup and sit down."

Judith found a mug, filled it, and dropped into a chair. "I've been at the college. I did what you said. I ran down a couple of Dawn's friends—girls I'd met when we were together—and talked to them." I noticed that her face was pale and her eyes had a wild, angry look. "I am so damned *stupid*. I should have suspected that something like this was going on."

"Suspected?" Darlene asked. "Something like what?"

Judith seemed to brace herself, as if she knew that there was chaos and darkness in the answer to Darlene's question. "Dawn was seeing somebody else. They were obviously . . . having sex. He got her pregnant."

Darlene was staring at her, dumbfounded. "Pregnant? *Dawn*?"

"Yeah, right," Judith said bitterly. She made a gesture of futility. "Pregnant. Expecting a baby. She wasn't too far along, either. Three months, maybe four. Can you beat that? Here I was, thinking that it was just the two of us, and all the while she—" She broke off, looking at me as if she'd just realized I was there.

"China knows." Darlene was matter-of-fact. "She guessed, even before I told her." She smiled slightly. "You haven't exactly gone to great lengths to hide it, you know."

Judith turned her head aside in a gesture of pain and desperation. "I just don't understand," she said brokenly. "I was so sure she *wanted* to be with me. We had so many plans. She told me she loved me, right up to the end. I swear, I never even suspected she was involved with somebody else, especially a *man*." The word seemed to burn her tongue like poison. "I've been betrayed."

"So where has she gone?" I asked quietly.

"Gone?" She gave me a withering look. "How the hell should I know? It doesn't matter, anyway. She's . . . gone, that's all. Like Alice Ann says, she's run off somewhere. I guess she decided she couldn't face me or face what she'd done. Or maybe she ran off with him, whoever he is." She dropped her head into her hands, tormenting herself. "That's probably what happened," she said in a muffled voice. "The two of them went off somewhere together. Hell, maybe they even got married."

"I know this isn't any of my business," I said, "but if I were you, I'd have another talk with Alice Ann. There might be an entirely different explanation for all this, you know."

Judith looked up, glaring at me. "Different?" she growled. "Like what?"

"Like maybe Dawn has gone somewhere to get an abortion," I said. "I'm just guessing, of course, but it could be that she's planning to come back and go on, just like you were before."

"That's right, Jude," Darlene said. "It's a possibility you ought to consider."

Judith frowned, fierce and disdainful. "Go on, just like before? Come on, get real! If Dawn meant to come back, she would've told me why she was going, where she was going, when she'd be back. She had to know I'd be frantic."

"Frantic? Is that what it is?" I gave her a small smile. "Maybe she knew you'd be *jealous*. Maybe she'd already broken up with the baby's father and didn't want you to know because she was afraid you couldn't handle it.

Maybe she figured that the only way she could hold onto your relationship was to get an abortion and keep you in the dark about it."

Judith stared at me, afraid to hope. "Do you think so?" she whispered. "Do you really think that's what happened?"

"I don't know," I said honestly. "I don't know Dawn or what kind of person she is. But there's always another side to every story. Before you make any judgments about what she's done, you ought to hear what *she* has to say."

"I agree with China, Jude," Darlene said firmly. "You need to have another talk with Alice Ann. She and Dawn are close. If you confront her with what you heard from Dawn's friends, she'll have to tell you what she knows. And I'll bet she knows where Dawn is at this very moment."

After a brief, deep silence, Judith said, in a low voice: "All right, I'll do it." Her lips tightened in a wry and painful smile. "And I won't let on that I'm every bit as crazy jealous as Dawn knew I'd be."

Darlene put her hand on Judith's arm. "Don't think about her being pregnant," she said. "Just think about her being in trouble, and needing you to help her get through a bad time."

"Right." Judith's tight face loosened and tears brimmed in her eyes. "Thanks," she said gratefully. She pushed her untouched coffee away and rose, putting her hand on Darlene's shoulder and looking at me. "Thanks, both of you."

I put my hand out. "Before you go," I said, "there's something I've been wondering. It's about Wiley."

I could sense, rather than see, the tensing of Darlene's muscles. Judith's head came up quickly.

"What about him?" And again there was that same

fierce, inward-turning look of concentration, as if she were remembering something she had seen or heard, and with it a look of quickly suppressed jubilation. I had the idea that my unexpected question had reminded her of something she had almost forgotten, or perhaps tucked away in the back of her mind to be attended to later, after she had located Dawn.

"What about him?" she repeated brusquely.

"When I told you yesterday about his drowning, I got the feeling that you might know something." I made my voice casual, but I was watching her carefully. "Like maybe you saw him driving down toward the fishing camp on Saturday night. Like maybe there was somebody with him."

She shrugged and a mask slipped over her features. "Uh-uh," she said briefly, shaking her head.

I leaned forward, no longer casual. "If you saw anything at all, no matter how trivial, it might be important. The police took a statement from Aunt Tullie this morning."

That got her attention. "But they can't possibly think *she* had anything to do with it!" she exclaimed. "She's a sick old lady. She gets pretty upset sometimes, but she couldn't—"

"But they *do* think she was involved," I said. "They know that Wiley was here, and that she hit him with her cane hard enough to knock him out. The autopsy report says that he suffered a concussion. The cops figure that she contributed to his death." Ignoring Darlene's questioning glance, I paused to let that sink in. "If you have any information that might help explain what really happened, I'd sure like to know. It could take Aunt Tullie off the hook."

She was torn between her gratitude to Aunt Tullie for giving her a place to live and some private reluctance. After a moment of silent struggle, she said, almost sullenly, "I didn't see him or his truck. But I did see somebody walking back along that road late Saturday night, in the direction of the highway."

"Oh, yeah?" Darlene asked. "Who?"

"Who do you think?" Judith pushed her chair away from the table and stood up. "May Rose, that's who. Dawn's mother."

"May Rose," Darlene said blankly, when Judith had gone. "What on earth could she have to do with Wiley?"

"Who knows?" I said. I gave a dismissive wave. "Maybe Judith just thought she saw her."

"Or maybe," Darlene said quietly, "Judith really did see her, and now she realizes she's got some leverage."

"Maybe you should be writing murder mysteries. But I'll pass it along to the deputy, just in case."

Darlene raised her eyebrows, but that was all. We talked a little longer, then she went home to work on her book. I had planned to spend the rest of the morning reading Pearl's journal, but now I had something else on my mind. I went outside and walked through the garden, looking at Judith's neat, well-tended beds and the variety of plants she had brought in. There was no doubt about it—she had a green thumb and a garden-designer's eye.

But I wasn't here to admire the garden. I was looking for the path, the one that Darlene and Wiley and I used to take to the fishing camp, a half-mile or so away. I expected it to be completely overgrown by now, an impenetrable tangle of elder bushes and ground willow and poison ivy, so I wasn't hoping for much. But when I found it at last, hidden behind a large rhododendron that was smothered with pink blossoms, I saw to my surprise that someone—Judith, I supposed—had cleared the path and kept it clear. While the hummocky, soggy trail wasn't exactly easy walking, the only serious problems were an occasional bush slapping my face and the incessant mosquitoes that kept me busy slapping at them.

After a few yards, the wilderness closed around me in a dim green gloom, as if I were under water. The day was cloudy, and what little light filtered through the clouds was filtered again through a layered canopy of green leaves. The only open space was the path ahead, like a winding corridor between walls of trees. To the left was the swamp that edged the Bloodroot, its shallow water black and still, studded with the stumps of downed cypress and home to unthinkable hundreds of water moccasins and copperheads and rattlers. I heard the chittering of a chickadee and caught a glimpse of a large woodpecker hammering on the trunk of a dead sweet-gum tree. To the right, the land rose up, the dense woodland lit here and there by saucer-sized blooms of viburnum, glowing in the dimness. It was easy to imagine that this was the same landscape that Judith's great-great-grandmother had seen as she walked along the bank of the Bloodroot, easy to think that she would find this path familiar. Which might be why Judith had cut it here, I thought: so she could walk through the forest as Rachel Weaver had walked here—except that a century and a half ago, you wouldn't be walking this path without a shotgun to defend yourself from the wild creatures and from the likes of Jed Coldwell. Now, there were no bears, no panthers, and very little to be afraid of, as long as you watched out for the snakes.

And yet, I reflected as the trees thinned and the path

opened out into the clearing around the fishing camp, a man had died here. And easy as it might be to accept the official explanation—that Wiley passed out from the concussion Aunt Tullie had given him and his truck slid into the river—I was having trouble with it, mostly because I couldn't quite imagine what Wiley Beauchamp was doing here on a Saturday night, and why he had come here alone.

But *had* he been alone? The passenger door had been open. I stood on the grassy ramp and thought about this as the brown river, the color and consistency of a chocolate milkshake, slipped slowly and silently past. And if Judith was telling the truth, May Rose had been here with him, or at least nearby. But the two of them hadn't been fishing, because there was no fishing tackle in the truck. Maybe they'd come to enjoy the mouse-eaten bunk in the old cabin, as he and Darlene once had. That wasn't such a farfetched idea, actually. He had his share of ladyfriends, the Colonel had said. Maybe May Rose was one of them. Did they have a lovers' quarrel? Had May Rose done whatever it took to put Wiley and his truck into the river?

I turned to my left and began to walk upstream toward the edge of the clearing, my eyes on the ground. I had no idea what I was looking for—certainly not telltale footprints or marks of a struggle, for the soft earth was crisscrossed by the raw scars of truck tires and tramping feet, mute testimony to the rescue party's work on Wednesday night. Here, a truck had gotten stuck in the mud, the back tires spinning out a deep cut. There, someone had slipped and fallen down the bank, leaving a trail of broken grass and leaves.

As I glanced in that direction, however, a silvery glint

caught my eye. I stepped closer and saw a silver chain caught on a bush. I went down on one knee and teased it free. The cheap chain had not been unfastened, but broken. From it hung a small silver-plated medallion, the silver rubbed through from much wearing, a heart engraved on one side and an inscription on the other. Holding it by the chain to avoid smudging any prints, I looked at it carefully. Some of the letters were out of line, as if it had been stamped by one of those engraving machines they used to have in Woolworth's back in the early sixties, where you put in a dime and turned a lever to stamp each letter. "To Juliet from Romeo," it said.

Romeo. The photograph of a shy young Wiley on Darlene's shelf, "from Romeo" written in the corner. Darlene saying, "When I was in high school, we put on *Romeo and Juliet*. Momma, she flat loved it. Cried buckets when May Rose died. She was Juliet."

I⊤ was still early in the afternoon. I didn't think May Rose would be at home, but it was worth a try. Alice Ann might be around if her mother wasn't—or I might even get lucky and find Dawn there. I didn't. The garage was empty, the door was locked, the drapes were drawn. If mother or daughter was hiding inside, she didn't come to the door when I knocked. For good measure, I went around the back and banged at the back door. Still no response.

I went back out to the car, turned the key, and made a complete circle around the block, parking a couple of doors down from May Rose's house, where I could watch the front door without being seen. After five minutes, I put the car in gear and drove away.

*   *   *

MARIE Louise's chickens were still scratching in the front yard and the canary was warbling inside when I rapped on the screen door. This time, the canary kept on singing until Marie Louise said, "You jes' *hush*."

When she came to the door, she didn't say hello or even seem surprised to see me. She just pushed open the screen and said, "Dat bird, he'd sing till de Resurrection, if somebody didn't throw somethin' over him." I glanced at the cage in the corner of the small living room. A green pillowcase hung over it, and the bird was cheeping sullenly.

"I found the grave," I said, "and the double marker. I'd like to know the rest of the story. Will you tell me?"

"I'm fixin' me a cool glass o' lemonade," she said. "You want one?" Without answering me or waiting for my answer, she beckoned me to come after her through the house: the living room, followed by an even smaller dining room, followed by a kitchen. A pink-flowered curtain was looped to one side of the doorway at the back of the kitchen, and through it I could see a bedroom with a chenille-covered bed beside the open back door. A typical shotgun cottage, one room wide and four rooms long, so-called because you could fire a shotgun in the front door and out the back.

But for all its miniature size, the place was cozy: the kitchen windows hung with blue-checked curtains, the table and two chairs freshly painted white, a braided rug on the floor in front of the sink, a bowl of red peonies on the kitchen table. Marie Louise shuffled to the small refrigerator, took out a pitcher, and poured two glasses of lemonade. She brought them to the table, then a plate with three cold biscuits and a knife. I took one chair, she took the other.

I raised my voice slightly. "I said that I found Brent Holland's grave, in the Coldwell cemetery. I've also found out that Aunt Tullie had his baby, a little girl, and put her up for adoption."

"There's no call t' shout," Marie Louise said mildly. She pushed a beehive-shaped yellow ceramic honey pot toward me. "They wuz married in N'Awlins in March of 1942. The little girl wuz born dere in December. Her name was Enid. Miz Tullie, she named her after Mister Brent's dead momma."

Enid. Enid Freeman Gleason, Amanda had said. The Freemans had retained the baby's birth name when they adopted her. I sipped my lemonade. It was cold and tart, just sweet enough. "Why didn't Aunt Tullie keep her?"

"Why?" Marie Louise rolled her eyes. "Cain't you guess, girl? Where's yore brains? That father o' hers, he wuz de reason why. Said he wuzn't gonna have no Beauchamp baby livin' in a Coldwell house. Tol' her to git rid o' hit. Have an abortion." She shook her head darkly. "Dat Clancy, he wuz a mean man, an' poor Miz Tullie, she was near scairt to death o' him. But she wuzn't gwine to kill her baby, 'cause dat was a pure sin. So her 'n' me, we took de bus to N'Awlins an' stayed in a roomin' house till hit was her time. When de little girl was born, I took her to de sisters at St. Anne's, and me 'n' Miz Tullie rode de bus back home. Mister Clancy, he never said a word, jes tol' her to take off her hat and git on with her work, and dat was de end of hit. Almost," she added, so low that I wasn't sure I was supposed to hear.

I broke open a biscuit and drizzled honey on it with a spoon. The honey had the scent of lavender, and when I tasted it, the flavor of lavender, warmed by the sun. "And then what? What happened after Brent Holland came home from the war?"

A fly buzzed against the screen. The old woman shifted in her chair, her eyes lowered, not meeting my gaze.

"Colonel Blakeslee says he knows what happened," I said softly. "My grandfather told him."

Her glance came up to my face. Her mouth was twisted to one side. "Hit's a shame to say," she replied disgustedly, "but yore gran'paw wuz a no-count drunk. Didn't do one lick o' work around dat place. If'n Miz Tullie hadn't been such a good hand to keep things up, de Chic'ry bank would've come in an' took over, long time ago."

She picked up her glass and drank thirstily, the pale liquid dribbling down her chin. She wiped it with the back of her hand and added emphatically, "*Course* he done hit. Mister Howard, he allus did what his daddy said, no matter what. Hit happened on July 4, on de annivers'ry of de fall of Vicksburg, at dat old fishin' camp on de Bloodroot. Howard 'n' Homer got Mister Brent drunk, and when he passed out, yore gran'paw, he picked up his pistol an' fired hit straight into Mister Brent's heart. Dey loaded him on a cart and drug him up to de house and—"

"And buried him beside the old pergola," I said quietly. Inside, I felt sick. The nightmare that had haunted me— the dark figures clustered at the foot of the garden, Aunt Tullie's grief, the bony hand—was nothing compared to this monstrous truth.

"Dat's right." She reached for the flyswatter hanging on the wall between a calendar from Bygoods Feed Store and a plastic-framed picture of Jesus. "Homer, he planted a bed of iris on top o' pore Mister Brent. Bloomed right purty fer years, until Miz Tullie made Homer dig him up." With expert aim, Marie Louise smacked the fly that was crawling across the table. "But you know dat part already, 'cause you wuz dere dat night." She made a face. "Shouldn't've been, but you wuz. Gracious sakes, you wuz curious. Allus wantin' to know what wuz what. Never would take no fer an answer."

"How did Aunt Tullie find out where he was buried?"

"Her brother Howard, he tol' her, on his deathbed."

On his deathbed. Of course—now I remembered. I had been at Jordan's Crossing that night without Leatha, because my mother was at the hospital, where my grandfather was dying.

"Yessiree, he tole her." Marie Louise chuckled darkly. "Reckon he figgered hit was his last chance to git straight wi' de folks he'd wronged, afore de good Lord took him outta dis life."

Or get back at someone he resented, I thought. The disclosure hardly seemed like an act of kindness. If he had truly loved his sister, it would have been better to have died with it on his conscience.

"Hit didn't do one bit o' good, though," Marie Louise added serenely. "I got faith in de Lord's good judgment. Mister Howard, he's fryin' in de fires of hell, right next to his daddy, both of 'em jes' cookin' away, like catfish fryin' in hot fat."

So Howard had told his sister what he had done, and she'd come back to Jordan's Crossing and compelled Old Homer to dig up her husband's body. It was all beginning to come clear now, except for one more thing.

"Back in 1946, when my grandfather shot Brent Holland—did Aunt Tullie know about it?" I asked.

Marie Louise shook her head. "She only knew what her daddy tol' her."

"Which was—"

The old woman didn't answer right away. When she did, her voice was bitter. "He tol' her dat he paid Mister Brent five hunnert dollars in cash to leave dis place an' never come back."

My breath caught in my throat. What a contemptible lie! With his words, Clancy had not only obliterated all his daughter's hopes of happiness, but had condemned her to a lifetime's belief that her husband had allowed himself to be bought off, that he had traded her heart for five hundred dollars. I wasn't sure which was worse, the murder or the lie. Together, they were almost too awful to imagine.

"But Miz Tullie got her revenge, God bless her," Marie Louise said, with grim satisfaction. She reached for the plate of biscuits and the honey pot.

"She did?" I asked, startled. This had escaped me. "How?"

She squinted at me, her grin showing stained teeth. "I would of thought you'd of figgered dat out, too, whiles you wuz up at de graveyard, stirrin' up dem ghosts." She paused. "D'you know what day it was dat Mister Clancy died?"

"Clancy? I don't think I—" I frowned. "Yes, as a matter of fact, I saw it on his monument last night. July 10, 1946." Then my mouth dropped open and I sat there, stunned. He'd died on July 10, only six days after he had ordered his son to shoot his daughter's husband.

I lowered my voice as if we were conspirators in the

crime. "Are you saying that Aunt Tullie got her revenge by *killing* her father?"

Marie Louise shrank back with a horrified look. "Now, how I gwine know a thing like dat? I wuzn't dere when hit happened, wuz I?" She popped a piece of biscuit into her mouth and chewed reflectively for a moment before she said, "All I know fer sure is, two days before dat wicked old man fin'ly give up de ghost, somebody dug up a mess of dem bloodroots out by de 'zalea bushes."

I stared at her. "Bloodroot? But it's *poisonous*."

"It'll shore kill you if'n you git enough of it," Marie Louise agreed cheerfully. "My momma used to make hit up with cornmeal and slip'ry elm in a poultice for cuts and abscesses, but she never would give hit by mouth, fer fear of givin' too much."

"I see," I said quietly. I wondered if Howard had any suspicions about what had happened to his father—although there would have been no easy way of proving it, under the circumstances.

There was a moment's silence while Marie Louise licked the honeyed crumbs off her fingers. "By de way, dat double marker in de cemetery? She tole me she put a paper with her will, sayin' she wants to be buried 'longside Mister Brent. She wants her name on dat marker, too. Missus Petulia Holland."

"If that's what she wants, that's what she'll have," I said.

The old woman gave me a crooked smile. "Well, Miz Smarty-pants, you ever figger out who else is wantin' to know 'bout Mister Brent?"

I straightened up. This was one question I could answer. "Yes," I said. "Her name is Amanda. She's Enid's daughter. She's been searching for her mother's family for several years, and now she's found us." I paused. "How did you know about Amanda?"

"I don't know how I knows, I jes' knows," the old woman said. "My momma had de gift, an' she 'queathed it to me, 'long with her good looks." She sat for a moment, her eyes shut. Then she opened them and a wide grin split her wrinkled brown face. "Enid's girl," she said happily. "I been waitin' fer dis day ever since I left dat little girl wit dem nuns. Thank you, Lord!" She lifted her eyes and raised her hands. "De Lord be praised!"

I wondered if she would still be praising the Lord if I told her about the disease that Aunt Tullie had passed on to her daughter and granddaughter—the disease that Leatha and I might also have inherited, along with the other tragedies the Coldwells had handed down as part of our bloody inheritance.

But as we said good-bye at the front door, Marie Louise had the last word, even more oblique than usual and delivered with an inscrutable look. "Dat other thing you's worryin' 'bout," she remarked, "hit's gwine to be all right. You can rest easy. Miz Tullie, she ain't who you think she is."

"Excuse me?" I said, surprised. What was *that* supposed to mean?

But she had closed the door in my face, and I was left with yet another unanswered question.

Chapter Seventeen

One legend associated with the lily of the valley comes from Sussex, England. The hermit St. Leonard battled a dragon that was the devil in disguise. He struggled for four days and finally summoned the strength to cut off the dragon's head, not before, however, his adversary's strong claws had torn through his armor and spilled his blood. Lilies of the valley sprang up from the drops of blood, and pilgrims to the site could trace the path through the fields and woods where the battle had raged. Every year since, lilies of the valley bloom each May on the battleground.

Bobby J. Ward
A Contemplation Upon Flowers

White bud! thou'rt emblem of a lovelier thing:
The broken spirit that its anguish bears
To silent shades, and there sits offering
To Heaven the holy fragrance of its tears.

George Croly, nineteenth-century poet
"The Lily of the Valley"

 It was after one o'clock, and Marie Louise's honey biscuit, tasty as it was, hadn't gone very far toward filling me up. So I stopped at Elmer's Bar-B-Q and got a combo plate: spicy sausage, saucy ribs, red beans, and coleslaw. Elmer's has occupied the same run-down frame building in Chicory ever since I was a kid, with a worn linoleum floor, a fly-specked front window, and a cork bulletin board layered with items of local interest: a photo of a missing hound dog named Booter, an ad for a milk goat for sale, a flyer inviting everybody (especially sinners) to attend next week's Baptist revival.

But it's not class that accounts for Elmer's longevity, it's good down-home cookin' and lots of it. You pick up your loaded paper plate (piled with enough chow to fill up a starving company of Confederate soldiers), pour yourself a quart jar of iced tea, and carry all this to one of the pine picnic tables, where generations of Chicory folks have carved their initials into the wood.

The place was almost empty, so I found a spot under one of the lazily turning ceiling fans and ate slowly, savoring my food and thinking about my conversation with Marie Louise. The old woman had cleared up the rest of the mystery surrounding the death of Brent Holland. I knew who had killed him and why and where, and how he had come to be buried in the garden. But Marie Louise's hints about the bloodroot had given me something new and compelling to think about: the possibility that a despairing Aunt Tullie, believing that her father had enticed her husband to abandon her, had poisoned the old man. And if that's what she had done, I thought bleakly, I certainly couldn't blame her. I had read enough of Pearl's journal to know that Clancy had been a thoroughly bad character long before Brent Holland had the misfortune to fall in love with his daughter.

I was still thinking about this latest plot twist in the

bloody saga of the Coldwell family when a heavyset, moon-faced woman in a green apron came over with a pitcher of iced tea. Her name—Marge—was embroidered in flowing script across the bib of her apron. I put my hand over the top of my glass to signal that one quart of tea was enough, remarked that the ribs I'd just eaten were the absolute best I'd had since the last time I was here, and let her take my empty plate.

Then, prompted by a sudden intuition, I said, "Too bad about Wiley Beauchamp, wasn't it, Marge?"

She frowned as she collected my used silverware, as if I might be a Yankee spy, and I added, slipping into the slow and easy dialect of my youth: "Wiley and me, we used to hunt snakes 'long the Bloodroot, way back, when we was kids. I was real sad when I heard he got drownded."

Her suspicions vanished. "Yeah, me too. I was shocked near to death when I heard. Wiley, he used to come here lots. Allus got a double on ribs and a couple of Buds. Matter of fact, he was here on Sattidy evenin', havin' an early supper." Sadly, she pointed to a table by the window. "Sat right there, he did. Said he wanted to keep a eye on that fine new truck of his. Make sure none of them motorcycle kids dinged it. They got a habit of parkin' too close." She fished in her apron pocket for my ticket. "You want a piece of pie, hon? We still got some lemon meringue."

"Lemon meringue, huh? That plate filled me up, but you might could fix it to go." I pushed back the bench and stood up. "Guess I can't think of a better place to eat my last meal," I said, with a little laugh. "I sure hope Wiley got a piece of pie. And I hope he didn't have to eat it alone."

"O 'course he got pie. Coc'nut cream." Marge cast a prissy look at Wiley's empty table. "And I never saw that man eat alone, not once. Them girls, they was after him, big time. You can bet there's some broken hearts in Chic'ry, now that Wiley Beauchamp's gone to his reward."

I followed her as she carried my dishes back to the counter, dumped the paper plate in the trash, and dropped the silver into a sink of soapy water. "I wonder, did May Rose happen to be with him that night?"

"May Rose?" Marge opened the glass pie cabinet. The slice of lemon pie, its meringue a lofty caramel-tinged white cloud, was large enough for two people. "Oh, my stars, no. Wiley, he liked 'em a lot younger'n her." She put the pie into a box and handed it to me over the counter. "It was Alice Ann came in here and sat down with him that night—although I got to say, in my 'pinion, she was a mite *too* young for him." She took my money and headed to the cash register, an old manual model that was probably even older than the one I had at Thyme and Seasons. "I'm sure her momma wouldn't of liked it much," she added, ringing my ticket with two fingers. "And I cain't say as I blame her. Wiley was old enough to be her daddy."

I pocketed my change. "Thanks, Marge," I said. "That was a great meal."

"Have a good one," she replied cheerfully. "Come back 'n' see us, now, y'hear?"

On my way back to Jordan's Crossing, I swung by May Rose's house and rapped on the door again, with more urgency this time. If May Rose wasn't home, I'd settle for Alice Ann. My curiosity was about to get the better of me. Exactly what was the connection between Wiley and May Rose—and Alice Ann?

But the house was still closed up and there was no answer to my knock, except from the next-door neighbor. She was out with a broom, sweeping the leaves off her front walk.

"They won't be home till after six," she called helpfully, over the hedge. "Alice Ann is in school, and May Rose is at work. I ain't seen Dawn around for a while."

I thanked her and got back in the car and drove home. I wasn't expecting Leatha and Aunt Tullie before early evening, so I put the pie in the refrigerator, went upstairs to my room, and opened the windows to the afternoon breeze. Then I took Pearl's journal out of the drawer in the bedside table and carried it to the rocking chair. When the storm had knocked the electricity out the night before, I had just gotten to the part where Clancy had blackmailed Tobias into giving back the land by framing him with a fraudulent charge of embezzlement—if you believed Tobias, that is. Of course, he could have been lying. But knowing what I now knew about my great-grandfather, I was inclined to give Tobias the benefit of the doubt. A man who could order his daughter's husband's murder could hardly be trusted to do the right thing by his bastard half-brother. I still felt sick when I thought about what Clancy had done to Brent and Tullie.

I turned the pages, found the place where I'd left off, and continued reading Pearl's story, written in her steeply slanting script in faded sepia ink.

And that is how Clancy, who at the time of this occurrence was scarcely 25 to Tobias's 37, dispos-

sessed his half-brother of his birthright. Worse yet, Clancy (since without his brother's skills & experience, the plantation was likely to fail) forced Tobias to remain as his manager, on the threat of bringing charges of embezzlement if he should ever attempt to leave. And as Tobias says, he knew those charges would follow him to the ends of the earth, so he had no choice but to stay and work for the brother whom he now hated with all his heart.

And worst of all, when Abner's grand mansion burned & was to be rebuilt, Clancy determined to construct it on the ground his father had given to his brother: a flagrant & contemptuous gesture which (as Tobias says) has been an affront & an insult to him every day since the house was built. For each time he enters to do the business of the plantation he is forced to say to himself: this is my brother's house, built on land he has stolen from me, & I am powerless to get it back.

I put my finger on the page to hold my place and looked out the window, wondering which of these men must have hated the other more: Clancy for the love and preference his father had shown toward Tobias, or Tobias for the terrible wrongs Clancy had done him. And yet they had worked together every day of every year until one of them died.

But this was the kind of poisonous hatred that could outlive even death, I thought sadly. And God only knew what other crimes it had brewed, what other ways it had warped these men's lives. I went back to Pearl's narrative.

As I have said, this long and bitter enmity between Clancy and Tobias began before I was born & even longer before 1908, the year when I was married to

Clancy. Our marriage was not of my choosing (although I suppose this hardly matters), for Clancy was thirty years my senior & my father's friend, not mine. I must confess that the difference in our ages did not so much matter to me at that time, for Clancy was a handsome man even at 53 & (yes I must confess this also) quite a wealthy man, which pleased my father and of course myself. He offered me his heart & this house, which he had built for his first wife, Margaret, whom he wed the year after his father's death & whom he divorced after twenty-five years of a childless marriage on charges of unfaithfulness.

I paused again. I had completely forgotten about Margaret, who had never figured in our family's story because she had not produced an heir and because Clancy had divorced her on the grounds of infidelity, some time around 1905. It had been a great local scandal, apparently, and I had never heard Margaret spoken of except in whispers. But now that I knew about Clancy's other crimes, I wondered whether Margaret had been another one of his victims. Had Clancy framed her, as he had framed Tobias, so he would be free to marry a wife who could produce an heir to Jordan's Crossing? I went back to my reading.

But of course as I now know, words about love & fidelity come easily to a man when he is eager to marry & are as easily forgotten when the passion has passed and he has what he wants. And I was very young & had no experience with which to judge the truth of the things he told me (particularly about the reasons for his divorce) & no power to choose for myself or to resist his persuasions or those of my father & mother who desired the mar-

riage. And so I became his wife & have dutifully borne him four children—three sons, two of whom died before they walked and only Howard is now living, and one sweet daughter, Hattie. And these two dear, dear children I do regret to leave & would not if I could bear to stay behind with them, as a mother should.

But in my despair, I cannot. I cannot bear to be Clancy's wife now that I have heard Tobias's most recent & most awful revelations, which only confirm the suspicions I have lived with for nearly three years: that Clancy, not content with taking his brother's birthright and holding him in his employment as if he were a slave, has now got a child, called Petulia, on Tobias's wife Sapphire, our children's nursemaid.

I gasped. Aunt Tullie was *Sapphire's* daughter? It couldn't be! It wasn't possible! But Pearl's writing was clear and firm. She didn't seem delusional. She had to know who her children were. And Aunt Tullie herself, just yesterday, had made that odd remark about Pearl: *Anyway, she's not my mother.*

But if this were true, if Aunt Tullie was indeed Sapphire's daughter, how had she come to be so thoroughly accepted as a member of the family, a sister to Howard and Hattie? I hurried on:

There is no question in my mind that Petulia is Clancy's daughter, for she has his features and coloring, and not those of Tobias. Nor do Clancy's actions deny his paternity, for he clearly favors Sapphire's child and has brought her so often into this house as a playmate for Howard and Hattie that my children think of her as their little sister. And in-

deed, there may be other, older children of this liaison, for Tobias says that Clancy has lain with Sapphire often and it cannot be told which of the sons she has borne have been fathered by Clancy and which by Tobias. But Clancy has not lain with her out of love, I am sure (for Clancy is utterly incapable of love), but out of contempt for Tobias and a despicable imposition of la droite du seigneur, as was the taking of his brother's birthright and the building of this house upon the stolen birthright.

And now Sapphire has grown desperately ill with some terrible sort of disorder, St. Vitus dance or something dreadfully like it, and is no longer able to care for my children, or even for her own. Because of this illness, Clancy has brought his daughter Petulia to me to rear with Howard and Hattie as their sister, as our own child. But I refuse to accept this child who is inflicted upon me against my wishes, as Clancy imposed this house upon Tobias and his carnal will upon Tobias's wife. The girl would be a continual affront, an insult, a daily reminder of my husband's faithlessness and perfidy, and of my own weakness and inability to stand against him.

But I am not weak as Tobias has been weak, and I am not willing to endure the daily effrontery of Clancy's misbegotten child. And since I cannot take my own children and go (to whom would I go? my parents are dead and I have no family, no friends to provide any sort of hospice), I have determined to end my life. Clancy will see to the good care of his children, I have no doubt of that. But I refuse to live any longer the unwilling prisoner of my husband's will, or to seem by my silence to be complicit in his actions. And so I speak up here, in these pages, and through the act of taking my life, which

I intend to accomplish by some natural poison. I am
told that a strong tea brewed from the fresh leaves
of lilies of the valley . . .

And that was the end of it. After that last unfinished
sentence, the despairing cry of a woman who had reached
the end of her endurance, the remaining pages were blank.
They would stay that way for all eternity.

I sat there for a very long time, Pearl's journal on my
lap, poignantly aware that she had almost certainly written
those words in this very room, at the table that stood not
three feet away from me. And suddenly I was also aware
of the strong scent of lilies of the valley, *not* wafted
through the window, on the breeze that carried nothing
with it but the fresh scent of new-mown grass and the
shrill trilling of a wren, but behind me, in the room itself.
I turned swiftly, but there was nothing there, no soft
movement, no ghostly shape, no shadow—and then the
scent was gone, too, as swiftly as it had come.

Lily of the valley. Yes, lovely as the plant is, it can
also be a deadly poison. Before the foxglove, *Digitalis*
purpurea, became the best treatment for heart disease, lily
of the valley was widely known to be a useful cardiac
tonic. It is still used for this purpose by skilled herbal
practitioners. But it is also known to be extremely dangerous, its cardiac glycosides making it as deadly as digitalis in the hands of someone who doesn't know how to
use it, or who is bent on self-destruction. A strong tea
brewed from the leaves would almost certainly be fatal,
if you drank enough of it. I sat there for a long moment,
thinking how sad it was that Pearl's beloved lilies of the
valley—the plant she treasured, the fragrance that de-

lighted her—had also borne her down the silent path to death.

But if I trusted Pearl's own testimony, perhaps her death was not sad, for it was a release she sought from a life that burdened her, from a husband she had come to hate. And she had not gone silently after all, I thought, closing the book and holding it in my hands. She had left her story behind as a legacy, a witness to her determination to be her own woman, to set herself free. The greatest sadness lay in the fact that she couldn't find a different way to declare her independence.

And as I sat there, holding Pearl's journal, I realized that her story had yet another significance, perhaps the most important of all. It freed my mother and me from the awful possibility that one or both of us would inherit Aunt Tullie's disease. For if Tullie was Sapphire's daughter, she must have inherited Huntington's from her mother who, as Pearl wrote, had been desperately ill with "St. Vitus dance or something dreadfully like it." This meant that my grandfather, Pearl's son, did not have the gene, and that Leatha and I were not at risk!

I closed my eyes and felt the tears streaming down my cheeks, tears of relief and joy. Leatha would probably want to be tested to be sure, but I was confident that both of us were miraculously, blessedly free of what I had come to think of as the Coldwell curse.

And then I thought of something else. Since neither Howard nor his sister, Hattie—Pearl's children—had ever seemed to know that Tullie wasn't their full sister, it was quite likely that Tullie herself had not always known this. Once Pearl and Tobias and Sapphire were dead, only Clancy would have known whose daughter she was. Had he refused to allow Tullie and Brent to marry because he knew they were *related*? Brent was Sapphire's sister's son, according to Leatha, so he and Tullie would have been first cousins. And if Brent's mother had the Huntington's gene, too, it was entirely possible that Tullie's daughter, Enid, had inherited it from *both* her parents. Was that what Clancy had tried to prevent by refusing permission for the marriage? And when he discovered that they had married anyway and that Tullie was pregnant, by ordering her to get an abortion—and telling her why? And finally, when all his commands and edicts had failed, by directing his son to murder Brent Holland?

But while these questions took me a little further toward a possible understanding of Clancy Coldwell's motives, they were essentially unanswerable. I didn't know— I could *never* know what had compelled my great-grandfather to do the terrible things he had done all those years ago. His motives were lost forever, as lost as the Old South to which he and his father had given their hearts.

And there was something else I didn't know, either. The image of Marie Louise came into my mind, standing at her front door and saying, with that inscrutable look of hers: "Dat other thing you's worryin' 'bout, hit's gwine to be all right. You can rest easy. Miz Tullie, she ain't who you think she is."

Miz Tullie, she ain't who you think she is.

But how did Marie Louise know what I was worrying about? And how could she know who Aunt Tullie was?

How could she know? How could she *possibly* know?

Chapter Eighteen

Sir James Frazer, in *The Golden Bough*, suggests that
the tradition that mistletoe can extinguish fire may
be traced back to the Druids, who believed that the
herb was an emanation of lightning. In Scandana-
via, mistletoe was hung beside the hearth to contain
the blaze; in the American South, mistletoe was sus-
pended from the rafters of the home to protect it
from fire.

At five-thirty, I went down to the kitchen and made
a sandwich with some of the chicken salad Darlene
had left for our supper, and washed it down with a glass
of milk. I left a note for Leatha on the hall table, telling
her that there was lemon meringue pie in the fridge and
that I was leaving for Chicory to talk to May Rose. I was
heading for the door when the phone rang. I ran back to
the office to answer it.

"China," Darlene said abruptly, "I've been thinkin'
about what Judith said this morning. About seein' May
Rose walkin' back from the fishin' camp on Saturday
night. I'm thinkin' that it would be a good idea for you
and me to have a talk with May Rose."

"Well, maybe," I said cautiously. I hadn't intended to
take Darlene with me to confront May Rose with her me-

dallion, but it might not be a bad idea. "What do you think we'd accomplish?"

"Hell, I don't know." Darlene sounded frustrated. "All I know is, Wiley's dead and that woman maybe knows how he got that way. And she sure as the devil ain't gonna tell the sheriff."

"She probably won't tell us, either," I retorted. "It'll be a waste of time."

"I got time to waste." Darlene's voice was resigned. "I don't love Wiley anymore, but I sure hate to think of him drownin' in the river. With this on my mind, I can't write worth beans." She sighed. "But if you don't want to come, it's okay by me. I'll let you know tomorrow how it turns out."

"Hey," I said hastily, "I didn't say I didn't want to come. I just said we're probably wasting our time." This was true. I hadn't really expected May Rose to tell me anything—I just wanted to watch her face while she tried to come up with a lie that would explain how her medallion came to be snagged on a weed by the riverbank. "How about if I drive?" I added. "I can pick you up on the way into town."

And on the way to May Rose's house, I told her what I had found at the fishing camp.

THE drapes were still drawn, but there was a car in the drive and when Darlene knocked on the door, it was finally opened, as far as the chain would allow.

"Go away," Alice Ann said tearfully. "Go away, or I'll . . . I'll call the police."

"What?" Darlene asked. "What you talkin' 'bout, girl?

Open that door and let us in. We need to talk to your momma. It's important."

"Mom isn't here," Alice Ann said. "She went off with . . . Judith made her go—" She gulped back a sob. But it didn't stay gulped, and erupted in a cascade of half-hysterical wails.

Darlene was gruff. "Alice Ann, you open this door this minute, you hear? If you don't, I am gonna come through it, open or not." She raised her voice and slammed the flat of her hand against the door for emphasis. "And don't you think I won't, neither! You want your nice neighbors to see a black woman break down your door?"

Sobbing, Alice Ann opened the door and let us in.

Darlene and I gasped in unison. The living room was in shambles. A chair and the coffee table had been over-turned; a lamp lay on the floor, the shade askew, the bulb smashed; the TV stared blankly up at the ceiling; the phone cord had been ripped from the jack and the phone flung at the wall, where it had gouged a hole in the Sheet-rock.

"Hell's bells," Darlene said devoutly.

"Did your mother and Judith have a fight?" I asked Alice Ann.

Alice Ann stuffed her fist into her mouth, her eyes wide and frightened. Her face was so white that her freckles stood out like measles. Her pale hair was braided in strag-gly pigtails and she looked as if she were about twelve years old.

Darlene reached for her hand and jerked it out of her mouth. "Now, you listen to me, girl," she growled. "You tell us what happened here and you tell it fast and straight, or we're callin' the cops. And that ain't no empty threat, neither."

Alice Ann was trying to pull herself together. "No, don't," she begged. She swallowed her tears. "Judith swore she'd kill Mom if I called anybody!"

"Don't act like a stupid kid," Darlene snapped. "Judith ain't gonna kill *nobody*. She ain't got it in her."

"Why would she kill your mother, anyway?" I asked in a reasonable tone. "What's she mad at her for?"

Fighting for composure, Alice Ann turned to me as an ally in the face of Darlene's anger. "She's mad because she . . . because she thinks Mom knows where Dawn is. She's trying to make her tell."

"Well, does she?" I asked.

Alice Ann looked at me, her eyes red-rimmed, chewing on her lower lip. "Mom was going to tell her, but Judith blew up and pulled out a gun. She's drunk—not a lot drunk, but enough—and we were both too scared to—"

"A *gun*?" Darlene was goggle-eyed. "Judith pulled a gun? I don't believe it."

"What kind of gun?" I asked. It's always good to know what fire power you're up against.

Alice Ann hiccupped. "A little gun. Silver. It looked sorta like a toy. I wanted to jump her but Mom held me back."

"Saturday-night special," I said to Darlene. Which didn't make it any less dangerous, especially at close range and in the hands of someone who'd been drinking. If Alice Ann had tried to tackle Judith, she might be dead right now. We were just damned lucky that we hadn't opened the door on a bloody murder scene.

Alice Ann was smearing her tears with the back of her hand. "Judith's gone crazy. I mean it! She's crazy and she's drunk." She shook her head, desperate and pleading, her eyes like round dark holes in her white face. "You've got to get Mom away from her, Darlene. When she tells what happened to Dawn, Judith will *kill* her!"

Darlene stared at her. "What happened to Dawn?"

Alice Ann straightened her shoulders. "You'll have to ask Mom," she said staunchly. "She made me promise not to tell."

"I'm asking *you*," Darlene said, "and you're going to tell me or I'll—" She took a step forward, but I yanked her back.

"Can that," I gritted. "We have to find them before somebody gets killed." I turned to Alice Ann. "Where'd they go?"

"I don't know." Alice Ann shook her head. "I have no idea, honest. They just left a couple of minutes before you got here. You must've passed them. They're in Judith's truck."

"Come on," I said urgently to Darlene, and headed for the door. When she didn't move, I turned around. "Come on, damn it! Let's *hustle*."

"I'm coming, too," Alice Ann said.

"No way." Darlene was on the move at last. "You stay here."

I considered quickly. I didn't want to put the girl in danger, but that was her mother out there, and she might be useful. "You can come if you swear you'll follow orders," I said. "And no talking back."

"I swear," Alice Ann said.

As the three of us piled into the car, Darlene asked, "Where the hell are we going? We don't know where to look."

"We can guess," I said, and spun away from the curb.

* * *

FRESH vehicle tracks in the lane suggested that I'd guessed right. About fifty yards short of the fishing camp, I nosed the car off the lane and cut the engine. We climbed out. I opened the trunk and handed Darlene a tire iron. I took the jack handle.

"What do I get?" Alice Ann asked nervously.

"You get to keep your friggin' mouth shut," Darlene said in a low, stern voice. "You want her to hear us?"

"How about some rope?" I whispered. There was a small coil of clothesline in the trunk, left there from a camping expedition with McQuaid and Brian. I gave it to Alice Ann, putting a reassuring hand on her shoulder. "Remember what I said about following orders?"

She took a step closer to me. "Yeah, right," she said.

Darlene looked down at the weapon in her hand. "You sure we need to get Rambo'd up like this?" she asked uneasily. "I mean, can't we just talk to her?"

"We *are* going to talk to her," I said. "But before we do that, we need to get hold of her gun. Now, listen up, guys. We're going to get as close to the camp as possible so we can see what's what. But we don't want to be heard, so don't make a sound. Got it?"

A few minutes later, we were creeping quietly through the trees, with me in the lead, then Alice Ann, and Darlene bringing up the rear. It wasn't six-thirty yet, but the sky was thick with gray clouds and the dense green woodland around us was filled with twilight shadows. It didn't take much imagination to believe that the ghosts of Judith's ancestors were there, too, slipping behind the trees, murmuring low as they plotted how to burn down the log trading post and take back the land from the Coldwell thief who had stolen it. I felt the skin on my arms prickle.

We circled around the camp so that we came up as

close as we could to the old log cabin. A beat-up brown Ford truck was parked out front, the key still in the ignition, the cab doors hanging open. Judith's truck.

"Where are they?" Darlene whispered. "In the cabin? In that old shed?"

And then we heard voices from inside the cabin. May Rose's was thin and high, scared. "I keep telling you, she's staying with her aunt in Florida!" She was sobbing hopelessly. "If you'll just let me get to a phone, I'll call her and you can talk to her."

Alice Ann made a move to step forward. I grabbed her arm and shook my head, hard. She stepped back, her lips pressed tightly together, her eyes frightened.

Judith's voice was a savage growl, and her speech was just slurred enough to tell me that she'd been drinking. "She's pregnant, isn't she? Who's the father?"

"Stay here," I whispered. I moved stealthily to the left, to a point where I could see through the small front window. It was dusky inside, and Judith had lighted the old pump-style gasoline lantern in the middle of the wooden table. She was standing with her back to the stone fireplace, her feet wide apart, the gun in her hand. May Rose was seated in a straight-backed wooden chair between the table and the fireplace, facing Judith, her hands behind her. I couldn't tell from where I was, but I guessed that her wrists were tied, ankles too, probably. To Judith's right was the back door, closed. To her left was a small window, the only other one in the cabin. It had been shuttered on the inside, to make it harder for people to break in, but one of the shutters was hanging loose. I couldn't see the bunks, but I remembered that they were stacked along the wall opposite the fireplace, which had no windows. A plan began to form in my mind.

Inside, they were talking again. "Who got her pregnant?" Judith's voice was louder this time, and more cruel. Her face, its fierce planes illuminated by the light of the lantern, might have been the face of her great-great-grandmother, strong and severe. May Rose said something I couldn't catch, and Judith replied angrily.

"Don't you lie to me, May Rose. I know damn well she's pregnant. I heard it from her friends, and if they know, you do, too. So what happened? Did she run off with the son of a bitch? Or did you pack her off to have an abortion—and get her away from me?"

"I did what she wanted," May Rose said wearily. "I did what I thought was best." She lifted her head and dredged up some bravado from somewhere deep inside. "I'm her mother. I have a right to protect my daughters from evil influences, don't I?"

"So you sent her away." Judith leaned forward, a note of jubilation in her voice. "And you wouldn't let her get in touch with me because you couldn't bear the idea of my being with her, of us being together." It wasn't a question.

May Rose choked out something I couldn't quite hear, but whatever it was, it seemed to satisfy Judith, because she straightened up, her shoulders less rigid. "Well, good. If you'd said that in the beginning, we wouldn't be here now. So all you have to do is tell me where she is, and you can go home." There was a silence, and her voice sharpened. "Where is she?"

May Rose cried out, one long, heartbroken wail so shrill with grief and desperation that it made me shiver.

But the cry didn't seem to reach Judith. Her face tightened, her shoulders tensed, and she took a step forward. The light glinted dully off the gun, a short-barreled revolver. "Remember what I said?" she gritted. "If you don't tell me where Dawn is, I'm going to tell the cops what I know about Wiley Beauchamp's death. I'll leave you tied up here and drive to the sheriff's office and tell them you've admitted to killing him. And don't think I'm foolin', either, May Rose. I'll count to ten. One, two—"

Oh boy. So Judith had already coerced a confession out of May Rose—and she still hadn't revealed Dawn's whereabouts? This was one tough woman. Except that she didn't sound very tough just now. She sounded panicked.

"Oh, please," May Rose cried. "No, please, don't go to the police!"

"Three, four—"

I stepped back away from the window to where Darlene and Alice Ann were waiting. "Okay," I whispered. "Here's what we're going to do."

It took only a moment to sketch out the plan. I had no idea whether it would work, but we had to give it a try, and quick. I didn't believe that Judith would really go for the cops, but we couldn't wait to see whether she meant it or not. And even if she did, she wouldn't get more than fifty yards before she saw my car and came roaring back with that gun.

I nodded to Darlene. "Let's go." To Alice Ann, I said, "Wait for my signal. You know what to do then?" When she nodded, I said, "Okay. Be careful. And stay behind that truck. She might open fire, and I don't want you to get hurt."

She nodded again and Darlene and I split. With her tire iron in one hand, Darlene crept to the right to take up her station at the window beside the fireplace. I took my jack handle, which felt disconcertingly light and ineffectual, and circled the cabin to the left. When I got as far as the back door, I scooped up a pebble and threw it over the low roof.

From the front of the cabin, I heard Alice Ann slam the door of Judith's truck, then her voice, shrill and excited. "I'm here, Mom! I've brought the cops!"

At the word *cops,* Darlene yelled "Police! Come out with your hands up!" and smashed the window with her tire iron. In the same instant, I kicked the back door open and crashed through. Judith was facing the window, her gun raised, her back to me, in a crouch. She whirled when she heard the door fly open and got one shot off, but my jack handle had already caught her wrist and the shot went wild.

At that point, several things happened at once, although when I think back on these events, I see them in slow motion, as if somebody were playing a film frame by frame. May Rose screamed in pain, a high, warbling sound that seemed to echo endlessly around the little room. The lantern danced, gasoline spraying in all directions over the table and onto the floor. Almost instantaneously, the vapor ignited with a massive *whumph* and the table and the floor were covered in a blanket of curling flame. The front door crashed open and Alice Ann ran in, with Darlene close behind. Together, as if they'd rehearsed it, they grabbed the chair to which May Rose was tied and dragged it outside. Judith had flung both arms across her face and stood there, frozen, her pants flaming from ankles to knees, and the right leg of my jeans was on fire, too. Not stopping to think, I grabbed Judith and shoved her out the front door, tumbling with her into a deep mud puddle in the front yard, left over from the recent rains.

In a moment, the flames were out. One leg of my jeans

was charred around the hem, but I'd been wearing socks and my skin wasn't badly burned. The mud felt cool and lovely, though. Beside me, Judith lay on the ground, moaning.

"It's all right, Mom," Alice Ann was saying to May Rose, as she and Darlene worked her ropes free. "You're not hurt. It looks like the bullet just nicked your ear. There's some blood, and your hair is singed and you've got what looks like a bad sunburn on the back of your neck, but that's all. You were really lucky. You'll be all right."

"Oh, God, baby," May Rose cried, sitting on the ground. "You shouldn't have come." And then, panicked: "And I can't believe you brought the police when I told you—"

"It's just me and China," Darlene said reassuringly. "It was a trick. We had to get Judith's gun." Still kneeling, she glanced over her shoulder. "We sure as hell didn't mean to burn the place down."

At that moment I became aware of a rushing, crackling sound and the smell of burning cypress. I glanced up. Through the open front door, I could see that the whole interior of the log cabin was engulfed in orange-red flame, and that fire was spouting up the chimney. Suddenly, I was swept by an eerie, irrestible feeling of déjà vu, as if I had witnessed this same event before, on this same spot, long ago. I shook my head to clear it, but the feeling persisted, as if I were caught in a time warp. Shadowy figures crept through the woods behind me, one of them carrying a burning torch. They had taken revenge on Jed Coldwell, and he was somewhere in those flames, burning to death, while the rest of us stood helplessly by, not able to—

"Darlene?" Judith rolled over and pushed herself up, looking groggily around. "China? What are you—" She looked down at her legs. "Oh, God," she moaned.

Alice Ann had jumped to her feet. "I'll go call the fire department! Where's the nearest phone?"

I was suddenly jerked back into the present. Even if the pumper truck had been there to spray down the flames, the cabin was already a total loss. I pointed toward the woods. "There's a path over there. It'll bring you out at the Big House. But don't bother with the fire department. Just tell them to send—"

"Wait." Darlene jumped up and grabbed Alice Ann's hand. "Nobody's hurt bad enough that they're going to die right away. I want to know about Dawn." She looked from May Rose back to Alice Ann. "Come on, now, come clean. Where is she?"

The silence was broken only by the crackle of flames and then a loud crash, as one of the rafters burned through and part of the roof fell in, a crescendo of sparks erupting into the sky. At last, Alice Ann said quietly, "We might as well tell them, Mom. People are going to have to know. We can't keep it secret any longer."

Judith looked up. Her face was bright red, as if she'd been sunburned, and she had no lashes or brows. I wondered fleetingly whether I'd lost mine, too. "Tell us what?" she cried. "What have you done with her?"

May Rose's shoulders slumped and she covered her face with her hands. Alice Ann knelt down beside her, one arm around her shoulders. She looked at us. "Dawn is dead," she said simply.

Judith gave a long, helpless groan.

"Dead?" Darlene was incredulous. "How?"

"You don't think somebody's going to die from a legal

abortion," Alice Ann replied, "but that's what happened." In the orange light of the flames, her face was strained and set, and she looked suddenly older. "Mom didn't want anybody to know she was pregnant, so Dawn decided not to have it done in Jackson. She went to a clinic downstate, instead. But she put it off because of the twenty-four-hour waiting period, and when she finally went, she was about fourteen weeks." Her voice was so low I had to strain to hear her. "They told her she had to have a D and C."

Judith had dragged herself into a sitting position, bracing her back against a pile of log sections. "What's a D and C?" Her voice was dull, with no inflection.

"It's a surgical procedure," Darlene said grimly. "They scrape you out with a knife."

May Rose was crying now, big wracking sobs that shook her shoulders. Alice Ann took a deep breath and went on. "The doctor apparently nicked her uterus. Then everybody went to lunch and left her alone in the recovery room. She . . . bled to death."

"*Bled* to death?" Darlene whispered, her eyes large.

Judith made a low sound. She'd wrapped her arms around herself and was rocking back and forth, her burned legs stretched out in front of her.

Alice Ann stood again and looked down at her mother, her face stony. "Dawn wouldn't have been alone if you'd let me go with her," she said. "Or if you'd gone yourself. She didn't have to die. If somebody had been there, they could have called EMS."

"*I* could have been with her," Judith cried.

May Rose didn't look up. "I didn't want . . ." she whispered. She swallowed. "I couldn't let . . ."

"You couldn't face up to the fact that your daughter wasn't perfect by your standards of perfection," Alice

Ann said, her voice low and level. "That she got pregnant and had to have an abortion."

May Rose scrambled to her feet. Her frizzy hair was tangled and singed, her face smeared with blood, her clothes covered with mud. "But they're going to go to jail," she cried. "The doctor and the clinic administrator. They've already been charged with manslaughter. They'll pay for what they did!"

"That won't bring Dawn back," Alice Ann said sternly. "It'll only cause more pain." She looked at her mother as if their roles had been reversed, as if she were the mother and May Rose a wayward child. "Like what you did to Wiley Beauchamp. What were you thinking, Mom? You only made things worse."

May Rose's face twisted. "Shut up," she hissed. "You don't know what you're talking about, so just shut up."

Darlene stared at May Rose. "What did you do to Wiley?"

May Rose half turned away. "I didn't do anything," she said defensively. "She's just a kid—she doesn't know what she's talking about. Alice Ann, we're not hanging around here any longer." She started for Judith's truck. "Come on. We're going home."

Alice Ann folded her arms. "I'm not going anywhere until you tell the truth," she said flatly. "I'm sick and tired of lies and deception. Dawn deserves better than this."

May Rose had reached the truck. "I don't know what you're talking about," she said. "There's nothing more to tell." She looked in the truck and saw that the keys were in the ignition. "Come on, Alice Ann. Let's go."

"Can it," Judith said harshly. "You've already told me you killed him."

"But that's because you were pointing that gun at me!"

May Rose exclaimed. "I would have told you anything you wanted to hear, just to get away. It isn't true. I lied."

"That won't work, May Rose." I stood up, wincing at the sudden pain in my leg. "We know you were here the night Wiley died. Judith saw you walking down the road, and I found your medallion beside the river, where you lost it. It's inscribed. 'To Juliet, from her Romeo.'"

"Juliet?" Darlene took a step forward. "*You* killed him?"

May Rose frowned at me. "Medallion?" She flicked her tongue across her lips. "I didn't lose any—"

Alice Ann's voice cut through her mother's words like a knife. "It's no use trying to cover up, Mom. Tell them what happened. If you don't, *I* will. And when I've told them, I'm going to tell the police. We have to tell the truth. We owe it to Dawn."

May Rose sagged against the truck as if all the strength had gone out of her. "All right," she said in a leaden voice. "I can see that you hate me so much that you're determined to destroy me. Go ahead, tell them."

"I don't want to destroy you," Alice Ann said quietly. "I just want us to do what's right, for Dawn's sake." She waited for a moment, and when her mother still said nothing, she swallowed hard and went on. "Wiley came over about seven on Saturday night, after he'd been to Jordan's Crossing. He wanted to talk to Mom about Dawn. He wanted to know what happened to her."

"Why didn't you tell him when the two of you had supper together at Elmer's?" I asked Alice Ann.

If she was surprised that I knew, she didn't show it. "I couldn't. After Dawn died, Mom made me promise not to. She thought it would be better if everybody thought Dawn had just decided to move away. That she'd got a job in Memphis, or gone to school somewhere else, or something like that." She gave her mother a hard look. "She said it would keep Dawn's memory unsullied."

"So Wiley came over." Darlene's voice was tense. "So then what?"

"So then he and Mom left. About nine-thirty, she came home alone." Alice Ann's words were coming faster. "She said she and Wiley had a big argument and she killed him. She said she got mad at him and pushed the truck into the river so he'd drown. She said she stood there and watched while it—"

"That isn't the way it happened," May Rose said wearily. She straightened up. "You weren't there, Alice Ann, you don't know."

"Then *you* tell us," I said.

She sighed heavily. "Wiley and me, we came out here together for some privacy." She looked accusingly at her daughter. "I was just trying to protect Alice Ann, that's all. She's still a young girl. I didn't want her to have to hear all the dirty . . . everything that would be said."

"You don't know anything!" Alice Ann cried fiercely. "You think I'm still a virgin? Well, think again! I—"

Darlene put her hand on the girl's arm. "Be quiet, girl," she said gently. "This is bad enough. You don't need to make it worse."

May Rose wrenched her glance away from her daughter and turned back to me. "So he parked the truck on the ramp, and we had a . . . we talked, for, oh, maybe ten, fifteen minutes. But toward the end, he wasn't acting quite right, like he was woozy or something." She bit her lip. "He said he had a headache, and that Miss Tullie had smacked his head with her cane. He showed me this place where he was hurt. It wasn't bleeding or anything like that, but I could see he'd been hit pretty hard. I said maybe he'd better go to the emergency room, and he agreed, if I would drive him there. But then he . . . he put his forehead on the wheel and sort of passed out. I sat there for a minute, and then I—" She stopped.

"Go on," Darlene said urgently. "What did you do?"

She looked from one of us to the other, as if she were looking for help or reassurance. "I . . . I don't know what came over me," she said desperately. "I really mean it. I don't know."

Judith was still sitting on the ground, leaning against the pile of logs. She broke her silence. "Tell them," she said harshly. "Tell them what you told me. Tell them how you *murdered* him."

"It wasn't murder. It was just—" May Rose cleared her throat. "The truck was a stick shift. I put it into neutral and got out."

"And left the door open?" I asked.

"I guess," May Rose said. "I don't remember."

"And then?" Darlene prompted tensely.

"And then I went around to the back and pushed it," May Rose said. "Well, I . . . I didn't push it, really, I just sort of leaned against it. When it began to coast down the ramp, I stood back and . . . and let it go." She was crying again, the tears running down her muddy cheeks. "I had no idea how deep the water was. For all I knew, it was really shallow out there, and the truck would just coast out and get stuck and he'd have to get it towed out. But then it picked up momentum and it sort of floated in the water and I could see from the angle that it was going in all the way. Really deep, I mean. Like the water was going to be over the roof of the cab."

Darlene made a noise deep in her throat, and I gave her

a compassionate look. I could see how much it hurt her to hear this.

May Rose wiped her nose with the back of her hand, smearing mud and blood across her face. "When the truck started settling into the water, that was when I realized that Wiley was actually going to drown. I got really scared. I scrambled down the bank, thinking I could maybe swim over and pull him out. But then I thought, Why should I risk my neck for this bastard? He deserves to die. So I left him there, and walked out to the highway and got a lift home."

Darlene's mouth was trembling. "Why did you do it, May Rose?" she whispered. "What did Wiley do to you?"

"What did he do to me?" May Rose cried. "He got my little girl pregnant, that's what he did! If it hadn't've been for him, Dawn would be alive right now. I'm glad he's dead. The bastard can burn in hell for all I care!"

"Oh, God," Darlene said.

"Wiley?" Judith whispered. "*Wiley* did it to her? So that's why he wanted me out of the cottage. He didn't want us living together!"

Behind us, the cabin roof caved in with a thundering roar and a shower of bright sparks.

Chapter Nineteen

According to Daniel Moerman, in *Native American Ethnobotany*, the Iroquois Indians employed blood-root as a ceremonial witchcraft medicine. The smoke from the plant was used as a purifying wash to cleanse someone who had seen a dead person.

The night didn't end there, of course. Right after the roof fell in, the county's Volunteer Fire Department showed up with a pumper truck and half a dozen men. Leatha had seen the smoke from her bedroom window, realized that the old log cabin must be on fire, and called 911. While the firefighters were sluicing down the burning cypress logs with water pumped from the Bloodroot, Alice Ann and Darlene got in my car with Judith and started off for the emergency room at the Chicory hospital. It turned out that Judith's burns were extensive and painful but neither deep nor terribly serious, and she was kept overnight and released the next morning. As for her abduction of May Rose, it seemed better to simply forget that the whole thing had happened, especially since the cabin was the evening's worst casualty. May Rose was not keen on this, of course, but she was hardly in a position to bargain.

I'd already decided what had to be done about May

Rose. When Alice Ann and Darlene drove off, I put her into Judith's truck and headed for Jordan's Crossing, where I phoned Colonel Blakeslee and got him out of bed. I sketched out the situation, and fifteen minutes later, May Rose and I were sitting in the kitchen of his house. It was eleven by that time, and he was in his pajamas and robe. When he heard her story about what had happened the night Wiley drowned, he agreed with me that at the very most, it might warrrant a charge of criminally negligent homicide. He thought he could convince the county attorney to accept a plea in return for maybe six months jail time plus a couple of years of community service, especially since the county wouldn't be put to the expense of a trial. When May Rose tearfully gave him her pledge that she'd show up, he phoned the sheriff, arranged for her to surrender at eight o'clock the next morning, and sent us both home. I dropped her off at her house and headed back to Jordan's Crossing. It had been a very long day.

THE next morning, Leatha and I had a long, serious talk. I read her the whole of Pearl's journal, and we drew up an amended version of the Family Record page in the Coldwell Bible, showing that Tullie was Clancy and Sapphire's daughter and adding the names of her daughter, Enid, and her granddaughter, Amanda. Of course, we also talked about what this meant for us—that Leatha's father was Tullie's half-brother, and that he couldn't have inherited a gene that had come from Sapphire. Which meant that Leatha and I were not at risk.

"After all these months of fearing the worst," Leatha said tearfully, looking down at the new lines of descent we had penciled into the Family Record. She took a deep

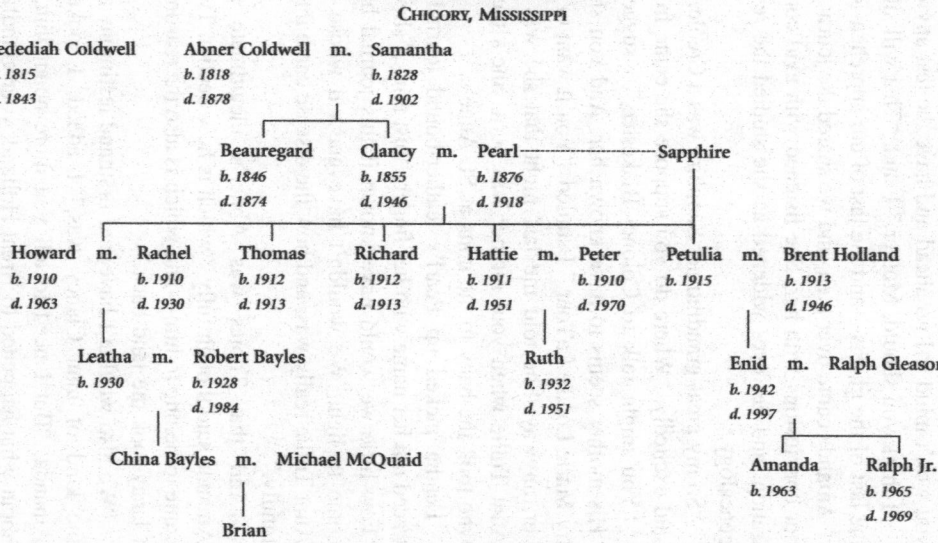

FROM THE COLDWELL FAMILY BIBLE
JORDAN'S CROSSING PLANTATION
CHICORY, MISSISSIPPI

Jedediah Coldwell
b. 1815
d. 1843

Abner Coldwell   m.   Samantha
b. 1818   *b. 1828*
d. 1878   *d. 1902*

Beauregard   Clancy   m.   Pearl ------------------ Sapphire
b. 1846   *b. 1855*   *b. 1876*
d. 1874   *d. 1946*   *d. 1918*

Howard   m.   Rachel   Thomas   Richard   Hattie   m.   Peter   Petulia   m.   Brent Holland
b. 1910   *b. 1910*   *b. 1912*   *b. 1912*   *b. 1911*   *b. 1910*   *b. 1915*   *b. 1913*
d. 1963   *d. 1930*   *d. 1913*   *d. 1913*   *d. 1951*   *d. 1970*   *d. 1946*

Leatha   m.   Robert Bayles   Ruth   Enid   m.   Ralph Gleason
b. 1930   *b. 1928*   *b. 1932*   *b. 1942*
               d. 1984   *d. 1951*   *d. 1997*

China Bayles   m.   Michael McQuaid   Amanda   Ralph Jr.
                                                                             b. 1963   *b. 1965*
                                                                                          d. 1969
Brian

breath. "It's hard to believe that we've been spared. I hope you won't mind if I go ahead and have the test anyway."

"I think you should, Mother," I said. "That will silence the last of the ghosts—and the last of our apprehensions."

Amanda came over then, and we shared the journal and our conclusions with her. She listened with avid concentration, and her eyes widened as she studied the revised genealogy.

"So my great-grandmother Sapphire was a Creole," she said excitedly. "Where do you suppose she came from?"

"You might talk to Colonel Blakeslee," I suggested. "His mother seems to have known her. And you should try Marie Louise LaTour." I smiled. "You'll want to meet her, anyway. She told me last night that she was with Aunt Tullie when your mother was born. She's the one who took the baby to the nuns at St. Anne's."

Leatha picked up Pearl's leather-bound journal and traced out her name with her finger. "Just think," she said, "how little we would have known if this journal hadn't come to light. We wouldn't have guessed whose child Aunt Tullie really was, and how the disease came into the family."

"And that Tobias was Abner's illegitimate son," Amanda said thoughtfully, "which is how Section Twelve came to belong to him—and which is also the reason why Clancy took the land back."

"We also wouldn't have had firsthand testimony about the kind of man Clancy was," I added. I looked at Amanda. "But I need to tell you more about him, and about what happened to Brent Holland, your grandfather. And why your mother was put into an orphanage. You see, Clancy couldn't abide the thought of a marriage between . . ."

That chapter took several moments to relate, and when I was finished, Amanda's eyes were wet. Leatha let out her breath in an angry puff.

"I can't believe that my father and grandfather would have done such a wicked thing!" she exclaimed. Then she added, frowning, "No, I'm afraid I can believe it. I've always known that my father was a weak man. He did everything his father told him to do. I just don't *want* to believe it, that's all."

"Clancy might have suspected that Brent inherited the same affliction that killed his aunt Sapphire," I said. "He couldn't have known that Sapphire's disease was genetic. DNA wasn't discovered until the early 1950s. But he certainly knew that Tullie and Brent were first cousins, and he might have been afraid that their children would inherit the sickness that apparently killed Tullie's mother—and perhaps Brent's mother, for all we know."

"Don't make excuses for him, China," Leatha said angrily. "Clancy was evil. I am *disowning* him." She frowned. "Can you disown an ancestor?"

I covered her hand with mine. "Let's not be rash, Mother. Anyway, it's all in the past. We just need to live with it for a while and see if we understand it any better." I paused. "But there are some things I wish I knew right now. For instance, how did that journal get from the drawer where I put it onto my bedside table?"

"Come to that," Leatha replied, "how did the journal get into the drawer? After Wiley brought that deed over, I went through everything there, thinking I might discover a document that could help explain the deed. It wasn't there then—I would have seen it, I'm sure."

"And my old pajamas," I said, "and that scent of lilies of the valley. And the way Marie Louise seems to *know* everything." I could have mentioned the twist of smoke in the corner that might or might not be Uncle Jed, but that was probably my imagination.

"I guess there are some things we just can't explain," Amanda said soberly. "And some mysteries that just can't be solved."

Let all dem ol' ghosts lie, Marie Louise had said. *Ain't much you kin do 'bout 'em now, anyways.*

She was right. I had to leave it there.

THAT afternoon, Leatha, Amanda, and I packed a picnic supper and took Aunt Tullie, the lawn mower, a bucketful of garden tools, and some painting supplies to the Coldwell family cemetery. Leatha and I cut the weeds, clipped around the headstones and monuments, and painted the rusty fence while Amanda walked with Aunt Tullie around the graveyard, listening as she pointed out who was buried where.

After a while, we moved the iron bench next to Brent's grave and the two of them sat down, while Amanda quietly told Aunt Tullie who she was. I had been afraid that Aunt Tullie would be distressed by the news, but it didn't seem to affect her, one way or the other. She listened without expression to Amanda's story, staring off into the distance as if she were seeing into a long-ago past. But after a while she turned and kissed her granddaughter's forehead, as if she were a child, then got up and clumsily brushed the grass clippings off her husband's marker. Amanda, looking on, silently wept.

Pray, love, remember, I thought, watching the two of them mourning together. At least now, there would be someone else to remember Brent Holland.

By the time we spread out our picnic on an old quilt under a black oak, evening was falling and the cemetery looked neat and tidy once again. "I think Judith can manage it from now on," I said, as I sat down on the grass.

"Grandmother and I can do it, at least for a while," Amanda replied. She looked at Aunt Tullie. "I'd like to come and stay with you for a few months, if you don't mind."

"Suit yourself," Aunt Tullie said brusquely, but her face was softer as she picked up her paper plate. She ate quickly and then went back to sit on the bench again, refusing Amanda's offer to sit with her.

"If I didn't know how Huntington's affects people, I'd think she didn't like me," Amanda said wryly, when Aunt Tullie was out of earshot. "But Mother behaved the same way, and the doctor told me that it was typical of the disease. People seem to get disconnected, emotionally."

"So you plan to stay here for a while?" Leatha asked, pouring another round of iced tea from the thermos into our paper cups.

"Unless you have some objection," Amanda said. She looked at me. "I know you'll want to do some more checking to assure yourself that this isn't a case of mistaken identity. I'll cooperate all I can."

Leatha and I looked at each other. "I don't think it's a major problem," I said, and Leatha added, "I have to confess that I'll be glad to get home. I'll come back as often as I can, of course."

"It's hard to say how long she'll be able to stay here," Amanda said. "Mom's doctor offered to recommend a couple of homes that have experience in caring for Huntington's patients, and when that time comes, we'll just have to do what we think is best." She gave Leatha a small smile. "You've borne this burden for quite a while. It's my turn now."

Wordlessly, Leatha patted her hand. "Will you be able to take time off from your work to stay here indefinitely?" I asked.

"I've decided that I'm not going back to work right away," Amanda said. "When I'm ready, I can probably get a teaching job somewhere. I still have money left from Mom's insurance, so that's no problem." She paused. "I'm hoping Darlene and Judith can stay on, too, part-time. They'd be company for me, as well as a help. And we don't want to let the place run down. At some point, I suppose it will have to be sold, don't you think?"

"Yes," Leatha said firmly, "Jordan's Crossing should be sold. I used to believe that it ought to be kept until the last Coldwell was gone from the face of the earth, but I've changed my mind." She looked out over the grave-yard and beyond it, to the flat, fertile land of the Yazoo Delta and the green band of trees and swamp that marked the meanderings of the Bloodroot River. "There are too many ghosts here, and no way of righting the old wrongs. They cut too deep, they're too painful. I'm ready to let go of it. All of it."

"I am, too," I said, reaching for my mother's hand.

Resources, References, and Recipes

RESOURCES AND REFERENCES

Most of China's herbal mysteries, at least so far, have used as the "signature herb" relatively familiar plants that belong to the western European tradition. Bloodroot, however, is an eastern North American plant, unknown to the Europeans until the early colonists adopted it. It was used extensively by at least eighteen different Native American tribes for medicinal and ritual purposes and as a dye plant. It continues to be popular in traditional practice, although its uses have not been affirmed by modern research. There is, however, some interest in the plant's primary alkaloid, sanguinarine, for potential use in antitumor compounds and in the reduction of dental plaque and gingivitis. Please do *not* experiment with this toxic plant.

If you'd like to learn more about native peoples' uses of plants that grow in your local fields and woods, you might begin by making a trip to your library to consult anthropologist Daniel E. Moerman's excellent compilation of the work of nearly two centuries of firsthand studies of American Indians. His book, *Native American Ethnobotany*, surveys over four thousand plants, with over forty thousand different usages by almost three hundred tribes. For your own home library, you might want one of Alma R. Hutchens's two works, *Indian Herbalogy of North America* or *A Handbook of Native American Herbs*. For the eastern and southeastern United States, *A Reference Guide to Medicinal Plants: Herbal Medicine Past and Present* (John K. Crellin and Jane Philpott) is very helpful. And don't overlook the wildflower guides for your local area. While the authors of these guides probably won't call these plants "herbs," they frequently annotate the plant's description with its known uses by local tribes.

The setting for this book is quite different from Pecan Springs, and I had plenty to learn about the landscape of the Yazoo Delta and its history, especially that of the Choctaw people. Books that I found useful include: *Providence*, by Will D. Campbell (the history of one square mile of Holmes County, Mississippi); *The Yazoo*, by Frank E. Smith (the river and the people and places along its banks); and *After Removal: The Choctaw in Mississippi*, edited by Samuel J. Wells and Roseanna Tubby, (the life and culture of the Choctaw who resisted the government's efforts to remove them). I was first introduced to this landscape and its people, however, through fiction: William Faulkner's unforgettable saga of Yoknapatawpha County. Among his finest novels are *Light in August; The Sound and the Fury;* and *Absalom, Absalom*. For Southern women's experience, I turned to the book Darlene mentions to Amanda (*Within the Plantation Household: Black and White Women of the Old South*, by Elizabeth Fox-Genovese) and to *The Plantation Mistress*, by Catherine Clinton.

One of the major plot strands in this book has to do with Huntington's disease, which I happened on by accident on a web-surfing expedition. I found several important websites; a daily exchange of E-mail by HD sufferers and their caregivers and loved ones; and two compelling books: *Mapping Fate: A Memoir of Family, Risk, and Genetic Research*, by Alice Wexler, and *Faces of Huntington's*, by Carmen Leal-Pock. I am indebted to those who have so fearlessly shared their pain. No fictional account of this dreadful disease can substitute for their real-life stories.

RECIPES FOR THE DISHES SERVED
BY MARTHA EDMOND

The Edmond Family's Favorite Tomato Pie

Recipes for Tomato Pie have been handed down from mother to daughter in as many different versions as there are family traditions. If you don't want to make a bread-crumb crust, use a pastry crust instead. With the herbs and cheeses, you don't need additional salt, although you can add it if you wish.

2 cups fine bread crumbs (5 slices of day-old bread,
    crumbed in a blender)

1 teaspoon dried basil

½ teaspoon dried oregano

¼ teaspoon dried thyme

¼ teaspoon garlic powder

6 large tomatoes, sliced thin and drained on paper
    toweling

¼ cup chopped fresh basil

¼ cup chopped green onions

2 cups grated Cheddar or Swiss cheese, or a combi-
    nation of both

3 eggs, beaten

¼ teaspoon nutmeg

½ cup grated Parmesan cheese

5 slices lean bacon, diced (precook for two minutes to
    remove fat, if you like)

Preheat oven to 325 degrees. Mix the bread crumbs with the dried herbs and press half of the mixture on the bottom of a buttered 9-inch pie plate. Arrange half the drained tomato slices, overlapping them. Top with half of the fresh basil and green onions and half of the cheese. Repeat for a second layer. Drizzle the eggs over this layer and add the remaining bread crumbs. Mix nutmeg and Parmesan and sprinkle over bread crumbs. Top with diced bacon. Bake for 40–45 minutes, until bacon bits are crisp. Cool 15 minutes, slice and serve. Serves 8.

Martha's Cold Cucumber Soup

Martha's cucumber soup is easy but elegant, especially when it's garnished with a dollop of yogurt, cucumber circles, and sprigs of fresh dill. Ideal for make-ahead convenience.

> **2 medium cucumbers (about 1 pound), peeled, seeded, and diced fine**
> **½ teaspoon salt**
> **2 cloves garlic, finely minced**
> **1 tablespoon snipped fresh dill (or 1 teaspoon dried)**
> **4 cups (1 quart) low-fat yogurt, unflavored**
> **salt to taste**
> **dill, cucumber slices, and yogurt for garnish**

Mix the diced cucumbers and salt in a colander and place in the sink to drain for about 20 minutes. (The salt drains some of the liquid out of the cucumbers.) Mix drained

cucumbers, minced garlic, dill, and yogurt in a large bowl
and chill for at least one hour. Taste and add salt, if desired. If the soup is too thick, dilute with a little cold milk
or water. Spoon into serving bowls, garnish, and serve.

Easy Herb Bread

   1¼ cups water
   6 tablespoons butter or margarine
   1 envelope dry yeast
   2 tablespoons nonfat dry milk
   2 tablespoons sugar
   1 teaspoon onion powder
   ¼ teaspoon pepper
   2 cups wheat flour
   1¾ to 2 cups white flour
   3 tablespoons dried parsley flakes
   1 teaspoon dried basil
   1 teaspoon dried thyme
   ½ teaspoon dried rosemary, crushed fine

Combine water and 4 tablespoons butter in a saucepan
and heat over low heat until lukewarm and butter is soft-
ened. Pour into large bowl. Add yeast, dry milk, sugar,
onion powder, and pepper. Beat at high speed with electric mixer for two minutes. At low speed, beat in wheat
flour. With a wooden spoon, stir in just enough white
flour (about 1½ cups) to make a soft dough. Knead on
lightly floured board for about five minutes, or until the
dough is smooth and elastic, adding the remaining flour

as necessary. Place in lightly greased bowl and turn so that greased side is up. Cover with a damp towel and let rise in a warm place until it is double in bulk. Punch down.

On floured board, roll dough into a 15" × 9" rectangle. Melt remaining butter and brush it onto the dough. Combine the herbs and sprinkle evenly over the dough. Roll up like a jellyroll, from the narrow end, and place seam-side down in a 9" × 5" loaf pan. Cover with a damp towel and let rise about 45 minutes, until double. Bake at 350 degrees about 45 minutes, until the bottom sounds hollow when it is tapped and the top is golden brown. If the top gets too dark, cover with foil. Remove from pan and cool on a wire rack.